With a
Little Luck

Anne Baker

D0994410

HEADLINE

First published in 1999
by HEADLINE BOOK PUBLISHING

First published in paperback in 1999
by HEADLINE BOOK PUBLISHING

10 9 8 7 6 5 4 3

ISBN 0 7472 6139 3

Printed and bound in Great Britain by
Mackays of Chatham plc, Chatham, Kent

HEADLINE BOOK PUBLISHING
A division of the Hodder Headline Group
338 Euston Road
London NW1 3BH
www.headline.co.uk
www.hodderheadline.com

With a

Little Luck

Book One

Chapter One

15 April 1928

As she washed up the dinner dishes at her scullery sink, Edith Luckett smouldered with vexation. Her eldest son Len was taking advantage of her good nature. He should have been here an hour ago to take his daughter Alice home. She'd been looking after her two granddaughters all week, and he knew she'd be in need of a rest by now.

A shout of triumph from the back yard made her look up through the window. The girls had drawn chalk marks on the concrete and were seeing which of them could jump the furthest.

Alice was getting ready to make a run, her teeth biting her lower lip in concentration. She went flying down the yard on legs like sticks. Her jump fell noticeably short of her cousin Maddy's. Edith wasn't surprised. Alice was a poor stunted little thing, pale and whey-faced, with fair wispy curls. She took after her mother. There was no way Alice would ever jump as far as Madeleine.

'You're miles short,' Maddy was crowing.

Edith watched Alice pick up her large toy monkey and cuddle it, disappointment in every line of her body. As she turned, she saw the dirty marks on the clean blue frock she'd let the girl put on because her father was coming.

Edith grunted with irritation. All the washing and ironing she had to do! Anger welled up in her throat. It was asking a lot of a woman of sixty-two to look after two nine-year-old children during a whole week of school holidays. She didn't have the energy to run round after them now. It was not what she wanted to do with her life, and she didn't have the patience with her grandchildren that she'd had with her own.

She did it because the family meant everything to her. She put their interests above her own and always had, devoting her life to her three boys. She'd had a pair of twins, with her third son coming along many years later, and wanted to see all of them get on and go up in the world.

She'd been looking after Madeleine, Frank's daughter, for years, whether she was at school or not. Frank paid her ten shillings a week to do it because his wife was a hairdresser with her own business. Alice came to live with them off and on for months at a time, and Edith never saw a penny towards her keep. She had to do it out of the goodness of her heart.

She felt another rush of irritation when she thought of Len, her eldest by twenty minutes. He hadn't half the gumption of Frank, her second twin. Len had agreed to come for his dinner and collect Alice when he finished work today. It was Saturday and he had a half-day, yet here it was, gone two o'clock, and he hadn't turned up. It was hurtful.

Len took after his father; he'd no sense and no go about him. Beryl, his wife, had been a millstone round his neck from the beginning. Not a local girl at all, she came from some poor part of London. She gave out that her mother was a widow and a consumptive; when she took bad, she had to go home to look after her.

Edith didn't believe her. According to Frank, Beryl went off with other men from time to time, leaving Len to bring up their daughter by himself, which meant his mother had to help. Len always seemed cagey about where Beryl went, but he had said that she'd caught consumption too. Beryl had been a disaster for them all.

Edith peeped through the window again. Alice was a strange child, obsessed with that stuffed monkey, a horrible thing with bare patches in its fur. She called it Wobble because its head wobbled round, and she treated it as though it was human. She wouldn't be parted from it, wanting it beside her on the next chair at every meal.

She saw Alice prop it up against the yard wall while she jumped again. It wore baggy trousers with real pockets in them and stood two and a half feet high. It had a red fez and a red waistcoat with gold braid; all its clothes were shabby and spotted with grease. Edith wished she'd washed them before letting Alice take it home. She wanted Len to think she was taking proper care of the girl and her things while she was here.

There was another triumphant scream from Madeleine. 'I've won, I've won!'

Alice had already lost interest and had turned away. She was trying to entice next door's ginger tom down from the dividing wall. Edith gave another cluck of irritation as it landed in the yard with a thump, sounding like a bundle of wet washing being thrown down. Alice bent to stroke it.

'I can jump further than you.' Maddy was trying to goad her. 'I can run faster and skip better.'

Madeleine was a very different specimen from Alice. Her hair was a magnificent shade of deep bronze. She had eyes the colour of tawny sherry, creamy skin and rosy cheeks. Maddy was well fed and glowed with health.

Edith surmised that having a settled home and healthy parents made a big difference. Maddy was only a month older than Alice, but she was inches taller and a stone and a half heavier.

Edith reflected that Maddy was also a lot more trouble to look after. A bit of a handful really, noisy and boisterous, perhaps a little spoilt. She wouldn't play by herself as Alice would.

Not that Alice was easy; she was a fussy eater who pushed

the food round her plate, while Maddy ate everything put before her. Edith had tried to feed Alice up while she'd been here this week. The child was so like her mother that everybody was afraid of her going into a decline too, and she'd look better if she weren't so waif-like. Her grandmother had put generous platefuls of food in front of her at every meal and said:

'Come on, Alice, do your best. See if you can finish it. Sausage is good for you. You want to grow big and strong like Maddy, don't you?'

Alice was a slow eater, but she'd been finishing what was on her plate. Not that she looked any better for it.

Edith didn't like next door's cat coming into her yard. An enormous fat thing and she was sure it had fleas. As she watched, she saw Alice hold something out to it. She was gripped by such a wave of anger that she shot to the scullery door.

'Alice, what's that you're giving it?' The child's hand swept behind her back.

Maddy's pretty face smirked up at her: 'Sausage. There's some mash too, and some of the apple pie.'

Edith was shaking with outrage. 'Is that your dinner? You naughty girl!' The devious little madam!

'I couldn't eat it.' Alice's eyes were round and green, too big for her tiny face. 'I couldn't get it down. It stuck in my throat.'

Maddy was hopping around on one foot. 'She wouldn't give it to me. I'd have eaten her sausage. She wanted to keep it for Ginger.'

'I did try, Gran. It was too much.'

'Wasting good food like that! Do you know what food costs?'

Madeleine looked up coyly. Edith knew that look. It wasn't the first time Maddy had told tales.

'She hides it in Wobble's pockets.'

Edith was choking with ire. 'That damned monkey!'

6

All that shopping and cooking, and what for? What was the point in trying with Alice? She knew now why the monkey's trousers were stained with grease. No wonder Alice wanted it by her at every meal. It caused nothing but trouble.

Maddy had tried to take it to play with herself. That had caused hair-pulling and a fight that Alice had managed to win. Of course, Maddy only wanted it because Alice loved it so much. Anyway, at nine they were both too old for soft toys.

'Sorry, Gran.' There were tears glistening in Alice's eyes. A deep red flush ran up her neck and into her cheeks.

Edith retreated to the kitchen, breathing fire. Monty, her husband, stirred in the rocking chair in front of the range. That was as far as he'd moved from the table after dinner.

'Leave her be, Edith. She's a good little thing really.'

Alice had followed her in. She looked paste white now, as though she'd had the stuffing knocked out of her.

'Isn't Dadda here yet?'

'He won't be long now.'

'Can I read my horoscope, Grandpa?'

Edith tried to stifle her irritation. Horoscopes indeed! Alice got all that nonsense from her mother.

'Course you can.' Monty flapped the pages of his newspaper, finding the place for her. 'There you are. Let's hear you read it out.'

'Where's Leo? Yes, it says: "There will be disappointments and delays this week . . ."'

Monty chuckled. 'Well, that's true enough.'

Alice went on reading: '"If luck is not coming your way now, keep to your usual routine and don't take on anything new until after the new moon."'

She took a deep breath and turned to Monty. 'The disappointment is that Dadda hasn't come.'

Her face screwed with sudden horror. 'But he will, won't he?'

'Yes, luvvy,' her grandfather reassured. 'It says delays, doesn't it? Not that he won't come.'

Her tears were about to brim over. Alice was a pathetic scrap of humanity. Even though she was infuriating, her plight pulled at everybody's heartstrings.

'Go out and play with Maddy till he comes,' Edith told her, pushing her out on the step and closing the door against her back.

It didn't help that Alice took after Beryl and not their side of the family. A shame really.

Alice felt the door bump against her shoulders and bounce back an inch. She huddled on the step with her eyes closed, shaking with fear, silently imploring the powers that be: 'Please come for me, Dadda. Please come for me now.'

Maddy was skipping, the rope sending up whirls of dust from the concrete yard. 'Thirty-six, thirty-seven . . .'

Alice could hear Gran's voice inside: 'I'm getting worried about our Len. It isn't like him not to come when he's said he will.'

She felt perspiration break out across her forehead. That Gran was worried made everything seem worse.

'I kept his sausage and mash for him but it's gone cold now. I'll have to fry it all up again. Did you see him this morning?'

Alice knew that both her father and grandfather worked in Lever's soap factory at Port Sunlight, but Dadda's job was tending a machine that packed Vim into canisters, while Grandpa was a clerk in the main office. She pushed the door to make it open another inch. It seemed vital to hear what they were saying.

Grandpa's newspaper fluttered. 'No.'

Grandpa infuriated Gran as often as Alice did. He had an almost permanent smile that seemed to show he was well contented with life.

Gran barked: 'When did you last see him?'

'Thursday, I think. Or was it Wednesday? Going for the bus, he was.'

'I thought you saw him in the canteen every day?'

'I don't go to the canteen anymore.'

'So where d'you have your dinner?'

'The cafeteria. Len can't eat there, it's for office staff.'

'I thought you said the canteen was better value?'

'I don't want such big meals these days.'

'You don't want a proper dinner? Why not? I do wish you'd take Alice home.'

'Len will come when he's ready. Why don't you put your feet up for five minutes? You try to do too much. Here, have a look at the paper.' Alice heard him get to his feet.

'Where are you going?'

'Down to the allotment.'

'Take the girls with you. If Len gets here, it won't hurt him to walk down for Alice.'

Grandpa cleared his throat. 'I'd rather not. Alice might be all right by herself – she'd do a bit of weeding – but not Maddy. I'll just get my cap.'

Gran sounded vexed. 'It wouldn't hurt you to take them off my hands for an hour.'

'They'll race about, make nuisances of themselves.'

'They make nuisances of themselves here.'

'Come on, Edith, they're not much trouble. Not while they're both together and playing outside.'

Grandpa was coming out. Alice pushed herself off the step, hurled herself at Wobble and hugged him to her, her heart thumping.

Maddy hadn't stopped skipping. 'Seventy-four, seventy-five . . .'

Grandpa stood on the step, surveying Alice. He had a thick mop of grey hair that was turning white, and a big droopy moustache one shade darker, more iron grey. Alice thought he looked like a Mexican bandit. She thought her

9

dad did too; he had an even more droopy moustache, that tickled when he kissed her.

Grandpa smiled at her. 'Don't you worry about your dadda. He'll get here sooner or later.' He was feeling in his pocket.

'Here.' Alice felt a halfpenny being pressed into her palm. 'Get yourself some sweets.'

Maddy stopped skipping and came closer. He gave her the same. The next moment he'd gone and closed the yard gate behind him. Maddy whooped with joy.

'Come on.'

Alice followed slowly, still hugging Wobble. All week she'd been looking forward to Saturday dinner time, counting the days till Dadda would come. Gran didn't like having her here, she didn't want to be bothered with her. Every time Mummy went away she had to come, and she lived in dread that Dadda would go away too. What would she do then?

When Monty left, Edith collapsed on the rocking chair, the only comfortable one in the narrow kitchen. She knew she wouldn't be able to rest until Alice went home. There'd be no peace.

She tossed her apron over her head, closed her eyes and thought of her sons. They'd been such lovely boys. She'd lost two brothers in the Boer War and had called her twins Len and Frank after them. She'd done everything she could to make them happy and successful. She'd wanted them to have the good lives her brothers had missed.

Her Len had started work as a clerk at Cammell Laird's at fourteen. She'd expected him to follow in his father's steps and keep his white-collar job. It was the Great War that had done for him. He'd been shell-shocked in the trenches, and in a pitiful state when he'd come home. Never been able to take any pressure after that.

He'd wanted a job without stress and had taken a labouring job in the Hovis flour mills. Edith had been disappointed, she couldn't say otherwise. He'd done very well at school. She'd nagged Monty to get him a better job at Lever's, expecting it to be in the office, but Len had wanted to go in the factory. There'd been a price to pay for the war, and Len had paid over the odds; he should have been given a disability pension. It had ruined his health.

She hadn't liked any of the girlfriends he'd brought home. Each one had seemed worse than the last. She'd told him straight out that he could do better than Beryl Briggs. A barmaid, and a tart if ever there was one. There'd been no talking him out of it, though she'd tried.

Got married in white, Beryl had, though the gown had been straining across her stomach. Holding her bouquet in front of it hadn't hidden that. Edith had felt embarrassed for her. Even more so when Alice had been born four and a half months afterwards.

She never had trusted Beryl; she'd seen it coming, though Len wouldn't listen. Flighty, there was no other word to describe her. Flashing her big green eyes at other men. Len had given her everything she could possibly want. Forgiven her, and taken her back twice. Edith was afraid they'd had rows with the child cowering there, listening to it all.

The first time Beryl went, Edith had had to take Alice in. Len couldn't cope with the child, not when he had to work. Alice had been even more pathetic at three.

'Want my mummy,' she'd cried, looking up at her grandmother with troubled green eyes. 'Want her. Where's she gone?'

Edith didn't know. She only knew what Frank had told her, that the barman from the Lighterman's Arms had gone too. She hoped that wouldn't be noticed by anyone else.

She said quickly, 'Your mam's down in London, with your other gran.'

That's what Len had said, but she didn't believe him because his eyes wouldn't meet hers. She always knew when he lied.

11

The marriage had seemed to be on rocky ground right from the beginning. Beryl had never acted as though she was Len's wife; she seemed to distance herself from him. They'd done nothing for Alice. Practically ignored her. It had been Monty's idea that she should come here. He thought Len and Beryl needed time alone to work things out. Edith had had to look after Alice for months at a time.

Len had tried to please Beryl. When they'd both been working in the North End, he'd got her a nice new council house there, even though the rent was six shillings a week. Now he had miles to travel to work. Not that Edith would approve of a council house anywhere for herself, but Len couldn't afford to buy. Beryl had had the nerve to complain that it didn't have a proper bathroom.

The lavvy was outside but against the house, so she didn't have to go down the garden, but there was no satisfying Beryl. He'd rented a lovely gas cooker from the gas board because she'd fancied that too. It hadn't stopped her leaving.

Alice had had little loving care from her parents. She was far too thin and peaky, and if Edith didn't watch her, she'd sit in a corner all day reading her books. It was good for her to have Maddy to play with, though Maddy was inclined to lead her into mischief.

Edith leaned over to poke the fire and suddenly realised there were no sounds of play from the yard. She got up and went to the window. It was empty. It bothered her when she couldn't see the girls. It was a responsibility looking after other people's children, even if they were family.

She went up the narrow hall and into the parlour. Everybody else insisted on calling it the front room, but she'd made it a real parlour, with a piano and a Victorian horsehair sofa in green velvet. It had the stuffy atmosphere of a room that was rarely used.

She kept the plush curtains partly closed to avoid fading the red and burgundy carpet square. She had to move the aspidistra to get close to the window, but she couldn't see the girls in the road either.

Clucking with annoyance, she went out through her front door and on to the pavement of Woodchurch Lane. From here she could see up to Storeton Road and down past the row of shops, in one of which Maddy's mother carried on her hairdressing business. The family lived in the rooms above it.

She let out a pent-up breath of relief. The girls were peering through the salon door. Little devils! They had no business to go away without telling her. As she watched, Madeleine went inside and Alice, still gripping Wobble, turned towards home, her head low in misery.

Alice crept in through the back door. She'd kept going for the last ten minutes by telling herself that Dadda might be here by now. As soon as she saw Gran reading the paper, she knew he wasn't, but she couldn't help asking:

'Has he come yet?'

'Not yet, dear.'

Gran was tired of telling her that, she knew from her voice. Alice felt cold inside.

'Maddy's gone home. Uncle Frank's there.'

'You should have told me before leaving the yard. I don't like you wandering off by yourselves.'

'Sorry, Gran.'

'Would you like to go down and play with Maddy? Uncle Frank likes to have you there.'

'No.'

'All right, then we'll go to the shops.'

Gran splashed water into the enamel bowl in the scullery sink. Alice felt the cold wet flannel swish across her face, then more carefully across her palms, and lastly it scrubbed at the dirty marks she'd made on her frock.

Gran always went shopping at this time on a Saturday afternoon. She said shopkeepers were glad to get rid of their produce at this time and often threw in little extras for their customers.

She followed Gran upstairs and watched from the doorway as she took off her apron and changed her frock. Gran had to sit on the side of the double bed to see herself in her dressing-table mirror. She dabbed powder on her large Roman nose and redid her iron-grey hair into the tight roll that rested along the top of her collar. She was thin-faced and gaunt, and her hands were red with housework.

Gran got up suddenly. Alice felt a comb scratch through her hair. She asked: 'Can't I stay here? In case Dadda comes.'

'It'll do you good to have a little walk. You can help me carry the shopping.'

'But Dadda . . .'

'If Dadda comes while we're out, he'll wait.'

Gran was skewering her hat to her head when Alice heard the back-yard gate scrape open. She raced to the back door.

Uncle Peter, the younger of her two uncles, still lived at home. He was wheeling his bike into the yard. Alice gulped with disappointment as she saw him prop it against the wall. She'd thought Dadda was coming at last.

'Hello, kid,' he smiled.

Peter took after his mother rather than his father, though he hadn't inherited her Roman nose. His was straight and thin, and his eyes were brighter blue and more kindly.

He worked in a bakery up on the main road and didn't come home for his dinner. He said there was more than enough food on the spot, and old Mr Best thought he ought to taste what he baked. Now he was sliding a bag off his handlebars. He always brought the bread Gran ordered home with him.

Alice felt hope die. Dadda wasn't going to come. Tears were burning her eyes. She rushed to the lavatory and locked herself in. She didn't want Peter to see her cry.

Tears scalded her cheeks as she pulled herself up on to the scrubbed wooden seat. She mopped them up with one of the squares of newspaper she'd helped Gran thread on the string.

Edith reached over to the kettle that was singing on the hob. Peter always wanted a cup of tea when he came in.

He had to be at work by five in the morning to start baking, and was usually home just after three. He was taking off his bicycle clips. She could see by the way he bent down that he was tired.

Peter was fourteen years younger than Len and Frank. They'd been growing up; she'd thought of her family as complete, and it had changed everything for her when she was caught on the change with Peter.

She'd welcomed him once she'd got over the shock, of course she had. Her family was everything to her. It had been more than a shock, all those nappies and wakeful nights again, but Peter was a delight, everybody liked him.

He was nineteen now, and old Mr Best was relying on him more and more. Peter was ambitious like Frank. Edith could see him taking over that bakery in a few years, when Mr Best wanted to retire.

'Hello, Mam.'

His hair was straight and light brown until the summer sun put bright streaks in it. Whatever he did with it, it always fell over his face.

She said: 'No wonder they make you wear a cap at work. You ought to get that hair cut.'

'Give over, you're always on about my hair. I'd still have to wear a cap even if it was short.'

He had a gentle, good-natured face, although he was not quite so obviously handsome as his brothers. He reached for the tea pot she'd put on the table for him.

'It won't be brewed yet.'

15

He went on pouring. 'It's fine. Just as I like it. I'm parched.'

Alice let herself into the kitchen and went to sit at the table with him.

'You still here then?' he asked.

'Dadda didn't come.' Her face was blotchy with tears.

'I expect he will.'

'Will he be much longer?'

'I don't know, kid. Fetch a cup and I'll pour you some tea.'

Alice shook her head. 'Don't want any.'

Edith sighed. 'Will you take her home, Peter? She's dying to go.'

'Mam! I'm dropping, I can't. You take her.'

'I've got to go shopping.'

'I need a nap.'

Edith knew he'd flake out on his bed after his early start. He'd sleep now until about five. It was Saturday, and tomorrow was the only day in the week he didn't have to get up before five in the morning. He'd want to go out and enjoy himself.

Alice was curling up in misery.

'Later then. After you've had your nap.'

'Oh, Mam! I'm going out with Eric.'

Eric Ainslie lived next door, and though he was more than a year younger than Peter, they'd been friends since they left school.

'It's all arranged.'

'Where are you going?'

'There's a do on at the rugby club.'

'You'll have plenty of time to take Alice home first, and it won't be much out of your way.'

'It's miles out of our way, and we were going to have a drink first. For goodness' sake, Mam, it's Saturday night.'

'I can go home by myself,' Alice said defiantly.

'No,' Gran retorted. 'You've got to change buses at

Woodside and there's your case to carry. Anyway, I want to know what's happened to your father.'

'What has happened?' Alice's face was full of fear.

Peter sighed. 'It's OK, Alice. Let me have forty winks, and if your dad's not here by the time we've had tea, I'll take you home.'

'That's settled then.' Edith pulled herself to her feet. 'Come on, Alice, we'll go down to the shops.'

Peter felt guilty as he went upstairs. He couldn't help feeling sorry for Alice. He remembered the first time she'd come to stay with them. She'd only been three; little more than a baby. She had stayed with them on and off after that, and for a long time when she was six. Almost every day she'd asked him: 'Will Mummy be coming home today?'

'I don't know, kid.' What else could he say?

There'd been dozens of questions he couldn't answer.

'When will she be coming back? Where's she gone?'

He'd had to shake his head. The solemn face and imploring green eyes had gone through him. It hurt to see such longing and suffering in one so young.

Every time Beryl went away, Alice went through the same agony: 'Dadda wants Mam to come back. He told me he does.'

'Of course he does.' Peter had squeezed her hand. 'I do too.'

'Why does she go away all the time? Where does she go?'

Where indeed? Peter had wondered too. Len didn't confide in him. To Len he was still a half-grown lad. Peter was almost sure he didn't confide in their parents either, but he thought Frank knew more.

During Peter's growing years, there'd always seemed to be some new rumour about Beryl. When he went into a room, Mam and Dad would stop talking abruptly, and he'd know they'd been discussing Beryl. As though there was something they didn't want him to know. He knew they didn't like her.

He felt close to Alice, but taking her home on Saturday night was still a bit of a bind. Why Len had let Mam talk him into a job at Lever's, he didn't know. He'd given himself miles further to travel to work. Now he was trying to swap his house in the North End for one in Bromborough, and he was on the list for a house in Port Sunlight. Len never thought anything through. He'd been down in the dumps since Beryl had gone away again, dragging himself round.

The North End was miles out of their way. They'd planned on having a drink first at the Swan, and tonight was a big night. They'd met two girls at a dance last week who'd said they'd be going to the rugby club tonight. He really fancied the little dark one. Julie, she'd said her name was.

At tea time, Alice looked with dismay at the big slice of ham Gran had put on her plate. Beside her, Uncle Peter was yawning but making good headway into his share. Gran was cross because Grandpa hadn't come back from his allotment.

'I don't know where he gets to,' she fumed. 'He said he'd bring some salad stuff back with him for tea. He knew I was going to buy tomatoes to go with it. Never gives a thought to anyone else. He knows you go out on Saturday night.'

'We won't go hungry on this, Mam.'

'Salad makes it go further. Serve him right if there was no ham left.'

Alice didn't know how she was going to get through what was on her plate, because Gran had made her leave Wobble on the rocking chair by the fire and her own dress had no pocket. She was chewing and chewing but the meat wouldn't go down. She didn't want food, she wanted Dadda; she was afraid he'd gone away too.

'You'll feel better when you get that inside you,' Gran

said. 'Come on, eat up. Let's have no nonsense about feeding it to that cat.'

When she got up to fetch the tea pot from the hob to refill their cups, Alice watched Uncle Peter's fork come over and hook the rest of her ham on to his plate. When Gran took the tea pot back, a piece of tomato followed. Alice swallowed what was in her mouth and looked up in relief. Uncle Peter winked at her.

There was a knock on the back door. Peter got up to let his friend in.

'Just finishing my tea. Won't be long.'

'Have a cup in your hand?' Gran invited. 'While you wait.'

'No thank you, Mrs Luckett. Just got up from the table myself.'

Eric sat on the rocking chair and pulled Wobble up on his knee. He was darker than any of the Lucketts, and more squarely built. His hair usually had a slight wave to it but now, still damp from his bath, it was combed straight back.

Alice knew him. He lived next door and often came round to see Peter. His eyes were dark brown, friendly and gentle. He was wearing his best Harris tweed jacket, with grey flannel slacks that he'd made himself. His white shirt was soft-collared and his tie dark blue.

'I want Peter to take our Alice home first,' Gran told him. 'Before you start your night on the town.'

'I've brought my bike round. Thought we were going on our bikes.'

'Alice could sit on my crossbar,' Peter suggested.

'There's her case and that great toy. And a pie I've made. Len'll have no food in. Better if you take her on the bus,' Gran said.

'They stop running at midnight. It's easier . . .'

Alice froze. What if they suggested she wait until morning? Eric's fingers were pulling something sticky from

Wobble's fur. He didn't look pleased, but it seemed they were agreed. They'd take her, and they'd go by bus.

Then it was all fluster as they got ready to go. Gran was wiping Alice's face and hands over again with a flannel. Uncle Peter brought down her case, while Eric hurried her arms into the coat with the velvet collar and tried to put the matching hat on her head. She had to pull it straight.

She walked down Woodchurch Lane between them, trying to swallow back the apprehension that was rising in her throat. Ever since Mam had gone she'd had this awful dread of what would happen to her if Dadda went too.

Her dress was damp and clung to her bare legs because Gran had sponged it again. She'd been cross because the dirty marks hadn't come out the first time.

The bus was crowded as they rode into town. Eric had to stand, but Peter found a seat just inside and pulled Alice up on his knee. He held her close to show affection.

'Uncle Peter, if . . .'

'Don't call me Uncle. It makes me feel ancient.' He grinned at her. 'Just Peter.'

'Peter, what if Dadda isn't home yet?'

'He will be by now.'

'Then why didn't he come and fetch me like he said he would?'

'I don't know, kid. But we'll find out when we get you home.'

'Perhaps he forgot about me?'

'Perhaps he's just fallen asleep in the chair, something silly like that. We'll soon find out.'

Alice felt frightened. Dadda was supposed to call for her on the way home from work. He must have forgotten about her, otherwise he couldn't have got home to fall asleep in his chair.

When they got off the bus and walked down Gautby Road, Eric wanted to give Wobble a piggy-back but she wouldn't part with him. It made her forget for a few moments.

Then she was leading the way round the back of her home. Miraculously, everything seemed all right. She wanted to laugh out loud. Dadda's bike was in its usual place, leaning up against the side of the house. He must be here.

The back door was tight and always difficult to open. Uncle Peter had to put his shoulder to it. Alice, feeling all excited and eager, pushed past him and ran inside.

'What a funny smell,' she laughed, but then it caught in her throat and seemed to burn. It was darker inside and it took a moment for her eyes to get used to it.

'Dadda? Dadda! Oh!'

The next instant she felt Peter take a firm grip on the collar of her coat and jerk her back outside.

Chapter Two

Eric wasn't pleased that Peter had been talked into taking Alice home. Without their bikes, they'd have to leave the dance before the buses stopped running or face a long walk home in the small hours. He knew Len, and he felt sorry for his child, but he hadn't wanted Peter to take her home and he hadn't wanted to go with them. It was a waste of time on a Saturday night.

Going round the back of the house, Eric had been bringing up the rear, his mind anywhere but on what they might find, but the moment he heard the child scream, he recognised the smell. It was gas. It was coming out of the door in choking clouds. It was everywhere, and Alice was screaming and coughing and spluttering and waving her thin arms about.

She was shouting, 'Dadda, Dadda,' over and over. When he saw her plucking at the inert figure lying across the kitchen floor with his head in the gas oven, his heart turned over.

He had a momentary glimpse of Peter. He'd thought him paralysed with shock, but suddenly he leapt to life, grabbed at Alice and started dragging her out.

Eric could feel himself shaking but he knew what had to be done. He took a deep breath and dashed in to turn off the gas and throw open the window. He had to get out again to fill his lungs with clean air, and he knew he had to pull Len Luckett outside as soon as he could. Alice was screaming at full pitch the whole time.

Len was heavier than Eric was himself. He couldn't budge

him until Peter came back to help. Together they dragged him to the back door and down the step to the weed-filled garden. Alice was at them like a mad thing, pushing to get at her father.

'Dadda, wake up! He's not dead? Tell me he's not dead?'

Her shrieks were bringing out the neighbours, and a woman came and threw her arms round Alice to take her away. Eric could still hear her screaming from the next-door house; the sound was turning his blood to water.

'Dadda, don't die! Don't let him die. Don't let him die.'

Len wasn't moving, but he didn't look dead. As Eric remembered him, he'd been sallow. Now he had rosy cheeks and pink lips, and he looked healthier than he had done for a long time. Peter looked a lot worse. He was as fraught as Alice.

'Len, Len, wake up!' He was slapping his brother's face, trying to bring him round.

'What can I do?' His frightened eyes swung up to Eric's, imploring him. 'What can we do?'

Other people were gathering. 'Artificial respiration,' someone suggested.

'How do I do that?' Peter cried. Eric didn't know. Nobody seemed to know exactly how it should be done, but they were pushing on Len's ribs, trying to drive clean air into him. Soon a small crowd was filling the garden.

Eric took another deep breath, held it, and rushed back into the house. He propped the front door open to get a through draught. Threw open some more windows.

Realisation was beginning to dawn on him. Len Luckett had tried to kill himself. He wondered what could possibly have driven him to such an awful step. He felt cold with horror. It was impossible to breathe inside the house even now, and he rushed out to the garden again. Len was still inert, though two men were working on him.

Another man asked: 'Shall we send for an ambulance?'

'Yes please,' Eric said. 'And what about the police? Do we need them too?'

'I think so.' Peter was bent over in agony and shock.

Eric came out in a cold sweat himself as he remembered that both he and Peter had been smoking as they'd walked down from the bus. He'd dropped what was left of his Woodbine in the gutter outside the garden gate and ground his heel on it. If they'd had lighted cigarettes in their hands when Peter had opened the door, they could all have been blown sky-high. He tripped over Wobble in the crush round Len. Alice was still screaming next door.

'Take her home,' Peter gasped. 'Take her back to my mam. Don't let her see her dad like this.'

'Right.'

'We can't do anything. It's no good. We're too late.'

'Mustn't blame yourself.' Eric tried to comfort him. 'Not your fault.'

'It is. Mam wanted me to come down at three o'clock,' Peter wailed, unable to drag his gaze from the still form of his brother. 'I knew he was depressed. We all did. We shouldn't have let this happen.'

There was nothing Eric could do but pat his friend's shoulder. Peter looked unsteady on his feet; he was holding on to the waist-high fence.

'Go on, take Alice back. I'll have to stay here and see to things. Talk to the police.'

'What shall I tell your mother?' Eric was aghast at the thought.

'Anything. She'll have to know. Anyway, she's tougher than the rest of us put together. I'll come as soon as I can.'

Eric ached for Alice as they walked up to the bus stop. She'd been so eager on the journey down, looking forward to getting home and seeing her dad.

She'd gone quiet now, her little face sad and bewildered, like that of a miniature adult. As though what she'd seen had made her grow up instantly. He had her firmly by the hand, her suitcase in his other. He didn't know what had happened to the pie but Wobble had been restored to her care. For once she was letting his feet drag along the pavement. Eric's stomach churned with sympathy.

'Where are we going?' she asked, as though she'd only just noticed they were going anywhere.

'Back to your gran's.'

'Is my dadda dead?' Her eyes, red and swollen with crying, searched his face. There was no point in lying; she'd seen too much.

He said as gently as he could: 'I'm not sure, Alice, but I think he might be.'

'So do I.'

Eric didn't know what to say next. He felt agonised, still in a state of shock himself.

'Will my mam come back for me, do you think? Now Dadda's dead, there's no one else.'

'I don't know. You must ask your gran.'

'She won't know either.' Her voice was matter-of-fact. 'Who will look after me now?'

'Your gran will.'

'She won't want to. I'm a lot of work for her.'

Eric tightened his grip on her hand. How did he comfort the poor child?

'Your Uncle Peter will help to look after you. He likes having you in the same house.'

'Perhaps. Yes, perhaps he might.'

'I'll help too. I want to.'

When they reached the bus stop, he put an arm round her thin shoulders and pulled her close. Finding that her father had gassed himself was the worst hell he could think of for a nine-year-old child. He didn't know how to offer comfort.

She was clinging to him. On the bus, she buried her face in his jacket, his best Harris tweed too. She was twisting it, pulling the material out of shape. He knew she was crying again, but silently now. He pushed his handkerchief into her hand. It was all he could do to stop his own tears running down his face.

Eric knew his step was slowing as they turned into Woodchurch Lane. He was dreading having to tell Mrs Luckett what had happened. He was tempted to go straight to his own house and keep Alice there until Peter came. But it was too late; he could see Peter's mother walking up from the shops to her front door. She was staring at them, her eyes wide with surprise.

From thirty yards she called: 'What are you bringing her back for?'

That made Alice cry again. Eric hurried closer.

'What's happened?'

There was nothing for it, he'd have to tell her. 'Let's go inside.'

'Well, for heaven's sake! Tell me what's happened . . .'

'Dadda's dead,' Alice whispered, her face twisting with agony.

'What? Glory be! No, he can't be. Don't be telling such stories.'

'Let's go inside.' Eric urged her towards her own front door, relieved that Alice had got the words out, because he'd never have been able to. His own mother doted on him; he knew it would be the end of the world to her if anything happened to him.

He followed Edith up the narrow hall and urged her into the rocking chair in the kitchen. The colour had drained from her face.

'Is it true? Our Len . . . ?'

'I'm afraid it might be. They were still trying artificial respiration.'

'But what happened? Tell me.'

'I think he wanted to take his own life. Gassed himself.'

'Oh my God!' Edith flung her apron over her head and sobbed noisily. 'Not our Len?'

Eric felt even less capable of comforting her than he had Alice, who was crying noisily again and clinging to him. He couldn't prise her fingers away from his jacket and there was no other way to loosen her grip. He put a comforting arm round the child's shoulders and pulled her closer. He felt helpless in the presence of such grief and didn't know what to do.

'Shall I fetch my mam?' he asked.

'Frank,' Edith gasped. 'Go for our Frank. He's at home, I've just come from there. Took them a cake I'd made.'

'All right.'

Eric was glad to get away, glad to have something useful to do. He had to take Alice with him; she wouldn't loosen her grip.

It was Cecily, Frank's wife, who answered the door. He said as little as possible, just that Frank was wanted at home.

She frowned. 'His mother was here a minute ago. What does she want?'

'Something's happened.'

'What?'

'She'll tell him. Ask him to go straight away.'

Eric had made up his mind to keep out of it. He'd go home and take Alice with him for a bit, but he'd hardly turned back when he heard Frank's footsteps running after him.

'What's the matter? Is it our Len?'

He had to tell him then. He couldn't pussyfoot about any more. Frank was a grown man and could handle it. When Eric and Peter were small and they did something Frank didn't like, he used to bang their heads together. Eric wasn't all that keen on Frank.

'Oh my God!' Frank was visibly shocked. 'He was dead when you found him?'

'Shush,' he said, nodding down towards Alice's head. 'Peter will be home soon, he'll tell you all about it. Your mother wants you now. She's upset . . .'

'Damn it, I'm upset. He's my twin . . . Look, get my dad for us, will you? Mam'll want him. You'll find him in the Halfway House.'

Eric didn't need to be told where Mr Luckett would be. It was common knowledge that he walked to the local pub almost every evening.

'All right. Will you go in with Uncle Frank now?' He put a finger under Alice's chin and made her look up at him.

She was shaking her head. 'Want to stay with you.'

'You won't be able to come into the pub with me. They don't let children in. You'll have to wait outside.' Nothing would budge her little fingers. She was clinging to him like a limpet.

'I'll tell Mam she's with you,' Frank said.

That meant he'd have to take her. Eric felt for her hand, took it firmly in his, and strode out.

'I shouldn't have brought you,' he worried. 'It's much busier up here on the main road, and it's dark now.'

She sniffed and he felt her fingers tighten in his.

'You won't be frightened to stay outside by yourself?'

She was shaking her head. From making so much noise, now it seemed she couldn't make any sound at all.

'I won't be long then. You stay here. Don't go away.'

Eric pushed the door open. The convivial sounds grated tonight; he wasn't in the mood for jollity. But horror had made his mouth dry, and his tongue felt like old leather. The smell of beer was tempting. What couldn't he do with a pint?

He walked through the tap room to the lounge, looking for Monty Luckett. He was nowhere to be seen. Eric stood with his back to the bar and let his eyes travel from one table to the next. He couldn't see the shock of grey hair, nor the familiar flat cap in brown checks.

He turned and shouted to one of the two barmen: 'Has Monty Luckett been in tonight?'

They were busy, and he had to repeat the question.

29

'Not tonight.'

He watched the man fill a pint tankard and the froth spill over. 'Are you sure?'

'Course I'm sure. Monty Luckett never comes in on a Saturday night, does he, Charlie?'

'No, don't see as much of him as we used to.'

Somebody guffawed. 'Got better things to do, has Monty.'

Eric wanted the taste of beer on his tongue. He jingled coins in his pocket.

'Give me . . .' But he mustn't. Alice was waiting outside. 'Five Woodbines,' he finished. As he put them in his pocket, his best Harris tweed jacket felt damp where she'd buried her face in it. There was an ominous dark and twisted patch; he hoped it would be all right when it dried.

Reluctantly he went out. Alice was shivering, hunched against the wall of the pub, her head buried in the fur of her monkey. She hadn't moved an inch.

'Your grandpa's not here,' he told her, feeling for her hand. 'Come on, let's go home.'

She looked up at him with green eyes so full of tragedy, he felt his throat tighten all over again.

Alice felt as though the end of the world had come, yet somehow she'd survived. Nobody knew where Mam had gone, and now Dadda had gone too. Terror was curdling her stomach; she felt abandoned and alone. She couldn't think what would happen to her now. She knew nothing could ever be the same again.

Her eyes felt hot and sore, and her legs ached; they were tired from all the walking about. She felt ready to drop, but she couldn't leave go of Eric. He'd been there when she'd found Dadda. He understood what had happened and was being kind.

She took comfort from the arm round her shoulders, but he was taking her to Gran's house. She dragged her feet.

When his hand went out to the knocker on her front door, she twisted round to look at him.

'No,' she pleaded. 'Grandpa isn't there, or Uncle Peter. Not yet.'

He looked taken aback, quite shocked really, and she felt him hesitate.

'Where d'you want to go then? I'm shattered. Surely it's time you were in bed?'

'Not yet.'

'I'm going home. I've had enough. D'you want to come with me?'

Alice nodded and took a firmer grip on his hand as he turned to the next-door house. Alongside the front door was a large wooden board that read: 'Mrs N. Ainslie, High-Class Dressmaker. Curtains and upholstery undertaken.'

During the hours of business, their front door always stood open. A sign on the lobby door invited everybody to enter. That door pinged like a shop door every time it was opened.

Propped up in the hall was an even larger notice that was put outside every morning. It listed the prices Eric's mother charged for her work and invited customers inside.

Gran did not approve of it. She said it was lowering the tone for neighbouring houses and shouldn't be allowed. If Nell Ainslie wanted to run a business, she should move to a shop.

Alice had been inside with Peter many times and knew Eric's home was very different. She followed him into the front room, where his mother was still at work. Her treadle sewing machine was racing up a long seam on a vast expanse of red velvet.

Alice had never seen so much lovely material and couldn't resist putting out her hand to stroke it. It felt soft and comforting. Softer than Wobble's fur. She saw a small offcut on the floor and picked it up.

'You shouldn't still be working at this hour,' Eric said wearily. 'You take on too much.'

31

'I wasn't expecting you back before midnight.' Nell Ainslie was a plump, motherly woman. 'And curtains are easy, I can do them when I'm tired. Hello, Alice.'

She had a soft and gentle voice, not like anybody else Alice knew. Enough of her accent had rubbed off on Eric to make him sound a little different too. She watched his mother's grey eyes, kindly behind her rimless spectacles, slide to Eric.

'What's brought you home so early?'

Alice buried her face in Eric's jacket again. She didn't want to hear what he would tell his mother. The next moment she felt herself enveloped in a hug and half carried to the fire in the kitchen.

'You poor little mite. Some cocoa? Would you like that?'

Eric collapsed on a chair.

'Are you all right, Eric? It must have been a shock for you.'

'Worse for Alice,' he sighed. 'And Peter. It's been a terrible evening for us all. Could you go next door and tell them Monty isn't at the Halfway House, and that Alice is here with us? I can't face . . .'

Alice sank down to the hearth rug and leaned against his legs. It helped that Eric couldn't face things either.

Chapter Three

Monty Luckett had a spring in his step as he came out of Rita Hooper's house in Carlaw Road. She'd bought it quite recently, a lovely new house, quite a big one.

He turned for home. He'd had a good day, and tomorrow promised to be even better. He was quite proud of the way he was managing to keep both sides of his life under control. Edith hadn't the slightest idea. He'd be home right on time tonight. The pubs had just closed.

He'd been visiting Rita for the last two years though Edith believed he was going to the pub. He felt he was living two separate lives. It made him feel on top of his form, bursting with the energy of a man half his age.

As he turned into Woodchurch Lane and glanced down at his own house, he felt his first misgivings. Always, when he came home at this time of night, he saw a pink glow from the upstairs bay window. Edith was a creature of habit. She read the paper in bed until he came in. Tonight, there were no lights on upstairs, but the hall light burned. Edith's thrift didn't usually allow her to leave that on.

He turned his key in the front door and went in. He could hear voices from the kitchen. He hooked his cap on the hall stand with a sense of foreboding, afraid that something had happened.

Edith called. 'Is that you, Monty?'

The small kitchen seemed crowded. Frank, Cecily and Peter had pulled dining chairs close to the range and the fire had not been allowed to die. That and their sorrowful faces warned him that something very bad had happened. Edith's eyes were red from crying.

'Where've you been?' she demanded angrily.

The question was the one he dreaded most.

'Just out for a drink. You knew that.'

'We've been looking everywhere for you,' Frank said. 'You weren't in the Halfway House.'

Monty felt his heart begin to pound.

'No, it got crowded. Why d'you come looking for me? You knew I'd be back just after eleven.'

Of his three sons, Frank was the one most like him to look at. Tall, with wide shoulders, easily the most handsome, with the same thick, glossy head of hair Monty had had in his youth, the same luxuriant moustache. Though Frank was more confident and aggressive than his father had ever been. More determined to get what he wanted in this world.

Frank's steel-blue eyes stared into his; there was something confrontational about them. He was getting uppish, too big for his boots.

'Where did you go?'

Monty could feel anger rising in his throat. He turned on him savagely.

'Down to the Swan. What is this, an inquisition? What's happened?'

'All right, Dad. There's no need to blow up.'

'Is it Len? Has he had an accident or something?'

'Worse than that.' Tears were rolling down Edith's cheeks. 'He's killed himself. Committed suicide.'

That knocked the breath out of him. He groped for a chair and sank down on it.

'Wha-at? No! Not our Len. He's not the sort.'

But he knew he was, he was exactly the sort. He'd never got over his war-time shell-shock, and Beryl's goings-on had driven him near the edge. It was only a few weeks since she'd gone again. He hadn't seemed all that upset at the time, but clearly he must have been.

'Gassed himself,' Frank added.

Monty moistened his lips. 'Who found him?'

Peter's agonised eyes met his. 'Alice. I took her there.' Monty heard emotion break in his son's throat.

'It was dreadful. Enough to give me nightmares. I wish she hadn't seen him.'

'Isn't it awful?' Cecily dabbed at her eyes.

'What did he have to do that for?' Monty asked indignantly, looking round his family. 'We could have helped.'

'He left a note.' Edith pushed a sheet torn from an exercise book across the table to him.

Monty felt too agitated to read it. 'What's he say?'

'He asks Frank to look after Alice.'

'Frank? Why you, Frank? We always look after her. Is that all? No reason . . . ?'

'Just that he couldn't go on. That things were getting too much for him.'

'Oh my God! The silly fool. Why didn't he tell us? He could have come here for a bit till he'd got over it. Whatever was troubling him.'

Monty could feel sweat breaking out on his face. They were all staring at him accusingly.

Edith's face was twisting with agony. She took a deep, shuddering breath.

'If you'd gone down to his place right after dinner, when I asked you to, you might have been able to stop him. But no, you had to go to your precious allotment instead.'

Monty felt a tide of guilt run through him. His face felt fiery. He hadn't been to his allotment. He hadn't owned an allotment this last year. Rita had one of those big new semis with a large garden. He grew vegetables for her and brought some home for Edith, to keep her believing that things hadn't changed.

Anger made him turn on her: 'You could have gone yourself. Why didn't you take Alice home?'

'I've got enough to do here. Looking after this house, and

35

all the cooking and washing for two men. And there's been no school; don't forget I've had two children to look after all this week.'

'I'd have thought you'd be glad to get out of the house for a change. Ride down there on the bus.'

'I get tired too. I can't do everything.'

'We could all have gone down sooner,' Peter said gravely. 'But we didn't. No point in trying to blame each other.'

'I blame Beryl.' Edith spat the name out. 'Yes, Beryl's got a lot to answer for. She's driven him to this.'

Monty sat back in his chair. He blamed himself. He'd been too wrapped up in his own interests to offer even token help to Len. He should have done more, but what? The lad was grown up, he could be prickly if anyone asked questions. Len hadn't wanted his father to interfere.

Edith was crying again. 'I remember my own mother, I thought her heart would break when my brothers were killed in the fighting. This is worse, much worse. Taking his own life like that. He must have known what this would do to me.'

Monty felt shaky; he was appalled at what had happened. Len must have been in a very black mood to do such a thing, must have felt terrible. Poor Len, he hated to think . . . He must put it out of his mind.

Cecily swung the kettle over the fire. 'Shall I make some more tea?'

Monty watched her take the tea pot out to the scullery sink to empty the slops. If Len had married a girl like Cecily, she'd have kept him on an even keel. Cecily was a good-looking girl, with pale-brown hair which benefited from frequent camomile rinses to bring out its golden highlights. She knew how to enhance her looks. She'd been taught to do facials and paint fingernails and things like that, and she had good dress sense.

She had a stylish gloss, the sort that usually cost a lot of money, and he was proud to call her his daughter-in-law.

But it wasn't just her looks. Cecily had a lovely warm manner. She seemed to care for people, give out affection to everyone.

He'd watched her hand go out to touch Frank many times, and her eyes could shine with love when she looked at him. He envied Frank, he had to say that.

'Tea?' Cecily pushed a brimming cup in front of him. He was usually careful to refuse when he was supposed to have come straight from an evening on the beer, but tonight his mouth was dry with shock. He needed it.

Edith ignored hers. 'I don't know how I'm going to hold my head up in front of the neighbours. It was bad enough having to admit his wife had upped and walked out on him again. But now . . . I'll be ashamed to admit he's done for himself like this.

'I did my best for him. Always did my best for you all. I've spent my whole life . . .'

Frank said: 'I know, Mam. Don't upset yourself again.'

Monty felt a prickling of irritation with Frank. There were times when he seemed to take over as head of the family. This was one of them. There was no doubt that Frank was very capable, and he willingly took on responsibilities and duties. He was quite the opposite of Len. Hard to believe they were twins. Not that they were the identical sort.

For a start, Frank had both feet on the ground. He'd been a physical training instructor in the army, and when he'd been discharged at the end of the war he'd been very fit. He'd married well too. Cecily was a lovely girl.

'I am upset. All I've ever wanted was to bring up my family decently. I wanted you all to get ahead, have decent lives.'

'Mam, we do have decent lives,' Frank assured her.

'Len didn't, but I did my duty. We've nothing to reproach ourselves with, have we, Monty?'

'Of course not,' he told her. But he could have done more, and so could she. Edith just didn't see it that way.

'Family meant everything to me. Still does.'

'There's Alice to think of now,' Peter reminded them.

'Alice?' Edith looked up, aghast.

Monty knew that Peter had thought his mother would be pleased that there was still family needing her.

'Where is she?' he asked.

'I put her to bed here,' Cecily said. 'In the middle room. She was terrified. Our Maddy's keeping her company. It's like three in the bed, with the monkey on her other side. She'll be all right.'

'I suppose there'll be no getting rid of Alice now?' Edith's ravaged face turned to Frank. 'Len seemed to think you . . .'

'You wouldn't want to get rid of her,' Monty said gently. He felt full of pity. He'd never wanted to do more for Alice than he did at that moment.

'I'll do my duty by her, just as I did by the others.' Edith's face was stiff with reluctance. 'It's just that she'll stop us doing what we want. It'll be years before she's off our hands. I had such plans for you and me, Monty. For when you retire.'

Monty could feel himself shaking. He knew Edith was after a new bungalow. The last thing he wanted was to move from here. It was just the right distance from Carlaw Road. A short walk, yet far enough away for those living in one not to know the occupants of the other.

He didn't want to retire, he hated to think of it, yet Edith never stopped talking about it, planning for it. He didn't like admitting he was as near to it as he was. He was five years younger than his wife, only fifty-seven.

Rita wanted him to spend more time with her, but he didn't know how to extricate himself from Edith after thirty-four years. He was torn between loyalty and doing what he really wanted.

'This is the best place for Alice,' Peter said. 'She's used to us. I'll try to take her off your hands a bit at the weekends,

Mam. Really I will. Poor kid. She couldn't wait to get home, could she?'

'I'll help,' Cecily said.

'What can you do?' Edith sniffed into her handkerchief. 'I have to look after your Madeleine when she's not at school. You can't do much, not with your shop. There's always something to stop me doing what I want.'

'She can come and spend the night with us from time to time,' Frank said. 'It's no harder to get two up for school than one.'

'She'll be company for Maddy,' Cecily smiled. 'And they're both getting older.'

'If everybody takes a turn, it won't be too much for you.' Monty tried to comfort Edith.

'Perhaps not.' She sounded reluctant to admit it. 'And you'll be able to take her down to your allotment with you.'

That made him run with guilt again.

At breakfast the next morning, Alice watched Maddy tucking into her boiled egg and toast while she struggled to swallow hers. Gran's eyes were red and swollen; all the grown-ups seemed on edge. Alice wondered if they all felt as she did, as though they were living a nightmare.

'You've got to do something about the house,' Gran was saying.

'What house?' Grandpa was irritable.

'Len's house, of course! You'll have to let the council know tomorrow. Otherwise we'll have to pay the rent. You'll have to get his furniture out.'

Alice watched Grandpa stroke his moustache. 'I suppose so, but what can we do with all his stuff? We haven't got room for it here.'

'It'll have to be sold.'

'We can't do that in ten minutes.'

'There's my things,' Alice put in faintly.

'Course there are, love,' Gran said fiercely. 'We'll have to fetch your clothes up. Honestly, Monty, what are you thinking of? If you aren't going to do it, I'll talk to Frank. He will.'

At that moment, Alice heard Uncle Frank and Aunt Cecily coming through the back door. Maddy ran to her mother for a hug.

Alice had always seen a lot of Uncle Frank; he was often round at their house. She'd heard him order Dadda about and knew Frank could make him do things even if he didn't want to. He'd made Dadda nervous, and sometimes she'd thought Dadda was afraid of his twin.

They were not much alike. Frank was much bigger and stronger, and always wanted his own way. He was more handsome too, with confident blue eyes that had a way of looking at her as though she was one of his possessions.

Alice didn't know how to take him. Sometimes Uncle Frank was cold and cruel and wanted her out of his way. At other times she could feel his love, strong and more intense than Dadda's.

He was always generous with pennies and sweets, and sometimes, if he was in the mood, he'd play with her, lifting her up on his shoulders. It made her feel ill at ease in his company, wary of him.

'How are you, Alice?' Frank bent down to kiss her cheek and give her a hug. He was too rough and hurt her arm.

'Feeling a bit better this morning? Did you have a good night's sleep?'

'Yes,' she whispered, though she'd had a terrible night.

Uncle Peter smiled encouragingly from across the table. He'd crept in twice in the night to offer comfort. Maddy had slept through it all.

Frank straightened up. He always held his shoulders back and his head high.

'We've got to do something about Len's house. Sort his stuff out and close it down.'

40

'Thank goodness for someone with sense,' Gran said.

'That's why I'm here so early. I thought I'd go down this morning.'

Alice said: 'I want to go with you.'

'No need for that, love,' Gran and Grandpa said together.

'I want to go,' she said more fiercely. 'It's my home. I want to get my things.'

'All right, all right.' Uncle Frank rocked back on his feet in his superior way. 'You'd better come, Mam, to help Alice pack.'

'We'll all go,' Peter said. 'We'd better take suitcases.'

'No need for you,' Frank said pointedly. 'There's nothing of yours there.'

'He can help,' Gran said. 'We'll need all the help we can get.'

In the end, Cecily decided to stay at Gran's to put her Sunday dinner in the oven for her. She kept Maddy with her. Monty said he was going to his allotment as usual.

On the journey down, Alice wondered why she'd wanted to go back home again. She felt for Uncle Peter's hand as Frank unlocked the front door. All the inside doors stood open. She held her breath; she couldn't stop her eyes going to the kitchen. Somebody had closed the oven door.

Gran clucked with impatience.

'What a mess! You'd have thought Len could have washed his dishes.'

'He had other things on his mind,' Peter said, his voice tight.

Alice felt Gran take hold of her other hand. 'We'll go up to your room and pack your things.'

The suitcase they'd brought was opened on the bed and Gran began taking her clothes from the wardrobe. Before packing them she held each garment up to examine it.

'Not worth taking,' she said of every other one, and threw them in a heap on the floor.

Alice kept her toys in two old shopping baskets, one of which had lost its handle.

'Do you really want to take all that?' Gran was eyeing them with distaste.

'Yes.' Alice took a pile of books from the windowsill and packed them in too.

'Those old books aren't worth taking.'

'I want them,' Alice insisted.

'I don't know how we'll get them home.'

Peter had come upstairs. 'Tuck a towel over the top and then I'll string it up.'

He threw open the door to the front bedroom, that had once been Beryl's.

'What's all this?'

Uncle Frank was hot on his heels. 'No need to bother about what's here.' He was trying to close the door. 'Just stuff Len was looking after for me. I'm taking it back to my place. I've asked Tommy Brent to bring his cart round this morning.'

'What is it?' Peter asked, his hand against the door.

'Stuff for the salon. Soft soap to make shampoo, setting lotions, hair tonic and stuff like that.'

'But why bring it here?'

'Len offered. He had the room to store it, didn't he? We're stuffed like sardines over the shop.'

Alice ducked under Peter's arm to look at the six wooden crates. The sight of them brought a torrent of memories flooding back.

'Dadda was frightened of them, I know he was. Frightened of the man who brought them.'

'Nonsense,' Uncle Frank said. 'It's just stuff Auntie Cecily uses. It wouldn't scare anybody.'

Alice wailed: 'Dadda didn't want them here. He told you to take them away before he got into trouble.'

She felt Frank's strong arms lifting her up and carrying her downstairs.

'Leave me.' She fought against his grasp, drummed her feet on him. His arms tightened their hold.

Gran said: 'I knew she'd be a nuisance. We shouldn't have brought her.'

Peter came to her rescue. 'Give her to me.'

Alice felt his arms lifting her away from Frank. He collapsed on a chair, holding her against him in a comforting hug.

'Don't fret yourself, Alice. It is only Cecily's stuff, I've had a look.'

She wasn't convinced. 'I know Dadda was scared of it. That's why he killed himself, I know it.'

'No, he wouldn't be afraid of hair tonic, love, would he?' Peter held her tight until her sobs began to subside.

'Come on, come and see for yourself. It's only shampoo. There's nothing to worry about. Nothing to worry anybody.'

Alice could feel her heart thudding as he led her back upstairs. Uncle Frank was on the landing, eyeing her anxiously.

'What a fuss about nothing,' he said, but she could see she was making him nervous.

'Dadda told you he was frightened,' she insisted. She'd heard him one night when she'd been in bed. 'Mam was frightened of them too.'

Frank blustered: 'There now, your mam was gone long before these came.' He looked up at Peter. 'I told you, the child doesn't know what she's saying.'

Alice couldn't argue with Uncle Frank – even Dadda hadn't been able to – but she knew she was right. There'd been other crates and boxes, they'd been coming for years. Mam had pleaded with Dadda not to let any more come.

Her gaze settled on an old metal steamer trunk. 'That tin box isn't yours,' she told Frank. 'It's full of Mam's things.'

Peter stepped over to it and lifted the lid. It was blue

43

on the inside. Alice felt tears prick her eyes again as she caught sight of the fur tippet. She could see the black silk shawl beneath it, and could picture her mother wearing them now.

'There, I told you,' Alice wailed. 'They're Mam's things, you can't have them.'

'I don't want them. I've no intention of taking them.'

'I want them,' she sobbed.

Gran clucked with irritation. 'Don't be a naughty girl. Making a fuss about nothing.

'I knew we shouldn't have brought her. It's just Beryl's cast-offs. What she didn't want to take.

'You'd have been better off at home. Bound to be hard for you, love, isn't it?'

'They're my mam's things.'

Sometimes while she'd waited for Dadda to come home, she'd peeped inside that trunk. She'd taken out some of Mam's frocks and shoes and even tried them on. It brought Mam closer.

'If she wants Beryl's things, there's no reason why she shouldn't have them,' Peter said. 'Be reasonable, Mam.'

'There's more I want.' Alice wiped away a tear of gratitude and swept half a bottle of Carnation scent and a framed photograph of Mam off the dressing table. 'Her jewellery too.'

She pulled open a small drawer and took out a cigar box full of beads and brooches.

'Jewellery,' Gran sniffed. 'Stuff from Woolworth's. Just tat.'

Alice tossed them into the open trunk. 'There's Dadda's things I want too. His clock.'

If she didn't take them now, she'd never see them again. Gran would throw them away. Spurred on by a feeling of urgency, she shot to his bedroom and snatched up the alarm with two big bells on top. She grabbed too his mottled red fountain pen that reminded her of corned beef. She saw her mother's writing case on his bedside table with some letters inside as well as half a writing pad and some envelopes. She took them all back and put them inside Mam's trunk.

Gran fumed. 'It's a load of rubbish and look how it upsets her.'

'I want them. I want my mam. Tell her I need her, Uncle Frank.' She could feel tears stinging her eyes again. 'I want her to come back.'

'Shush,' Gran told her. 'He doesn't know where she is. None of us do.'

'He does,' she insisted.

'No,' Frank said firmly. 'No, I don't.'

Alice gulped. 'You can find out. You can do everything, Uncle Frank. I wish you'd help me find her.'

Gran took Alice home on the bus and grumbled at her all the way, but Uncle Peter had promised to see that everything she wanted came up on the cart with Frank's stuff.

'I don't know where we're going to put it all,' Gran muttered under her breath. 'Oh dearie me, what a mess.'

When they got off the bus, Gran towed her down Woodchurch Lane as fast as she could. Alice had been struggling to stop tears rolling down her face for what seemed like hours. Now she gave up and let them flow.

As soon as they were indoors, she was given an aspirin and hustled upstairs to bed. She slept then, right through Sunday dinner.

Chapter Four

Frank helped Peter manoeuvre Beryl's tin trunk downstairs and add it to the pile of boxes building up in the narrow hall. He felt desperate. Beryl would be at his throat when she came home, but what else could he do? She'd turn on him, blame him for Len's death. She'd let the whole awful story out and blame him for everything. He quaked at the thought; she could ruin everything he'd built up.

And he hadn't expected Alice to make such a fuss. It had drawn the family's attention to his stuff. Exactly what he didn't want.

'God, this is awful.' He wiped the perspiration from his face, thinking of his own predicament. Then he saw Peter's eyes on him, assessing him, and said: 'Poor Len.'

'What made him do it?' Peter sounded angry. 'Why didn't he think of Alice?'

Frank felt his stomach muscles tighten. Len had thought of Alice. He'd written in his suicide note, 'Frank, please take care of Alice, I can't do it any longer.'

He'd nearly died when Peter had shown that to him, and it had been giving him palpitations ever since. He'd been waiting for one of the family to ask why. It had made him get down to Len's house as soon as he could, to hide anything that might help them draw the right conclusions.

He started to bluster: 'It's like part of me has died. A twin is a twin. So close . . .'

'But you weren't all that close.' Peter's eyes were staring into his.

'Closer than me and you.'

'You bossed him around. Made him do what you wanted.'

Frank knew he was defensive. 'One always leads and the other follows. That's the way of twins. Anyway, he wouldn't listen to me, wouldn't take my advice.'

'Frank, he was too ready to do what everybody wanted.'

'I wanted to help him.'

Yes, he had, it had mostly been for Len's benefit, but he wondered now if he'd pushed him too hard. That thought had kept him tossing and turning last night.

'I felt sorry for our Len. I knew he wasn't coping, but I never for one moment thought he'd do this.' Frank sighed as he looked round.

'There's nothing here worth having. Nothing to show for all the years he worked. Everything he had, it's all so pitifully cheap and shabby.'

'Len wasn't concerned with this world's goods.'

'No.'

'Not like you,' Peter added.

'What's wrong with wanting to get on?' Frank knew he was being too sharp. 'You do too.'

He wished Tommy Brent would bring his cart to the door. He had to get those boxes out of this house before anybody else saw them. If he wasn't careful, he could land himself in trouble.

Peter asked: 'Do you want a hand to get those crates of yours downstairs?'

Frank stiffened. He didn't want them in the hall in view of everybody. Tommy would help him take them straight out to the cart. Then he'd cover them as soon as he could with other things.

To deflect Peter's attention he said: 'Shouldn't we be sorting through Len's clothes? Seeing what's worth keeping and throwing out the rest?'

He'd just got Peter started on Len's wardrobe when he heard cart wheels rattle outside. Thank goodness Tommy was here. He showed him the six crates and explained he wanted them dropped off first.

Tommy said: 'Better start by loading the other stuff. Those can go on the back.'

Frank hoped he was doing the right thing by taking them home. Whatever he did with them now could be dangerous.

He hoisted up one end of Beryl's trunk. Getting it outside wasn't too bad; lifting it high enough to slide on to the cart took superhuman effort.

Frank closed his eyes. The clip-clop of the horse's hooves was soporific as the cart swayed and creaked through the Sunday streets. Beside him, he heard his younger brother sigh. He hoped Peter wasn't going to probe any further about those crates. He'd get them inside quickly and lock the door again.

'We'll drop them off and leave them just inside the shop,' he told Peter and Tommy, as they dragged off the first one. 'I'll put them away later.'

'What's all this you're bringing in?' Cecily had come home and was shouting down to them. When he didn't answer, she came down to look, but by then Peter had gone out for another of the crates, so he was able to shut her up.

He was tired and hungry and it was dinner time, but at least he'd been able to pick up Beryl's letters without anybody seeing him. He patted his pocket and hoped he'd got them all. There were things he had to keep to himself.

If Mam had the slightest hint, she'd be on at him, asking question after question. On his back for the rest of his life. He'd never live it down. It had scared him, having them all there, particularly Peter; he was quick at picking anything up like that. It was a weight off Frank's mind that he thought he'd got away with it.

Clearing Len's house was a miserable job, and they hadn't

49

got half his stuff out. Frank would have liked to send Peter home alone on the cart, but he didn't want to appear less interested in what they were taking home. He'd have to help Peter unload that too. He jumped on the back of the cart as Tommy moved it up the road.

He was manoeuvring one end of Beryl's tin trunk through the lobby when Mam came rushing from the kitchen.

'I'm not having that about the place,' she said sharply. 'Put it straight up in the loft.'

Peter struggled with Frank to get it upstairs. 'Mam, there's no harm in Alice having it.'

'It'll only bring more heartache. You saw how upset she was. Better if she doesn't see it. She's asleep now, so be quiet. Anyway, there's no space for it in her room, what with the toys and books and clothes you're bringing.'

'What about these chairs?'

'Up in the loft too. Put everything you can up there out of sight. I don't want her to see any of it.'

Frank said: 'There's another load back at the house. I've sold a bed and a wardrobe to Tommy, but we won't be able to get much more up in the loft. There's that big sideboard.'

'We'll make space for it in the spare bedroom. It might come in handy for Peter when he sets up home.'

After dinner, Frank watched listlessly as Maddy's clock-work crocodile crawled noisily across the living-room lino, snapping its jaws as it went. It jammed against the table leg. Maddy crawled after it and set it going again. It whirred to a standstill against his foot.

'You do it, Daddy.'

He reached for the toy and wound it up, turning the key until the spring was as tight as it would go. He felt just the same, wound as tight as anybody could be.

Having a twin brother die the way Len had done was like finding oneself cut in half. It didn't matter that they weren't identical; he'd been closer to Len than any other human being.

Frank felt guilty. Silently he begged Len for forgiveness. He should have known what was in Len's mind, and he hadn't. He of all people could have talked him out of it.

Frank's thoughts went back to the childhood they'd shared at the turn of the century. He considered they'd had a deprived upbringing, though many had thought their family comfortably off. Mam was good at managing the family purse and putting on airs and graces, so that the neighbours thought otherwise.

Not that they'd ever gone hungry. There'd always been a fire in the grate and they'd had warm clothes and boots in winter, but there'd been no treats and no luxuries. No trips to the seaside in summer or the pantomime at Christmas. Presents were always useful things like socks and pullovers. They'd had precious few pleasures; Mam's thrift didn't allow for anything but bare necessities.

She was stronger than Dad and had delivered the discipline. She thought helping with the housework a useful training for all boys. She'd given Frank the job of bringing buckets of coal from the yard to the hearth and finding morning sticks. That meant he had either to walk to the woods where they could be gathered, or beg an orange box or two to break up from the greengrocer's down the road.

Dad did nothing but tend his allotment and go to work. He found his enjoyment in going to the pub. He had a few pub cronies and drank and played darts with them. He never took Frank and Len anywhere, or Mam either, come to that.

He and Len had talked about this and decided Dad went to the pub to get away from Mam's economies and their demands for pocket money. They'd both learned by five years of age that it was no good asking Mam for halfpennies.

Of course, Dad was a clerk, a white-collar worker, and that gave the family status. Even greater status came when they moved to the Woodchurch Lane house, which they were buying on a mortgage when everyone else rented. They were going up in the world. Before the Great War, the house was considered comfortable and the district good. Only the family knew this was made possible because Mam held the family purse in a fist of iron.

Frank detested the spartan lifestyle but enjoyed the status. He was determined that when he grew up he'd be rich and have even more status. There were really big houses in Prenton, just up the road, where gentlemen lived and employed servants. In fact, some of the houses like theirs in Woodchurch Lane, even if they were only rented, ran to a live-in general maid. Mam was quite indignant.

'They're only skivvies, but it's the height of lunacy to have them living in. They have to feed them too.'

In those distant days, many people employed a woman to clean or do their washing. Mam did hire a washerwoman for a while, but decided she could do it better at less cost. She said she wasn't wasting good money on letting others do her work. They'd get rich at her expense.

Frank knew he didn't have his mother's patience. He wanted a good time now. He couldn't scrimp and save for decades to get it. He would have liked to be honest and upright like his father, but he wasn't going to work for peanuts all his life. What had Dad ever done except work?

Cecily came bustling in from the kitchen where she'd been washing up. 'I thought you were going down to Len's house again?'

Frank shot guiltily to his feet. 'I said I would. Tommy will be there at four.'

As soon as he was out of the door, he could see Peter coming down to meet him. Peter was silent and sombre. Neither of them was looking forward to this. The thought of clearing Len's house was bringing a lump to Frank's throat.

Len had been the companion who had followed him

everywhere; he'd been his audience when he showed off, his accomplice when he did things he shouldn't. He'd had to provide the treats for himself and his twin. How many times had he stolen oranges and chocolate from the shops up on Woodchurch Road, with Len as his lookout?

Len had also kept watch when he'd taken pennies out of Dad's pockets. They'd never touched Mam's purse because she knew to the last farthing how much she had in it.

Dad's overcoat and mac both hung on the hall stand, and he could only wear one at a time. He also owned a camel coat, worn thin and bare of wool just above the pockets. It was too shabby for the office, but he said it was warm and comfortable and like an old friend. He wore it to the pub and to his allotment, and occasionally he left a few coppers in the pockets.

Frank had never been caught. They called him Lucky at school. They called him and Len the Lucky twins.

'With a name like Luckett, what d'you expect?' Len had asked, but Frank always felt lucky. He felt Lady Luck looked after him before anyone else.

When they were thirteen and leaving school, Len wanted to work in Dad's office. Mam nagged that an office job was the thing to go for and only achieved by a few. Frank felt he couldn't face a life like Dad's.

'I'm not sitting at the same desk for years on end, waiting to grow old and draw my pension. I'm not having any of that, even if it means Len and me being parted. I want to see a bit of life.' He thought there was hardly a flicker of life left in his dad.

He'd revised his opinion about that when Peter was born later that year. That had been an object lesson in sex. He and Len had thought their parents well past all that.

Dad accused Frank of being wild. Mam said he had a loud mouth on him and predicted he'd come to a sticky end. Frank was determined to do better for himself. Now he'd left school, he wanted to live it up.

At that time, before the Great War, wages were low. He found a job working in a dairy at eight shillings a week. For that he had to separate out the cream and help make butter and cream cheese. He also had to help with the bottling, and it was all done by hand. Then every bottle had to be wiped down and packed in a wooden crate. They ran a milk round, with a piebald pony dragging the float. Milk cost tuppence a bottle then.

There was a shop too, where all these things were sold over the counter. Eggs and cheese were bought in to increase the choice. There were two old men and three lads working there, and Frank quite enjoyed it, but he knew after a couple of weeks that it wasn't going to work out.

Len had started at ten shillings and was soon earning twelve. He had a nice warm office to go to at eight o'clock, while Frank had to be at the dairy for six when the milk was coming in.

True, he was allowed home early in the afternoon while Len had to work on, but Dad and Mam kept saying he should have seen sense and it was his own fault if he didn't like what he'd got. Furthermore, it was seven days a week, and while there was some sort of a rota and fewer of them worked on Sundays because the shop was closed, his turn came round alternate Sundays. Len had every Sunday off, as well as a half-day every Saturday.

As if that wasn't bad enough, Frank missed Len's company. Up till then, Len had always been two steps behind him. They slept in the same double bed and ate meals together. It seemed strange not to have him like a shadow, always with him.

'Who's Lucky now?' Len had goaded him. 'Reckon it's running out on you.'

Frank had been desperate for more money and asked his boss for a rise. He was given a rise to ten shillings a week. It wasn't nearly enough and made him decide he'd have to look for something that paid better.

He didn't want another job that entailed getting out of bed early. Nothing was worse than getting up quietly in the dark and tiptoeing down to the cold kitchen, leaving Len tucked up in bed for another couple of hours. Frank wanted to push his working hours to the other end of the day so that the boot would be on the other foot.

He finished at the dairy and got a new job at the Argyle Theatre, starting the following day. He sold programmes and chocolate from six in the evening to eleven, but the pay was only six shillings. He loved the job; he could come home and tell Len about the famous people he'd seen. That he'd been paid for the time he spent watching them made it even better.

It was there he started to short-change people. In the semi-darkness of the auditorium, it wasn't easy for people to see what they were being given. He managed to make another few shillings for himself each week. It was much better than working in the dairy.

Mam didn't like him lying in bed all morning, although he had a good excuse because it was usually midnight by the time he got home. She said it was unhealthy. He got himself a job in a greengrocer's on Friday and Saturday mornings, but lost that within a fortnight for short-changing a woman by a farthing on a bunch of beetroot. She swore to his boss that he'd done the same to her the previous week.

It made him much more careful down at the Argyle. He didn't want to lose that job.

He soon replaced the greengrocery job with gardening work three mornings a week at a house up on Pine Walks. He cut the grass and weeded the flowerbeds if it was fine, and mucked about in the greenhouse if it wasn't. He liked being out in the fresh air, and in the winter all that was needed was to keep the place neat and tidy.

He studied Mr Brand, his employer, as well as the other well-heeled gentlemen he saw in that part of Prenton. It seemed they could get all the good things in life. He wanted to be like them.

Frank also tended the vegetable patch, which was screened from the house by a rose hedge. Mrs Brand would ask him to bring carrots or parsnips or a cabbage to the house. He took a few vegetables and flowers home too, and sold them to Mam and to Mrs Ainslie next door. He reckoned that by then he was drawing even with Len as far as cash went, and he was having a better time of it.

They were back at Len's house now, packing and sorting through his possessions. Frank did it with only half his mind. It was Peter who was making the decisions.

Len had been his life for thirty-three years. For most of that time he'd had to look after him, stop others bullying him, though perhaps he'd bullied him himself. Len should have been in his prime now, should have been enjoying life. Frank wasn't sure that he ever had.

The last things worth taking were tied on the cart. Tommy had brought a friend round who'd bought some bedding and some dishes.

Frank counted the few silver coins they'd paid. 'We ought to buy something for Alice with this.'

'Mam'll want to open a savings account for her.' Peter sighed. 'I wish you'd talk to Alice about her mother. She's always asking me, and you knew her so much better.'

Frank turned away to hide the tide of red that was running up his cheeks. He felt even guiltier about Alice than he did about Len.

'What's she want to know?'

'About Beryl. That she didn't run away from her and Len. I keep telling her she went to look after her other grandmother in London, who was very ill. That she had to go, there was nobody else.'

'I can't tell her anything different.'

'Tell Alice her mother couldn't take her because she was afraid she'd catch consumption too. Well, we didn't want her to, all the family were against that. Particularly Mam. That's why she kept taking her in.'

Through the kitchen window Frank could see Tommy and his mate turning over the mound of stuff they'd put out in the back garden for the bin men to take away. Checking that they weren't throwing out anything of use.

'I'll do my best,' he said. Frank knew his voice sounded strange.

'Just reassure her. You know what Mam's like; she never did like Beryl, and she's let Alice see that. It's upset the poor kid.'

'All right.' Frank was running with guilt about Alice and must be careful not to let Peter see it. It was a miserable ride on the cart going back to Woodchurch Lane in the dusk.

Mam was making it pretty clear she didn't relish the prospect of providing Alice with a home on a permanent basis, but she was strong on family and wouldn't turn her away.

Frank's conscience told him he ought to take Alice into his own home and bring her up with Maddy. Mam had imparted enough of her obsession about the family to make him see that.

He was worried more about Cissie. She seemed to like Alice, and always made a fuss of her, but he was afraid she wouldn't want to take her into their home. She might if she knew the truth, but he was scared of telling her.

When Beryl came back, the balloon could go up anyway. He couldn't bear to think of that.

Chapter Five

Alice had stayed with Gran and Grandpa, off and on, for as long as she could remember; for several months when she was three. She remembered crying for her mother and being comforted by Peter and allowed to ride on his back, but he usually tired of the game before she did.

He was ten years older than she was, and Gran was always asking him to look after her while she did her work. She had memories of being handed over to Auntie Nell next door, who gave her cuddles and read stories to her.

She came again for a whole year when she was six, and again when she was seven. She remembered Eric and Peter building a crystal set in Peter's bedroom and letting her listen through the earphones. Gran used to take her up to his room and persuade them to play Snap and Ludo and tiddlywinks with her.

She'd inherited some books of fairy tales from Eric; dominoes and a spinning top from Peter. The best thing Peter had handed down were his roller skates. She played with them a lot.

This time, when Mam left home, she'd stayed with Dadda. Everybody said that, at nine, she was old enough. She'd wanted to stay at the same school and Gran thought she'd be a help to Dadda.

She didn't mind being alone in the empty house. Dadda had to leave to go to work long before she went to school, but he always woke her up before he went out. She could get herself dressed and cut a slice of bread and marmalade for her breakfast before she went.

He used to leave a sandwich and a glass of milk on the kitchen table for her to eat when she came home alone at dinner time. Or he did when he remembered. Sometimes, on very cold days, Mrs Smith next door would bring her a bowl of soup for her dinner.

Alice thought she managed well enough; she always had the potatoes boiling for Dadda when he came home at night. Then, when he got home, he'd open a tin of corned beef or pilchards and warm up a tin of peas to go with them.

They'd been up in Prenton having Sunday dinner just before Easter, and Grandpa had said:

'Alice, you'd better come and stay with us for the school holidays. What d'you think, Len? She can't spend all day by herself.'

'Is that all right?' Dadda had asked Gran.

'Course it is,' Grandpa had assured them warmly. 'Maddy will be here. It's just as easy for your mam to look after two.'

'All right,' Gran had agreed with a tight little smile in Alice's direction. 'You can help me by playing with Maddy. Keep her occupied.'

Alice hadn't seen a lot of Maddy over the last few years. Sometimes when she and Dadda were invited to Gran's they might find Maddy and her family had been invited too, but not always.

Maddy seemed to have grown since she'd last seen her. She was much bigger and much prettier. She had big brown eyes and lovely dark-red hair which she wore in one thick plait down her back.

'I'm glad you'll be here all the holidays,' Maddy had said. 'My daddy says I need a friend. Someone my own age. Grown-ups are always working and never want to play.'

Alice had warmed to Maddy; without her mother she'd

felt very much alone. She'd wanted to have Maddy as a special friend; she'd never needed a friend more.

On Monday morning Gran said: 'Better if you start at your new school straight away.'

Alice didn't want to. She felt tired, unable to think of anything but Dadda. She wanted to be quiet, by herself.

'It'll all be so new . . .'

'No it won't.' Gran's voice was hearty. 'You've been to Maddy's school before, when your mam went away.'

Alice swallowed hard: 'But I hardly remember . . .'

'Well you did. You had to go when you came here; when you were too small to be at home by yourself. Maddy can take you in tomorrow. I'll give you a note for the teacher. You'll only mope if you stay at home with me.'

Alice heard her mutter to Grandpa:

'Better if she's out of the way for the inquest and the funeral and all that. She's too young. It'll only give her more nightmares.'

Gran thought being with Madeleine was good for her and was pushing them together all the time. Alice thought Maddy was strong-willed; she always wanted to choose what they'd do.

All week, Maddy had wanted to show off her long jump. She gloried in the fact that she could jump fifteen inches further than Alice. The chalk marks were still on the concrete of the yard to prove it. Maddy was also better with the skipping rope; she could skip a hundred times and not trip up. Uncle Frank was keen on sport and encouraged her. He'd taught her to run faster than anyone else of her age.

Alice knew she couldn't compete at such things. She wanted to go indoors and paint at the kitchen table, but Maddy didn't want to and Gran didn't want them there. She sent them back to the yard to play with their yo-yos. Alice wasn't much good at that either.

Today, at school, the teachers thought Maddy would be a

comfort for her too, and sat them side by side in a long desk. Alice stole a glance at her now. Maddy was on the edge of her seat, listening to the teacher's every word, looking keen and alert. She was always one of the first to put her hand up to answer a question.

'I'm top in class,' she told Alice airily. 'Best at everything.'

'Not everything,' Alice was stung to retort. 'I'm better at painting.'

'Painting? Who wants to be good at that?'

Alice wanted to give up. She wanted peace to think about Dadda. She wished she could get away from her cousin.

After school on Wednesday afternoon, Madeleine came back to Gran's house with Alice as usual. Gran made a pot of tea and they made toast over the hot coals in the range.

Alice liked to kneel on the hearth rug and feel the hot glow against her cheeks, but Maddy ate quickly and wanted to toast another slice for herself. There was only one toasting fork and she tried to take it from Alice before her toast was brown enough. Gran scolded them both for horseplay and said they were too boisterous.

Maddy went off home without saying another word, and that vexed Gran. Maddy was supposed to stay until five o'clock, when her mother's shop closed.

'You girls! Why can't you play nicely?'

Alice wanted to escape. 'Can I go next door for a bit? Auntie Nell said I could, whenever I wanted to. She says she's always at home because she's sewing, and she'd be glad of a bit of company.'

Gran grunted: 'I doubt that, you're more trouble than you're worth, but you can go and see.'

Alice felt shy now as she went in. She could hear the sewing machine racing along a seam. It stopped as soon as the lobby door pinged. Nell Ainslie looked up and smiled.

'Come in, Alice, I'm glad to see you.' Her voice was low and gentle; she sounded as though she meant it.

The front room was bright with afternoon sun. There was a different atmosphere here. A low table in the bay of the window was piled high with things Nell had made. Alice went over to look at them.

'I spend my time making those when I've nothing else to do,' Nell told her. 'I make them from the bits left over from dresses and curtains. Customers see them when they come in and buy them for presents.'

Alice examined each one in wonder. There were tea cosies, needle cases, pot holders, cushion covers, aprons, peg bags and lots more.

'You can make anything,' she said in wonder.

'Not everything,' Nell laughed, and the sun sparkled on her rimless spectacles. 'I can't do tailoring. Well, not very well. Eric is learning to do that. He's apprenticed to Wetherall's in Bold Street, in Liverpool that is. When he's done his time, he'll able to make suits and coats. Then we'll be able to do everything between us. It'll be a good little business.'

'Eric's going to work with you?'

'That's the plan at the moment.'

'I like Eric, he was very kind . . . when . . .' But Gran was right, she mustn't keep thinking about all that. She gulped: 'Do you have lots of bits left over? To make presents like this?'

'Boxes of them.' Nell nodded towards the boxes in the corner. Alice opened one up; it was full of small pieces of cloth.

'Can I have a look?'

'If you like.' The treadle whirred. Alice began opening out pieces of cloth. Half a yard of cotton, printed with blue roses on a cream background.

'This would make another apron, wouldn't it?'

Then almost a yard remnant of grey wool flannel and the same of scarlet velvet. Alice stroked the velvet.

'This is lovely lovely cloth. You were making curtains of it when I came last time.'

'They're finished now.'

Alice followed her nod. There were three big bundles of them, now neatly pressed and folded.

'They'll be collected today.'

'But they're fawn now, not the same.'

'That's just the lining, pet.'

'What could you make with this piece?'

'I was just wondering that.' Nell got up from behind her machine and held it against Alice. 'I might be able to make something for you. There might be enough for a skirt with a bib. A pinafore dress? Would you like that?'

Alice couldn't believe her luck. 'For me? I'd love it. But . . .' She was blinking back her tears.

'What's the matter?'

'I've no dadda now. Nobody to pay you for making it.'

'Oh, your poor mite.' Alice was pulled into a hug. 'I don't want to be paid for it. I meant it as a present.'

Alice didn't know what to say. She tried to tell her she was as kind as Eric. Nell spread the material out on her table and took up her scissors.

'Not too many gathers in the skirt,' she said. 'It's thick material. I'll make it slightly flared. It'll be warm when winter comes. Look, I can use this little square as a bib and there's plenty of long strips to make straps to cross over your back. I think you'll look very nice in it.'

Alice watched fascinated as Nell cut it out, then held the pieces against her to see if they'd be big enough.

After a week or two at school, Alice was more than tired of seeing Maddy's hand shoot up first to answer questions. Maddy was so big-headed about what she could do.

She knew Maddy wasn't as good at drawing and painting as she was, but she wanted to be good at other things; the things Maddy was good at, the things Maddy thought important.

Her horoscope in Grandpa's paper said: 'Your ruler, Jupiter, brings powerful aspects to your aid on Tuesday. You feel you can achieve more.'

She decided to try harder in class; she sat up straighter and tried to concentrate on what Miss Desmond, their teacher, was telling them.

Today the lesson was on wild flowers. Alice managed to get her hand up first when the teacher showed them a picture of a flower and asked if anyone knew its name.

'Daisy,' she said triumphantly, knowing she was right.

'We all knew that,' Maddy muttered behind her hand.

The next picture was of a dandelion and Alice got her hand up first for that too. Maddy managed to get her hand up first for bluebell, though Alice's was only a fraction behind.

She decided she could be just as good as Maddy, and hoped that if she tried really hard, she could be better. From then on, in every lesson, it was a race between them to see who could get her hand up first.

After school, and after Maddy had gone home at five o'clock, Alice was sent out to the back yard to play by herself. The chalk marks they'd made on the concrete weeks before were still faintly there. She took as long a run as space allowed and tried to equal the distance Maddy had jumped. She couldn't do it.

Uncle Peter saw her through the kitchen window. He came out and coached her in how best to run and keep her legs up. He'd been good at sports when he was at school.

'You're smaller,' he explained. 'You have shorter legs and they're not as strong as Maddy's. You don't do badly. You just need to grow a bit and then you'll be able to jump just as far.'

Alice practised hard after he'd gone back indoors and

knew she was improving. Maddy's manner was getting up her nose. She had a habit of putting everybody else down, boasting about how quick she was at reading and how clever at sums. She thought herself very superior at everything. Alice was determined to show her that she was mistaken. That at some things she, Alice, was better.

To Frank, the nights seemed endless. He couldn't sleep. Cissie was usually curled up in a ball and breathing evenly when he got home from the cinema where he worked. She rarely stirred when he got into bed. Night after night he tossed and turned beside her sleeping body.

He knew it was Len's death that troubled him. He couldn't get his twin out of his mind. He needed to talk about him, about Beryl and Alice; he needed Cissie.

Deliberately he pulled at the bedclothes, taking more than his share. He tossed over roughly, shaking the bed, sighed heavily.

Cecily's deep breathing stopped; he heard her swallow. 'Frank?'

He moved closer, put out a hand to touch her.

'Are you all right? You're thrashing about the bed.'

He sighed. 'Can't sleep. I'm missing Len. Can't help blaming myself.'

She put her arms round him then in a comforting hug, her voice full of sympathy. 'You mustn't. You've always done your best for him.'

Frank grunted; he'd told everybody that, but it wasn't true.

Cecily murmured: 'He was depressed, the coroner said so. Took his life while his mind was disturbed. It was the war . . .'

'Yes, the war.' He could blame that. 'Our Len wanted to volunteer. I told him he was daft; that all those clerks he worked with were a bad influence, that they were bored and looking for excitement.'

'But you were wasting your breath? Did he know how much he'd be paid as a private?'

'He knew there was no money in it. He said some in his office were applying for commissions and he knew how to go about it.'

Cecily stifled a yawn. 'Did he?'

'No, fat chance he'd have had. I told him he'd be better staying at his desk, waiting for promotion when those employed higher up left.'

Frank sighed. He'd had no plans to spend his time marching round in heavy boots. Since leaving school he'd moved from job to job and had learned the knack of assessing the benefits or lack of them attached to each. He was afraid very few benefits were likely to accrue to Len, and gave him a strong talking-to.

'He volunteered all the same, with a couple of lads from his office. I don't know what he was thinking of; he wasn't the sort for rough-and-tumble of any sort. I'd have thought the last thing he'd want was to have the Germans firing at him.'

Frank had let everybody know he had a weak chest and really wasn't fit enough to fight for his country. The trouble was, he looked a lot fitter and stronger than Len ever had. He'd filled out by the time he was eighteen and looked a man.

'Poor Len, he was still just a stripling. He couldn't look after himself, not without me.'

'You couldn't help him at work.'

'Dad did that, and all the time we were growing up we spent our spare time together. I'd never have dreamt of going out without Len.'

'But he was all right then? Happy, I mean?'

'Ye-es. We both wanted a good time but we couldn't go in the Halfway House because Dad was always there with his cronies, cramping our style. We went to the pubs downtown.'

By their mid-teens, Len had been as keen on girls as he was. They'd sought them out and tried to impress them. Frank was much better at it than Len. They seemed to like him. Poor Len didn't have the knack.

Sometimes, when he grew tired of one, he'd hand her over to Len. Len picked up the pieces after him, made his apologies, covered for him. They'd been inseparable because he'd needed a helpmate like Len always on hand.

Frank was afraid he'd used Len. 'Yes, it was the army that did for our Len.'

Before four months had passed, Len was in France. Lucky twin or not, from then on his luck was out. Already the news from the front was of hardships in the trenches, and the death toll was mounting. Frank didn't expect Len to survive the war.

Frank wanted to stay well out of it, but the attitude of those around him was changing. There was open talk of cowardice and anger against those who didn't go to fight for their country. Several men he knew received white feathers. Women gave him knowing looks and no longer wanted anything to do with him. He was driven into it, but he was careful. He wasn't going to get too close to German fire if he could help it. He wanted to come through the war. All he wanted was the uniform, and he managed by a stroke of luck and some fast talking to become a physical education instructor in a camp near Blackpool.

Frank reckoned he was the sporty type. Games had always interested him and he'd read up all the rules. He'd kicked a ball about in the school playground and called it football. In the summer, they called it cricket, though played with any ball they could get their hands on, usually a soft one. He thought exercise would broaden his chest and make him look more of a man. As usual, Lady Luck looked after him; he'd come home from the war fitter and stronger than ever.

Poor old Len. Frank had made him play games too, but it had done nothing to strengthen him up. He spent a lot of the war in hospitals with injuries that were not quite bad enough to invalid him out altogether.

'And then a month after getting home he went down with a bout of the flu that was sweeping the country. It left him weaker than ever. It was a long time before he was well enough to go back to work, and by the time he was, there were no more vacancies. Office jobs were highly thought of. He'd lost his confidence anyway. He took a job in the flour mill and then Dad got him one that paid more in Lever's, filling canisters with Vim.

'Mam kept nagging at him. Telling him he'd be better in the office where he could sit down all day. That it wouldn't be nearly so tiring.'

'I bet you did all you could to cheer him up.'

'Took him round the pubs, I was so pleased to have him back. Really missed him.'

'And you got yourself a job at the Lighterman's Arms.'

'Yes, Beryl Briggs was one of the barmaids there.'

He'd shown her how to short-change so gently that customers didn't notice. If someone noticed and pulled you up, all you had to do was to say you were sorry and count out the correct money.

'You even introduced them, gave him somebody of his own.'

'Yes,' he agreed, though that wasn't what had happened.

Beryl was like Len; she'd followed Frank round with melting eyes and did whatever he wanted her to do. Nobody short-changed him. He always counted up what he was given. He wanted to be rich. The war was supposed to change everything, but for the working classes it hadn't.

Cecily gave a gentle snore. She was relaxed in his arms and breathing evenly again. Trust her to nod off before he'd said what he wanted, but of course, she had to work hard. She had a bit of go about her, worth two of Beryl Briggs; he'd chosen the right one. He pulled his arms from round her, cleared his throat and turned over on to his back.

Cecily stirred. 'Poor Beryl,' she murmured. 'Such a sad couple, but not your fault, any of it.'

Frank took a deep breath. 'I worry about Alice too. Feel a bit guilty that I should do more for her.'

He took another deep breath. He had to ask. 'How would you feel about having her here with us?'

'When?' He knew from her voice that sleep was overtaking her again.

'I meant bringing her up with our Maddy.'

Cissie gave a little grunt. 'Bringing her up? Beryl could come back at any time.'

Frank suppressed a shiver; that was his worst nightmare. He made himself say: 'Beryl would soon be off again. Alice needs a settled home.'

'She's settled with your mother. She's used to being there, she won't want to change.'

'You like her, don't you?' He felt there was some urgency about this. He'd feel better if he was doing something for Alice.

Cecily was breathing deeply again, her voice a whisper. 'Feel sorry for her.' He strained to hear. 'Felt sorry for Beryl too, who wouldn't?'

There was a long pause and then: 'Born loser, like your Len.'

He raised himself up on his elbow. 'The trouble is, Mam doesn't really want her there.'

'No space here . . . Can't . . .' Cecily was snoring softly again and he hadn't got round to settling anything for Alice.

Frank thumped his pillows into shape and tried to sleep too. He was afraid Cissie was right; there wasn't a lot of space here. It looked as though she was going to dig her heels in for that reason.

70

Chapter Six

May 1928

The next Saturday morning, Madeleine came up at nine o'clock, when the shop opened. It was a damp morning, and Gran sent them up to Alice's bedroom to play.

'It's not a very nice bedroom,' Maddy said, looking round. 'Everything's old.'

'Your dad and my dad slept here when they were small. That's their fort in the corner.'

'Who'd want that? It's old and broken, and anyway it's boys' stuff.' Maddy wrinkled her nose in distaste. 'Is that your blackboard and easel?'

'Yes, Uncle Peter brought all my things from home.'

'Let me see the rest.'

Alice was hugging Wobble to her. 'My paintbox and a colouring book.' She got them out of the wardrobe. 'Shall we do some colouring?'

Maddy prodded at her paints. 'You've used up all the bright colours. There's only these browns left. And the black.'

'There's a bit of white; you can make more colours if you mix that in.'

'I've got much better paints.'

'Would you like to do my jigsaw? It's a picture of fishing boats, there's only two pieces missing.'

'No, I don't like jigsaws.'

Maddy was tetchy all morning and wouldn't play with anything for long. She kept going downstairs to Gran who wanted peace to cook the dinner. Eventually she let them help and they made pastry men.

When the meal was finished and Grandpa had gone out again, they played in the yard for a while, but there was another shower and Gran sent them back to Alice's bedroom.

'I'm bored here,' Maddy said. 'Let's go down to my house. I've got some lovely things to play with.'

'Can we? I mean, aren't you supposed to stay here?'

'Mam won't mind. Not if you're with me. She just wants me to be happy.' They ran down the road and into the shop.

'Hello, darling,' Aunt Cecily opened her arms to Maddy as soon as she saw her. She kissed her and gave her a little hug.

She always called Maddy 'darling'. Always stopped what she was doing to kiss her the moment she came into the shop. Cecily called Uncle Frank 'darling' too. She seemed to overflow with love for her family. Alice envied Madeleine that. Maddy seemed to be loved much more than she was.

'Hello, Alice.' Cecily kissed her warmly too. 'Maddy's been looking forward to having you here to play.'

Cecily was freer than Gran with kisses and hugs. She seemed to exude affection and she never went away and left Maddy. Alice liked Aunt Cecily. Last night, she'd dreamed about her. A fantasy dream where Cecily was her mother and not Maddy's. Where Cecily loved her best.

'Cecily loves children,' Gran had told her.

Alice knew that Maddy had once had a little brother called Robin. He'd been an invalid all his short life, and died when he was three.

'Such a loss,' Gran had breathed heavily. 'That's why Cecily loves Maddy so much.'

'Uncle Frank too?'

72

'Of course. It made them draw closer together, closer to Maddy. They spoil her.'

Maddy asked: 'Is it all right if we play upstairs, Mam?'

'As long as you don't make a mess.'

Alice thought their flat was lovely. So clean and tidy, not at all like her own home. Once Mam went, it was never clean and tidy.

The fire was lit in the living room. It looked comfortable and homely and a lovely place to live. She said so.

'No it isn't. This is over the shop. We're hoping to move soon. To a better place, a proper house with a garden. You had a garden, didn't you?'

'Yes.'

Maddy and her mother had only been to Alice's house once. Alice wasn't going to mention that her garden had been overgrown with weeds and rank grass. She knew what gardens should be like. On one side of her house there had been flowers and lawn, and on the other orderly rows of vegetables. She'd heard both neighbours complain to Dadda about his weeds.

Maddy had a bedroom full of lovely toys. Alice hadn't seen so many since Dadda had taken her to the Christmas grotto. She had a doll's house and a doll's pram and a row of dolls, even a golliwog. Far more than Alice had ever owned herself.

'Do you want to see my frocks?' Maddy opened her wardrobe.

Alice was amazed, and fingered the clothes hanging there. 'This coat is lovely,' she breathed.

'Don't you have any nice clothes?'

'Yes, I love my best frock. It's got birds on it.'

Maddy's big brown eyes were watching her carefully. 'Brownish birds?'

'Sort of, on a cream background. With branches of trees too. That's my favourite.'

Maddy laughed derisively. 'That was mine. I had it last year. I grew out of it.'

'No!'

'Yes, Mam chose those bronze birds to match my hair. It can't be your best one, it's just one of my cast-offs.'

Alice felt cold.

'I think you'll be getting my school coat soon, then I'll be able to wear this one to school.'

'I don't want it,' Alice said quickly. Really she admired it, but it was bright red and everybody there would recognise it as Maddy's.

'Mam says you're poor and you need it.'

'I don't then. There's nothing the matter with my blue one. Saying things like that isn't nice. You said you were my friend.'

Maddy looked contrite. 'I want to be. I'll give you one of my toys to prove it. Which one would you like?'

Alice's eyes went round the array set out about the room. She liked most of them. The china sleeping doll was beautiful; it had eyes that closed when you laid it down. She wondered if Maddy would let her have that.

'What about this one?' Maddy picked up a small stuffed doll with a painted face and hair of yellow wool. It was rather tatty.

Alice stifled her disappointment. At least it was a doll. Once she'd had a china one too, but she'd dropped it and it had broken.

She said: 'It hasn't any clothes. If it was dressed, it would be nicer.'

Maddy rummaged in her toy box and found a torn dress. 'This belongs to it.'

Alice dressed the doll carefully. Maddy produced a squashed bonnet. She put that on too. Perhaps Eric's mother would help her make it some new clothes.

'What's her name?'

'It hasn't got one. You can call it what you like.'

'Judith. Do you think that's a nice name?'

'Not bad. Do you like the doll?'

To be polite, Alice said: 'Yes.'

'Would you give me a present then? In exchange? To show we're friends?'

Alice smiled. 'I would, but you say you don't like my toys.'

'I like Wobble. Will you give him to me?'

'No! Anything else. Not Wobble.'

Maddy turned her nose up in disgust. 'You haven't got anything else I want. It's all rubbish.'

Alice took a firmer grip on Wobble and went rushing downstairs. She shot through the shop without saying a word to Aunt Cecily, and out into the street.

Rain was sweeping down on the wind and she'd left her coat behind. She wasn't worried about getting wet herself, but she was anxious that Wobble should not, because Gran wouldn't let her play with him if he was damp. She'd say it would give her a cold. Tears of desperation were clouding her vision as she ran up the road. She didn't see Eric coming down on his bike. She almost ran into him as they both turned into the narrow passage that divided their houses and led to their back yards.

'Hey – what's the matter?'

'Nothing.' Alice caught on to his coat for support.

'There is,' he said gently. 'Even I can see that. Come on, we can't stay here, it's teeming down. Come into our house for a bit.'

It felt warm in the Ainslies' scullery. Eric dried his face on a roller towel and pushed her in front of it to do the same.

He laughed, a great trumpet of delight. Alice felt his strong arms lifting her.

'You'll have to grow a bit before you can reach.'

Alice wiped her tears away on the towel too, and blinked hard to stop any more coming. She could hear the sewing machine racing away in the front room. She watched Eric refill the kettle, poke the fire in the kitchen range into a blaze and prop Wobble up with his back against the oven door.

'He'll dry off there.' Eric took her hand in his. 'Let's go and find Mam.'

As he led her into the front room he said: 'I've brought someone to see you.'

'Hello, Auntie Nell,' Alice said shyly. The first thing she noticed was the little pile of red velvet, neatly folded on the shelf.

'I've run up your pinafore dress. I was waiting for you to come and try it on.' Nell's voice was soft and low and she sounded every syllable clearly. Gran called it speaking posh. She said Mrs Ainslie had come down in the world.

'Does your gran know you're here?'

Alice shook her head.

'Eric, run round and let her know. We don't want her worrying about you, do we?'

'Righto, and I'm making some tea.'

Alice felt her spirits lift as Auntie Nell slid the dress over her head.

'Now then, does it fit all right?'

She pulled the bib up into position and took the straps over Alice's shoulders, crossing them in the middle of her back. Alice thought it looked beautiful.

'I want to put some pins in. To mark where the buttons must go. That's about it. Now the other side.'

'It's a bit too long,' Alice said, hating to find fault because everything else was perfect.

'There's no hem on it yet.' Nell had a laugh that was a softer version of Eric's. 'Let's see how long you want it. A touch longer than this dress? How about that?'

Aunt Nell pinned it and then led her into the middle room, where the dining table was kept fully extended and piled high with pattern books and samples of materials. This was where her customers tried on their new clothes. The middle-room window looked into the yard and was much more private than the front. Alice found she was standing in front of a full-length mirror.

'It looks lovely,' she breathed. 'Even Maddy will think it's lovely. It feels so soft.'

'You need a blouse to go with it. We'll have to see if we can do something about that.'

Alice was taken to the kitchen then, to sip tea with them. Eric and his mother seemed to be offering the love and comfort she wanted. They were much kinder than Maddy.

When they all went back to the front room, Eric tipped out the contents of one of the boxes that contained remnants.

'Now then, how would you like to make a new suit of clothes for Wobble? Which material would he like?'

Alice fingered the pieces of cloth hungrily, then held up a piece of black satin.

Eric shook his head. 'That will be slippery to sew. Too hard for your first attempt. Besides, Wobble's got black trousers, he'll want something different, won't he?'

'While you've got the bits tipped out,' his mother said, still sewing hard, 'look for a piece big enough to make a blouse for Alice. Something white.'

'This is beautiful.' Alice pulled out a piece of white satin from the bottom of the pile.

'I made a wedding dress of that.' The machine slowed to a halt. Eric opened the cloth out.

'There isn't enough of it, kid. Not unless we can find some more.'

'I think that's all there is,' his mother said.

'There's this cream poplin. I reckon there's plenty of this.'

'Perhaps poplin would be better for a little girl. I'll use that, it'll wash well. Put it on one side, Eric.'

Alice continued to look through the pieces of cloth. She came across a small triangle of cream cotton with bronze-coloured birds on it.

'Did you make Maddy a dress from this?' she asked Aunt Nell.

'Why yes, I did, last year.'

'I've got it now.'

'Don't you like it?'

'Yes. It's my best frock. It was my favourite but not any-more. I like my red velvet better. I wish we could find some red velvet for Wobble.'

'There won't be any more.' Aunt Nell was treadling hard again.

There were hundreds of others pieces to choose from. Alice finally settled on red plaid in fine wool and ran to fetch Wobble to undress him.

'He can still wear his red fez,' Eric said seriously. 'It'll go well with his new suit.'

Alice watched as he measured Wobble's trousers and waistcoat. He laid them out on the new material and cut into it. Then he took a needle and cotton and tacked the pieces together with huge white stitches.

'Now it's your turn,' he told Alice, handing her a needle threaded with matching red thread. 'Can you sew?'

'No.'

'This is what you have to do. We call it back stitch. It'll make a firm seam for Wobble's trousers.'

Alice sat down on a stool near Auntie Nell's machine and started to sew.

'That's a piano stool,' Eric pointed out. 'The seat lifts up; it's meant to be a place for storing music. You can leave your sewing inside. It'll still be there when you want to sew again.'

When she looked up, Eric had finished stitching up the hem of her velvet skirt.

'Come and choose two buttons to fasten the straps,' he said, tipping out the contents of their button box.

Alice picked out two gilt ones, which Eric stitched in place. Then he pressed the dress on the ironing board that was permanently set up.

Alice couldn't wait to try it on again. Eric helped her pull it over her frock and she ran to the dining room to see herself in the mirror. It was the nicest thing she'd ever owned.

'Suits you.' Eric was behind her. She looked at his reflection in the mirror. His dark eyes smiled into hers, then his lips widened into a grin. Alice felt she'd found a friend of her own. She much preferred him to Maddy.

'Right, I'm going to have a bath now and get ready to go out.'

'With Uncle Peter?' Alice was flushed with hope. 'Can I come with you?'

He was shaking his head. 'Not this time.'

'Where are you going?'

'Nowhere we can take you, kid. It's Saturday, our night out.'

She said desperately: 'You took me out one Saturday night.'

'Yes.' She could see from his straightening lips that he didn't want to remember that.

'Your Uncle Peter needs taking out of himself too. You can come with us some other time.'

They took her the very next day, on a bicycle ride to Heswall beach. Alice perched in front of Peter on his crossbar. The bar bit into her thighs and was very uncomfortable, but it was exciting too, to have the wind whistling through her hair as the bike bowled along. She felt quite safe with Peter's arms one each side of her.

She'd never been to Heswall beach before. It was high tide and the choppy waves filled the estuary. The sun glinted on the water and the sea birds called overhead.

She sat between them on the sand, watching the water swirl up the channel and the little sailing boats skimming over the water. Peter pointed out the coast of Wales to her. Afterwards, they pushed their bikes up the hill to the village. Eric bought them all an ice cream from a little shop on the way.

She sat on Eric's crossbar for the trip home and loved the

closeness of him. She could feel the effort it took him to pedal her weight along in addition to his own. She could feel him breathing deeply, and if she leaned back against him, she could hear his heart thumping away inside his chest.

Chapter Seven

Frank had several jobs. Being a cashier at the Carlton Hall Cinema was his main one. He sold tickets before each of the two evening performances from a booth in the foyer. There were also matinées on Thursday and Saturday afternoons.

He was on the bus going to work one evening. As he stood up to get off, he saw Hilary, his sister-in-law, heading for the Carlton Hall too. She was easy to pick out because she had dark-red hair like Maddy's. It was bouncing as she walked.

Once off the bus, he called to her and she turned and waited. Hilary was six years younger than Cecily and worked as an usherette. As they went into the foyer, Frank sniffed at the strong smell of disinfectant. He didn't like it; it got on his chest at times.

He went upstairs two at a time and smoked a Gold Flake in the gents' cloakroom. It was what he always did. Bert, the projectionist, was there smoking too, while Percy, the commissionaire, was changing into his very grand suit with gold braid epaulettes. With his peaked cap on, he looked like a Ruritanian general. To see him now, no one would believe Percy also had to act as janitor. He looked after the new central heating system, changed light bulbs and unblocked sinks.

On his way down to the cash desk Frank met Hilary running up.

'I'm on the left-hand side of the balcony as usual,' she hissed. She was now wearing her uniform too, and the maroon colour didn't flatter her auburn colouring.

Frank shut himself into the pay box. It was hot and airless

on this warm summer evening. Mr Butterworth, the manager, came in with the float. He was a dapper little man, shorter and slimmer than average. Frank towered over him.

While Frank sorted the coins into their compartments in his drawer, Butterballs checked the ticket machine. This issued numbered tickets, and the cash Frank took had to equal the number of tickets sold. If it didn't, then he had to make it up from his own pocket. That was the agreement he'd had to sign when he'd been offered the job here.

The Carlton Hall had opened in Argyle Street as the Gaiety Music Hall in 1888, just a few doors away from the New Theatre Royal. It became the Pavilion Theatre in 1905 and was famous for its drama productions. It was still the Pavilion when he'd started working here.

In 1920 it was turned into a cinema and renamed the Carlton Hall. The dress circle was called the balcony thereafter, and refurbished with tip-up velvet seats and carpets. The price of the seats in the front stalls was reduced from three shillings to sixpence. The furnishings were deemed more than adequate for that price.

Occasionally Frank had been able to sell more tickets than his accounts showed. As far as he was concerned, the more expensive the seats the better he liked it. He knew it would be easier to make a little on the side once he didn't have to allocate seat numbers as he sold the tickets, but then he found a new ticket machine had been installed as part of the refurbishment.

'The very latest design,' Mr Butterworth, the manager, had patted it fondly. 'It makes it easy to be accurate every time. Less work and worry for you.'

Frank got the message. What the boss meant was that the ticket machine made it impossible for any cashier to fiddle the takings. He'd tried hard, but whatever he did to it, the machine recorded the numbers of the tickets as he sold them.

It had taken him a long time to figure out how to beat that machine. The idea, when it came, was very simple:

he had a few rolls of tickets printed at his own expense, ordering them to look as near as possible to the genuine article.

The originals were printed by a firm of security printers and the numbers were carefully logged. His privately printed ones had a similar sequence of numbers on them, but they meant nothing.

He gave his own to old ladies who wouldn't be likely to notice that they came from a drawer rather than the ticket machine. The money he took from them, and the change he gave, had to be kept separate too.

He thought Mr Butterworth ineffective. How could he be otherwise when Frank had been getting away with a share of the takings for years? He'd let the rest of the staff grow lax about such matters as timekeeping and pressing their uniforms. They all called him Butterballs, but not to his face of course.

Percy, the commissionaire, passed majestically through the foyer to open the main doors, and the public started to stream in. It was time to start.

The film today was Somerset Maugham's *Sadie Thompson*. Two ladies in late middle age came to Frank's window and were the first to ask for seats on the balcony. He always felt a little thrill when he handed out his own tickets, more alert and thoroughly alive. He and Hilary were pitting their wits against the world. Apart from everything else, it kept him from being bored.

It was Hilary's job to meet people at the door to the balcony, show them to their seats and tear their tickets in half. She was instructed to keep the side showing the printed numbers and thread them on a string, so in the event of a discrepancy the numbers sold could be checked.

Hilary colluded with him to pick out the privately printed ticket halves and dispose of them. As soon as she could after the show started, she flushed them down the lavatory in the public toilet. She'd laughed and said she'd found that to wrap them in toilet paper first ensured that they all disappeared from view.

That way, they left no clues as to what they were doing. It wasn't that simple, of course. The number of seats he could sell for his own benefit had to be nicely judged. They had to be spread thinly through the seats on one side of the balcony only. If there was a full house, the returns handed in had to reflect that. For his own purpose, he liked their shows to be popular but not too full.

Many of the cinema audience were elderly, particularly those who could afford the balcony. On a good night, he could leak in twenty to thirty seats at each show.

Frank felt he had a good system. He was very careful to bring in no more of his own tickets than he expected to sell in any one night. He and Hilary covered their tracks. If they were caught, there was no way it could be proved they'd done it for more than that one performance.

But he didn't want to be caught; it augmented his wages, gave him a few luxuries, made it possible for him and Cissie to do a lot of things. It would be the end of a nice little earner and he didn't want to wind up being charged with theft.

He felt he could trust Hilary; she was meticulously careful. It was no secret at the cinema that she was his sister-in-law, but they hardly spoke to each other here. He had little chance to talk to any of the staff once he was shut in the pay box.

Cecily was the only other person who knew what they did. 'That's fraud,' she'd said, wrinkling her nose. 'Dishonest.'

That hadn't pleased him; he wanted her approval. She'd said a lot more about involving Hilary in his money-making schemes; she didn't think he should. She even had a go at Hilary, but it made no difference. Hilary was a real trouper.

'It's all right for the toffs to have ideals,' Frank told her. 'They've never had to go hungry. It's different for us.'

Cecily had never known her father, and her mother had died when she was eighteen and Hilary twelve. She'd been an apprentice then, and they'd been desperately hard up, but she had her standards. Frank knew they were higher than his.

He thought the working classes had put up with poverty for far too long. Men like him and girls like Cecily were still being paid less than they were worth, while employers lived in the lap of luxury. They had to turn a penny where they could, and this was proving to be one of his better ideas.

Another week passed. Edith didn't like Saturdays because she had the children with her all day. It exhausted her. What she really needed was a few hours to herself, but she was vexed when Madeleine didn't come up as she usually did. She didn't want to lose the ten shillings a week she was paid to look after her.

When Edith had started looking after Maddy, she'd earned every penny. She'd had to collect her from school every day at dinner time, give her something to eat and take her back. Then collect her again at half past three, and look after her until Cecily closed the shop at five. For the last few years, Maddy had been coming and going under her own steam, and that made it easier. Except in the school holidays and on Saturdays.

Cecily had said she thought Maddy was old enough to do little jobs in the shop now, hinting that it wasn't the problem to look after her it had once been. Edith was afraid she might soon lose her little income. She intended to go down and collect Maddy. She'd say she was company for Alice.

Not that Alice was anything like as much trouble. She'd washed up the breakfast pots and peeled potatoes for their dinner. Peeled them too thickly, of course, and wasted some, but no doubt she'd learn. Edith looked at the clock. It was ten o'clock already.

'We'll go down and get Maddy. Come on, you don't need a coat to go that far, it's a nice morning. You don't need that monkey either, Maddy's got plenty of toys. Too many really.'

Edith took off her apron and put on her outdoor shoes. She never ran to the shops in her slippers, though she saw many who did. This morning, as she went into the shop, Cecily turned to smile a welcome. She looked smart and businesslike. Her nose was carefully powdered.

As she closed the door behind her, Edith saw the draught take the collection of hair clippings and roll them up the lino. There were a lot. Saturday was Cecily's busiest day.

She had two assistants, who wore pink smocks. One washed hair and swept up, but the other was an experienced hairdresser. Cecily wasn't pinned down in the shop as much as she made out. They lived in the flat above, so she could be upstairs if she wasn't busy.

Edith had to admire her. Cecily was not only running her own business but was ambitious to go further. She spoke eagerly of exchanging her suburban salon for one in Grange Road in the centre of Birkenhead.

'That's where the top-class salons are. I'd be able to charge more. Much more.'

Cecily had her own hair cut at a smart salon in Liverpool. She had it shampooed and set every week by her assistant.

'I've got to have the best,' she'd explained to Edith. 'I'm an advert for my own salon, aren't I? Can't just screw my hair up into a bun on top.'

'You're a wonderful advert,' Edith assured her.

'Lots of customers say: "I want you to cut my hair just like yours."'

'I can imagine.'

Cecily was an attractive girl of thirty; she had style and elegance. She'd make her fortune if she could turn out the housewives of Prenton in her own image. This morning they were attending to three customers, and a fourth was reading *Woman's Own* as she waited.

Cecily was giving a perm; winding special curlers into a customer's hair which would then be attached to the new

Eugene perming machine she'd just bought. Edith watched with interest; she'd been told that the customer would emerge with permanent curls. Well, semi-permanent, because they always grew out.

Cecily smiled at her. 'When are you going to let me perm your hair?'

Edith couldn't make up her mind whether she should at her age. She'd worn it in its stiff little roll for the last twenty-five years, and with all that practice she found it quick and easy to do. Cecily had laughed when she said that. She was always at her, wanting to cut and perm it.

'You ought to be more fashionable,' she told her. 'It would suit your face to put a few curls round it. Knock years off your age.'

Edith stared at the notice advertising perms for a guinea and was tempted. 'But it would need more looking after.'

'I'll set it for you every week,' Cecily offered.

At the moment, Edith came once a fortnight to have it washed. She didn't want to put on Cecily or give her any reason to suggest a cut in the ten shillings she paid her because she was having more hairdressing.

The new hairstyles had been very good for Cecily's business. She'd had to learn to cut them, of course, but with long hair, most women had thrown it over their shoulders and cut off two or three inches when it was growing too long. Edith had been doing that for years. She could get it nearly straight, and what did it matter if it wasn't exactly so? By the time it was up in its roll or a bun, nobody knew whether it had been cut straight or not.

These new bobs and Eton crops were a different matter. Nobody could cut their own hair when it was short, and style was everything now.

Cecily laughed and said: 'Furthermore, short hair needs cutting regularly, every six weeks or so.'

'A boon to hairdressers like you. What with the new perms too.'

'There's more salons opening up. I'm afraid there might be too many soon.'

'Go on with you, look how busy you are.'

'At the moment.'

'What about you, Alice?' Cecily turned to her. 'Do you want your hair cut?'

Edith watched the child's hand go up to touch her hair. It was poor, wispy stuff, never looked anything.

'I could tidy it up a bit. Make it look prettier.'

Alice was shaking her head. 'Could I grow a plait like Maddy's? Would it take long?'

Cecily's head went on one side to consider.

'Yes, a very long time. Your hair's very fine; it'll never be thick enough to make a good plait. It suits you better short. Shall I trim it?'

Alice's fingers were plucking indecisively at her wisps. Edith watched her big green eyes going round the salon, taking it all in.

'No? Well, there's no hurry, you can come another time when we're not so busy.'

'We've come to fetch Madeleine,' Edith said. 'Alice wants to play with her.'

'She's upstairs with Frank.'

Edith's spirits fell. 'He hasn't gone to work?'

'No. Go up, he'll tell you all about it.'

Cecily had wound all her customer's hair on to curlers and was now attaching each curler to the perming machine.

'Right, ready to switch the electric current on now.'

Edith didn't trust electricity; that was something else that put her off having a perm. She took Alice by the hand and headed for the stairs. She wanted to talk to Frank. She was proud of him, and thought he worked hard. He said he was saving up to help Cecily move to a better salon.

The living room was tidy, the breakfast pots had been cleared from the table. Frank was stretched out in an easy chair, listening to the new wireless they'd just bought.

Although he said they were saving, Edith thought they spent pretty freely.

'Hello, Mam.' He pulled himself upright in the chair.

Frank had always been the best-looking of her three sons. He took after Monty. At thirty-three, he was in his prime; tall, with broad shoulders, his muscles rippling under his shirt, every inch a man. His hair was glossy brown and very plentiful.

That Frank and Cecily were doing well went some way to staving off the disgrace Len had brought on her. Frank and Cecily had a firm marriage. He adored her, there was no danger she'd run away, and they both thought the world of Maddy. It was a close family that Edith could be proud of.

'D'you want a cup of tea, Mam?'

'I wouldn't mind.' Edith pulled out a chair at the table and sat down. Alice was snuggling close against her. 'Why aren't you at work?'

Frank's job at the Carlton Hall gave him a good deal of free time during the day. He said he didn't enjoy it because Cecily was at work all the time. He'd always had several part-time jobs to add to his earnings. Like his father, he enjoyed gardening, and did a few hours each week at a big house in Reservoir Road.

On Friday and Saturday mornings he'd been working in a grocery shop up on the main road.

'Decided to give up the shop job. It's too much. It'll give me two mornings to myself.'

'Give it up?' Edith couldn't imagine herself doing any such thing. 'Give up that money?'

'They didn't pay much. We aren't that desperate.'

'Lucky for you,' Edith said, a little sharply.

'Mam, I never have a minute to myself. I only ever meant it to be short term, to get a bit together.'

He disappeared into the kitchen to put the kettle on.

'Where's Madeleine?' Edith raised her voice.

'Maddy?' he called. 'She's in her bedroom. Maddy? Alice is here to play with you.'

Edith saw her come to the living-room door.

'Off you go and play.' She put a hand on Alice's back and gave her a little push. She didn't want her to hear what she was about to say. If Frank thought he had plenty of money, she had to speak up. She went to the kitchen and closed the door.

'Isn't she quiet?' Frank said. 'Not like our Maddy. Needs feeding up, poor kid. Needs to put a bit of weight on.'

Edith was stung; it sounded like criticism.

'I'm doing my best. She's got the appetite of a bird and she wastes food. Did I tell you how she stuffed it into Wobble's pockets? That toy monkey she's so fond of?'

'Yes, several times.'

'We've taken her in, Frank. I know it's my duty to give her a home, but we'll have to feed and clothe her until she's fourteen. We aren't finding it easy. Your dad's near retirement age; we need to save while we can.

'Our Peter's offered to give me an extra half-crown each week, but that won't cover it, we're still hard pressed.'

Frank put the filled tea pot down on the kitchen table and stood over it for a moment, smoothing down his moustache. She'd noticed him do that when he was on edge.

'I suppose I could help a bit,' he said, not looking at her. 'How about five bob a week?'

Edith felt a surge of pleasure. 'Thank you.'

Then the doubt nagged. 'As well as the ten for looking after Maddy?'

He seemed defensive. 'Five bob to help feed Alice, nothing to do with looking after Maddy. That's quite different.'

She watched him pour out the tea. 'That'll help a lot, thank you.'

Edith realised he hadn't promised to keep paying for Maddy, but she could hear Cecily's step on the stairs and didn't want to press it further. It was easier when Frank was alone.

Chapter Eight

When the door closed behind his mother, Frank threw himself back on his chair. To hear Mam going on about looking after Alice set his stomach churning. And to be thanked for offering five bob a week to help feed her? That had made him cringe inside. Mam would lambaste him if she knew!

His mind went back to that terrible time ten years ago when he'd felt he was taking hard kicks himself. Beryl weeping and blaming him, imploring him not to cast her off. What could he do, when Cissie was in the same condition? He'd done the right thing by choosing her.

He spent the rest of the morning staring into the fire, creased with guilt. Len had taken Beryl's part, and pleaded for money for her and the coming baby. Over and over, just at a time when Frank needed every penny he could get his hands on to set up home for Cissie.

He'd done all he could for Beryl. For Len to take her on was the best thing, though it hadn't worked out as well as he'd hoped.

At twelve thirty, he went out to buy fish and chips for himself and Cissie. It was what he usually did on Thursdays and Saturdays. When there was a matinée, he didn't have time to come home for the dinner that Cissie cooked once she'd closed the shop.

He no longer enjoyed going to work when everybody else had finished for the day, but as Cecily said, it was worth persevering with this job. They had to put up with the inconveniences. He changed into his uniform. He hated wearing the maroon serge suit; it was a suit of servitude. He decided, as he knotted his maroon and gold tie in front of the mirror, that he looked better than he felt.

Cecily was inclined to flatter him. She was always telling him he was a handsome man. She took care of his hair, cutting it carefully every three weeks, so that he always looked well groomed. She didn't really approve of him having a moustache, but she trimmed it for him, and put a professional gloss on his looks.

All the Luckett family had blue eyes, but while his father's smiled out at the world with a rather fatuous enjoyment, and Len's had shown the misery in his soul, Cecily said Frank's were astute and assessing.

Hilary, her sister, had laughed when she'd heard her say that. 'They look as though you're watching out for the main chance. Sort of wily.'

When it came to wits and drive, Frank knew he was much better endowed than anyone else in his family. It was just that Len's death had knocked the stuffing out of him.

Cissie came in with their fish and chips set out on warmed plates. She liked to do everything with as much style as possible. She paused for a moment at the window as she walked past.

'Maddy's out there playing. Yes, and Alice too. They must have had their dinner. Isn't she growing to look like Beryl?'

Frank suppressed a shiver. She was, and it was making it harder to put her out of his mind. He looked across the table to Cissie, who was forking up her chips hungrily.

He said: 'What d'you say, Cissie? Should we give her a home?'

'I thought you'd just offered your mam five shillings a week to help with her keep. You're doing your bit.'

'But if she came to live with us . . .'

'Where could we put her?'

'With Maddy.'

'There's no room for another bed in her room.'

92

'I've thought of that. What about bunk beds? Maddy would love to sleep on top.'

'It's not just in the bedroom.' Cissie's voice was a little sharper. 'The flat's a bit of a squash for us now. We need more space. That's the top and the bottom of it. We haven't enough room as it is.'

Frank thought about it as he ate. 'Perhaps you're right, this place is too small. We ought to move somewhere bigger.'

'And better?' Her smile was dazzling. 'We can afford it?'

'Why not? We're having to afford everything else.'

'Your mam's always going to batten on you.'

'We could get a place with three decent bedrooms and plenty of living space. It's what you want.'

'It's what you want too.' Cecily gurgled with excitement. 'A really good house in a good area.'

'Think what it'll mean to Maddy – being brought up in a place like that. Give her a good start in life.'

'She could marry well from a house like that. Get herself a well-to-do husband.'

'A professional man. I'll try and find time to run up to the estate agent on the main road this afternoon.'

Before Cecily reopened her shop, Frank had to catch the bus into town. He got off a stop earlier than usual to buy a newspaper to look at the property pages. He could feel a ball of excitement in his stomach. He and Cissie had talked of buying a house many times. He wanted to get a place they could both be proud of, but it was a big step to take.

He'd seen it as something to look forward to in the future, but surely they'd waited long enough? If they had more space, Cecily would be more willing to take Alice in, and that might go some way to appeasing Beryl when she came home.

He was studying the houses-for-sale columns when the manager brought the float to his airless ticket booth.

'There's a couple of letters for you.' Mr Butterworth was looking at him strangely as he put them down on top of his paper.

Frank felt his heart miss a beat. He'd notified the post office that Len's letters should be redirected here rather than to Woodchurch Lane. His first thought was that they must be from Beryl, but he saw that the envelopes were typewritten. He hadn't yet told Beryl about Len.

'Thanks.' Frank slipped them in his pocket. He didn't care how strange Mr Butterworth thought it that he received letters here. He couldn't possibly have Cissie picking them up at home. Her questions would be much more searching, and she wouldn't let him get away without answering. All the same, anything to do with Beryl shook him up. He didn't know how he was going to cope with her now Len was gone.

He did what he always did: sorted the coins of the float into the compartments in his drawer. He could hardly wait to see the manager go. As soon as the door closed behind him, he ripped the first of the letters open. Now he'd had time to think, he could guess what it was.

He'd been giving Len money to pay for Beryl to stay in the sanatorium. They had to pay towards her keep. Since his brother's death he'd done nothing about that. It would be another bill.

He was right; he was now weeks in arrears. He felt like tearing it up and forgetting about Beryl. It wasn't as though money grew on trees, and he'd need every penny he could put his hand on if he bought a house. The trouble was, when she was well enough, Beryl would be back. There'd be real trouble then. She knew too much. His heart was pounding.

With shaking fingers, he opened the other letter. It was from the medical superintendent to say that Beryl's condition was deteriorating and giving concern. That the added burden of pregnancy was proving too much for her.

He felt his spirits perk up. If Beryl died . . . It would solve the problem. He hoped she'd die before the baby was born. He didn't want to be landed with another baby to keep. Then he felt sorry for her and ashamed of himself.

It was always like this with Beryl. One moment he wanted

94

to be rid of her and all the trouble she brought him, and the next he couldn't do enough for her. Damn it, he was fond of her.

He remembered that it was her birthday next week; she'd be twenty-eight. It was no age to die. He'd get her a card and put in a note to say Alice was well and happy and doing well at school. He wouldn't tell her about Len. It wouldn't do her any good to know what had happened to him. And he'd pay the hospital bill. It was the least he could do for the poor girl. They'd had some good times in the past.

'Two back stalls, please.'

Frank rammed the letter back into his pocket. His face was running with sweat. How was he going to explain another child? He'd been so devastated by Len's death that he hadn't been able to think clearly. Only when it was all over had he wondered whether he should have said something about Beryl having another. He could pass it off as Len's, but Beryl might say different when she came back.

Beryl wasn't like Cissie; she blew hot and cold. Full of love for him one day and out for revenge the next. It had always been like that, and perhaps he shouldn't blame her.

Frank could see a line forming outside his ticket window and tried to speed up, but the letters had shaken him up and his head was whirling. An elderly lady with a high-pitched imperious voice asked for four seats on the balcony and then turned to say something to three equally elderly companions. He couldn't bring himself to reach for his private tickets – not tonight, he wasn't up to it – though she was the sort who wouldn't notice. It helped to do his routine work. By the time the show was underway, he felt calmer.

Hilary came running down an hour later. 'What's the matter?' she hissed through the ticket window.

'Forgot to bring my own tickets,' he lied.

'You clot! Talk about wasted opportunities . . .'

'Can't be helped.'

He couldn't go into it with Hilary. He couldn't get Beryl

out of his mind. His head was spinning with memories of her, most of them bad.

In a way they'd been kindred spirits. They'd wanted the same things, to have a good time and more money to spend. Even at eighteen years of age, when they'd both worked at that pub down by the docks, Beryl had had a fragile look about her. It had made him want to look after her. She'd been attractive then, and they'd soon had a good thing going.

She'd seen him short-change a customer one night; she wasn't daft. She'd giggled afterwards and asked him how often he did that. The customers soon got too drunk to realise what was happening, but it should have taught him a lesson. If Beryl could see what he was doing, the landlord would be able to too. That happened a month later, and he was dismissed on the spot.

He soon got himself a better job, in the Hippodrome Theatre in Grange Road, and it made him try other ways to make a bit on the side.

Beryl reckoned shoplifting was easier and paid better. He'd taken her to the big shops in Liverpool, Chester or Southport, where they weren't known. Beryl shoplifted things to order. A leather handbag for Cecily's Christmas present once. He wasn't proud of asking her to do that.

He knew somebody who would take expensive things like gold watches and jewellery. Not top-class jewellery that could be traced, but good middle-market stuff. They'd made quite a bit from that. He still wore the watch she'd got for him. But Beryl had got caught in Southport. Lucky that she'd had to go to court there, because the Birkenhead newspapers hadn't reported the case. Nobody knew about it. He'd paid her fine, but she got caught again and then a third time, and had been sent to prison for the first time when Alice was three.

Beryl was caught again when Alice was six. It was while she was in prison that time they found out she had TB. She spent most of her sentence in the prison hospital. He'd promised to look after Alice for her. He felt he owed her that. Beryl wasn't much good at shoplifting. Wasn't much good at anything really.

Hilary Belling was selling programmes and chocolates at the Hippodrome where he'd gone to work. Through her he'd met Cecily, and she'd knocked him sideways. Cissie had a touch of class. She'd been taught how to make people look good, but she also had more go about her than Beryl.

It was rotten luck that he'd got them both in the family way at the same time. That had been a dreadful time for him, and he hadn't known which way to turn. He was fond of Beryl; he had to take care of her. Like Len, she wasn't the sort who could look after herself. It had seemed a good idea at the time that she should marry Len. He'd hoped it would solve everything and that they'd settle down together.

Beryl was jealous of Cissie; he should have foreseen that. She turned quite nasty too, even though he'd fixed it for her so that she had a roof over her head and three meals a day, and was able to bring up her baby. She even had Len to make it all socially acceptable. It was much the best thing for them all, but Beryl couldn't accept that. They still worked together, Beryl still wanted the good things of life, and she wasn't going to get them on Len's wages.

Cissie was more honest. Frank couldn't tell her everything he did to turn a penny. She was likely to throw up her arms in horror and worry that he was going to be caught next week. It was kinder not to tell her everything.

When Beryl was down – and she always was when she got caught – she could turn nasty and talk about revenge. She'd threatened once to go to the police and tell them about the stolen goods he was storing in her house.

He'd only been able to stop her because that would have got her and Len in trouble too. It was their house. It had made Frank uneasy all the same. She didn't love Len but he was supporting her and was kind to her. They had a lot in common, those two.

It was odd to see them together at Mam's house, having

Sunday dinner. Both his daughters sitting up to the table and Beryl making little digs at him from the other side. Good job she was timid; it made her digs small, so that his family hardly noticed. He pretended to take it all in his stride.

At one time she wanted to take her daughter and leave for good. Her mother was ill with TB, down in London, and she planned to go down there and look after her. He'd managed to persuade her not to take Alice in case she caught it too. He'd heard it was very infectious.

He hadn't wanted Beryl to come home once they knew she had it. TB was a terrible thing. She'd got on the wrong side of him by then.

He'd written to her: 'Don't come back here infecting all my family. Stay away. I've given you all you're getting.'

It made him feel guilty now. She'd accused him of using her, and perhaps he had, but he'd gone on sending her money. Frank sighed. His family was always asking for money, so he never had enough. It was almost as if they knew . . .

To see Alice alongside Maddy, who was so much more robust, talking her into doing things in the same way he'd done with Len . . . It took him back in time. It was like history repeating itself.

He'd promised to look after Alice, and he would. She was his daughter and he should do for her what he did for Maddy. He wanted the best for both of them: a happy childhood, good health, a good husband and prosperity.

By the following weekend, Gran had given Alice what she called 'little jobs' to do in the house, such as polishing the letter-box and holy-stoning the front step. When she'd finished them on Saturday morning, Alice opened Grandpa's newspaper to look at her horoscope.

'It says: "You're unshouldering a burden. The new moon brings you unrivalled opportunities. The only mistake you could make would not be to strive for them."'

Alice felt she was striving hard and was determined not to give up. 'When's your birthday, Gran?'

'That's a lot of nonsense.'

'No it isn't. It tells you what's coming. It really does. When is it?'

'January the eighth.'

'You're Capricorn then, the Goat.'

'What's my birthday got to do with goats?'

'It says: "The past year has proved a trying time. Last month's difficulties were caused by your ruler Saturn's confrontation with the moon, but Friday's new moon brings no relief. Expect further surprises, even shocks, this week."'

'I don't want to hear any more,' Gran told her briskly. 'That's enough.'

'Can I go next door to see Auntie Nell, then?'

'Don't be long,' Gran said shortly. 'Maddy will be up to play with you soon.'

Edith was glad to see the back of Alice, with her horoscopes. The past year a trying time! She didn't need a horoscope to tell her that. It had certainly taken it out of her, what with looking after the children, Len's funeral and the inquest. The last things she needed was to be told to expect more shocks.

She was still grief-stricken too, of course she was, but the fact that Len had taken his own life mortified her. It reflected on her as his mother; she hadn't, after all, brought him up as well as she'd thought. Edith put the kettle on for a cup of tea and picked up last night's *Echo*. She turned quickly from the horoscopes to the property pages.

Moments later she was captivated by an advertisement for new bungalows being built in Bebington, each with two bedrooms, gardens front and rear and an optional garage. It was a dream she'd had for years: Monty retired and just the two of them living in a nice little bungalow somewhere quiet. But there couldn't be just the two of them, not now. There was Alice to think of, and Peter hadn't yet left home.

Edith didn't know Bebington well and tried to visualise where the site might be. On the number 64 bus route, the paper said. She'd love to see those bungalows.

Maddy came bursting into the kitchen, slamming the back door, making more noise and fuss than Alice ever did. Edith sighed. There was no let-up for her, no time even for a quiet cup of tea. There was no getting Maddy to wash the cabbage for dinner either. She'd no sooner told her to take it to the sink than she was screaming in panic because she'd seen a slug in it.

Edith felt she needed a lift, a little treat. She decided to take the girls into Birkenhead.

'Go and fetch Alice from next door,' she told Maddy. 'Tell her we're going into town now.'

She'd pay some more into her account at the Liverpool Savings Bank. It was a joint account; Monty's name was on it too, though he did little to add to it. She was saving for their retirement and in particular for the new bungalow she wanted so badly.

She paid in every penny she could. All the money she earned by looking after Maddy, as well as what she could save from her housekeeping money. She'd pay in two whole pounds today. Monty was giving her five shillings extra to pay for Alice's keep, so now with what she was getting from Frank and Peter, she had more than she needed to spend.

Edith knew exactly how much there was in the account; she didn't need to look. After today there'd be two hundred and seventy-four pounds and five shillings. She felt she could look forward to a life of luxury when Monty retired. For years, she'd been doing everything she could to make that possible.

She tied her shoe laces and was ready to leave. It made her cluck with impatience that there was no sign of the girls. She couldn't trust Maddy to do anything. She'd have to fetch them herself.

She went out of the front door and turned to survey her

own property, a solidly built turn-of-the-century house in the Victorian style. Built of red brick, it had two substantial bay windows one above the other, and the brass knocker on the front door was the most highly polished in the road.

It was semi-detached, but appeared to be part of a terrace. Narrow paths with solid gates level with the front door separated each pair and gave access to the back yards.

She'd been very proud of having a bath in those early days. It was in a cold, narrow room next to the scullery, plumbed in, but only for cold water. She'd had to boil kettles and pans and carry them from the kitchen. Then, after the Great War, they'd had a new range put in. It cooked a treat and also heated the water. It ran hot in the scullery and into the bath. Then, a few years after that, they'd had the house wired for electricity upstairs and down, even though it had cost eight pounds ten shillings. It had seemed the height of luxury at the time, though everybody had it now.

The house had been her choice all those years ago, and her idea that she and Monty should buy it on mortgage. She'd never stopped congratulating herself on doing that. It was paid off now, and they owned it outright.

Monty didn't want to think of retirement, but she was five years older and past her retirement age. What Edith wanted most was a chance to slow down. She yearned to sell this family house and buy a small new one.

Monty was dragging his feet about this, wouldn't even come with her to see the new bungalows. He wanted to stay where he was and had suggested that instead they should have the smallest of their four bedrooms turned into a proper bathroom with a lavatory inside.

Edith bristled with resentment. Monty was a disappointment to her. He'd worked all his life as a lowly clerk. He'd let the family down because he hadn't got on. True, he was a white-collar worker. She built up his job and responsibilities for the neighbours, but he wasn't well paid and had no ambition. It was only her thrift that allowed them some prosperity now.

You couldn't push Monty, you couldn't persuade him either. He was going to do his own thing. He could boil up in a rage if crossed. One minute he'd be sitting there with that fatuous smile on his face; the next he'd be purple with rage. He left all family decisions to her and had the nerve to complain that she was always telling him what to do. If she didn't, he'd never do anything.

She'd known for years that she'd married beneath herself, but it was no good thinking about that now. She had to make the best of things. She was in command of the family home and finances. She could cook well; she cleaned to perfection, and could paper and paint, sew and mend. She'd made thrift a high art. Her father had been a tram conductor but it didn't do to think about that. Her mother had married beneath her too.

Chapter Nine

July 1928

On her way to Nell Ainslie's house next door, Edith noted that the gate to the passage they shared needed another coat of paint. She'd get Peter to do it.

Nell's head was visible through the window, bent over her sewing machine. The lobby door pinged as she went in. She saw Maddy engrossed with the left-over remnants. She'd spread them out everywhere, across the cutting-out table and the ironing board.

She barked at her. 'Maddy? What are you thinking of? I told you to fetch Alice home. You knew I wanted to take you both out.'

Alice looked up from the stool where she was sewing quietly.

Maddy came instantaneously to Edith's side. 'We were just coming, weren't we, Alice?'

'She didn't say,' Nell smiled at them in her motherly fashion, 'or I'd have sent them.'

'All these pieces of cloth, they'd make all sorts of nice things,' Maddy breathed.

Edith said: 'You can't leave them like that. Go and put them back where you found them.'

'I didn't get them all out,' Maddy grumbled, but she went back. Alice had put her sewing away in the piano stool and went over to help.

'Isn't this lovely, Gran?' Maddy held up a piece of brocade. 'I'd love a dress made from this.'

Nell laughed. 'It wouldn't do at all for you. I'll make needle-case covers from that bit when I've nothing better to do.'

'You shouldn't let them make a mess like this,' Edith told her. She didn't know why Nell put up with it. 'How can you work with these two here?'

'We aren't any trouble,' Maddy told her. 'Mrs Hardy down the street has a dress of this stuff, and I've seen somebody in this blue.'

'Come on with you,' Edith told her, beginning to lose patience. 'Never you mind who has her dresses made here. You're a nuisance to everybody you are, both of you.'

''Bye, Auntie Nell,' Alice said.

'Alice is never a nuisance.' Nell's grey eyes followed her fondly.

To me she is, Edith thought ruefully, as she took them home. Not such a big nuisance as Maddy, but a nuisance all the same.

On the bus, with Maddy hemmed in against the window and Alice on her knee, Edith began to feel better. After they'd been to the bank, she took the girls down Grange Road to look in the big shops. That was part of her treat, but window-shopping was all she allowed herself. Maddy kept asking for sweets but Edith didn't give in. They'd only spoil her dinner anyway, and she'd make liver and onions for them all when they got home.

After they had eaten and Monty had gone off to his allotment, Edith felt restless. The girls were running up and down to Alice's room and she couldn't stand the pounding on the stairs.

'Get your coats,' she told them. 'We're going out again.'

'Where?' they wanted to know. Both were eager to go out.

'Somewhere nice.'

'Can we go to the seaside?' Maddy asked, her brown eyes dancing. 'Daddy took us to New Brighton once and . . .'

'No.' Edith tore the page from the newspaper. 'Somewhere nicer than that.'

They all liked bus rides, and it was a sunny afternoon. Bebington looked lovely. There were lots of leafy trees planted in the pavements, and behind the houses Edith could see lush fields and woods. It was easy to find the new estate; there were big signs to direct her. Some of the bungalows were finished and already had curtains up. She was filled with longing.

They were built in pairs, but with more space between them than in Woodchurch Lane. All more or less the same style, spanking new, very smart and pebble-dashed. She saw a little cabin with a sign saying it was the sales office. The man inside gave her a sheet of paper with more details printed on it. The bungalows cost £525, a little more if she wanted the attic converted to a big third bedroom, or to have a garage in the back garden.

Edith marvelled that she had almost half of what these bungalows cost in her account now. But when they sold their present house . . . Perhaps if she saved enough, Monty could buy a car too, to drive her round, and they'd still have a bit put by for later.

There were several almost-built bungalows that she could look through. The salesman pointed them out to her. Edith was eager to see inside. The scent of drying plaster and fresh paint was like balm as she went in. She loved the living room, a long room at the back with a french window leading to the garden.

The kitchen had a white glazed sink and was fitted with shelves. The bedrooms were at the front; the biggest would suit her and Monty down to the ground. Edith caught her breath as she opened the bathroom door. It was small, but there was a bath and a washbowl and a lavatory, all fitted in so neatly, with tiles on the floor and the walls. She sighed with delight. It was perfect.

She couldn't resist going inside another one. Alice trotted behind her.

'Will we be coming to live here?'

'Perhaps. Would you like that?'

'I'd rather stay where we are.' Alice's green eyes wouldn't meet hers. The child knew it wasn't what she wanted to hear.

It was then Edith noticed that Maddy was no longer with them, and she rushed out to look for her. The girl had no business to go wandering off, but she hadn't gone far; she was kicking over the bare earth that would soon be a garden.

'Serve you right if you got left here by mistake,' Edith told her, though they all knew it was only a threat. She couldn't leave Maddy here, not when she was being paid to look after her.

'Come on, don't you want to see inside this one?'

'It's exactly like the others,' Maddy grumbled. The path to the door had not yet been paved and was muddy. To avoid this, she walked close against the wall of the house and didn't look where she was putting her feet. There was a drain full of muddy water that hadn't yet had a grid cover put over it. Maddy put her foot in it, soaking her shoe and sock.

'You naughty girl!' Edith couldn't keep the words back. 'You'll ruin your shoes and they're almost new. What'll your mother say?'

Her shoe squelched all the way home. The girls laughed, of course, and thought it a huge joke.

'Wait till you have to pay for shoes and socks for yourselves,' Edith told them. 'You'll take better care of them then.'

Madeleine was infuriating. Edith liked children who did as they were told. Cecily wasn't nearly strict enough with her. What Maddy needed was a good spanking. If she'd been her child she'd have got it, but Maddy was the sort who went running home to tell tales. She had to be careful about that sort of thing; she didn't want to get into Cecily's bad books.

Edith felt vexed with Maddy. She'd had to wash her sock

106

and she hadn't been able to get it as white as its partner. Steam was rising from it in little whorls as it dried over the oven door of the range. She'd made Maddy dry her shoe on a piece of old towel. Now it was stuffed with newspaper and laid on the fender. She'd had to lend her Alice's slippers to put on her feet, so now she couldn't send them out to play in the yard.

Alice was spending more time next door with Auntie Nell. She particularly liked to go when she knew Eric would be there too.

'It'll be Maddy's birthday soon,' she told them as she looked through the collection of needle cases and stuffed toys that were kept on show on the table in the window.

'She'll be ten. I want to give her a present. I've saved tuppence . . .'

'You could make her something,' Auntie Nell suggested.

Alice refolded the apron she'd spread out. 'But what? Maddy wouldn't want an apron, and she's too old for stuffed toys.'

It was Eric who showed her the pictures in a magazine his mother had bought. A pattern was being given away free for a nightdress case in the shape of a dog lying down with his head on his paws.

'Mam's got some brown plush fabric left over. It'll be just the thing.'

'But could I do it?' Alice turned the picture round. 'Maddy would like that, I'm sure. I'd love to make it, but it looks hard. All those pieces in the pattern.'

'It's complicated, but if you like it, I'll help you,' he said, his dark eyes shining with kindness.

'Oh, please! Would you?'

Eric cut the pieces out and stuffed the terrier's square head with wadding. Alice did a lot of the sewing herself, both of the plush fabric and of the blue taffeta lining. Auntie Nell put the zip in for her and went over some of the seams with her sewing machine to make them stronger.

When it was finished, Alice thought it was as good as the one in the picture. She took it home to show Gran, who found some tissue paper to wrap it in. It was Maddy's birthday the following Thursday, and because it was early-closing day, she was able to have a tea party.

'Only five guests,' Cecily had stipulated. 'We haven't room for more.'

Alice was pleased to be one of them. She knew the others; they were from her class at school. On the way there that morning, Maddy told her all about the bike her mam and dad had given her. It was bigger than a fairy cycle, but not quite full-sized.

After school, Alice hurried home to change. Auntie Nell and Eric had finished her cream blouse just in time, and she was able to wear it with the velvet pinafore dress. It made her feel like a princess. She went to Gran's bedroom to look at herself in her mirror. The velvet was really gorgeous.

She ran down the street with the present she'd made. The door to the hairdressing salon stood open; it had been cleaned and tidied and there was nobody to be seen. She could hear sounds of merriment in the flat above. Alice went up the stairs.

The little hall seemed packed with children. Maddy looked very pretty, with her red hair loose from its plait and full of waves. She had a new party dress of blue taffeta, but the other girls admired Alice's red velvet and wanted to touch it. Even Aunt Cecily did.

'I'd like a velvet pinafore dress too,' Maddy said. Alice breathed a sigh of satisfaction. If Madeleine said that, it meant she truly admired it.

Maddy seemed pleased with all her presents and was thrilled with the nightdress case. The other girls cooed over it and nobody knew, until Alice told them, that she'd made it herself. They were all peeping round the living-room door at the balloons tied to the curtain rail and the feast set out on the table.

'Tea in five minutes,' Aunt Cecily said. 'And we'll play games afterwards.'

First, Maddy took them all off to her bedroom to see her very best birthday present. Leaning against her bed was her new bike, all glittering chrome and bright paintwork. Along with all the others, Alice fingered it and tried the bell.

'It's lovely,' she whispered. 'You are lucky.'

It was so beautiful it took her breath away. A real bike was something they all longed for but knew was outside the reach of their families to provide. Nobody but Maddy could hope to have a bike of their own.

'Now I'll be able to go out with Uncle Peter on Sundays.' Maddy smiled slowly. Alice knew she was watching her. 'Now I've got a bike of my own, he and Eric will take me with them.'

'I wish I could have a bike like this,' one girl sighed. They were all very envious.

Alice was trying not to be. A bike was something she longed for but could accept she wouldn't have. But Eric was different. He was her special friend and she didn't want him to take Maddy out without her.

She knew Maddy was going round to his house more and more, whenever she could give Gran the slip. Eric had told her she'd been there several times.

Alice said: 'They won't want to take you along very often. Eric and Peter can go faster and further on their own.'

'Daddy will ask them. Mam said I mustn't go very far on my own. She wants Peter to look after me.'

Alice's heart sank.

Another guest asked, 'Maddy, can you ride a bike already?'

'No, but it won't take me long to learn. Then I'll go out with them every week.'

Alice knew Maddy's brown eyes were still watching her. 'Eric thinks I'm more fun than you.'

Alice didn't think that was true, but she didn't like Maddy trying to worm herself into his affections.

The next day, Auntie Nell asked her how she'd enjoyed the party.

'It was lovely,' she smiled. 'The tea was grand, with cakes and jellies. Peter came to organise the games because Uncle Frank had to go to work. We had musical chairs and Maddy loved her nightdress case.'

She then went on to tell her about Maddy's new bike, and that Maddy was expecting Eric and Peter to take her out for rides on it on Sundays.

On a Saturday night a fortnight later, Eric and Peter went over to Liverpool to a dance. This was the real thing, with a sprung floor and a sparkling globe in the ceiling that flashed diamond-sharp lights on the dancers.

'Good band too,' Peter said. It was an eight-piece playing in strict dance tempo. He was watching a little blonde girl in a red dress twirling with expert ease.

Eric was standing beside him; they always took stock first. This was better than the church hall or the rugby club. He said: 'Peter, can you stop Maddy from coming round to our place all the time?'

'Is she?'

'She's always there.'

'Is she making a nuisance of herself?'

'Not to me.'

'I know not to you. To your mother?'

'No, to Alice.'

'But they're friends. They play together.' Peter wondered if the girl in the red dress would dance with him. Was she with her boyfriend?

'Alice feels they're thrown together too much.'

'They seem to get on together all right.'

'Alice needs something of her own. She likes to come round and sew. Mum's taken to her.'

Peter said: 'You have too.'

The girl in the red dress was a very good dancer. Better

than he was. He wondered if she'd think him a clumsy clodhopper.

'Yes, well, wasn't I with her when we found her father? I saw what she went through. Anyway, Mum needs somebody to mother now I'm grown up.'

Peter frowned. 'Maddy's certainly one to push herself forward. She keeps asking me to take her with us on Sundays.'

'With Alice, you mean? We don't want to make a habit of that. We can't go far with them.'

Peter dragged his mind back. 'Without Alice. Just her. She wants what Alice has.'

'That's what I mean,' Eric said. 'Maddy keeps coming round to our place, trying to elbow in. Alice feels she's having her nose pushed out.'

'What?'

The tune finished and the dancers were walking off. Mostly the girls sat at the little tables while the men hung about in groups round the door. Peter was pleased to see that the girl in red had separated from her partner. So he wasn't a boyfriend; it would be safe to ask her.

'Two kids are too much for Mam. I mean, she's got work to do. Stop Maddy coming.'

'How am I going to do that? Can't you drop a hint?'

'I've dropped plenty. Maddy takes no notice.'

Peter said: 'Mam's paid to look after her. She shouldn't let her go round to your house all the time. I'll tell her.'

'Tell Maddy it worries your mother if she doesn't stay at your place.'

'Right, I will. I'm going to ask that girl in the red dress for the next dance.'

'What if it's the Black Bottom?'

'I'll wait.'

The band broke into an enthusiastic Charleston. Peter set off purposefully across the floor.

Chapter Ten

August 1928

Over the next few days, Alice was often next door. She liked being with Auntie Nell and spent many hours on the stool beside her machine, sewing clothes for Wobble.

She found Aunt Cecily had bought a length of green velvet and asked Nell to make Maddy a pinafore dress.

'I know Maddy wanted one like mine.'

'Cecily thinks green will go better with Maddy's bronze hair,' Nell told her as she started to cut it out.

'Good job I made yours plenty big enough round the waist. You're putting on a bit of weight now, and growing too. It must be your gran's good food. You'll soon be as big as your cousin.'

'I think I'll be a dressmaker when I'm grown up.' Alice watched, engrossed. 'It must be lovely to sit here and sew all day long.'

'You could do worse.' Nell looked up and smiled. 'I'm pleased you want to follow in my footsteps. It'll give you a trade; you'll always be able to earn a living.'

Alice asked: 'Would I have to do what Eric's doing? Go as an apprentice to Wetherall's?'

'You'll be taught properly if you start as an apprentice. That's the best way. It doesn't have to be Wetherall's; there are other places.'

'But that's the best?'

'Definitely one of the best.'

'That's what I'll do when I leave school then.'

'You ask Eric, he'll tell you all about it.'

'But he won't be there then?'

'No, he'll be finishing his apprenticeship soon.'

It was Friday afternoon, and Edith was setting the table for high tea. Upstairs, she could hear Peter moving around his bedroom.

It was time Maddy went home, and she wanted to see Frank. Friday was the day he paid her. It didn't do not to go down for it. It would be only too easy for him to forget what he owed. She was in the hall, putting on her coat, when Peter came downstairs.

She said: 'Just popping down to Frank's, I won't be long. I'm taking Maddy home.'

'Is she here?'

'She's playing in the road. On her new bike.'

Edith opened the front door just in time to see Alice wobble past on the bike, with Maddy running behind her.

Peter had seen them too. 'I'll come with you,' he said.

'Only as far as our shop. Then it's my turn,' Maddy called.

The girls seemed to be arguing on the pavement. 'It's my bike,' Maddy was saying.

'You said two turns to my one.'

'No, three to your one,' Maddy corrected. 'That's only fair. It's my bike.'

The salon was about to close, the customers had all gone. One assistant was sweeping the floor and the other cleaning the washbowls.

Edith saw Cecily's face light up when she saw them. It always did, but she never came up for a chat. It made Edith wonder if the show of pleasure was an act she put on, and she was so used to doing it for customers, she put it on for her too.

114

'Maddy, love.' Cecily left her cashing-up to go to the door. 'It's time to put your bike away and come in.'

'Oh, Mam! Just ten more minutes, I'll come then.'

Cecily turned and caught Edith's eye. 'Frank's upstairs if you want to go up.'

Peter was already on his way. Edith followed. There was a savoury smell coming from the kitchen. The table in the living room was set nicely for high tea. Frank, already wearing his maroon Carlton Hall uniform, was stretched out on his chair drinking tea.

'Do you want a cup?'

'Yes.' Edith never refused tea. Frank got up to pour two more cups for them.

'I've come for my wages,' she told him, and he took his wallet out of his pocket straight away and counted out two half-crowns and a ten-shilling note.

Edith held the note between her fingers. 'You want me to go on looking after Maddy then? Cecily was saying she was old enough to stay with her, perhaps help a bit in the shop now.'

'We don't want you to stop,' he said. 'It's very handy her going to you for her dinner every day. And after school, giving her a bite to eat and keeping her for an hour or so. That's what you want?'

'Yes.' Edith breathed a sigh of relief. 'It's just that it's more expense for you.' She'd worried that they wouldn't want to go on paying.

'She's happy to play with Alice and it suits us very well.'

'So you're doing all right?' Peter asked. 'Going up in the world?'

Edith couldn't see how Frank could deny that, not after agreeing to all this expense for Maddy, and buying her a fancy new bike too.

'You'll be real toffs soon,' she laughed as Cecily came upstairs.

Cecily smiled. 'What's wrong with that? Tea? Jolly good, I'm parched.' She shot to the kitchen for another cup.

'I don't suppose,' Peter was choosing his words carefully, 'that you're doing well enough to get a bike for Alice too? It's her birthday soon.'

Cecily's smile slipped. 'Maddy's cost nearly three pounds.'

Peter's blue eyes gleamed; they had an over-innocent look Edith recognised.

'Maddy needs someone to go for rides with her. She's asking me and Eric to take her and it isn't on. We don't want a kid like her hanging on to us. She needs to go with someone her own age.'

Cecily frowned. 'I don't want Maddy to go far.'

'I was cycling all over the Wirral when I was ten,' Peter beamed, 'wasn't I, Mam? You won't be able to stop her now you've bought her a bike. She'd be safer with Alice; you don't want her to go by herself.'

'I'll pay something towards it.' Frank sounded cautious. 'But it's only fair you stump up something too. And you, Mam.'

'You know I'm trying to save,' Peter said, 'but I could manage five bob. I think I could persuade Eric to give that much too.' He pulled out some coins from his trouser pocket. 'I've spoken to Dad about it, and he'll put in a pound. What exactly did it cost?'

'Two pounds twelve and six.'

'I'll give half a crown,' Edith offered. She didn't want to seem mean, not when everyone else was giving.

Peter beamed. 'That only leaves one more pound to find. You'll not mind giving that to get Alice a bike?'

'All right.' Cecily's face softened. 'We'll get her one much the same as Maddy's, won't we, Frank?'

'Exactly the same,' Peter insisted. 'We can put a mark on it so they know their own.'

'Has Frank told you then?' Cecily was smiling at Edith.

She almost said yes. Frank just beat her to it. 'No.'

That made her stiffen. 'What d'you mean? He's told me that you want me to go on looking after Maddy.'

116

'We're buying a house, Mother-in-law.' Cecily giggled with excitement. 'In Oxton. A lovely house. We've made an offer and it's been accepted.'

Edith's tea cup crashed on to its saucer. She was running with envy, boiling with it. She'd never made any secret of how much she wanted a new bungalow, but they'd kept this from her. It wasn't fair. They were young, they could afford to wait. She'd been waiting and wanting for years.

'It's got three bedrooms and a lovely garden.'

'I thought,' Edith's voice was harsh, 'that you wanted a salon in town? That you were saving for that.'

'Well, yes, I do.' Cecily laughed again, showing perfect teeth. 'We are, but I only wanted to earn more so we could have a nice house. Nobody really wants to live over a shop.'

'But it's very handy for you.'

'It is that, but I'm hoping to get a lock-up shop in town. We'd have to have a house first.'

'You're planning on having everything, then?' Edith heard the envy in her voice.

Frank said: 'We've been saving for this for years, Mam, and there's two of us working for it.'

'Glad I thought of asking you to tip in for Alice then.' Peter tossed his brown hair back off his face and grinned.

Edith felt awash with jealousy. She'd worked and saved for years and hadn't yet achieved her goal. Cecily prattled on about the lovely bathroom the house had, making matters worse.

When she heard the girls clattering up the stairs, she couldn't get away quick enough.

'Cecily must be earning a packet,' was all Peter said on the way home.

Edith couldn't get it out of her mind that Frank and Cecily were going to beat her to it. She couldn't wait for Monty to come home. She was incensed with the injustice.

'Our Frank's buying a house.' She didn't wait for him to take his hat off. 'Would you believe that?'

'A house?' Monty collapsed on the chair to change into his slippers.

'A house in Oxton. Isn't he, Peter?' She was choking with envy. 'They've made an offer and it's been accepted. Wouldn't you have thought they'd have said something before now?'

'It could have fallen through.' Monty went to the table. 'What's for tea?'

'Cecily came right out and said: "We saw what we wanted, so we thought we might as well go ahead."'

'Why not? They're going up in the world.' Monty stroked his moustache. 'Isn't that what you want?'

'Monty, I've seen a lot of houses that I want and fat chance I have of getting them.'

'Cecily's business must be doing better than we thought.'

'That's what I said,' Peter put in. 'Anyway, why not, if they can afford it?'

'She's always on about getting a shop in Grange Road, or better still, central Liverpool. I don't understand why she's suddenly changed her mind and decided on a house.'

'Blame yourself for that, Edith. You're always going on about new houses. You've convinced Frank it's the best thing he can do. He's changed her mind. Talked her into a house instead.'

'He wouldn't talk her into anything. It's the other way round. He idolises her; eats out of her hand, does anything she wants. She only has to hint.'

Alice made a pot of tea and put it on the hob to keep warm. Monty pulled out a chair and sat down. 'What's for tea? I'm hungry.'

Edith bustled into the scullery. 'It's coming. It's meat pie. Where are they getting all this money from? That's what I want to know.'

She dished up furiously, slapping pie and mashed potato on to four plates.

'They know how to spend. Gets her everything she wants,

and they both want Maddy to have the earth. They spoil her.'

Edith was too vexed to enjoy her meal. 'When are we going to get our bungalow then? That's what I want to know.'

Alice was feeling better. It was her tenth birthday, and by dinner time she'd been given three birthday cards, a block of chocolate and a silver sixpence. The parlour door had been locked for two days. Maddy told her her biggest present was being kept out of sight in there.

Maddy was at her most teasing; she said she knew what it was, she'd seen it, but had been put on her honour not to tell her.

Alice started guessing. 'Is it a doll?' She really fancied a sleeping doll, but Maddy wouldn't say any more.

Gran said there wouldn't be a party this year but she'd make a special tea and Maddy could stay and have it with her. After school, Maddy went home to change into her blue taffeta dress and brought Alice a present. It was a scarlet wool cardigan that matched exactly the colour of her pinafore dress. Alice was thrilled with it.

When Grandpa and Uncle Peter came home, Gran cooked fish and chips because that was her favourite. There was jelly and a lovely sponge cake with pink icing to finish.

Then Uncle Peter got the key to the front room from a jug on the kitchen dresser and took her by the hand. The family crowded behind her as she went in.

Alice could hardly believe her eyes when she saw the new bike, all glistening chrome and black paint, propped up against the couch.

'For me?' She stroked the saddle, rang the bell.

'It's exactly like mine,' Maddy said. 'I knew you'd like it.'

There was a fancy luggage label tied to the handlebars. Alice started to read it.

'It's from everybody,' Gran told her. 'All the family.'

'And Eric and Auntie Nell,' Alice breathed. 'It's the most wonderful present.' The fact that everybody had chipped in gave her a feeling of warmth.

'Can you ride it?' Peter wanted to know.

'Yes, Maddy's let me try on hers.'

'She's not as good at it as I am. My daddy says she needs more practice.'

Peter said: 'Do you want to have a go now?'

'It'll get muddy.'

He laughed. 'It's bound to get dirty if you use it. You don't want to leave it propped up here.'

A few minutes later, they were all out on the pavement.

'Be careful.'

'Watch the traffic.'

'Don't go down on Borough Road.' Everybody was giving her advice.

Alice started to pedal carefully down Woodchurch Lane. She passed Maddy, who was running home to get her own bike. She felt on top of the world; she'd been given the best birthday present ever.

She and Maddy rode round in a circle, up Prenton Road West, along Storeton Road and down Woodchurch Lane again. She soon began to feel more confident. Before bed, she went to thank Auntie Nell and Eric.

'It's the most marvellous present anybody could have. I absolutely love it.'

While she still missed her father and mother, she was beginning to feel that life could be good again.

Alice heard all about Maddy's new house. Maddy couldn't stop talking about how grand it was, and how much bigger her bedroom there would be.

She knew Gran was tired of hearing about it too. She kept saying hush when Maddy started on again about the garden or the garage.

One Sunday afternoon, Uncle Frank took them all to see

the outside. They couldn't go in because the owners were still living in it.

'I've had to ask them to let me and Cissie in several times – to measure up for curtains and furniture. I can't ask them to let you lot traipse through.'

Alice was impressed and could quite understand why Maddy was so delighted with it. The houses in that part of Oxton were all big and set far apart in well-kept gardens. She thought it would be like living in a park.

Gran exclaimed at its size. 'Think of all the furniture you'll need and the curtains for all these windows . . .'

'It'll take us a bit of time to get settled,' Cecily said. 'But it'll be very nice then.'

'Very posh,' was Edith's verdict. 'But not what I want.'

It was Georgian in design, but built in Victorian times. According to Frank, the rooms were larger and better proportioned than in Edith's house in Woodchurch Lane.

'Once we're half organised,' Frank said, 'you must all come round here for your Sunday dinner.'

'Yes,' Cecily agreed. 'We can't do it at the flat. Impossible to get more than four in comfort round our table, but we'll have plenty of room once we move here. You must come to us sometimes.'

Alice thought Gran didn't look too pleased at that. Gran saw it as her role to bring the family together round the same table for Sunday dinner.

Grandpa wasn't with them; he'd said he was going down to his allotment again.

Later that afternoon, Gran came out when she saw them riding their bikes up and down the road. She asked them to go down to the allotment to ask Grandpa for some carrots and onions to put in a stew for the next day. She was cross when they returned empty-handed. They were still out in the road when Grandpa came home for his tea.

Maddy asked him: 'Where is your allotment, Grandpa? Me

and Alice rode down there on our bikes and we couldn't find you.'

'You couldn't have looked very hard,' he laughed. But Alice knew they had. She thought another man was digging on Grandpa's patch.

She heard Gran tell him about Uncle Frank's house over tea. When she said they'd soon be going there for Sunday dinner, his face twisted in a wry smile.

'They just want to show off. Frank wants to impress you, make you envious.'

Alice knew he was right. Gran was awash with jealousy. It made her nag at Grandpa all through tea. If Frank could do it, why couldn't he?

'All you want to do is wait, and I'm sick of waiting. Haven't I been waiting for years?'

It had sent Gran round the estate agents, searching for something that would please both her and Grandpa.

Chapter Eleven

October 1928

Usually Frank didn't like weekends. Fridays and Saturdays were his busiest days. The Carlton Hall often had full houses.

Today, he was feeling better, although it was Friday. He'd come into town late in the afternoon to call at the estate agent's and collect the key to his new house. The formalities were completed; they could move in. Not tomorrow, because Saturday was a busy day for Cissie too, but he'd go round first thing in the morning, and take a few bits and pieces.

He kept this news to himself as he smoked his Gold Flake with the projectionist and the commissionaire. The less they knew about his personal business the better, but he felt he was getting somewhere at last.

All his good humour went in a flash when Mr Butterworth came down with the float and threw another letter in front of him.

'Why have them sent here?' he asked coldly. 'You'd get them in the morning's post if you had them sent to your home.'

Frank felt the strength drain out of his legs. Again it was addressed to Len, and the envelope had been typewritten. The baby wasn't due for another three weeks, and the thought of it was giving him nightmares, but he'd paid Beryl's bills and wasn't expecting another letter just yet. It would come as a shock to the family to find Len had a posthumously born child.

Frank had had sleepless nights because he didn't know whether Beryl was well enough to look after a new baby. He'd read somewhere that they didn't let consumptives keep their babies with them because of the risk of infection.

Anyway, she had no home to come back to. He'd told the council he didn't know her whereabouts when Len had died. He'd had to; it was what the family expected, and they'd have been stuck with paying the rent on that house if he'd said otherwise.

He couldn't see his mother accepting another grandchild into her home, and Cecily didn't have the time for a newborn, even if she was willing. It would have to go to an orphanage. He'd lived in a state of dread about this from the moment he realised Len was gone. He had nobody to rely on now. Nobody to support him.

Customers began to trickle in, wanting tickets. He had to put off opening the letter, but it filled his mind, paralysing him with dread. The first house had started when he got round to ripping the envelope open.

Dear Mr Luckett,

It is with deepest sympathy that I write to tell you that Mrs Beryl Luckett died peacefully at 4 a.m. this morning.

Yesterday evening, at 9.15 p.m., the 19th, she gave birth prematurely to a boy child of 3lb. 5oz. who unfortunately lived only until midnight. Our hospital padre, the Reverend Arthur Middleton, baptised him with the names William Francis, which we understand was his mother's wish.

We offer our sincere condolences.

May we please know by return your wishes regarding burial?

Relief was exploding within him. Beryl was dead! The baby was dead! He was off the hook.

He'd been almost out of his mind with worry. He'd have been able to pass it off as Len's, of course, but now there was no need. The poor bugger hadn't lived. He was free of all that. He wasn't nicknamed Lucky for nothing.

His mind raced. Yes, of course he was sorry – in a way. He felt as though a sword had been hanging over him, threatening to fall and chop off his head. Now it had fallen and missed him. He could relax and get on with his life. He took a long, steadying breath and stood up; he wanted to sing, wanted to jump about, but there was no room to move in this cramped compartment.

He felt the elation drain away almost as quickly as it had come. Hadn't Len accused him of signing Beryl's death warrant when he'd got her pregnant for the second time?

'She's not strong enough,' he'd burst out angrily. 'It'll kill her. Don't you ever think of anybody or anything but your own pleasures? You ought to be ashamed of yourself, using her like that. You've got a wife of your own. Why can't you keep your hands off Beryl? You've ruined her life as it is. You've ruined mine. You're an animal.'

Len knew how to make him run with guilt, but he mustn't let him. Mustn't think like this. He'd let Beryl down, but she'd asked him to look after Alice and he'd do that to square his conscience.

Should he tell the family or keep the whole thing to himself? It would be easier to say nothing . . . But if he told them, it would put an end to their speculation about Beryl.

Better for Alice, who was always talking about her coming back, and if Cissie knew Beryl was dead she'd be more likely to agree to bring Alice up. Especially now they could give her a decent home.

He'd do his best for Alice.

On Saturday morning, Frank heard Cissie's alarm go off

125

a couple of hours earlier than usual. She got up, full of boundless energy, eating her breakfast before six o'clock so she could walk over and take a look at the new house before opening the shop.

Frank hadn't slept well. He pulled the blankets over his head and turned over as soon as she was gone, but he couldn't get back to sleep. He lay there worrying about what he'd done to Len and Beryl. He'd loved them both; they'd played a big part in his life, and he missed them now.

Cissie came back in a euphoric mood to make a cup of tea for him and give Maddy her breakfast. Frank walked over to see the house. It took longer to get there than he'd thought. He saw this as a problem; it would take time out of Cissie's day.

The empty rooms made the house look forlorn. He thought of how much more money they'd need to live here. The mortgage alone would take some meeting. He'd have to think of more ways to earn it.

He'd save a bit by not having to pay for Beryl, of course, but he wanted to keep Alice from now on. Surely looking after her wouldn't cause too much extra work for Cissie? Would he have to tell her the truth?

Frank walked slowly home, but with all the packing to do, he couldn't settle to anything. He felt overwhelmed and didn't know where to start on the jobs facing him. He was wound up tight again.

What he'd done to Len and Beryl was terrible; it was preying on his mind. He'd never dared to breathe a word about it to anybody, but now he might have to tell Cissie. Explain why he wanted Alice to live here with them. It was no good beating about the bush; he'd probably feel better if he confessed. He was silly to worry about how she'd take it.

Cissie loved him, he couldn't doubt that. She was always giving him little smiles of approval; little hugs and kisses. They made a good team, always pulled together. She'd understand and want to do her best for Alice too, once she knew.

Frank couldn't move from his chair. He felt paralysed with dread. All right, he had let Beryl down, but now he mustn't do the same to her daughter.

Alice had the look of Beryl, her slight figure and white-blonde hair. She was quiet, and her big green eyes could stare at him in the same way, wary and full of reproach.

Len had always followed his lead, Beryl too. He'd expected her to play second fiddle and run round after him. He'd been able to persuade them both to help with his money-making schemes.

He'd always had this power to talk people into doing what he wanted. He'd had his first taste of it at twelve years of age when he'd had a confrontation with Dad and come out on top. He liked the feeling of being top dog.

Money had been important to Len and Beryl too; being able to get it for them added to his power. But they'd become scared, lost their nerve once Beryl had been caught. She'd wanted Len to move right away with her before he ended up in prison too.

Len had broken the web Frank had spun, preferring to kill himself rather than carry on. Frank blamed himself for that and it had catapulted him into a crisis. He no longer felt in control.

Last night, he'd been so uptight he hadn't been able to sell his own tickets. Hilary had sneered and asked if he was getting cold feet. He'd come home to bed and tossed and turned for half the night, trying to decide whether he should show the letter to Cissie or keep it all secret. He was late getting up and still felt sleep-sodden.

At mid-morning he heard his mother wheezing as she climbed the stairs. He knew what she was coming for. He hadn't paid over this week's money. She'd missed him yesterday afternoon because he'd gone out early to see the estate agent.

'I could do with a cuppa,' she said. She was always more inclined to ask for things if Cissie wasn't about. He made her

127

some tea and she sat on for half an hour, although she was supposed to be looking after the girls and there was no sign of them.

He wondered if he should tell her about Beryl. Whether he should or shouldn't was going round in his head the whole time. He couldn't bring himself to do it; he wanted her to go.

'So what do you reckon then?'

Mam was staring at him; he was aware she'd asked that twice.

'About what?'

'The hole in Alice's shoe. She'll have to have a new pair. She could do with some new underwear too. I was wondering if you'd want to help me out with a few shillings.'

Frank felt ready to choke. It was as if she already knew. He was feeling in his pocket for a couple of half-crowns, but he felt he had to protest.

'It's an expensive time for me. The new house and everything.'

'You're doing all right, Frank. No need for you to scratch and save like us.' But at least she went on her way once she'd got what she wanted.

Frank collapsed back on his chair, wishing he'd never given her grounds for supposing he could afford this sort of thing. She was always asking for more. He didn't know how much time passed before he heard Cissie's voice down below.

''Bye. See you later.'

The shop door clanged shut and then she was running upstairs. He shot to his feet and whisked the tea pot and dirty cups to the kitchen.

Cecily had closed her shop for an hour's lunch break. He should have set out ten or fifteen minutes ago to fetch their usual fish and chips. He'd forgotten all about it.

Cissie came in, her face glowing with vitality, but her smile slipped a little when she saw he'd made no preparations.

'Is something wrong? Your mam said something to upset you?'

'Ye-es.'

'I thought she wanted more than her usual. She had that determined look about her.'

Cecily laughed. 'I'd better run out for the chips straight away. I thought I hadn't seen you go.'

'No.' Frank braced himself. 'Don't go, I want to talk to you.'

'But what are we going to eat?' She was already in the kitchen, filling the kettle to make tea.

'The usual sandwich will do.'

She was cutting bread. 'There's a tin of sardines, will you open it? And apple pie to follow. So what did your mother want?'

'Money.'

'Extra money? I might have guessed. What for this time?'

'To help buy shoes for Alice.'

Cissie's good-natured face turned to smile up at him. 'You should expect it; she's always on about the family having to support each other. I hope you told her we had a lot of expense ourselves with the house. How much did you give?'

Frank told her, and found himself sitting back on the same chair with a plate of sandwiches on his knee.

'Cissie, how do you feel about doing more for Alice?'

He stole an anxious glance at her. She'd taken off her pink overall. Her blue jumper and skirt were smart. She was eating her lunch hungrily.

He screwed up his courage. 'To bring her up with Maddy, surely it wouldn't be too much to ask? You could be mother to them both.'

Cecily was frowning. 'Your mam wanted that too? She might have consulted me. Coming here and putting it to you when I'm busy downstairs. Who does she think will have to do all the extra work?'

'No,' he said too quickly, then realised that to get what he wanted, he should be saying the opposite. 'Not exactly, but she'd like us to do it. All in favour, I'm sure.'

'What d'you mean?' There was suspicion in Cecily's eyes now. 'If not her, it's you that wants Alice here. You've been on about this before.'

Frank tried to pull himself together. 'Alice is family. Enough of Mam's feeling for family's rubbed off on me.'

She was staring at him. 'Never noticed that before.'

'You like Alice, you said so . . .' He'd have to show her the letter, tell her everything. He took it from his pocket and held it out.

'Read this.' He'd read it through so many times himself, he almost knew it by heart.

Cecily ignored it, leaping to her feet to cut the apple pie instead. He leaned forward and pushed the letter up against her plate.

She said: 'Of course I'm fond of Alice, but I never seem to have a minute as it is, and she's happy enough with your mam.' A large slice of pie arrived on his plate.

Frank said urgently: 'Beryl's dead. Read the letter.'

'Dead! I thought she was getting better?' Her hand went out for it.

He felt sick as he watched her read, her frown deepening. 'Two girls together; she'll keep Maddy occupied . . .'

Cecily's sherry-coloured eyes, deeply shocked, searched his face.

'Poor Beryl! She must have been lonely sent away like that. Why didn't Len say? We could have done something. Written to her, visited.'

He'd have to tell her. He took a deep breath.

'I'd like Alice to be with us. You could be mother to them both. Bring them up together.'

Cissie frowned. 'I don't think . . .'

'She is my flesh and blood.'

'Well I know . . .'

He said with more force: 'My flesh and blood, Cissie.'

She looked at him uncertainly. 'You're not trying to tell me . . . ?'

'Yes, I am.' He felt relief that he was making her understand at last. He wanted it all out in the open now. 'She's my daughter.'

She was shaking her head. 'Your niece . . . ? You're helping with her keep, that's all your mam wants.'

'I'm her father, I tell you. I've always provided for her.'

He saw that realisation had dawned on Cissie. The colour had left her cheeks, and her mouth sagged open.

'Good God! Beryl? I thought you felt sorry for her?'

'Of course I did. I got her in the family way, didn't I? I had to do something.'

'There's only a month's difference in their ages. Maddy and . . . You were going with Beryl when I . . . ?'

He had. He'd been afraid this would be the difficult part.

'Maddy's a month older. You were having sex with Beryl when I was already pregnant. I thought you loved me.' It was a cry from the heart.

'I did. I do. I married you, didn't I? I chose you and I've never regretted it.'

'But Beryl Briggs . . . You're going to say you loved her too?'

'No. It's you I love. We've been happy, haven't we? All this was ten years ago, eleven nearly . . .'

Cecily's eyes were shocked, horrified even. 'Tell me about it, Frank. Tell me about Beryl.'

'You know . . .'

'I don't. Quite clearly I don't.' Her cheeks were crimson now. She was angry. 'You got yourself a job in a pub and she was a barmaid there. That's all you've ever given out. I didn't know there was anything between you.'

Frank took a deep breath. There was a lot about Beryl he'd be wise to keep quiet, particularly since Cissie wasn't taking it as well as he'd hoped. He mustn't say he'd taught Beryl to short-change the customers.

'She was eighteen then, better looking. I was quite taken

with her . . . They were heady days at the end of the war when we all came back.'

In those days, Beryl had done whatever he wanted her to.

'She was Len's wife.'

'Yes.'

'You're always on about family feeling and how close you were to Len. Now you say Alice isn't his daughter. If you're telling me you shared his wife it's horrible. Disgusting.'

'Nothing like that!' He could see revulsion on her face. She didn't like that, wouldn't accept it. Well, he didn't have to admit to everything.

'Nothing like that at all. I had an affair with Beryl before she was married. Before I introduced her to Len. They were married just after us. You know that.'

Cecily's face had hardened. 'What about this baby she was having?'

'That was Len's. Nothing to do with me, honest. What d'you think I am?'

'You got us both pregnant at the same time? But you preferred me?'

Frank swallowed hard. Good grief, he could only marry one of them; you'd think Cissie would be grateful he'd chosen her.

'Then, fortunately for Beryl, Len fell in love with her and wanted to marry her?'

'Yes, that's right.' He wasn't going to say that he had had to talk Len into it, that Len and Beryl never shared the same bedroom; and above all he must never admit he'd touched Beryl since.

'Len knew she was carrying my baby when he married her. I owned up about that. I helped support them all.'

He'd never seen his easy-going Cissie look at him like this before.

'And this strong feeling for family you have – that made it almost as good for Beryl and Alice to live with your twin as to live with you?'

'No, it was nothing like that.'

Actually it was. Frank could feel his heart pounding. Cissie was so near to the truth, it was making him nervous.

'Neither of them seemed very happy to me. Not ever.'

'They were. Maybe not madly happy like us, but content with each other. The way most married couples are.'

He hoped she hadn't noticed that Len was miserable, depressed at times. That he felt he couldn't cope with either of them, particularly Alice, when she was too young to do much for herself. He'd always thought it a good thing that Cissie was pinned down by her work and unable to visit his relatives alone.

Cissie was looking at him in a strange way. She sounded hostile. 'Beryl went to prison, didn't she? She told me . . .'

That shocked him; he'd thought he'd kept that quiet.

'To hell with Beryl!' he burst out. 'What about Alice? Can I tell Mam we'll have her here?'

'No you can't! It makes me feel sick when I think of you and Beryl together. I believed you when you said you loved me. I'm not bringing up your little bastard. You've got a real nerve to ask.'

Chapter Twelve

Cecily bathed her eyes in cold water in the bathroom. She couldn't go back to work with red eyes. She didn't want her customers to know she'd been crying, and the next one would be arriving in ten minutes.

She didn't want to believe what Frank had told her about Beryl, but it all added up. She felt he'd kicked away her security; changed everything. Now she was searching, figuratively speaking, for something to hang on to, some means of support. However much pressure he put on, she was not going to bring up Frank's bastard. She'd made up her mind about that.

In her bedroom, Cecily powdered her nose and combed her hair. Her eyes still looked puffy but she had to open the salon. As she ran past the living-room door she saw Frank hadn't moved from his chair. He was going to be late for his matinée.

She found it helped to talk to her customers; to see the salon busy again. She picked up her scissors and set to work, but she couldn't keep up her usual light-hearted patter.

Frank had told her – not once, but many times – she was the only woman he'd ever had in his life. He'd said he'd never loved anyone else, only her. Now that he'd admitted having sex with Beryl, it soured everything. How could she feel love for him? And if Beryl, how many more? She'd thought she was happy with him, but how could she trust him after this?

There'd been other things over the years. She'd known there'd been little lies about where money came from. That he wasn't too particular where he got it, as long as it came.

She'd known he was a bit of a rogue. She should have listened to Beryl, who'd tried to open her eyes to what was actually going on.

Poor pathetic Beryl Briggs. Frank had always been power mad. He'd made Len and Beryl jump to his wishes. Beryl had got herself into a state and confided in Cecily one night.

Her story had been so outrageous Cecily hadn't wanted to believe it. Beryl had been het-up and tearful; Cecily had thought she was embroidering reality. She said Frank had made her shoplift for him. He'd point out what he wanted her to take.

'Frank can sell jewellery on,' she'd wept. 'He gets good money for the pieces I take. But I got caught in a shop in Chester. Frank said with luck there won't be a report in the local papers. Don't tell his mam, whatever you do; he'd kill me if he knew I'd even breathed a word.'

That had made Cecily smile. 'Frank wouldn't hurt anybody.'

'Not you, perhaps.' Beryl had blown her nose hard. 'He loves you, but he can be cruel. He makes me steal for him.'

'Just tell him you won't.'

'I try, but . . . He said nobody would see me. He made me a bag with a slit in the side so I can pop things in without being noticed. He keeps watch for me, but when I'm stopped, he disappears and I'm left on my own.'

'What?' Cecily couldn't believe that of Frank. He was the sort who stood by his friends. She was sure he was.

'I've got to go to court tomorrow and I'm worried stiff. What if they send me to prison?'

'It'll be a fine. Nobody goes to prison for shoplifting.'

'It isn't the first time,' Beryl had wept. 'It's the third. Frank pays the fines. I'm frightened; what if . . .'

The next thing Cecily knew, the family was in turmoil because Beryl had left home. Len had had to ask his mother to look after Alice.

Edith had been furious. 'Where's she gone?'

'Down to London to see her mother.'

'She never said anything about going. She wouldn't just up and leave the baby to go to her mother's. She knows you can't look after her when you have to go to work.'

It had been Frank who'd said Beryl had gone off with another man.

Cecily had faced Frank that night with what Beryl had told her, wanting to know if there was any truth in it. He'd dropped his head in his hands.

'I wish I could say no. Len wants it kept as quiet as possible. Don't breathe a word, Cissie.'

'Beryl told me you make her do it, that you tell her what to steal.'

'That's not true!' Frank's handsome blue eyes had met hers in an open, honest stare.

'She's shoplifting all right, and I've pleaded with her to stop. So has Len. You know how Mam feels about the good name of the family. Don't tell her.'

'What did you have to say she'd gone off with another man for? You knew that wasn't true. You're blackening her name.'

'Mam didn't believe our Len. I had to give her a reason she'd accept.'

'Her mother has consumption; you could have said she didn't want to take Alice there in case she caught it.'

'I was all shaken up, couldn't think straight. I had to take Beryl to court, somebody had to go with her. She's the sort who wouldn't be able to find the place, and Len was scared of going. I did the best I could for a hopeless case. Honestly, Cis, if I wanted somebody to shoplift for me, I wouldn't choose Beryl. She's a ditherer, the sort that's bound to be caught. It was an awful day.'

'More awful for Beryl, I'm sure.'

Beryl had gone away for three months. Their Christmas gift to Edith that year had been an expensive brown calf handbag. Frank said he bought it in Bobby's in Liverpool, but he didn't have a Bobby's bag. When he handed it over to her to wrap in Christmas paper, it was in a plain brown carrier, together with a wallet for Monty and three pairs of socks for Peter. It made her suspect the worst.

On Christmas Day, she'd unwrapped his gift to her and found it was another luxury leather handbag. She'd never been able to use it. It was still wrapped up in its fancy paper at the back of a drawer. She couldn't take to stolen property.

Cecily picked up the curling tongs to put a Marcel wave into her customer's hair. Of course, she'd known what Frank was really like, but he'd treated her like a princess until now. She hadn't wanted to think badly of him.

Beryl was caught again when Alice was six or seven, and was away even longer. Len gave the same reason for her absence, that her mother was ill with consumption in London and she'd gone down to look after her.

'Why doesn't she say she's going then?' Edith had demanded. 'Why doesn't she ask me to look after Alice herself? She knows I'll have to.'

'Must have forgotten,' Len said. 'She did ask last time, didn't she?'

'When she was only going to see her mother for a week. I don't know why she has to go at all. We don't want her bringing consumption back here to us.'

Beryl had caught it, they all knew that. She had to go to a sanatorium in Market Drayton for treatment. Alice spent more time with Edith then. They were all afraid she might catch it too.

It was no secret in the family that Frank helped Len to pay for Beryl's keep. Len had let it drop to his mother.

Cecily combed out a head of regular grey waves and sold the customer a hairnet to keep them in place under her hat on the way home. She moved to her next appointment. A trim as well as a set. She combed the damp hair through and took up her scissors.

She shivered. Ever since Len had taken his life, Frank had

seemed to change. He'd been on edge, had less patience with Maddy, less patience with everybody. If it had been anyone else, she'd have said he seemed nervous, and afraid, but Frank was never afraid of anything. He was bombastic, went into anything life could throw at him with his shoulders back. Frank seemed to be changing almost before her eyes, and it scared her.

She heard his footfall on the stairs. The only way out was through the salon. He nodded in her direction as he always did.

'See you later, Cissie,' and he gave her his usual little wave.

It was an act he was putting on for her two assistants. Just bravado. Pretending nothing had happened. But anyone could see he wasn't walking with his usual swagger, nor was he holding his head so high. He seemed suddenly much older, older beyond his years.

He was no longer strutting about, giving orders and expecting everybody to jump to his command. She was seeing Frank in a different light. Cecily thought she'd reached a crossroads in her life.

It made her ask herself whether there was more to Len taking his life than had appeared. Did Frank feel he was to blame? She was sure he was stricken with guilt.

She decided that in future she wasn't going to kowtow to him. He wanted her to bring Alice up to atone in part for what he'd done to her mother. Well, she wasn't having that. Even though he said he'd bought a bigger house so that she could.

She had her own daughter to look after. That was more than enough, especially now she couldn't trust Frank to pull his weight.

On Sunday, Edith was spreading her best white linen cloth on the oak table in her dining room. Monty insisted on calling it the middle room, though a dining room was what it was. She was proud of it, but it was only used when they were too many to sit round the kitchen table.

She liked to have Frank and his family to Sunday dinner. It meant a lot of extra work, quite apart from the cost, but she liked to see them all together. It made her feel like the kingpin uniting her family.

Today there was a special reason to invite them. Frank and Cecily had collected the key to their new house yesterday, but Saturday was a busy day for them. The furniture removers had been outside the shop at nine this morning, though they'd had trouble finding a firm willing to do it on Sunday, and had to pay extra. It was the one day of the week they had free.

Cecily would have no time to cook today, so Edith was doing it for them. Once dinner was over, they were all going back to help get the beds made up and the curtains hung.

When she came, Cecily looked flustered. Her nose was usually carefully powdered, but today it was beginning to shine. She was not so flustered as Frank, though. He really looked shattered.

'Aren't you well?' Edith asked him.

'Of course I'm well,' he retorted irritably. Edith knew he was on edge.

She watched her daughter-in-law tucking into the apple pie and rice pudding that she'd made to follow the roast beef.

Maddy pulled at her mother's skirt to get her attention. 'When we've finished dinner, can Alice and me go out to ride our bikes?'

'No, darling. I want you to come back to the new house. You can show Alice round and then I want you to arrange your things in your new bedroom.'

'That would be lovely,' Alice said. 'I can help you. We can ride our bikes any time.'

'No,' Frank said. 'Let them go out for ten minutes.' He put a hand on each of their shoulders and steered them towards the door. 'Do you good to run off a bit of steam. Don't go far now, we'll be leaving soon.'

When the back door slammed behind them, Edith watched him look round the table at each of them. He was white-faced, full of tension. She knew he was afraid.

'Our Len's had a letter,' he said quietly, taking it from his pocket. 'I asked the post office to redirect any letters on to me. It's from some sanatorium.'

'About Beryl?' Edith knew it must be.

'She's dead.'

'What? What happened?'

'Caught consumption. Died of it, like her mother.'

'Goodness!' Monty's eyes were filled with horror. 'Poor girl. Len should have told us.'

'He did. He told me,' Peter said solemnly. 'Ages ago. You wouldn't have it, Mam. Said it wasn't true. There were all sorts of other rumours about where she'd gone.'

'Off with another man.' Edith nodded.

'She was having another baby,' Cecily said. 'Read the letter . . .'

Edith picked it up. Her legs felt weak with shock. 'I bet it wasn't our Len's baby. That'll be why he did himself in. That baby wasn't his.'

Peter was very conscious of the atmosphere round the table. Nobody moved. Dad's face was filled with horror. Frank looked ill.

Len had told them all that Beryl had consumption. More than once. Mam hadn't believed him, she'd half-convinced them all it was just to excuse Beryl's absence.

'She never looked that bad . . .'

Mam wasn't shocked; he could feel her relief that Beryl was dead. Almost as though it could have been much worse, but he found it impossible to think of anything worse. It was a terrible death.

'Somebody's got to tell Alice,' he said. 'Will you do it, Frank?'

'Why me?' He spun round on Peter, full of aggression.

'You've told the rest of us,' Peter said mildly. 'She'll want to know. Poor kid, it's not long since her dad . . .'

Mam said, stiff-faced, 'You do it, Monty.'

'She'll be heartbroken,' Dad protested. 'You know how much she thinks of her mother.'

Frank said: 'You, Mam . . .'

Mam had barked: 'She's better off without Beryl. She wasn't worth bothering about. It's good riddance to bad rubbish.'

'Why?' Peter asked. He could accept that Beryl's death was fact, but he couldn't help wondering how much truth there'd been in all the other rumours. 'What did Beryl do?'

'She was nothing but a tart, but I can't say that to Alice, now can I? Better if you tell her, Frank.'

It was as though nobody in the family could bring themselves to talk about Beryl. Ten minutes later they were all walking round to Frank's new house and Beryl was forgotten.

Peter saw his mother's lips tighten as they went from room to room in the new house. He knew it was larger and grander than the one she wanted to buy herself. He knew she was very envious.

It was in a chaotic state because they were just moving in. There were crates and boxes everywhere, but Cecily would make it look lovely. He and Dad started to put the curtains up. Frank was going from room to room, doing nothing.

'I'll have to get a car,' he said, sounding overstretched. 'To run back and forth to the shop. It's not so convenient for buses here. We have to walk down to Borough Road.'

He saw Mam give a little smile of satisfaction that everything was not perfect.

Even now, Peter didn't understand why they'd left it to him to tell Alice. It made his stomach turn over to remember how he'd done it almost by accident days later.

Alice had come home and told him there was going to be

142

a concert at school, that she was going to recite a poem and Maddy was going to sing.

'I wish my mam would come back in time to see me do it,' she said. It had come like a kick in the guts to find she didn't yet know. 'Do you think she will?'

He'd held her close and said: 'I don't think so. Your mam was sick, Alice. She caught consumption from her mother. She was in hospital for a long time. That's why she couldn't be with you.'

There'd been a deep frown on the small face. She'd said calmly: 'And she died of it?'

He'd had to say 'Yes.'

'I was afraid this would happen,' Alice said softly. He could see the tears glistening in her green eyes.

'Why?'

'Nobody wanted to tell me about Mrs Hall next door when she went into hospital.'

Peter caught his breath. Mrs Hall had died in hospital too, in childbirth.

'It was different for your mam,' he told her gently. 'She was very sick.'

'But for me it's the same. I've lost her for ever now.' She wiped her eyes. 'You are sure?'

'Quite sure, kid.' He told her about the letter Frank had received from the hospital, and that she'd almost had a little brother.

Alice clung to him for a long time. He took her next door then, so that Auntie Nell and Eric could help him comfort her.

Alice felt everybody was being very kind to her because her mother had died. In truth, she'd felt much worse when it happened to Dadda. She'd always been close to him; she'd seen him doing his best for her, felt his love. She still missed him.

Her mother had been gone so long she already seemed a

143

distant dream. Alice had lived in hope that she'd come back, of course. It was what she and Dadda wanted, to be able to live with her again, and now that hope had gone for good.

'You've still got us, kid,' Peter had told her. 'And you've still got a home here. I'd miss you if you went now, d'you know that? So would Eric and Auntie Nell.'

It was Monday, but she didn't have to go to school. It was what the teachers called half-term. Alice spooned up her breakfast porridge in a more leisurely fashion than usual.

'Teachers' rest again,' Gran said. 'They seem to have so many.' It made her sharp because it meant she had Alice and Maddy about the house all day, but Alice did feel settled with her now.

She'd heard Gran arrange with Aunt Cecily to cut her hair. 'Make a fuss of her,' she'd said. 'Let her have the works, it might cheer her up.'

At five to nine, Gran said: 'Off you go now. Your auntie said nine o'clock and you mustn't keep her waiting. And tell Maddy to come up here. She needn't wait for you unless she wants to.'

Alice knew duty made her say that; Gran would prefer Maddy to stay away as long as possible. She skipped down the street. She liked going to Aunt Cecily's shop; she always seemed pleased to see her.

The shop was already open and she wasn't the first customer. Betty, one of the assistants, was already washing somebody's hair.

Cecily was standing stiffly by the little desk on which she kept her appointments book. She looked up at Alice in a distracted fashion, as though she didn't know who she was.

'I've come to have my hair cut,' she told her. She'd never seen her aunt look so outraged. 'You did say nine o'clock.'

'So I did. Get your coat off then.'

Usually Cecily gave her a welcoming hug and helped her off with her coat. Now her arms were being pushed roughly into the sleeves of a pink smock. A comb was tugged painfully through her hair. Alice could feel the irritation behind each tug.

Always when she'd come before Cecily had asked Betty to shampoo her hair first, and she was given a camomile rinse to make her hair bright and shiny, but it seemed that today she wasn't going to.

She watched Aunt Cecily in the mirror. She'd never seen her frown like this before.

'Who's been cutting at your hair?'

Alice swallowed. Gran had said it was too long and getting in her eyes; that she didn't know how she could see from under it to do her school work, and that she'd develop a squint if it was left like that. Alice had taken a pair of scissors and trimmed a bit off; Maddy had helped.

'You've been hacking at it and making a mess. Far better if you leave it to somebody who knows what they're doing.' Cecily sounded severe.

The cold steel of the scissors against her neck made Alice shiver. Something had upset Aunt Cecily. She worried about what she'd done to cause this sudden change.

Maddy appeared at the bottom of the stairs. 'I've swept out my old room, Mam, and thrown out the bits. It's all clean and tidy now.'

'There's a good girl. You go up to Gran's with Alice, darling.' Maddy was getting the loving treatment still, the kisses and the hugs.

Uncle Frank came down behind her with a sack of rubbish. He was cleaning all his stuff out of the flat.

'I won't be long,' he said.

'Take as long as you like,' Cecily snapped.

Alice breathed a sigh of relief. Cecily was in a temper, but after all it wasn't something she'd done. Uncle Frank was in her bad books too.

Book Two

Chapter Thirteen

July 1929

Frank spent most of Monday morning tending his own secluded garden, and most of the afternoon sitting in a deckchair looking at the jobs he still had to do.

'I wish I had time to sit in the sun,' Cissie said sarcastically when she saw his chair still out on the grass. 'When are you going to start doing a full day's work again?'

Frank had no energy; he felt he needed to take things easy. He needed time to think and time to relax. His nerves were stretched to breaking point.

He hadn't been selling many of his own tickets. His confidence had ebbed away. Hilary jeered at him and tried to push him to do more.

'No point in staying here if you don't. The pay's rotten and I'm sick of this job.'

Last year, Frank knew he'd have felt the same, but now he didn't feel he could cope with any changes. He was afraid he was getting more like Len. Over the last months, he'd told himself over and over he had nothing to worry about. Beryl was dead and buried. He had nothing to fear from her; he was starting with a clean slate.

But he wasn't. Beryl's death had knocked him for six and he'd opened his mouth too wide. He should never have told Cissie that Alice was his daughter. Everything had gone sour between them since she'd known. He'd expected her to take that in her stride, but she hadn't.

He hadn't enjoyed anything since they'd moved to this house. Cissie complained it wasn't so convenient for her. It took her twenty minutes to walk to her salon, and that made it hardly worth coming home when she closed the place at lunch time. It was taking Frank longer to get to work because they weren't on a direct bus route. He'd always wanted a car, and Cissie had pushed him into buying one.

It was costing much more than he'd expected to live here. He hadn't felt this short of money for years. The bills never stopped coming in.

Cissie was overflowing with energy, often wanting to slip out of her salon in the afternoons to drag him round the shops.

'Daisy can run the business for a few hours,' she told him. 'No need for me to be chained to the place. We need a new carpet for the sitting room, and I want to look at curtain material.'

Last week she'd wanted a bookcase and some easy chairs. The week before it had been dining-room furniture.

'Go easy,' he'd said. 'We can't afford it.'

That made her pull herself up. 'Before we bought the house, you said we could.'

'Not all at once.'

'We might as well fix it up comfortably now we've got it.'

Cissie often went down on the bus by herself and then paraded the new clothes she'd bought in front of him. She'd always been smartly dressed, but now she was spending more she looked really elegant. She didn't stint Maddy either, always buying things for her.

Frank found it was impossible to stop her because she had money from the shop. He'd always thought she spent sensibly, that she had a thrifty streak, but not any longer.

Since they'd moved out of the flat over the shop, he'd

wanted to sub-let it to Hilary. She'd even asked if she could have it. It was ridiculous not to – the rent would help with their expenses – but Cissie said no.

'I want to sell the business and get a bigger salon in the centre of Birkenhead. It'll make it harder to sell the lease and the business if there's a tenant in the flat.'

'But it's Hilary. When we're ready for that, we can ask her to move out.'

'I'm ready now,' Cissie said rebelliously. 'I've been to an agent; there's a shop in Grange Road I'm interested in. Right opposite Duckworth's.'

That had really taken his breath away. 'It'll be expensive there. The rates . . .'

'A lease on a shop in a good position doesn't often come up. It's a big shop too, I'd be a fool not to jump at the chance.'

He couldn't help but notice the difference in her manner. She now said 'I' when she always used to say 'we', with a fond look in his direction.

'A hairdresser's? A going concern?'

'No, I don't want a going concern. I'd rather fix the place up myself. I want everything up-to-the-minute, top-class, smart and expensive.'

'Cissie! We can't afford to take on more expense. Not so soon after getting the house.'

'We could if you didn't sit around all day doing nothing.'

She nagged him, demanded, wouldn't hear of waiting.

'I want it,' she said in the newly acquired imperious manner.

He started selling his own tickets again in the cinema, slowly and carefully. He had to try to keep up with Cissie's demands. He hadn't quite got his nerve back and was scared of being caught, but he felt better for doing it. It gave him back the upper hand with Hilary, as well as more cash.

Cissie always wanted more.

'You're always giving money away. Your mother has only

to ask. You almost throw it at other people. What about me and Maddy?'

But the worst thing she'd done to move out of his bed. She'd fitted up the spare bedroom with no expense spared. He'd taken her into Robb's to buy a new bed, and new wardrobe and dressing table, all of the best quality. Not to mention lino and bedside mats and curtains.

He hadn't complained because he'd been under the impression it could be for Alice, but Cissie had moved in herself and she'd fitted a bolt on the inside to stop him getting in.

'This is my room,' she'd said coldly, when he'd tried. 'I don't want you near me. Not if you won't help me get my new salon. You agreed years ago that I should. I'd earn more.'

He'd had to say he would. Had to agree to a lot of things. He'd tried to pull one of the other usherettes at the Carlton Hall, a pretty little thing called Mavis Cuthbertson. She'd seemed quite responsive at first, but Hilary had stepped in and foiled that. Told the girl he was her sister's husband and a dangerous womaniser. Mavis was giving him a wide berth.

Cissie had pressed on fast and was due to take over her new shop in Grange Road next week. She'd arranged for shop-fitters to go in and fix it up on a grand scale. She wanted her new salon to be the very best in Birkenhead. She was taking all the decisions and making the arrangements without reference to him. She'd insisted the lease be in her name alone.

'In case you get caught and sent to prison. Better if you have no connection with my business if that happens.'

That hadn't pleased him. He hadn't thought her capable of doing so much by herself. It made him feel she was cutting him out of her life.

She'd put the salon in Woodchurch Lane on the market as a going concern. It had been on the market for three weeks and they were both disappointed that there hadn't been one enquiry as yet. He'd been thinking about it today and he'd suggest she put a manager in and keep it open. It would more than pay its way, and keeping it on had other advantages. He hadn't yet told his employers at the Carlton Hall that he'd moved house. If they kept that business, he wouldn't need to. The flat over it was quite decent. Hilary could move in and pay them rent; it was better than the room she was living in now. She'd jump at the chance.

In the late afternoon he cut a few generous slices of beef off yesterday's joint and fried up some of the left-over mashed potato. He had to hurry then. He just had time to collect Cissie and drive her home after she'd closed the shop. She knew how to keep him running round after her. He couldn't believe that he was doing it. All wives seemed to know how to get what they wanted. Cissie was rationing his visits to her bedroom. Either he pleased her or he didn't get in. He felt she was cutting him down in size.

It made him furious, but if he showed the slightest sign of anger she'd go to her room and put the bolt on.

'Cool down,' she'd say. 'We'll talk about your needs tomorrow when you're feeling calmer.'

He'd let fly at her once, and woke Maddy in the next room. She'd come to her door all sleepy-eyed to ask:

'What's the matter, Mam? What's happening?'

Cissie had fussed over her, taking Maddy into her own bed, so there was no possibility of him getting there. He'd gone out for a walk alone; he didn't know what else he could do.

After that, she said: 'Calm down and be quiet or you'll wake Maddy again.' It made him feel more like throttling her than having sex. It was enough to put him off her for good.

It was sapping his confidence in other directions, making it harder for him to get back into his stride at the picture house. He needed to come up with some new ideas to make more money.

When he mentioned the idea of putting a manager in at the old salon he saw the corners of her mouth turn up in a smile.

'I've been thinking about that too. I was watching Daisy this afternoon. I could trust her to manage it, and the customers already know her. If I close the shop the business will ebb away. A shame, when I've worked so hard to build it up.'

'Can you run two at the same time?'

'If I can get the right staff for the new place, yes.'

He dropped her at home and drove on into town. He'd get himself a decent car once this new salon was up and running. He'd bought this second-hand Austin Seven and it wasn't the easiest thing to drive. It was three years old, a 1926 model. It swayed from side to side as the wheels went over bumps, and the brakes weren't much good. He'd taken it back to the garage and been told there was nothing wrong with it; all Austin Sevens were like that. They'd tried to sell him a new one, telling him it was better and the quirks had been ironed out, but he wasn't having that.

Frank sighed. He longed to own a really smart car, something with a bit of go in it. A car that would give him a bit of status. It was definitely on the list of things he meant to get.

He parked his Austin Seven in Douglas Street, which was just far enough away from the Carlton Hall to escape the notice of the staff. He'd never mentioned to any of them, apart from Hilary, that he had a car. Safer not to; he didn't want to look as though he earned more than old Butterballs, who was always telling them that business was falling off.

Tonight he'd make an effort to sell more of his own tickets. He'd been doing it for years without any trouble. It was almost foolproof. A good way of earning extra cash. He needed to get back into the way of selling as many as he could at every performance.

Monty was seeing much less of Frank now he'd moved further away.

'I miss him,' Edith complained. On Fridays now, Maddy

brought her a brown envelope with coins inside. This week she'd said: 'Daddy wants you all to come to have dinner with us on Sunday.' Edith found a note in with the money, inviting them for twelve thirty.

'They did promise,' Edith said. 'I still see Cecily from time to time, but sometimes she's quite off-hand. I don't think she's finding it so easy now she doesn't live over the shop.'

Monty had warned Rita that he'd not be able to spend so much time with her this Sunday.

Edith was looking forward to it. 'They'll have done a lot to their house by now. I can't wait to see it. Don't you go disappearing to your allotment this morning,' she told him. 'You never come back on time, and we don't want to be late. Not when Cecily's cooking for us.'

Monty went out to get the Sunday papers and then sat reading them in his rocking chair. It was a restful morning. Edith fussed over getting Alice ready and got them all there ten minutes before time.

The house smelled of new paint. Cecily had had it redecorated from top to bottom.

'Come and see my bedroom, Gran,' Maddy urged, pulling her towards the stairs before she'd taken her coat off. 'And you, Uncle Peter.' Alice followed them uninvited.

Monty heard Cecily say: 'It's looking quite different now. We're getting things the way we want them.' Of course she'd want to show it off. Prove how much more money she had than him.

He was left with Frank, who led the way to their sitting room. They sank down in opposite corners of the red velour sofa.

Frank said in a falsely social voice: 'Cissie's full of furnishing ideas. Having the time of her life.'

Monty had sensed a difference in the atmosphere over the last few months. A coolness. Cecily hadn't rushed to kiss any of them as she usually did. Frank seemed stiff and ill at ease. He wondered what had caused the rift.

155

'Mam will love what she's done to the house.'

Monty was afraid Edith would find it harder to accept the status quo at home after this.

He said: 'It's grand. Cecily must be doing very well with her hairdressing. I don't know how you manage it. All this must take a bit of paying for.' He'd noticed a splendid grandfather clock in the hall that hadn't been there on his last visit.

Frank said brusquely: 'Not just Cissie. I do my bit too.'

'I thought you weren't doing as much as you used to. Didn't you give up that job you had on Friday and Saturday mornings?'

'It was a waste of time. Didn't pay enough. Would you like a glass of beer?' Frank leapt to his feet to fetch it.

Monty sighed. He should have remembered Frank liked to feel big. He'd want to feel he was providing all this, not Cecily.

'Did you get something to replace it? The morning job?'

'No, I've given up my gardening job too.'

'How do you manage? I mean, all this . . .'

'There are ways.' Frank gave him a knowing nod and then, as he stared at him, a wink. 'Ways and means.'

Monty wished he had the magic formula for earning easy money. He said, without thinking: 'I wish I knew what they were.'

Frank's eyes slid sideways to his face. His tone changed. 'You know them, Dad. You know them all right.'

Monty didn't. 'What makes you say that?'

Frank laughed. 'That watch you're wearing, for a start.'

Monty dropped his arm to make the sleeve of his jacket hide his watch. He felt flustered; he should have known Frank would notice. He admired the trappings of wealth.

The oblong Rolex Prince had been a Christmas present from Rita. He kept most of the things she gave him at her house – the dressing gown and slippers and things like that

– but he'd wanted to wear the watch, and Rita thought it silly not to.

He'd been so careful for the first six months not to let Edith see it. He'd worn it at the office and at Rita's house and changed to his old cheap one every night on the bus coming home.

He should have known he'd grow careless. He was tucking into faggots and peas one evening when Edith said:

'That's a fancy watch you've got. Is it new?'

He'd gone stiff with horror, afraid she'd know it had come from a lady friend. He'd made himself act naturally.

'Yes,' he'd said. 'D'you like it?'

'Very nice, I'm sure,' she'd sniffed.

He'd had to rush in with an explanation then. 'The strap on my old one broke and it fell on the floor by my desk. Didn't even notice until somebody trod on it. I had to get a new one.'

'You've done yourself proud. Is it gold?'

He'd almost said 'rolled gold' but remembered in time it was stamped eighteen carat. It would only make her suspicious if he left it around and she saw that.

'Yes,' he admitted. 'Thought I might as well get a decent one while I was at it. The old one didn't keep good time anyway.'

Edith was innocent about expensive things. To her a watch was a watch. Monty thought she believed him. Frank certainly did not.

'You're up to something. You're not drinking in the Halfway House when Mam thinks you are. Haven't been doing it for ages.'

Monty felt his heart race. His mouth was suddenly dry.

Frank went on: 'So I asked myself what you could be up to that you didn't want Mam to know about.'

Monty gulped at his beer, horror clutching his guts.

'And I came to the conclusion that you were out making a bit on the side.' Another wink came his way. 'Hard cash.'

Monty could hardly get the words out. 'What makes you say that?'

'The night our Len died, Eric Ainslie couldn't find you in the Halfway House and you said you went down to the Swan because it was crowded.'

Monty knew what he'd said. 'That's right.'

'Well, Mam was in such a state that night, I didn't know what to do for the best. We wanted you at home, so I went to look for you too. I went to the Swan but you weren't there either.'

'I must have been walking between the two. I met Harry Jackson on the way and stopped to talk.'

Monty was awash with guilt. He could see Frank didn't believe him. He had that knowing smile on his face. Frank loved to get the better of him.

'The Halfway House wasn't all that crowded, though you said it was. I reckoned you must be out on some money-making exercise. That's why I said nothing at the time.'

Monty could hardly breathe. He mustn't deny that. If it wasn't money, there was only one alternative, and he didn't want Frank to think of that.

'No, you've got other fish to fry. They told me at the Halfway House that you don't spend as much time there as you used to.'

Monty gave him the wink then. Better that Frank should think that than arrive at the truth. The last thing he wanted was for him to find out about Rita.

He said slowly: 'I'd be glad if you'd keep your mouth shut about it. Say nothing.'

'Course, Dad. You bet.' Frank gave him another wink. The doorbell rang again and he got up to let Hilary in.

Monty was glad she'd been invited too. Frank was making a fuss of her, and it took the spotlight off him.

But he'd lost his peace of mind. He no longer felt safe. He was afraid his secret mistress would not be a secret much longer.

Chapter Fourteen

Monty was so agitated by what Frank had said that he couldn't think straight. Cecily served Sunday dinner with more style than Edith did. With Hilary there to help her, she made it look easy. She had her new big table extended to its fullest extent. Frank sat down to carve the joint at the table. It was all rather grand.

He heard Edith admire Cecily's new china dinner service and canteen of cutlery. All through the meal he saw Edith's eyes going round the dining room, taking in its silk wall-paper, fine Victorian sideboard and red carpet square. He knew she was envious, and that it would fire her own ambition to have a new house.

The roast lamb was good too, but he couldn't enjoy it. His mind was on fire. He'd been so confident that all his family would see his life as an open book. Now that wasn't so, and Frank had only to take another small step to come up with the right answer.

He wanted to leave as soon as dinner was over but knew he couldn't. Edith expected help with the washing-up after the Sunday dinners she provided, and would no doubt offer to do the same for Cecily.

He helped dry up to speed the process, but then Frank took them all out to see the garden. It was bigger than Monty remembered from his first look round, but it had been well cared for by a previous owner. There was a lot of lawn and several flowerbeds.

'You'll need a good lawnmower to keep all this straight,' he said.

'I've had to get one already. Come and see it.'

Monty wanted to get away. He couldn't settle here, and he'd made arrangements to see Rita that evening. Sunday was the one day of the week any of them had any leisure, and they all liked to sit round and take things easy.

At last he got them away. It took the best part of half an hour to walk home again. Edith wanted to assess every house they passed, and any with a for-sale notice delayed them for ages. She kept up a hymn of praise for Frank's new house and new possessions. She gloated on his success; felt some of it could be attributed to the way in which she'd brought him up.

'Didn't think much of the lamb though,' she sniffed. 'It was a little tough.'

The meal was Cecily's province, and she was competing directly with Edith.

'It was a lovely meal,' Peter protested.

'Especially the chocolate pudding,' Alice sighed.

Monty felt bound to add: 'Nothing the matter with the lamb.'

After the blow-out of a Sunday dinner, tea was always light. Perhaps a meat sandwich and a piece of cake.

'Let's have a cup of tea,' Monty said as soon as they got home. He took the kettle to the scullery to fill it.

'It's a bit early, isn't it?' Edith sat down to ease off her best shoes. 'You can't be hungry yet?'

He wasn't, but he wanted to get it over so he'd be free to go to Rita's. 'A bit of cake would be nice.'

'There's no filling you,' Edith complained, but with her slippers on, she fetched the cake tin and started to set out cups and saucers.

Edith believed in filling every inch of oven space if she lit it, and was in the habit of baking soda bread and currant cake alongside the joint on Sunday mornings. This week,

Peter had persuaded her not to bother making cake. He'd brought some from the bakery, but he ate so many cakes at work he never wanted them at home. He started making toast. Peter was at that age when he could be relied upon to eat at any time.

Monty bit into a custard tart, and it tasted so good he tried an Eccles cake too. Peter made excellent cakes, and had set his heart on running his own bakery one day.

He said slowly: 'I'm surprised they're going ahead straight away to get Cecily a better salon. They've got so much expense at home just now.'

Only then did it occur to Monty that Frank's sudden increase in income might not all be legally earned. Surely that was what he'd been implying? All that winking and nodding must add up to something. Frank was spending a small fortune and there seemed to be no end to what he could afford. It couldn't be Cecily's business that was paying for all that.

The Eccles cake he'd thought delicious a moment ago was like dust in his mouth. Was Frank getting mixed up in some sort of fraud? Was he taking money which didn't belong to him? Monty didn't know what it could be, didn't want to guess and certainly didn't want to know. He felt cold inside. He prided himself on being an honest man. He'd never stolen anything or broken the law in any way in his life. Yet Frank seemed to think he was capable of it.

He wouldn't have believed it of Frank! He'd brought him up to be honest, hadn't he? And Edith had been strict with all of them. And what if he should be caught? It might mean . . . prison?

Edith would be mortified, and so would he. The family meant a lot to her. She wanted them to be a tight, supportive group and the sins of one reflected on them all. Having Len kill himself was bad enough, truly terrible in fact, but if Frank should be caught thieving as well . . . It would tear the family apart.

161

He watched his youngest son teasing Alice. Peter had an open, honest face. Impossible to believe he'd do anything wrong, but Monty couldn't be sure. He'd have said the same about Frank.

He had to get away from them all, and anyway Rita was expecting him. He went into the scullery to splash water on his face.

'I'm going out,' he announced as he pulled the family comb through his thick mop of white hair in front of the scullery mirror.

'Where are you going?' Edith always asked.

'Down to the allotment.'

'Smartening yourself up to go down there, aren't you?'

Monty could have kicked himself. He was usually careful about such things.

'Said I'd pop in to the Halfway House after, meet some fellow from work.'

'Eh, you're always going out.'

He couldn't get out of the house quick enough, and strode down to Carlaw Road at a great pace. He felt just as agitated when he reached Rita's doorstep.

'I've been waiting for you, willing you to hurry,' she said as she let him in. She put her arms on his shoulders and kissed him. She wore a smart tea dress and exotic perfume. Edith rarely used perfume, and if she did, it would only be eau-de-Cologne.

Rita Hooper had been widowed after only three years of marriage and had been left well provided for. She'd bought this newly built house recently, because she thought the house she'd been living in was too big for one. She was twenty-six years Monty's junior and had a good job in the office at Lever's; secretary to one of the directors.

He knew Rita thought of herself as a plain girl. Her face was long and thin and her nose on the large side. She had quite a complex about that.

'Of course you aren't plain,' he told her. 'You've got

beautiful hair.' It was brown but with a rich depth of colour and golden highlights. Her skin was a little on the sallow side.

'Perhaps you're not chocolate-box pretty, but you've got a face with lots of character, and I love it.'

Monty thought youth had its own beauty. He couldn't take his eyes from her face. Not a line or wrinkle anywhere, no puffiness under her eyes, no slackness or hint of a double chin. He loved her firm young flesh and rounded limbs, her flat stomach and cheeky bottom. Her body was a delight. He couldn't bring himself to look at Edith these days. It was cruel what the years did to women. Being with Rita, stroking her peach-soft skin, made him feel decades younger.

'I've kept tea waiting for you.' She gave him another kiss and ruffled his hair. 'I've made some fairy cakes; come and try them.'

Monty could feel the last tea he'd drunk rising in his throat, but he couldn't refuse. Preparing for this visit had been the pivot of her day. He had to look as though he was enjoying what she'd made.

Her sitting room went across the back of the house, and the french window to the garden stood open on this summer afternoon. Rita had set afternoon tea out on her trolley, with an embroidered cloth, fine china and a fancy tea pot. The contrast between this and the tea he'd just had in the kitchen at home could not have been greater.

At home, the aluminium tea pot was kept in the hearth to keep warm, and they'd eaten Peter's cakes straight from the tin in which they were kept.

Here Rita was standing over him holding out the three-tier cake stand on which she'd set hers out. She placed a tea plate, knife and napkin on a small table at his side.

He loved to see her move; she had such grace. Her eyes, big and suggestive, played with his. He found her totally magnetic. She came to sit close beside him on the sofa, pressing her leg against his, talking all the time.

'Such a long, lonely day waiting for you to come.'

Monty hadn't enjoyed his day much either. Frank had given his confidence a jolt. Only now was his agitation being soothed. He felt safe here in her house, made familiar by frequent visits.

'I said it would be after five before I'd be able to get away.'

'I know, love, but time drags so when I'm waiting.'

'You should go out more,' he told her. 'Go to see your parents. They'd be glad to see more of you.'

Rita pulled a face. 'I know. I have tea with them on Wednesday nights and they're always asking me to come at other times, but I'd rather be with you. I can't think of anything but being with you.'

That was a lovely thing for her to say. He kissed her cheek and praised her fairy cakes. She'd gone to a lot of trouble decorating them. He knew everything she did was for him. He put his tea cup down and she put her hand in his.

'I want you here for whole days and nights. I wish you could spend more time with me.'

'I wish I could too.'

He meant it, he really did. He only felt truly alive when he was with Rita. When he was at home, he spent his time contemplating the utter bliss of a life spent here with her.

When he was with Edith, he spent hours watching her go about her domestic tasks, pondering on the best way to say he wanted to leave her. That was the difficult part, facing her about that. If only he could just pack a bag and move out.

But Edith wouldn't stand for it. She'd devoted her life to her family and he was its main bread-winner. He'd have to provide the new house she wanted and pay its running costs, and support her and Alice.

She'd give him a hard time too, wanting to know the ins and outs of everything; she always did. She'd say he was a disgrace and he'd let her and the family down. If he moved in with Rita, she'd find him. She'd leave no stone unturned until she did.

Monty knew he wouldn't be hard to find. He had to go on working for Lever's; he was earning a pension with them, and anyway, he didn't want to leave because Rita worked there too.

'You will tell Edith, won't you, Monty?' she wheedled now. 'I want all of you, all the time. Not just for the odd hour or two you can spare from her. I'll look after you if you come. I'll take good care of you, I promise.'

He took her in his arms and kissed her. Soon they would go upstairs. Monty put the problem of Edith out of his mind and gave himself up to the satisfactions of the moment.

Monty's desk was in the middle of the general office. There was always the clatter of typewriters and the shrilling of telephones. He had no privacy for anything.

He was earning more than Edith thought he was. He'd been promoted to senior clerk, and that had given him a big pay rise about which he'd said nothing. He preferred to spend it on his mistress rather than his wife. He bought her bottles of sherry and perfume, her two weaknesses. Just to think he had both a mistress and a wife gave him a lift.

He needed a lift, for although he'd had promotion, his wasn't an exciting job. He worked in the sales department, and for sixteen years had transferred the comments of several salesmen about sales outlets to a card index system. It was routine work and he'd found it deadly dull. Now he managed a whole lot of card index systems and had a typist who typed the comments on to the cards.

Rita worked up on the top floor. There was a gallery that ran round the general office, and any movement up there made him look up. Rita was coming out of her office now. She always looked very smart at work. Always a suit and high-heeled court shoes. Today she wore her navy serge. She had her handbag under her arm, which meant she was on the way to the ladies' to powder her nose.

She gave him a little signal, a flutter of her fingers; it acknowledged his glance. Monty hadn't told her he was twenty-six years older than she was. He'd knocked off eight. He reckoned he didn't look his age anyway.

He wanted to keep things exactly as they were. He was enjoying life and things were easier to manage if he knew what to expect. But both Edith and Rita were always on at him, wanting him to make big changes.

'You ought to be thinking about our retirement,' Edith was always saying. 'Making plans, looking for a nice bungalow.' She called it 'our retirement', but she meant hers.

Rita didn't know how bothered he was at the thought of retiring. He didn't talk about it to her, and anyway, she thought it was eight years further off than it actually was. All the same, it was creeping up on him; only three more years to go.

The last thing Monty wanted was to retire. Rita would be at work all day, and what would he do with his time? He didn't want to sit at home with Edith in her new bungalow, which would probably be miles away from Carlaw Road.

The changes Rita wanted to bring about were more immediate. She was constantly on at him to break things off with Edith and move in with her. The fact that she kept pressing him to do it excited him and made him keep turning the idea over and over in his mind.

He'd fantasised about telling Edith so many times, pictured her Roman nose quivering with indignation when he got the words out.

She'd shout at him, rave that he was disgusting. 'Only a few months older than Cecily, did you say? She's nothing but a girl! You should be ashamed of yourself, a man of your age!'

Of course Rita wasn't anything like so pretty as Cecily. Cecily could have men flocking round her if she wanted to, but looks were only skin deep, and Rita had a lovely personality.

He kept telling her that, but the truth was that men didn't beat their way to her door. Monty knew he might not have had a look-in if they had. Sometimes she teased him about his age, but more often now she needled him to leave Edith.

'Trust me, Monty. I'll take good care of you if you do.'

The truth was, he couldn't quite bring himself to trust her. Rita was so much younger, he was afraid she wouldn't want a husband who'd retired. The very word made him feel old.

Edith would say a lot more, of course. 'What's all this costing, I'd like to know? I bet you've spent a fortune on her. Money that should have gone towards our retirement.'

Once or twice when Edith was being particularly tetchy, the words had been on the tip of his tongue, but he hadn't been able to say them.

This year, he and Edith had been married for thirty-six years. He was nervous about throwing all that over at his time of life. Edith provided rock-like security. He knew what to expect from her.

He'd tried to explain all this to Rita, but she was a different generation. She didn't understand the loyalty that came from spending a lifetime together. Of course, Rita had been part of his life for a long time too. They travelled to work on the same bus, and ate their lunch in the office cafeteria.

There had been a time when he used to go to the works canteen and get a good hot dinner, but Rita didn't want to go there. She thought the men who worked in the factory were a rough crowd and had persuaded him to go to the cafeteria instead. Nowadays he had a sausage roll and a scone with her every day except Mondays.

On Mondays, a manager from the margarine company came in and took her to lunch in the staff dining room. Monty didn't go there, though he was entitled to. The same food was served as in the works canteen, but in the staff dining room they had waitress service and starched cloths on the tables.

167

It cost four shillings. Enough of Edith's thrift had rubbed off on him to make that out of the question. He couldn't afford it, and the price was set to keep the likes of him out. The managers and directors ate there; they didn't want it filled with clerks.

He didn't like Rita going to the staff dining room. He missed her company, and the manager was twenty years younger than he was and a good-looking fellow. He was jealous. He even wondered if that was why Rita went. She said they were discussing business, but he didn't believe that.

Today she'd be coming to the cafeteria with him. All round him, desks were being cleared and drawers slammed; Monty did the same, it was lunch time. The next instant Rita was with him looking bandbox fresh. He was proud to be seen eating at the same table. She favoured bread rolls filled with salad. She always cut them into bite-sized pieces. She was doing it now.

'Do you know what I'd like to do, Monty? I'd like you to take me out. We never go out at all.'

'You know why. It's safer to . . .'

'What's dangerous about going out once in a while?' Her hazel eyes were challenging.

'Being seen . . .'

'We're being seen here. What difference does it make?'

Monty found it hard to swallow his sausage roll. He was careful to keep his home life and office life separate. He knew some of his colleagues referred to Rita as his girlfriend. Behind his back, of course; nobody dared say it to his face. He was one of the old guard. Not only did he look like an elder statesman, with his white hair, but he'd also been working in the office longer than most. It gave him a certain seniority.

He was quite friendly with Jack Sharp, who'd been working in accounts for almost as long. He knew Jack lived in Wharfedale Avenue, which was close to Woodchurch Lane. He saw him round the shops and pubs of Prenton, but he never asked Jack to his home, and he was never asked to his. The two worlds just didn't meet.

'Outside, it's different,' Monty told her. He knew he'd be nervous in case they met any of his neighbours. Anyway, what he enjoyed was having Rita to himself in the privacy of her home.

'There's a good show on at the Carlton Hall this week. I'd love to see it. It's . . .'

'Not the Carlton Hall! Definitely not.'

He told her about Frank working on the cash desk. He couldn't go in there with Rita and buy two seats from his son. Not under any circumstances. That would be inviting disaster.

He had to agree to take her to the Royal Court on Saturday night. That was over in Liverpool. They'd be less likely to meet anyone he knew, but it would take longer to get back home. He never liked to be late. It made Edith ask a lot of questions.

Chapter Fifteen

January – September 1930

Since that Sunday the previous summer, Monty had tried to stay out of Frank's way, but he couldn't avoid him completely. Edith liked having the family round, and she felt she had to repay Frank and Cecily's hospitality. It wasn't long before she invited them back. It shocked Monty to hear her ask Frank to take turns with her to host Sunday dinner.

Frank, of course, wouldn't commit himself, and it didn't happen, but Edith went on asking them round regularly, just as she always had. They were coming again today.

Monty was nervous of being left alone with Frank. Nervous of receiving some confidence about where his increased wealth was coming from, and of being asked again about how he made money on the side.

When it was time for them to arrive, Monty got out a pack of playing cards and offered to teach Alice how to play whist; anything to keep her beside him, a buffer between him and Frank. Maddy sat down with them straight away; she wanted to learn too. Then she asked her father to come and make up the fourth.

Peter was talking to Cecily about business. He thought her very astute and wanted to learn what he could from her. It made Monty nervous when the talk turned to money.

'Money makes money,' Edith said from the scullery, where she was boiling sprouts and carrots.

Monty thought he had protection from Frank, until he looked up and found him smiling. The knowing smile he'd had since he was a boy.

'Certainly does, eh, Dad?'

Monty made vague sounds of agreement and tried to look as though all his attention was on the cards.

Frank said: 'You're not as interested in money as the rest of us. I see that now.'

Monty's palms were suddenly damp with sweat.

'No, it's women, not money, isn't it, Dad?'

Maddy's hand shot out to pick up the trick.

'That's ours,' Alice said quickly.

'No it's not,' Maddy objected. 'I took it.'

'I trumped it.' Alice insisted on spreading the cards out to prove it.

'I was daft not to see that before.' Frank was still smiling at him over the heads of the girls, as they grovelled together to count tricks. Frank loved to have the upper hand over him; he always had. Monty had felt their relationship as a power struggle ever since Frank was a pushy boy of twelve.

'We've won, Grandpa,' Alice told him triumphantly. Monty was afraid that was the last thing he'd done. He was afraid Frank had won again.

Shortly after this, on the evening of a long, hot Saturday, he was up in Rita's bedroom, lying on her bed, cradling her in his arms. They'd spent a leisurely afternoon there making love. He felt satisfied, and knew by the lazy, satiated smiles Rita was giving him that she did too. For the last hour they'd been lying together, discussing everything under the sun. As Monty heard the car come along the road and draw up outside, he felt Rita stiffen.

'That sounds like . . .' She rolled off the bed and went to the window. 'Oh my goodness!' She turned back to him, her face screwing with dismay.

'Who is it?'

'My stepfather's car. He's brought my mother round.' She was throwing on her clothes.

'Stay up here, Monty. She mustn't know you're here. Mind you don't make any noise. I won't let her come up.'

'They don't know about me?'

She gave an agonised gasp. 'No . . . A married man. They'd have a fit.' She flung her dress over her head and wriggled it down.

Monty slid off the bed to look. He could feel her panic; his own heart was pounding in sympathy. 'They're both coming up the path.'

Rita was pulling a comb through her hair when the doorbell rang. She flung it down.

'My shoes!' Monty remembered with horror. 'I took them off at the bottom of the stairs.'

She rushed to the door.

'The tea cups . . .' he hissed. They'd had tea in her lounge before coming up.

'I'll say I've had a neighbour in.' Her face was flushed and anxious. He'd never seen her like this before.

The door was shut firmly on him, he heard her go flying down. There were voices in the hall below. The front door slammed. Then silence.

Monty reached for his clothes. He felt vulnerable without them, and it would only add to the embarrassment if he were caught here without them. His security was shattered. This was the first time anybody else had come to this house while he was here.

He moved slowly and carefully, doing his best to prevent any creaking of the floorboards. He kept to the carpet as he pulled on his clothes. He could hear Rita walking about in her high-heeled shoes downstairs. She was drawing water in the kitchen. He guessed she was making tea for her visitors.

He crept to the window to look down on the bull-nosed Morris parked at her gate. Maroon, with a black hood and highly polished paintwork. He wondered how long

173

it would be before the visitors left. He felt trapped up here.

He crept round Rita's bed, making it very carefully, so that there was no sign it had been recently occupied. There were no more sounds from downstairs. He wondered whether it would be possible for him to leave. The lounge was at the back of the house; if he could open the front door quietly he might be able to get away.

He eased the bedroom door open carefully; the hinge squeaked. He held it still for two minutes but there was no further sound from downstairs. They couldn't have heard him. He peeped through the banisters; the lounge door was firmly closed. He wanted to go, but did he dare? The evening was going on, and Edith would be suspicious if he weren't home when the pubs closed. He was as regular as clockwork about that.

If he could be sure they'd go in an hour or so, it would be safer to wait, but he had no means of knowing that. He ventured down two steps from the landing, his ears straining for the first sound that would alert him to somebody coming out of the lounge.

He was halfway down when he realised his shoes weren't where he'd left them. Of course, Rita had had to move them, they'd have given away his presence upstairs.

He craned his neck to see along the hall. She'd have flung them out of sight, but where? In the cupboard under the stairs? He couldn't open that; its door was almost opposite the lounge door, and it was dark inside so he'd have to feel round for them.

He noticed then that his cap had gone from the hall stand where he'd hung it. Rita had removed all trace of him. Well, he could go home without his cap, but not without his shoes. He'd have to wait. Slowly and carefully he crept back to her bedroom and closed the door.

He was increasingly worried about being late home. He'd have to give some explanation of where he'd been if he arrived back well after the pubs had closed. Edith didn't just ask, she interrogated. He was scared of making her suspicious.

He rolled back on top of the bed he'd just made. It creaked under his weight, but there was nowhere comfortable to sit in the bedroom.

He was hungry. He'd eaten nothing since the dinner Edith had made for him. His mouth was dry; he'd give anything for a beer. A cup of tea would be very welcome, even a drink of water, but he daren't go to the bathroom and get one. There'd be the sound of water running in the pipes.

Perhaps the time would pass more quickly if he read? He reached for the book turned face down on Rita's bedside table. It was a romance, from Boot's lending library, but daylight was fading, and he daren't switch on the lamp. He lay back and tried to relax as he watched the night sky darken.

He knew Rita would come straight up to him when her parents left. He prayed it would be soon. He felt like a cornered fox hiding in a thicket. He couldn't keep still, and any movement made a noise. He was almost afraid to breathe.

At last he heard doors opening below him and the sound of voices carried up. Thank goodness, they were going! He almost put on the light to see if it was closing time. He just stopped himself in time. Rita came upstairs and put her arms round him.

'Of course it isn't closing time yet. Come down and have something to eat. I made a quiche.

'Monty love, you're a nervous wreck and so am I. We can't go on like this. You've got to tell Edith. Divorce isn't impossible; I want you to marry me. Then everything will be open and above board. We won't have to carry on like this.'

Monty had to agree. He felt sick as he walked home. He hadn't let himself think as far as divorce and remarriage. It seemed a huge and fearsome step to take. He wanted it, it was exactly what he wanted, but somehow it seemed beyond his reach.

Alice loved school and knew Maddy did too. They continued to sit side by side in class and compete against each other. She knew they'd have to leave once they'd had their fourteenth birthdays. They'd be twelve this year.

From time to time Grandpa pointed out articles to Alice in his newspaper. She'd read that the Government was discussing secondary schooling for all.

'Won't come in time for you, though,' he told her. It couldn't, until more prosperous times came to the country.

Already in class there was speculation about what they would do when they left. The number of unemployed was growing in the depression, but for school-leavers jobs were not impossible to find because they could be paid so much less than adults. It was important to choose the right job if they weren't going to be thrown out of work later.

Alice was hoping to be taken on as a dressmaking apprentice. Maddy didn't know what she wanted to do, but thought she'd have to be a hairdresser. She said that both her mam and dad thought it the best thing for her. She'd go as an apprentice to one of the top salons in Liverpool, and then help run her mother's business.

Then, without warning, both Alice and Maddy found they'd been picked out by the school to sit the merit exam. This was considered a great honour, because only a few of the most able pupils from each school were allowed to sit it.

If they were successful they would be allotted a free place at the higher grade school, where they would continue until they were fifteen. They'd be taught the usual subjects at secondary-school level, as well as commercial subjects. However, there were only twenty free places, and nearly sixty boys and girls competing for them.

Their teacher gave them homework every night, usually

questions from the previous exam papers. Alice wrote compositions and did the sums she was set very carefully. She felt she was competing directly with Maddy, and wanted to have the higher mark every day. She found it wasn't always possible. Maddy was striving for the higher mark too, and seemed to get it on alternate days, however hard Alice tried.

They had to go to another school to sit the exam, and Alice was glad of Maddy's company. Afterwards, Maddy said she thought the paper was easy and she'd done well. Alice wasn't so sure.

In the middle of the summer holidays, Alice had a letter to say she'd won a free place at Rock Ferry Higher Grade School.

'That's wonderful,' Gran told her. 'You're a clever girl.'

The news was still sinking in when Maddy burst through the back door waving a similar letter. She screamed:

'I've got it.'

'So have I!'

Alice felt euphoric. Maddy's face glistened with joy.

'Both of you!' Gran couldn't get over it.

The girls hugged each other, and danced round the kitchen until Gran said she couldn't stand any more.

'I won't have to be a hairdresser. Saved by the skin of my teeth.'

'What's wrong with hairdressing?' Gran demanded. 'Your mother's doing well at it.'

'She works too hard. Never stops. I don't want to work like that.'

When Grandpa came home from work that evening, he said to Alice: 'You're a lucky girl. We're all very proud of you.'

'Proud of Madeleine too,' Gran said, rubbing her hands with satisfaction. 'This shows what the Luckett family can do. Got a bit more on top than most of them round here.'

'You'll be taught commercial subjects there,' Grandpa smiled. 'And you'll be able to work in an office like me.'

'But I want to be a dressmaker.'

'You don't know what you're saying,' Gran retorted. 'An office job's much better. Better hours and better pay. You'll be quite the young lady if you can get an office job.'

'Course you will,' Grandpa said. 'You could be a secretary. You'll have a real career.'

Even Aunt Nell agreed with that.

'But I'd rather do dressmaking,' Alice protested. 'I'm sure I would.'

'I'd wait a bit before you make up your mind,' Nell told her. 'You might like typing more. Anyway, dressmaking's a wonderful hobby. When you're grown up, you'll be able to make all your own clothes.'

When the autumn term started, Alice was glad she had Maddy's company to go to her new school. Again they were put side by side in the classroom. Again Alice found herself competing with her cousin for the top marks.

They both decided they preferred the higher grade school. They enjoyed lessons in history and geography, though some of the boys liked general science better, but what all the pupils valued most were their lessons in commercial subjects. They learned bookkeeping, shorthand and typing.

'I'm glad I won't have to be a docker like my dad,' one boy said with satisfaction. 'It's our passport out of all that.'

'My dad's on the dole,' said another. 'They think that won't happen to me if I get office skills.'

Chapter Sixteen

January 1932

Eric watched his mother expertly cutting into a length of rich black silk that she was going to make up into a dress. She was quick. Quicker at it than he was, made so by long practice.

'Time is money,' she was always telling him, with her gentle smile.

Her dark hair was showing more grey now, and she had to wear stronger glasses because she'd strained her eyes over her sewing for more hours than she should have. He finished off the hem he was putting up by hand, and laid it aside.

'What about a cup of tea?' he suggested.

His mother's face came up from her work with such a look of love. 'Just what I need.'

Her affection warmed him as he got up to put the kettle on. She'd been doing this for him for years. Eric knew he was everything to her. He was pleased that things were working out so well now.

On his twenty-first birthday, he'd finished his apprentice-ship and been entitled to call himself a tailor. He'd been offered a permanent position by Wetherall's, who had trained him, but Mam had wanted him to join her in her business.

'I find it a bit lonely,' she'd said. 'Here on my own all day.'

'You have customers coming in for fittings all the time, and Alice is in and out. Never misses a day.'

'Yes, but I'd like to have you working alongside me. The two of us together, it wouldn't seem such hard work.'

'But will the business stand it? Would we be able to earn enough?'

'I think we could build it up.'

He got on well with his mother, and wanted to please her.

'All right, let's try.'

She'd bought a new sewing machine for him. A heavy-duty one designed for industrial purposes, the sort he was accustomed to using. They had to rearrange the furniture in the front room to fit it in. Alice had her own stool; she came to sew with them on many days after school.

The board outside had to be repainted to add his name: 'Eric Ainslie, Ladies' and Gentlemen's Tailor.'

It was her suggestion that he offer ladies' tailoring too, in case the gentlemen were slow to come in at first to order suits. She'd helped him find pattern books and suitable swatches of material, and their orders for tailoring were beginning to grow.

Eric was making a few suits and coats for ladies and felt his reputation was starting to spread. He knew he was being cushioned by his mother's business; she had more work than she could cope with and he could sew anything. They took on all the work they could get, and if it was ladies' dresses and blouses, Eric stitched those. He took on most of the hand-finishing: the sewing on of buttons and fasteners, the putting-up of hems.

Nowadays he was managing to do more sewing than she did, because she had to break off to get meals and do a little housework. Eric knew she enjoyed doing that, especially running down to the shops; it gave her a break from the sewing she'd done all her life.

Eric took the tea he'd made back to the front room. She left the pieces of black silk on the cutting-out table and sank into the old nursing chair near the window. She always sat there if she had hand sewing to do or a moment to relax. He'd moved in another easy chair for himself and placed it beside his mother's. The sun was warm on his face as he sipped the tea. It felt soporific, and he closed his eyes for a moment to relax.

Working close to his mother like this, the bond between them seemed to be tightening. They'd always been close. Closer, he thought, than most mothers and sons. He put that down to the fact that there had never been anyone else.

'Eric,' she said softly, 'there's something I have to tell you. About your father.'

He'd thought there was no more she was prepared to say. He'd gone through a phase as a child when he'd never stopped asking about his father. He'd asked how he'd earned his living.

'He was a solicitor.'

At eight years of age, he'd had to ask what that was. He didn't know any solicitors, and of all the boys and girls in his class at school, none had a father who was a solicitor. He'd also wanted to know how he'd died.

'In the Great War. He was a soldier by then. He was killed in the trenches.'

He'd noticed a change in her manner whenever he asked about his father. She seemed to tense and hold herself stiffly upright. She never mentioned him unless he asked.

He'd asked what he'd looked like and she'd shown him a faded sepia photograph of herself with a very tall and upright young man standing beside her. She'd looked incredibly young and happy in it.

Once he said: 'You weren't married for very long.'

She'd paused, her grey eyes staring down into his. He'd felt she was on the point of saying something momentous, but in the end she'd said nothing.

Now her voice was scarcely above a whisper. 'I should have told you years ago. All the time you were growing up, I told myself I'd do it on your twenty-first birthday when you were a man.'

181

'We went to the theatre. The Liverpool Empire. I was out of my apprenticeship as well as coming of age.'

'It wasn't the right moment. We were celebrating then. I put it off and I've kept putting it off.'

She seemed embarrassed and was twisting the wedding ring she always wore round and round her finger.

Eric felt cold inside. He said softly, 'You weren't ever married to my father? Is that what you're trying to tell me?'

She turned to look at him, her eyes glistening and bright. 'How did you know?'

'I didn't really.' He shook his head, embarrassed too now. 'I guessed. Everybody else has grandparents and aunties and uncles. I have no relatives. And what else could you be wanting me to know that was so painful?'

She took off her glasses and rubbed at her eyes. He felt full of gratitude for what she'd done for him, sympathy for what she'd endured.

'It must have been very hard for you.'

'I've managed.'

'But at great cost to yourself.'

She smiled and put on her glasses. She was herself again.

'Come on then,' he said. 'Aren't you going to tell me about it? What happened?'

'I loved him. I believed him when he said he loved me.' She couldn't look at him again. 'I'd always known him vaguely but we rarely met. My mother played bridge with his mother. He went away to be articled to a firm of solicitors. When he finished his time with them and came home, it was Christmas and we were invited to all the same parties. We started seeing more of each other. He bought me a ring and talked of marriage. I saw him as my future. I thought about him all the time . . .'

Her grey eyes had softened; they had a far-away look. She looked almost young.

'And then?'

'He met another girl. She was pretty and had wealthy

182

parents. He married her. His in-laws gave them a house as a wedding present, and set him up in a partnership in Liverpool.'

'He jilted you?'

'Yes. When I told him about you, he suggested I have an abortion. He said he thought he could fix it for me.'

'So I might never have been born?'

She half-smiled. 'There was never any danger of that. I couldn't have done it.'

'But he wouldn't marry you?'

'He'd changed his mind about me, met somebody he liked better.'

'But you loved him?'

'Love goes when something like that happens.' She gave a little shiver. 'I didn't want him back after that. I saw him in a different light.

'My father said I was a disgrace when I finally got round to telling my parents about you. They sent me away to a nursing home. They wanted me to have you adopted. I was going to, but once I saw you I couldn't part with you. You were a lovely baby. I just couldn't give you away to a stranger, so I was never allowed to go back home.'

Eric sat thinking of that in silent sympathy.

'My father ruined your life.'

'Let's say we both made a mistake.' She smiled again. 'But I was the one who paid most dearly. Your father did give me some money. Bought me off, you might say. I bought this house with it and set myself up as a dressmaker.'

'A jolly good one . . .'

'I never had any training, it was just a hobby.' She giggled girlishly. 'I'd worked in a bank. I was trained in typewriting, but they wouldn't have had me back if they'd known of your existence, and I didn't want to leave you. Sewing here, I could look after you at the same time.'

That made Eric feel very humble. 'I do appreciate what you've done for me.'

'I did what I wanted to. What I thought was for the best. You've gone without many things.'

'I bet you have too.'

'But I always had you.'

Eric marvelled that what he'd had in abundance was her love and devotion.

She went on: 'I couldn't tell you until you were grown up. It didn't seem fair to burden you with my guilty secret, and I was afraid you might unwittingly let the neighbours know and spoil things for us.'

Eric understood how strong she'd had to be.

'Do you think it's wrong that I pretend to be a widow? I'm living a lie, aren't I?'

He was shaking his head.

'I don't like doing it, but I had to, Eric. If I hadn't, I'd have been a pariah, isolated from society. I wouldn't have been able to set up as a dressmaker.

'If I'd been open about my state, customers wouldn't have come on moral grounds. Some husbands would have forbidden it. And you'd have been tainted by my sins too.

'That's why I came to Prenton in the first place. I knew nobody here and nobody knew me. I can go to church and get custom from my fellow churchgoers. I looked round at matins last Sunday and counted fourteen outfits that I'd made.'

Eric heard light footsteps running to their front door. His mother turned to look out of the window.

'Here's Alice coming. Poor Alice, I know what it is to crave love and not have it. Be kind to her, Eric.'

'I am,' he protested. 'I go out of my way to be kind.'

'Yes, of course you do. You're kind to everybody.'

Alice came in, bringing a rush of fresh air with her. She was all eager smiles and dancing eyes. He watched her cross the room, her face shining with affection for them both. He'd point out to his mother that Alice had found love. Not only here from them, but from her family; she and Peter were very close.

Eric had watched her grow up over the last four years. Now, at thirteen, she looked healthy and confident; she was as tall as Maddy and had filled out.

'Your hair looks pretty,' he told her. It was luxuriously thick and glossy now, and waved softly round her small face.

'I've just had it washed and cut.' Her fingers pulled at it.

'Your auntie does it for you?'

She shook her head, making her hair flutter. 'Daisy's been doing it for a long time. Her manageress, you know? Maddy reckons Daisy's as good as her mother; she does hers too. Makes hers look really beautiful.'

'She makes yours look beautiful too.' Nell peered at her through her glasses.

'Maddy's hair is such a lovely colour. Mine looks a pale, washed-out . . .'

'No, Alice!' Eric laughed. 'You're a natural platinum blonde! What more could you ask for? Film stars bleach their hair your colour. I think it's lovely. I bet Maddy does too. I bet she'd rather be platinum blonde than red.'

'D'you think so?'

'Sure of it,' he said.

Alice had long since progressed from sewing for Wobble to sewing for herself. She'd bought some flowered cotton in the market and he'd helped her cut out a summer dress. Now she opened the piano stool and took it out.

'Can I use your machine, Eric?'

His mother had taught her to use it. Alice never asked if both the machines were in use.

'Use mine,' Nell told her. 'I'm cutting out. I've some beach pyjamas to do as well as this dress.'

Perhaps, Eric thought, as he took their tea things back to the kitchen, everybody craved love. Alice wasn't alone in that. Though he felt enveloped by his mother's love, by affection from Alice and friendship from Peter, he still craved another sort of love.

He and Peter had been seeking it for years. Hadn't they spent their Saturday nights looking for desirable girls? They hadn't neglected opportunities on weekdays either.

He'd met Judy at a dance and taken her out for six months before deciding he didn't want to spend the rest of his life with her. Peter was going out with a girl called Dora at present, but Eric didn't think he was all that smitten. Neither of them had found the love they sought; they were both still actively searching for it.

Alice knew that Auntie Nell and Eric had worked very hard over Christmas and the New Year. They'd had almost more orders than they could cope with during the festive season. All their customers seemed to want a new dress for a party or a dance.

She'd spent many school holiday hours sewing on buttons and fasteners for them, pressing seams, putting up hems, helping where she could. She ran errands for Nell, helped put meals on their table, and cleared them away, so they could spend longer at their machines. But now the rush was over, it was January and they were able to take things more easily.

'We've had a good season,' Auntie Nell told Alice. 'Eric says we must celebrate. We never have much time to ourselves over Christmas.'

'Every year you say we will, but we never do,' Eric smiled. 'We even thought of going away for a few days. To London or . . .'

'At this time of the year it's too cold to go away,' his mother said.

'So we've decided to go out on Saturday night.' Eric's dark eyes shone with enthusiasm. 'Mam and me, Peter and you too, if you'd like to come.'

'Lovely,' Alice was thrilled. 'Where are we going?'

Nell smiled at her. 'Eric and Peter would like to see the

film at the Carlton Hall, but I'm not sure it's suitable for one as young as you.'

'It will be,' Alice said, determined not to be left out. 'Gran takes me sometimes and they're never films for children.'

Auntie Nell smiled. 'Alfred Hitchcock's *Blackmail* is on. It's said to be the first full-length all-talkie film made in Great Britain.'

'I'd love to see it. I've never been to a talkie.'

'It's that or the pantomime, *Cinderella*, at . . .'

'No,' Alice said. 'Peter won't like *Cinderella*. You won't either, Eric.'

'It's a thriller, are you sure?'

'I'm not a baby anymore! I'm thirteen.'

'Alfred Hitchcock it is then,' Eric said. 'We'll go to the first house, then we'll go to the Woodside Hotel for supper. I'll book a table.'

Alice felt very grown up as she got ready. She loved the pictures and wished Gran would take her more often.

After three years, Alice had grown and filled out, but she could still get into her velvet pinafore dress because Auntie Nell had made it so that both the straps and the hem could be lengthened.

She'd long since grown out of the poplin blouse. That had been replaced several times. For Christmas Gran had bought her a navy-blue jersey with a polo neck. With that, she was able to wear her velvet for special occasions all the year round.

She still had Wobble; he stood on the chest of drawers in her bedroom. He had a whole wardrobe of clothes but she no longer played with him. She was putting childish things behind her.

Alice had only once before seen Uncle Frank at work. She peered in his pay box as Eric bought their tickets. It seemed odd to see him wearing that servile uniform. Maddy's Aunt Hilary showed them to their seats on the balcony. It made Alice feel very important. She sat between Eric and his mother, and when the film got exciting she gripped a hand of each.

'You're wringing my fingers off,' Eric leaned over to whisper. She loved it all.

It was a rare night out for her. Even more exciting was the meal at the Woodside Hotel. It was the first time she'd ever been in such a place. She looked round the table and sighed with satisfaction; she was surrounded by the people she loved best in all the world.

She felt just as much at home in the Ainslie household as she did at Gran's. And although she felt closer to Peter than to anybody else in her family, it was Eric who was most special to her. He'd always seemed like a rock, someone she could cling to, a source of security for her. She didn't have to explain things to him; he knew what she was feeling and he always managed to support her, help her over the rough patches. She loved him more than anyone else in the world.

He'd seemed a grown man to her the night they'd found her father, but now she was able to work out that he was only nine years older, and the gap between them seemed to be closing.

Sometimes she fantasised about Eric. Wondered if he would wait until she grew up so that she could marry him. There was no one in the world quite like Eric.

Chapter Seventeen

March 1932

For Alice, time was passing quickly. She loved the higher grade school and really enjoyed her lessons in commercial subjects. She found she had quite a bent for bookkeeping and managed to be consistently top in that as well as arithmetic. She and Maddy were still in the same class and still competing to be best. They were both good at Pitman's shorthand. Maddy was the better typist.

Today was a school holiday, and Alice had been with Eric and Aunt Nell all morning, helping them with their sewing. Maddy didn't come to spend school holidays with her and Gran anymore. Uncle Frank said she was old enough to help Cecily in the salon. Maddy told Alice she hated sweeping up the bits of hair and making tea for the customers, but it was better than hanging about with her.

After dinner, Gran asked Alice to go up to the shops on Woodchurch Road to get a few things for her. Outside Best's Bakery, she stopped and took Gran's list from her pocket to check that she'd bought everything. Soap, furniture polish, matches and sugar, yes. Gran had given her the usual instructions that she must buy nothing extra.

She paused to look in the cake-shop window. This was where Peter worked. It was one of the smartest shops in the row, repainted every few years. The scents that came out were delicious, and it was crowded with customers.

Alice let her gaze linger on the custard tarts and cream buns, the scones and currant bread. Gran made almost all the cake that was eaten at home, and reckoned she could make it better and at half the price. Alice thought that what was on offer here was much more exotic.

Slogans in gold lettering glittered behind the window display: 'Best's Bread is Best', 'Best's for Everything Baked', 'Nobody Bakes Better Than Best's'.

It made her proud that Uncle Peter was in charge of the bakehouse at the back. She knew he was in there working, though she never saw him when she came on expeditions like this.

For all the years she could remember, Alice had listened to Peter talking about his ambitions; his plans for his future. She knew he wanted to take over this bakery. His eyes were bright and glinted with enthusiasm when he spoke of how he could expand it. How he could bake many more loaves and cakes than the business did now. How he could make it earn more profit.

It was only in recent months that she'd come to realise there was a stumbling block. Peter would have to buy the business when its present owner, Ted Best, retired. The sum required was likely to be high, and though he was saving hard with this in mind, it was likely to take many more years.

Suddenly she saw Peter lean over into the window and scoop three meat pies into a paper bag. He gave her a little grimace of recognition. Alice stepped back in surprise. For Peter to be working in the shop was very unusual, and he had an air of agitation about him. Alma, the young assistant he sometimes spoke of, was flushed and her hair was escaping from the cap she wore. Usually Mrs Best ran the shop, but she was nowhere to be seen. Alice wondered, as she turned for home, if something had happened.

At tea time, when they were all eating round the kitchen

table, Peter could talk of nothing else. Ted Best, his boss, had had a heart attack in the bakery. He'd been taken to hospital and was very ill.

'Mrs Best's in a terrible state,' he told them seriously. 'She says he's been doing too much for years, getting up in the middle of the night, working the clock round, ruining his health.'

She'd been very upset and had started shouting: 'What's it all for? He's going to kill himself if he carries on.'

'Mrs Judd had to be spared to go upstairs with her. She made her a cup of tea and found her some aspirins.'

'Is she all right?' Gran was shocked.

'Yes, she came down later and said to me: "I'm tired of telling him, we've got to get rid of this business. It's half mine anyway. We can't go on any longer."'

Alice waited. She could feel Peter's excitement. He was seething with it. He'd never made any secret that this was what he wanted. Even the Bests knew it was his ambition to buy their business when they retired. Ted had encouraged him to think he could.

'Mrs Best asked me formally if I want to buy it. She said that if I don't, she'll put it with an estate agent.'

'Now's your chance, lad.' Grandpa's fork chased the last of his bubble and squeak round his plate.

Peter said soberly: 'He's asking three hundred, just for the business.'

'Three hundred!' Edith exclaimed.

'And I've saved only ninety.' There was a note of defeat in his voice. 'I was expecting to have another few years to save. Ted always said he'd go on till he was sixty-five.'

'What about the shop?' Grandpa asked. 'He lives over it, doesn't he?'

'He's offered to rent the property to me. On a twenty-one-year lease.'

'It sounds like a lot of money.' Gran got up to refill

the tea pot. 'Sounds like you had ideas above your station. You've got a good job there, anyway. A job you enjoy.'

Alice could feel the disappointment pouring out of Peter.

'If someone else buys it . . . they might not want to keep me on. What if the new owner's used to doing all the baking himself? I was thinking of asking our Frank if he'd lend me the rest.'

'Is it worth it?'

Alice could tell from Gran's voice that she didn't think so.

'Yes, Mrs Best says they had it valued at three hundred and fifty pounds last year. Ted had a bad turn then and she wanted to sell. But when he felt better, he wouldn't hear of it.'

'We'll ask Frank and Cecily to Sunday dinner. You can put it to him then,' Gran said tentatively.

'I thought I'd go down and see him as soon as I've finished my tea.' Peter was eating quickly, looking as though he had no time to waste. 'No point in putting it off till Sunday.'

Alice felt for him. She knew this was his chance to get what he wanted, and he was afraid it would slip through his fingers because he couldn't raise the money. He drained his tea cup and stood up.

'There's no hurry,' Gran said. 'They won't have finished their own tea yet.'

'I don't want to miss him. Frank's got to go to work, hasn't he?'

As soon as Peter had gone, Gran got up to refill their tea cups again.

She grunted: 'Frank won't want to lend him money. He's always got something new of his own to finance.'

'He's doing well,' Grandpa said. 'He might.'

'Two hundred and ten pounds in cash? That's a lot.'

'Frank understands business. Look what he's earning from Cecily's salons. Peter could do just as well.'

192

'It's not all coming from the hairdressing. Frank's got a job too.'

'He won't be earning any fortune as cashier at the Carlton Hall.' Alice watched Grandpa put his cup down carefully.

'We could help him, Edith. We've got that money in the Liverpool Savings Bank. How much is there?'

He was on his feet in an instant, jerking open the drawer of the dresser. He riffled through the contents, reducing the order Gran maintained to chaos.

Alice could see she was affronted. 'That's for our retirement. For us.'

'We won't need it, Edith.'

'I want a new house. One with a lavatory inside.'

'Where's our bank book?'

'It's there. There's three hundred and seventy-two pounds in it. Now you know, perhaps you'll stop making a mess.'

'As much as that!'

'I've never made any secret . . .'

'Don't you see? That's plenty for everything! We can lend him what he needs.'

'Peter could be biting off more than he can chew.'

'Nonsense! He's got his wits about him. I'd back him against Frank any day. He's a master baker and a confectioner too. He knows how to run that business. He's got big plans.'

'You've never wanted to help the others.' Gran's voice had gone hard with complaint. 'What did you ever do for our Len?'

That made Alice wince; she saw it had caught Grandpa on a sore spot too.

'Perhaps if we had . . .'

'We couldn't. Couldn't afford to help our Frank either. Those two had to make their own way, stand on their own feet.'

'We could have tried – with Len.'

'Monty, you never try. You've never wanted to get on and

193

earn more so we could. No, you've sat back and taken the easy way. We've always had to scrape and save to manage on what you brought home.'

Grandpa's smile was gentle. 'We haven't done badly. I don't feel we've had to do much scraping.'

'Well, I do.' Gran was indignant. 'It's me that's scraped and saved while you've done nothing but spend.'

'Not scraped. Being thrifty is second nature to you. You'd still do it however much money you had.'

'I'd rather not . . .'

'Anyway, we've got a nice little nest egg saved in the bank.'

'And now you want to give it to Peter. Well, I won't stand for it. That's for our retirement.'

'I'll get a pension, Edith. I keep telling you.'

'What about an inside lavatory? I'm getting too old to go out to the yard on wet nights. It's bad for my rheumatism.'

'We can have one put in here and now. With this money there's . . .'

'Monty, I want a new house.'

'You can have that too when we sell this. Don't you want to help our Peter?'

'Course I do,' she snorted. 'But that's our house money. If Peter has it then we don't.'

'If Frank doesn't want to give him the lot . . .'

'He won't!'

'Then you agree we should chip in? We could give him half, give him a good start in life.'

'No,' Gran protested. 'No!' She stared at him, breathing heavily. 'We can't go on thinking of the children for ever. Anyway, looks like they'll both end up with more than we've ever had. It's time we thought of ourselves.'

Alice was afraid Peter was going to lose out. She'd never seen Gran so defiant. She was used to ordering the rest of the family around, but not Grandpa. He was the head of the family, the bread-winner and when he wanted something she was in the habit of bowing to his wishes.

'You're thinking of yourself,' he said. 'Just yourself.'

'Perhaps I am,' she burst out, her face flushed. 'Nobody else thinks of me. It doesn't matter what I want. Everybody takes it for granted that I'll put meals on the table for them and do their washing and ironing and cleaning. I'm expected to do more and more. I cook a hot meal every day. Sometimes I get sick of it. I want to sit back and have an hour to myself.'

Alice sank back into her seat. She'd have liked to creep away upstairs out of sight. She'd never heard Gran go on like this before. Never realised just how much she resented what she had to do for her family.

'I want a new house. I've been saving for it for the last ten years. And no, I don't agree that on the spur of the moment my savings can go on anything else. Not even our Peter.'

Monty felt more than put out. He had the bank book in his hand. He could hardly believe they had nearly four hundred pounds saved. It was ridiculous to keep all that money in the bank, doing nothing, when Peter needed it. To buy into that bakery was a wonderful chance.

Yet the sight of Edith, deflated now, stirred up feelings of guilt within him. She did work hard and she saved every penny she could. It really was her money. He flung the bank book down on the table in front of her.

He had to get out. He snatched his cap from the hall stand and let himself out through the front door. He was up on Storeton Road, near the Halfway House, before he asked himself where he was going.

Not to Rita's. She wasn't expecting him; it was her night to visit her parents. He hesitated outside the pub for a moment, but decided to go to Frank's place. To see if he was willing to lend Peter the money. That was filling his mind at the moment.

He'd worried himself stiff about Frank knowing too much, but no word about him having a lady friend had reached Edith's ears. She'd have fired off about it if it had. Frank had got the upper hand over him with that, but at least he wasn't spreading the news about. No need to worry about Frank probing further tonight; he wouldn't have time, he had to go to work.

Monty quickened his pace through the pleasant leafy roads of Oxton. It was four years since Frank had moved to this house. Every time he saw it, Monty marvelled at what he and Cecily had achieved. Smart, double-fronted and detached, with a large garden, it knocked Rita's house into a nutshell. It was being bought on a mortgage, of course, but Monty still didn't know how they managed it. The asking price had been nearly nine hundred pounds.

On top of that, they'd taken out a twenty-one-year lease on the shop in Grange Road and done it up to the nines, all within months. Monty had been even more alarmed when he heard Cecily was going to run two salons.

'If I get on all right, I might try and expand to a whole chain. I'll have to see how it works out.'

He'd noticed she wasn't including Frank anymore. Cecily was managing this on her own. It made Monty think that perhaps all the money was earned by her and Frank was getting jealous.

The Carlton Hall wouldn't be paying much for a cashier, and Frank had given up all the morning jobs he once used to do to augment his wages. He'd worked at the Carlton Hall for a good few years, but he'd be lucky to get four pounds a week, four pounds ten shillings at the most. Could be nearer three.

Monty had been afraid for them. He didn't understand how they could possibly afford to do so much all at once. He'd hoped they knew what they were doing. It all seemed a bit risky to him. Even more risky if Frank was up to something illegal.

Over the years it continued to amaze him that all seemed to be working out as they'd planned. Cecily was coping with her two salons. Frank said the new one was doing well. Rita became a customer and praised the service she received from Cecily. He, too, thought Rita's new hairstyle flattered her face.

Monty was always seeing advertisements for Cecily's salons in the local newspaper. Sandwich men walked round town advertising it on their boards, and Maddy was always pushing handbills through letter-boxes.

Cecily was getting a reputation now for providing the smartest hairdressing in town. He couldn't help but admire her business sense. He thought she must have some of Edith's thrift with money too, because Frank was inclined to splash it around.

He'd thought it the height of folly for Frank to buy himself a car almost straight away.

'Just an Austin Seven.' Frank had smiled deprecatingly. 'And second hand at that. It'll do for a start. We need it, Dad. It saves Cecily time.'

Monty had been envious of that. He fancied a little car himself. Rita was urging him to get one. He was a bit worried about whether he'd manage to drive it.

'I'll show you how,' Frank had offered. 'I've shown Peter, he managed fine, nothing to it. You want to do it soon, Dad; they're talking of bringing in a driving test.'

Rita had taken him to look at a few cars. Monty didn't mind admitting he'd come close to buying one. Edith had always talked of getting one for their retirement. He'd explained why it would be better to get it sooner, but Edith wouldn't have it. She wanted to buy a new house first. That was her number-one priority.

Monty reached Frank's house. As he turned into the gate he could see the garage doors standing open and the car gone, which meant Frank had already left for work. He hesitated. Cecily wasn't nearly so welcoming these days. Edith refused to go round unless she had an invitation, and there were fewer of those than there used to be.

But he thought Peter might still be inside. He'd be able to find out whether they'd be willing to help him or not. He rang the bell. Cecily came to answer it but didn't seem pleased to see him. Her hair was beautifully groomed and she wore a fresh flowered dress. She still took the time and trouble to look after herself even though she'd been working all day.

'Come in,' she said in a cool and regal manner.

When Frank and Cecily were first married, Cecily had told Monty that she'd been orphaned at eighteen and was very pleased to think of Frank's parents as her own. For years she'd called him Papa, in her ultra-friendly husky voice. Once she would have kissed him too. He used to like the way she showed affection to them all. Edith had never been generous with her kisses.

Now Cecily was stiff and cold. If he tried to kiss her in the way he used to, she pulled back. He couldn't believe anyone could change so much.

He was glad to see Maddy running to kiss him and pull at his hand. 'Uncle Peter's here too,' she told him.

'In the lounge,' Cecily added.

He noticed she didn't call it the living room as she had in the flat over the shop. It looked smarter than ever. He thought she'd had it redecorated again. There was a new Turkish carpet square with a wide surround of polished parquet.

'You've made it very stylish,' he told her. She'd always seemed pleased with compliments for her house.

'I was aiming at comfort,' she retorted, in a stand-off manner.

'We're going to get a piano,' Maddy added. 'And I'm going to have lessons so I can play it.'

Peter was stretched out on a red plush armchair. He looked exhausted but satisfied.

'Cecily and Frank are going to lend me some money to buy the bakery.'

'Not all of it, Peter,' Cecily warned. 'We can't do that. But . . .'

'Enough to get me going. A foot-hold in the business.'

'Only a toe-hold.'

'Frank thinks it might be enough.' Monty saw Peter's smile widen. 'He thinks he knows sombody who might lend me the rest.' He was doing sums with a pencil on the back of a used envelope. 'I'll have to pay interest, of course, but I'm sure I could manage.'

Cecily said: 'Frank thinks this person might be able to help Peter find new markets for his bread.'

Monty felt uneasy. 'Who is this man?' Nobody loaned money without a lot of strings attached. 'Do you know him?'

'Patrick O'Neill,' Cecily said. 'You've heard Frank talk of him?'

'Yes,' Peter said, but Monty had not. That brought another wave of guilt washing over him. He wasn't spending enough time with his own children.

Chapter Eighteen

March – September 1932

Peter had given more thought to borrowing money to buy the bakery business. He'd discussed it with his father, who'd suggested he approach a bank. He'd slept on this advice, and Frank's offer, and decided he'd prefer to be indebted to a bank.

He'd collected the account books for the last six years' trading from Mrs Best and approached two banks, but neither manager had agreed to do it.

'With the depth of the present depression, it's a bad time to go into business,' was their verdict. 'Safer to leave it until the economy picks up. We're lending very little money for this sort of thing at present.'

Peter refused to be swayed by their verdict, but it meant he had to rely on his brother. It was Sunday evening, and he'd arranged to visit Frank, who was going to introduce him to his friend, Pat O'Neill.

Since he'd had the bakery accounts, he'd spent every free moment poring over them, and what he saw filled him with satisfaction. It was a profitable business. He reckoned he could pay back the money he was having to borrow within two or three years on these figures.

If he could increase his turnover by making and selling more bread, then he might be able to pay off his loans even faster. He was keen to do this. Frank had told him

Pat O'Neill was just the person to help him with it; that he ought to consider employing him for a short time.

Peter stuffed the account books into his mother's shopping bag and set out, his step quickening as he went. He told himself he must not appear too eager, but as far as he was concerned everything hinged on whether he and Pat O'Neill could get on together. It was to be a business relationship, but he wanted to like the fellow.

'You will,' Frank had assured him. 'Everybody does. A very likeable person.'

'But how do you come to know him?'

'We've known him for years. He was working for Ledbetter's, you know, the firm who supply everything for the hairdressing trade. You remember what Cissie's first shop was like when she bought the lease?'

'It had been a greengrocer's.'

'Yes, we had to start from scratch. She chose all the stuff from Ledbetter's and it was Pat who handled her order and delivered it. He fixed us up with a man to plumb in the washbowls and fix plugs for the hair dryers and all that. Even advised about décor.

'We took to him straight away, and Cissie's been getting all her soft soap and camomile rinses through him ever since. Ledbetter's do everything for hairdressers, right down to curlers and clips.'

Peter frowned. 'If he works for Ledbetter's, he's never going to have time to build up my business. Finding new outlets for my cakes will take time.'

'But he will,' Frank smiled. 'That's the beauty of the whole idea. He's been laid off. Worked for them for years too. It's an ill wind and all that.

'This depression's the very devil. He's just the person to help you expand. Really he is. He even owns a van to deliver your stuff.'

It was Frank who opened the front door to him. Peter could hear Cecily talking to Maddy upstairs, but he was led straight to the dining room and the door was shut firmly behind them. This was going to be men's talk, a business meeting. Frank and Pat had been sitting at the table with tankards of ale in front of them.

Pat pushed his chair back and came towards Peter with his hand held out. He was thin and wiry and in his early thirties. His smile was friendly and lit up his blue Irish eyes. He had an untidy mop of brown hair that was naturally curly.

'I'm really keen on this,' he said. 'It sounds exactly what I'm looking for. A chance to work up a little business as a partner.'

'Hardly a partner,' Peter said, but he liked his enthusiasm, and his first impressions were that he could take to Pat. 'Frank says you've lost your job? Rotten luck.'

'Yes, specially after eleven years, but with this depression they're laying off people all the time, and it's hopeless looking for another job when there's millions looking too. The only way round it is to go into business oneself.'

Peter wondered if he'd misheard. He'd thought he was the one going into business, not Pat. Before he could take him up on that, Frank slid a tankard of beer in front of him.

'Peter's been lucky. His job's been safe enough. His boss took to him.'

'Thanks, but there's another reason. Everybody goes on buying bread. That's a huge advantage in times of depression. Our bread sales are actually going up. Here, take a look at this year's accounts.'

He emptied the shopping bag on the table and found the right book.

'People have to fill their stomachs with something, and when they can't afford meat they eat more bread.'

Frank said: 'They're asking three hundred for the business, right?'

'Yes, for the goodwill, equipment and fittings, that sort of thing.'

'But there's no delivery van?' Pat wanted to know.

'No. Up to now, everything's been sold through the adjoining shop, but I could easily bake much more. There's big ovens and plenty of space for more people to work there. The Bests only baked what they knew they could sell.'

'Right,' Frank said. 'Are we agreed then? We each put up a hundred pounds. Three equal partners in the business?'

To Peter that felt like a kick in the stomach. 'Hang on a minute.' He was shocked. 'That's not what you said.'

'No, you hear me out. You, Peter, continue to do your present job and draw your present wage. We'll agree a wage for Pat, who'll try to increase our profits by selling and delivering to small grocery shops.'

Peter felt a rush of anger. 'I thought you were going to lend me the money? That I'd pay you interest and pay back the capital too as soon as I could.'

Frank's smile grew wider. 'You're asking a lot, little brother. This way, if you grow richer, so will I. More in it for me, and it's only right there should be more in it for Pat.'

'But you know nothing about baking. What are you going to do?'

'Me? I'll be a sleeping partner.'

'No!' Peter wanted more than a third-share of this business. 'It's obvious that will mean less for me.'

Frank's handsome eyes stared back at him. 'Take it or leave it,' he said. 'It's your decision.'

'You won't be sorry.' Pat's grin widened, his leprechaun eyes danced.

'I'll soon create new markets for you. All you'll have to do is make me up a selection of your bread and cakes each morning, whatever's most profitable. I'll take them round and let the grocers see and taste them. I'll bring you the orders I get, and deliver the next day and ever after.

'I'm used to going round hairdressers, now it'll be grocers instead. Not so very different. It's still selling to the retail trade.'

'It could work out very well,' Frank assured them. 'We're right for each other.'

'I know Liverpool like the back of my hand,' Pat went on. 'Birkenhead, Wallasey, the Wirral and Chester too, and all of their suburbs. If it's anywhere near the Mersey, I've been around it looking for hairdressers. There's many more little grocery shops than there are hairdressers, and they'll be glad to build up their own trade with really good bread.'

'And cakes,' Frank added.

'Yes. Even the poorest have to eat, and a small cake brings a touch of luxury without costing the earth.'

'We'll have a formal agreement drawn up by a solicitor,' Frank added, 'so we'll all know where we stand.'

Peter stirred restlessly. 'You promised me a straight loan,' he said to Frank. 'This isn't the same thing at all.'

'We've thought better of it, haven't we, Pat?'

They were both stonewalling, not prepared to budge an inch.

'Then I'd like there to be an option for me to buy your shares back.' Peter looked from one to the other. 'In say three years.'

'No.'

Peter boiled over. 'You've got other irons in the fire. You don't need this, and you're not proposing to do anything to help.'

Frank was shaking his head.

Peter tried again. 'It was my idea to buy this bakery. I'm getting it cheaper because the Bests know me. I've worked in it, I know how to run it.'

'But you need my money,' his brother reminded him. 'You need our money, you can't do it on your own.'

Peter sank back on his chair. He wasn't pleased.

'I'll soon push up the profits,' Pat said quickly. 'You won't be sorry to have me as a partner. I'll earn my whack.'

Peter mused that Frank had always had an eye for a quick buck.

205

'You agree then? Three equal partners?'

'I suppose so.' Peter sighed as he stood up. 'All right, I agree.' He didn't like it, but he didn't have much option. 'I'm going home. Got to be up before five in the morning. Baking starts early.'

He had the feeling he was going to be done down. Certainly he'd be doing most of the work. Frank wanted easy profits, and he supposed the Irishman did too.

Frank saw Peter to the door and then fetched two more bottles of beer from the kitchen.

'I told you it would be all right,' Pat said as he refilled his tankard. 'I've sold him the idea.'

'Peter expects everybody to beaver away as hard as he does.'

'I'll work as hard.' Pat grinned at him. 'I need a straight business, something legit. Nobody can say I'm living beyond my income then. A private business like Best's – who's to say how much it earns?'

'And out on your own all day, finding new outlets,' Frank added, 'that'll leave you with plenty of time to do other things when you want to.'

'And provide an alibi if ever I need one.'

'Are you likely to?'

'Who's to say? Got to keep trying new things, so we have. Got to move on. Wouldn't do to get stuck in a rut, not for us.'

Frank frowned. 'Peter's as straight as a die. He won't approve of anything on the side, so don't let him know.'

'Strictly separate. I know he's your little brother, I won't let him down. I'll do a good job for him. Well, for myself too, and you. It might prove a winner.'

When Pat had gone too, Frank sat on over his beer, wondering if he'd done the right thing. Pat had been very keen to come in with them, and he'd had to let him – there was no other way to raise the money Peter needed – but it left him feeling uneasy.

He'd led Peter to believe Pat was a friend. Strictly speaking, that wasn't true. Cissie actively disliked him. For his own part, he had to think of him as a colleague. They'd worked together for years at jobs they couldn't talk about. Frank knew he'd never have got the money for this house together if it hadn't been for the jobs he did with Pat. He could talk his way out of a tight corner, keep his head when things went wrong, a sound partner for their joint ventures.

All the same, he couldn't say he liked him. Couldn't say he'd trust him to do the right thing for Peter. Pat always put his own interests first; he was a wily creature, could be slippery, and it wasn't always easy to keep on the right side of him.

Frank knew little about his background. Pat had told him once that his forebears had come over to Liverpool during a potato famine in the middle of the last century. Then, more recently, that he'd been brought up in Dublin. That he'd almost been caught when a job went wrong and had to hop on the next ferry over here. He certainly knew Liverpool very well.

If he were to tell the truth, Frank would like to drop Pat but he couldn't afford to. He was sick of the Carlton Hall too. He and Hilary had been working the seat racket for so long it was unbelievable that old Butterballs hadn't caught on.

He needed to find something new. What he'd really like to do was one big job, get enough cash to set himself up in comfort once and for all.

Then he'd turn over a new leaf. Live an honest life with nothing to worry about. All this was bad for his nerves.

Alice thought it a very exciting time. Peter was going round with a smile from ear to ear. He'd told Mrs Best that he was making arrangements to buy the business from her.

On the following Tuesday evening, over their tea of fresh

herrings, he told them that he was going to show Frank and his friend over the business.

'They want to see it before they put their money up,' he said. 'They're coming round tomorrow morning when everything's functioning – so they can see the shop open and the staff working.'

'I wouldn't mind seeing it,' his father said, sliding a bone out of his mouth.

Edith said hurriedly: 'You don't want to miss a day's work, but I'm doing nothing. I could come.'

'So could I,' Alice put in. 'I'm on holiday tomorrow.'

'Go on with you,' Grandpa said. 'You can go in any time once our Peter's got it.'

'Yes,' Peter agreed. 'We're going to talk business tomorrow. The boss is still in hospital, and Mrs Best is very fraught about him. If we're all agreed, we'll go to see a solicitor afterwards.'

He smiled round the table at them. 'You can all come and see it as soon as we sign. When it's ours.'

To Alice it didn't seem long before it was. She walked up with her grandparents one Saturday morning. Customers were standing three deep in the shop. Two assistants in white overalls and caps were serving briskly. Alice kept taking deep, deep breaths; the scent of newly baked bread and cakes was wonderful.

She knew what the shop looked like, although she'd never been inside before. Peter led them across the yard at the back to the bakehouse.

'What d'you think of it?' He had two big tables on which to work. One held cake trays full of cooling fairy cakes waiting to be iced.

'This is a new oven, it was only installed a few months ago, and this one's only two years old. We've been very lucky that way. All the equipment is up to the minute.'

Alice wasn't used to seeing Peter in his baking outfit; he looked less familiar.

'Mr Best had the building extended not so long ago, so there's plenty of space to work in. I could bake a lot more here. More than we could sell in the shop.

'That's where Pat comes in. He's got a van and he'll wholesale our cakes and bread to small general shops. I'm going to take on some help here and bake more cakes. We're going to expand. You'll see, it'll be a much bigger business in a year or two.'

Alice had never seen Peter look so excited. His face was flushed with enthusiasm.

'I'd love to come and help,' she breathed. 'A Saturday job. What d'you think?'

'We coped all right last Saturday. I'm trying to make my living from it,' he smiled. 'I won't do that paying out extra wages.'

Alice gulped: 'I'll do it for nothing.'

'I can't let you do that.'

'Yes you can. Haven't you done lots for me? I want to come and be part of this.'

He led the way back to the shop then. There were fewer customers. Peter introduced them to the two assistants, Flo and Alma Judd, who were mother and daughter. Flo had worked in the shop for fifteen years. Alma was now twenty and had been there since she left school.

'Mrs Best reckoned she managed the shop, but I think she more or less left it to the Judds. They're running the place between them now, nothing for me to do but cash up at the end of the day,' Peter said with satisfaction. 'They know the job backwards and I know they're trustworthy. Having them here made it easier to make up my mind to buy in.'

'What about the flat upstairs?' Gran wanted to know. 'I don't suppose we can see round that?'

'No, the Bests are still living there.'

'Should have moved to a house years ago.' Gran frowned. 'Not as though they couldn't afford it. Are they going to move out?'

209

'Yes, they want to get away.' Peter lowered his voice. 'Might take a bit of time; they've got to find somewhere, and poor Ted's not at all well.'

'Who'll live upstairs then?' Alice asked.

'I will.' Peter grinned at her. 'I'll have a place of my own at last.'

Grandpa was nodding his head wisely as they walked home. 'A good business. It'll set our Peter up for life. I'm glad he's had his chance.'

Alice felt almost grown up. Most of her contemporaries had left school and the lucky ones were already earning.

'In dead-end jobs,' Gran retorted. 'You and Maddy will get good ones when you start.'

Alice had turned fourteen and was in her last year at the higher grade school. She'd been living with her Gran for over four years, and though she could remember her parents, she couldn't visualise their faces anymore. She felt she'd managed to put the bad times behind her.

She still rode the bike she'd been given for her tenth birthday, but it was getting too small for her now, and she was saving up for a full-sized one.

She still did a lot of sewing next door at Auntie Nell's and had even made a dress for Gran – with a little help from Eric.

From time to time, she read her horoscope in the newspaper, but she didn't let Gran see her doing it now. Gran would only tell her it was a silly habit she'd picked up from her mother. On her birthday, she'd seen one for the whole of next year. It said: 'A volatile year of challenging developments. Do not lose sight of your goals. Vigilance is vital if you are to achieve them. You will need all your courage and determination to come through unscathed.' It didn't sound encouraging.

She asked Peter again if she could work in the cake shop on Saturdays. It was at its busiest then as customers came in for bread for the weekend.

'All right,' he'd grinned. 'Business is growing. Perhaps the girls could do with a hand. Come in next Saturday and see how you get on. Quarter to nine, before the shop opens. The first job is to set it up.'

She made sure she was there by twenty to, and Peter found her a white overall and a cap and introduced her to Harry, a middle-aged man he'd taken on as a full-time assistant. Harry had been working as a baker all his life.

The Judds arrived together: Flo was grey-haired and stringy, Alma plump and giggly. They started carrying great wooden trays of newly baked cakes into the shop and setting them out in the window and on the glass-fronted shelves that formed the two counters. Alice picked up a tray of tea cakes and was told to set them out next to the bread. She loved the bustling atmosphere and the heavenly scents of fresh baking.

She'd never been allowed her fill of this sort of cake. Gran thought them inferior to the plain cake she made at home. The coloured icing sugars sparkled under the shop lights; the thick cream and the blackcurrant tarts oozing juice made her mouth water.

At nine sharp the shop door was unlocked and customers began coming in. All the prices were marked on the shelves. Flo showed her how to work the till.

'Ask me if there's anything you want to know,' she said, and Alice found her very helpful when she did.

The time flashed past. She made herself useful where she could, and thought Flo and Alma went out of their way to be friendly. When the shop closed at five, Peter cashed up, while she helped the Judds clean the counters and wash the floor.

She knew Peter was paying out wages. As he handed her three shillings and sixpence for her day's work, he said:

'Flo says you're picking it up quickly and you're a good help. D'you want to come again next week?'

Alice did, though she rode her bike home on aching legs.

She'd been working there for three Saturdays before she

came face to face with Pat O'Neill. She was serving in the shop when she heard his Irish voice in the yard between that and the bakery. It struck a chord. It bothered her, though she couldn't think where she'd heard it before. There was a lull at the time, and curiosity made her go to see who was with Peter.

There was something vaguely familiar about the man who was carrying in more empty cake trays. Peter was joking with him. As she came in, he turned from the order he was making up.

'Alice, this is Pat O'Neill, the other partner in this business. My niece,' he explained.

Alice couldn't say she recognised him, and yet . . . That mop of brown curls? He had an engaging grin that was fading, and his blue eyes were staring at her as though he'd seen a ghost.

'Alice is Len's daughter. Did you know Frank's twin brother?'

She took a step back. Fear was making her feel weak at the knees, but she wasn't sure why. It was some sort of gut reaction. Her gaze locked with his.

'Hello, I think we might have met already . . .' She could see he wasn't pleased to see her either.

It came to her then: this was the man Dadda had been afraid of. She could hardly breathe. She had to get away from him.

'Have we? I don't remember.' She backed away and was glad to hear the shop bell ping again. 'Got to go.'

All day, as she served customers, she was plagued by unbidden memories. She hadn't thought about her life with Mam and Dadda for years, but now it wouldn't go away.

It bothered her that Pat O'Neill was one of Peter's partners. Peter was treating him as a friend. Alma Judd said he was good fun. She wondered whether she should say something to Peter, but she didn't quite know what she could tell him. Her memories were all so distant, so vague. She said nothing.

212

Chapter Nineteen

September 1932

Alice told Madeleine about her Saturday job. She knew straight away it was a mistake to say how much she was enjoying it.

The following Saturday morning, Maddy came in saying her mother had sent her to buy cakes. She hung about for a while, waiting for other customers to go so she could chat to Flo and Alma. Then she asked them to lift the counter so she could go and see Peter in the bakehouse.

Maddy had had her plait cut off. Her hair was a mass of shoulder-length curls. Alice thought it made her look very pretty and more like her Aunt Hilary.

At school on Monday Maddy said: 'I'd like to work in the cake shop. Do you think Uncle Peter needs two Saturday girls?'

'No!'

'I'm sick of helping Mam.'

Cecily had taught Maddy to be useful in the salon. She washed customers' hair, swept up cuttings from the floor and made tea. Before they'd started at the higher grade school, Cecily had said she wanted Maddy to follow in her footsteps and be a hairdresser, but Maddy had never made any secret about disliking the trade.

'Why don't we swap Saturday jobs?' Maddy asked. 'You'd like washing hair and handing curlers and things to Mam.'

'Aunt Cecily would rather have you there.'

'Sometimes I get tips. I had one and sixpence last week.'

'I'd rather stay in the cake shop.'

'My dad owns part of that shop,' Maddy said fiercely. 'I'll ask him to get me the job there.'

Alice thought about it all week, and when Peter told her Maddy was asking for her job, she said:

'I could help you in the bakery instead. I think I'd like that better.'

'You don't have to,' Peter said gently. 'We all know what Maddy's like. She only wants the job because you're doing it. I'll say no if you want to carry on with it. She's always trying to elbow you out.'

Alice felt reassured, though she'd guessed Peter would back her against Maddy. 'I'd quite like to learn how to make all those cakes.'

'You'd have to get up early with me. It's no joke getting up at five in the dead of winter.'

'I wouldn't mind. Not for one morning each week.'

Peter pushed his light-brown hair off his forehead. 'I could use an extra pair of hands about the bakehouse too on Saturdays. Pat keeps bringing in more orders and they're always bigger for the weekend.

'Harry's very experienced and dependable, and he'll get on with things on his own, but he's not a fast worker.'

After that, Peter woke her at quarter to five on Saturdays. Alice splashed cold water on her face to wake herself up, threw on her clothes and cycled up to the shop with him in the dark of pre-dawn.

'It's easier to get here and get started before we make a cup of tea,' he told her. 'Then we stop for breakfast about eight.'

She saw Pat O'Neill every Saturday now she was working in the bakehouse. He came in first thing in the morning, to pick up bread and cakes for the round he was building up.

214

'He's doing very well for us,' Peter told Alice. 'Trade's booming.'

One of Alice's jobs was to make up his orders and his small tray of samples. Often she saw him again later in the day, when he came back with a new order. She tried to take no notice of him. He said very little to her, preferring to joke with Harry or Peter. She was always relieved when he went.

She asked Harry: 'Do you like him?'

'He's Irish, isn't he? All the world loves the Irish. He's kissed the Blarney stone, that one. Always got a good story to tell.'

The Judds had taken to him too. If they weren't busy he often looked in on them.

Alice enjoyed baking. Peter said she had quite a talent for icing and decorating the cakes. He soon let her get on with that by herself, but seeing more of Pat O'Neill made her think more and more of the time he used to come to her house in the North End. He was awakening all sorts of memories for her. She remembered the time Uncle Frank and Pat had been drinking tea downstairs when her mother had taken her up to bed.

'I wish they'd go away and leave us alone,' Mam had muttered under her breath.

After her mother had kissed her good night and gone down again, there'd been the sound of cart wheels crunching out on the road, and then there'd been huffing and puffing on the stairs and the sound of beds being moved and something heavy being put down in the other bedrooms.

Alice had got up to see what they were doing. As soon as she went out on the landing, she'd seen Pat O'Neill coming up with his arms round a big demijohn. He'd dropped it on the landing and made a grab at her. She remembered him putting his angry face close to hers.

'What are you doing out here?' he'd roared. 'I told your mam to get you to sleep before we came.'

He'd twisted her flannelette nightdress tight round her throat, then half-thrown her across to her bed.

'This is none of your business, little girl. Keep your mouth shut, do you hear? You've got to learn to mind your own business, so you have. If you know what's good for you.' He'd slammed her door shut on her.

Alice had slid to the cold lino with a bump, then with pounding heart she'd climbed into bed and curled into a ball under her blankets, listening to the sound of more heavy things being brought upstairs.

Moments later, her door was flung open again and Mam came in to scoop her up in a hug.

'I haven't hurt her, sure I haven't.' Pat O'Neill was standing, legs apart, in her doorway, his bushy hair outlined against the landing light. 'Haven't hurt a hair on her head.'

Alice had burst into noisy tears, more frightened than hurt, and shy at finding herself the centre of attention.

'Don't fuss, Beryl,' Uncle Frank was saying. 'She's all right. You're all right, aren't you, Alice? Not hurt?'

'We told you to keep her out of the way, didn't we?' Pat was insisting.

'I thought she'd go to sleep.' Mam was rocking her in her arms. 'You frightened her.'

'We don't want her opening her mouth, do we? You know what kids are like.'

Mam's arms had cradled her, pulling her close against her own body to soothe her. Mam had stayed with her until the last of the stuff had been carried up, but even when everything had gone quiet again, Alice hadn't been able to go to sleep. Her stomach still churned.

She heard Uncle Frank leave the house and knew he had taken his friend Pat with him. She'd heard their voices as they went up the road. She knew her mother didn't like Pat. She didn't think she liked Uncle Frank much either.

Alice wanted to get things straight in her own mind now. She knew there'd been more trouble about storing those things. She couldn't stop thinking about them. She remembered peeping under her mam's bed the next day to find demijohns of setting lotions, bottles of bleach and hair dyes, packets of dried camomile leaves and hair nets and great earthenware pots of soft soap. There was the same under Dadda's bed in the next room.

She'd asked Mam: 'What's soft soap for?'

'To wash hair,' she'd said.

'Do I have my hair washed with it?'

'Sometimes.'

'Not ordinary soap?'

'Sometimes that too. Soft soap is better. It melts down in hot water to make a shampoo that leaves your hair nice.'

'Does Aunt Cecily use it in her shop?'

'Yes,' Mam had said, and given her a very strange look.

Alice knew her parents had argued about the things stored under their beds. She'd found some in Dadda's wardrobe too. There had been arguments about other things, and growing tension between them. Alice could remember pulling the bedclothes over her head as she heard them in the living room below.

'I don't want that man in my house. He's nothing but a thief.' She was in no doubt now that Mam had been referring to Pat O'Neill.

He and Uncle Frank had forced Dadda to do things he didn't want. Mam had wanted him to stop Uncle Frank coming to their house.

'He wants to control everybody,' she'd cried. 'He wants to get rich and he doesn't care what he does to anybody else.'

Eric was working on a fine worsted suit. It was the sort of tailoring he enjoyed most. All the time he'd been apprenticed and had to go over to Wetherall's in Liverpool every day, he'd thought working from home would be the ideal way of earning his living.

217

'I love having you working here beside me all day,' his mother told him. 'Somebody to talk to all the time.'

But now he was missing the companionship of a large staff and the feeling of being out and about in the world.

'It'll take a little time to settle,' Mam told him. She offered to let him go down to Benson's each Monday, but he knew she looked forward to that one outing in her week.

Benson's had a large shop in Grange Road and advertised that they could provide everything for the home dressmaker. Mam had persuaded them to give her twenty per cent discount on what she bought because she was in the trade and a regular buyer. They provided her with the pattern books and the swatches of material that covered their dining table, and which they changed with the seasons.

Some of their customers arrived with the material and patterns bought elsewhere, but others chose from those Benson's provided, and Mam went down to buy what was needed on Mondays when business in the shop was likely to be slack. She did other shopping she needed at the same time.

These days, Eric looked forward to going out in the evenings. He took his mother to the pictures on one night each week. He was going out more often with Peter, usually just for a drink on week nights because Peter wanted to be in bed by ten as he had to get up so early. Tonight was to be a big night; they were going to a party.

'It's Alma Judd's twenty-first,' Peter had told him. 'And as soon as Flo, her mother, said she was throwing this party, I offered to make the birthday cake and give her the cakes and pies she'd need.'

'Very generous,' Eric said.

'I thought it was the least I could do, when they've both worked in the shop for so long. Flo said I must come and bring some fellas. So I'm taking you. She's got three daughters and says their friends are mostly girls.'

'Sounds good,' Eric said. He knew Alma and her mother

and had spoken to them many times. He'd often been in the shop since Peter had bought into the business. He thought Alma was good for a laugh. He was looking forward to it.

Peter called for him at half past seven and they walked down to Gorsehill Road, where the Judds lived. It was a short walk, which meant they didn't have their usual worry about getting home before the buses stopped running.

Peter pointed out the house; it looked much the same as those they lived in. They could hear the buzz of voices and the dance music from outside. The front door was propped open, and Peter led the way in.

There were a lot of young girls in the front room. The gramophone was on a small table, but apart from that and a few chairs pushed against the walls, the rest of the furniture had been moved out to make room to dance.

Eric was used to seeing Alma in a white overall and cap, and he hardly recognised her with her dark hair all fluffed out and wearing a red dress with the latest sweetheart neckline. She was laughing and trying to introduce them to her friends. Eric tried to remember their names: Norma, Jean and Betty.

Then she wound up the gramophone again and Peter asked her to dance. Eric heard her say: 'We've put down lots of chalk on the lino, it'll be awful cleaning it up tomorrow.'

Flo came in from the kitchen, where she'd been laying out the food. While she was telling Eric how grateful she was for all the stuff Peter had given her, a girl on the other side of the room caught his eye.

'Who's that?'

'Don't you know Greta? She's my second daughter, Alma's elder sister.'

She shouted over to introduce them. Greta waved back, and mouthed, 'Hello,' but carried on dancing. She was partnering another girl.

Eric watched her spin round on the lino, her blue dress flaring out. She drew his attention like a magnet. He could see the family likeness in her features, but on her they were daintier than on Alma.

She knew he was watching her. Her laughing eyes played with his across the room. He'd ask her for the next dance. Then he decided it was silly to wait. He dodged round the edge of the dancers until he caught up with her, and excused himself to the girl who was partnering her. Moments later he had her in his arms.

'Hello, Greta.' She had such pretty dark hair, and was slim whereas Alma was plump. He could feel her slender body moving against his.

'Hello, Eric,' she smiled. 'I've heard all about you from Alma. You're Peter's friend, the tailor.' He couldn't drag his eyes from hers. They were hazel, with green flecks in their depths.

'Why has nobody ever mentioned you? Where do you work?'

'Robb's, in Grange Road. In their sewing room. I do alterations to the clothes they sell. You know, take up hems and make them fit better.'

'You sew!'

She giggled. 'Well, yes, have to.'

Eric giggled with her. 'I'm just so surprised we're in the same trade.' It seemed somehow fate.

Dancing wasn't easy with all those people in a room twelve feet square. Eric noticed they'd rolled up the hearth rug to make more space. It stood against the wall in the corner, and the grate was filled with paper flowers.

Greta pressed him into taking his turn to wind up the gramophone and put on the dance records they'd been collecting for years. She and Alma demonstrated the modern slow waltz. Greta was an extrovert; she was laughing and talking to everyone. Eric watched, fascinated, and wondered if his mother would like her. Surely she couldn't fail to? He'd never seen anyone like her.

Flo came in banging two pan lids to announce that supper

was ready. They helped themselves from the table in the kitchen, where Eric recognised most of Peter's products. This was a smaller house than his; there was no middle room. Greta perched with him on the stairs, as it seemed the only place left to sit down.

'Can I see you again?' he asked, biting into a pork pie.

'When?'

'Tomorrow afternoon?'

He was afraid Peter wouldn't be too pleased. They'd been spending their Sunday afternoons and evenings together for a long time. But cementing his acquaintance with Greta suddenly seemed more important.

'Do you have a bike?'

'Yes.'

'Good. Do you fancy a ride out to Thurstaston?'

'Love to, if it isn't raining.'

As soon as the gramophone was playing again, Eric asked her to dance, and he made up his mind to keep her by his side if he could for the rest of the evening.

At eleven, they switched on the wireless and had Henry Hall's dance band for a change. At midnight, he took her into his arms and kissed her for the first time. When he let her go, Greta reached up and kissed him on his lips in return.

'To let you know how much I liked it,' she laughed. From that moment, Eric couldn't get Greta Judd out of his mind.

Sunday afternoon was wonderfully sunny, and they lay on the grass up on Thurstaston Common. On Thursday, when she had a half-day, he took her to the Odeon in Birkenhead to see Clark Gable and Claudette Colbert in *It Happened One Night*.

On Saturday, he felt he had to go to a dance at the Methodist church hall with Peter, because they'd been going round the dance halls on Saturday nights for years.

'I'll meet you there,' Greta smiled when he explained. 'I'll persuade my friend Norma to come with me, to make a foursome. Peter won't mind that, will he?'

Peter didn't. Eric thought the evening went very well. Greta loved dancing and taught him some new steps. He asked Peter to see Norma home because he wanted to be alone with Greta. They left the church hall together and stopped to say good night in Highgreen Road, out of sight of her home.

'I'd like you to meet my mother,' he said. 'Come and have tea with us tomorrow.'

'Meet your mother?' Her eyes shone under the lamp. 'Already? Is it that serious?'

'It is for me,' he told her.

'I've only known you a week.'

He smiled. 'Plenty long enough.' Eric knew he'd fallen in love.

Chapter Twenty

Alice had had her tea with Gran and Peter. It was never substantial on Sundays, usually just the soda bread and cake Gran made to fill her oven while the weekly joint was roasting. When Peter went out and Gran settled down to read the newspapers, Alice decided to go next door to see Auntie Nell and Eric.

They didn't sew on Sundays. Auntie Nell said they needed one day a week away from it. It was the only day of the week that the front door didn't stand open. Alice went round the back, knowing they'd be in the kitchen. She tapped on their back door and went straight in.

She was crossing their scullery before she heard a girlish giggle and realised they had a visitor. It was too late to turn back.

'Sorry,' she said. She had a sinking feeling in her stomach when she saw the girl. 'I didn't mean to barge in.'

They were sitting round the table, eating cold roast beef with salad.

'You're not, Alice. We're always glad to see you.' Auntie Nell smiled.

'Not while you're eating.'

The best china and a clean damask cloth told her this girl had been invited. Surely she wasn't Eric's girlfriend? He'd never even hinted. Alice couldn't take her eyes from her.

'Sit down, I'll get another cup.'

'No, no thank you, Aunt Nell. I've just had my tea.'

She didn't know what to do with herself. She wanted to

turn and run. Eric pulled out a chair and signalled she should sit at the table with them.

'This is Greta,' he told her. 'Her mother and sister work in Best's Bakery. You know Alma?'

Alice tried to smile. Now it was pointed out, the girl did look a bit like Alma, but she was prettier.

'Alice is Peter's niece, they live next door.'

'I hear he's a very good boss.' Greta smiled at Alice.

'He's a very good uncle.'

Eric had never brought a girl home before. She was sure of that. Aunt Nell would have said if he had.

They were putting down their knives and forks. Auntie Nell took the dirty plates to the scullery and brought back extra crockery. There was tinned peaches and cream to follow. A small bowlful ended up in front of Alice.

'Alice is almost one of the family,' Eric said. 'The nearest thing to a little sister.'

That shocked her; she didn't want to be his sister. She'd never felt like that about Eric. She loved him. Eric was hers. He'd always shown her such attention, she'd thought he felt the same way about her. Had that been brotherly affection?

He'd always been ready to comfort her when things went wrong. She didn't know how she'd have got over what her father had done if it hadn't been for Eric. Hadn't Maddy tried to elbow her way into his affections and Eric had choked her off? He'd shown he liked her better.

She'd seen Aunt Nell as her closest friend, and Eric as something more. Their home had been her refuge, her strength and security. That he wanted Greta Judd in his life made it all collapse like a pack of cards. She felt betrayed, wounded.

She'd had her plans for the future and they'd included Eric. Now it seemed her future would be very different.

She ate the peaches, even managed a slice of sponge cake. It was easier to join in, easier to hide her feelings like this. Alice hardly knew what they were talking about. The way

Eric and Greta were looking at each other went through her, made her shiver. They were all surprised when the clock struck seven, and got up hurriedly from the table.

'Come on, Greta, we'll have to get going.' It seemed Eric had planned to take her out somewhere.

Greta went to fetch her hat and coat from the hall stand. She said: 'We're leaving you with the dishes. We shouldn't.'

Auntie Nell said: 'Go on with you. Alice and I'll have them done in a minute.'

Alice had already started to clear the table. It was what she always did, whether at home or here. Greta's face came round the scullery door to her.

'Goodbye. It's lovely meeting Eric's friends.'

Alice turned the taps on full. She didn't want to hear any more. She was jealous. Not just a little jealous; she was hideously jealous of Greta.

Auntie Nell came bustling in with a clean tea towel a few moments later, smiling indulgently.

'I think it must be serious. Eric bringing a young lady to tea when he's only known her a week.'

Alice went home as soon as the washing-up was finished, though Auntie Nell was trying to persuade her to stay.

'It was bound to happen sooner or later,' Nell said, as though she knew how Alice felt. 'Greta's a very nice girl, don't you think?'

It was all too sudden, too awful and too new for Alice to talk about it. And anyway, Auntie Nell was the last person she could confide in about this.

Gran was alone and reading by the fire when she went in. Alice picked up a book and sat at the table. She couldn't keep her mind on the printed page. She felt defeated.

What was very hard to take was that Eric preferred Greta Judd to her. Maddy hadn't been able to take him from her, but Greta had. Alice felt she couldn't compete. Greta was twenty-three, the same age as Eric, while Alice was still only fourteen. And even if she had been able to compete, she wouldn't. Not when Eric had made this choice.

She felt her horoscope had been right. It was proving a difficult year for her. Things had changed between her and Eric, and she was worried that Pat O'Neill would harm Peter.

It helped that school hadn't changed. Alice still enjoyed her lessons. She and Maddy continued to vie with each other to come top in the tests they had at the end of every term. As before, they seemed to take turns at it.

Alice still came top in bookkeeping – Maddy had been unable to beat her at that – but she didn't forget that office work had not been her first choice.

She'd seen herself dressmaking beside Auntie Nell and Eric. Living there with them, being part of that family. Now she had to accept that none of it was going to happen.

'I don't know what's the matter with Alice,' Edith said to Monty as they got ready for bed. 'She seems a bit down.'

'Hasn't come top in the latest test.' Monty unbuttoned his shirt.

'She's fretting about something.'

'She says she's happy and perfectly all right.'

'She's got that look in her eyes. You know, sort of apprehensive.'

Monty piled the coins from his trouser pockets on his chest of drawers. 'Perhaps she needs more company. She's on her own much more now Maddy isn't coming round.'

Edith bristled. She was missing the money Frank used to pay her for looking after Maddy. As soon as the girls started at the higher grade school Cecily had come round to say she saw no further point in it. Maddy was old enough to help her in the shop when she wasn't at school.

'Alice never wanted much to do with Maddy, and she isn't going next door to Nell Ainslie's as much now.'

Monty climbed into bed. 'Our Len was always one to fret and worry. He was a bit of a loner too.'

Edith froze with her flannel nightdress only half on. 'Are you saying she's taking after him?'

'He was about her age when we first noticed that he was getting depressed like.'

That scared Edith. 'I hope not.'

Eric found life was suddenly heady, though he spent his days sewing with his mother just as before. He couldn't get enough of Greta's company; it filled him with an inner excitement and seemed to promise so much. When he wasn't with her he thought about her, dreamed about her, fantasised about her.

He wanted to ask her if she'd marry him, but was afraid she might feel he was rushing her into it. He was more worried about how his mother would feel about him having a wife.

He knew her life had always pivoted round him. She had lots of acquaintants, lots of customers to pass the time of day with, but Alice was the only other person she was close to. He thanked the powers that be for Alice; he knew she'd still be coming in to keep Mam company, whatever happened.

Joining Mam in the business had tightened the bonds that held them close. Until he'd met Greta, they'd been mutually dependent for day-to-day company, for affection, for running the business and generating income.

The last thing he wanted to do was to upset his mother. He felt a duty, a responsibility for her continued happiness. He loved her still but he loved Greta too, and he very much wanted her. Eric was afraid his mother was not going to understand.

Apart from that, he wasn't sure he could afford to support a wife. His mother mustn't feel he was demanding more than his share of profit from the business she'd built up. He hadn't given this a thought when he'd decided to go in with her.

He looked at her, hunched over her sewing machine, seaming up curtains, treadling hard. The light sparkled on her spectacles, her hair more grey than anything else now. She'd devoted her life to him.

'I'll make some tea,' he said, and got up to put the kettle on.

With the cups ready, he got out the account book for a discreet assessment of what his income might be, before making any move about Greta.

They each kept an order book beside them in the front room. In that, they wrote the customer's requirements and measurements. When the work was finished and paid for, the amount was entered, together with the expenditure on material, pattern, buttons and thread.

The totals were added up every week. Mam encouraged him to do that. He knew turnover was well up on last year and that their profit was increasing. He and Mam discussed that often, with considerable satisfaction.

She said his coming into the business had given it a real boost, but what he wanted to look at more closely was how much he was actually contributing. He knew well enough that Mam's satisfied customers were persuading their husbands to come to him for their new suits. He wouldn't have found it so easy if he'd set up on his own.

He heard her step in the hall and leapt up to soak the tea.

'Oh, you're looking at the accounts.' Her grey eyes twinkled behind her spectacles. 'Any ulterior motive?'

His mother seemed to have this ability to guess why he did things. Right now it was a bit embarrassing to find she could read his mind.

'Well . . .'

She smiled. 'You can afford it if you really want it.'

He felt the flush run up his cheeks. 'How did you know? I mean, I was only thinking . . .'

'I know you think of nothing else.' She flashed him another smile as she lifted the tea pot.

He frowned in indecision. 'I haven't known her very long.'

'About a month.'

'You don't think I'm rushing things?'

'Actually – yes. You need time to get to know each other.'

Eric thought he knew all he needed to know about Greta. He'd never felt like this about a girl before. He loved her; he thought, he hoped, he was almost sure she was in love with him. He wanted very much to talk about it to Greta, but it was the last thing he wanted to discuss with his mother.

'You're looking to see whether the business would stand it?'

'It's your business, Mam.'

She shook her head. 'Yours too now. Let's call it ours. It's doing very well. Yes, you could afford to keep a wife, if that's what you want to know.'

'I don't want to take out more than my share.'

'I won't let you.' He knew from her smile that she'd give him anything he wanted. 'How far have you got? Have you popped the question?'

'No! No, not yet. I haven't said anything.'

'Then I wouldn't say you're rushing into it. But you want to?'

Eric ignored that. 'I don't know how you two would get on.' That was his biggest worry.

'You know her better than I do. What d'you think?'

Optimistically, he said: 'I think you'd take to each other.' Everything depended on that.

'Very clever of you to choose somebody who could work with us in the business.'

'I can't rush her into that.' Eric was alarmed. 'She mightn't like the idea.'

'You could find out. Put it to her. See how the land lies.'

'After one month?'

'Couldn't you do it without pinning her down?'

The lobby door pinged as a customer of Mam's came in for a fitting. Eric was left to wash up the tea cups. He felt heartened. He hadn't had to broach the subject of marriage. He knew he'd have been awkward and embarrassed if he had. His mother had brought it up and didn't seem resentful that he should want it. She was even telling him he could afford it. He felt his plans had taken a big step forward.

He rejected his mother's advice about waiting until he'd known Greta longer. Eric didn't want to take things slowly. It was high summer, and on fine evenings they could cycle to Thurstaston and climb the hill to watch the sun go down over the River Dee.

He loved those evenings, lying on the warm turf with Greta, the breeze fluttering her long dark hair so that it tickled his face. Her hazel eyes with their green flecks laughed up at him. They had privacy there; not many climbed the hill on week nights. There were outcrops of rock and little hollows where they could get out of the wind if it were too strong.

Eric spent much of the time there holding her in his arms, but they talked too, for hours on end. By the following week, he'd told her he loved her and wanted to marry her. She'd said there was nothing she wanted more. He laughed and said his mother thought they should take things slowly.

She told him all the things he wanted to know about her life. About her family, and about the girls who worked in the alteration room at Robb's with her.

He felt very pleased at the way things were going and was delighted his mother would accept Greta.

The following Sunday, Eric was walking with Greta along the promenade at New Brighton. It was a blustery day and the high tide raced in to hurl itself with tremendous force against the wall. The noise was deafening and water sprayed up in the air to splash over unwary walkers. He led her across the grass to a seat, far enough away that they wouldn't get wet.

'There's something I have to tell you now we're engaged,' he said.

Greta's hand rested lightly on his arm. He took it between both of his.

'A family secret, I suppose you'd call it. It's very important that you don't breathe a word to anyone. You will promise?'

'Of course I promise.' Greta's hazel eyes shone with sincerity.

'My mother wears a wedding ring and calls herself Mrs Ainslie, but she's never been married. Her family tried to persuade her to have me adopted when I was a baby, but she wouldn't part with me, so they cut her off, said she was a disgrace to them. That's why I have no other relatives to introduce to you.'

In front of him, the Irish Sea glistened in the sunshine and seagulls swooped and called over their heads.

'She knew looking after me on her own would be hard, but she wanted to do it. I'm telling you all this because . . . I don't want you to resent her presence in my life.'

'Of course I won't.'

'Resentment can build up . . . but I'm sure she won't resent you. I don't think she has an atom of envy or jealousy in her. She understands love, she knows I need you. She likes you, Greta.'

'I like her; she seems welcoming when you take me to your home.'

'She wants me to be happy and she knows I won't be unless you're happy too. I want us all to be happy. Is it asking a lot . . . ? Can you bear to live in the same house?'

Greta smiled serenely. 'I think so. Jane, my eldest sister, has been married for three years, and they still live with her husband's parents. They're saving for a place of their own, and she wants to get away now she's got two babies, but she was happy enough to start with.'

231

'I hope you won't want to get away from my mam. But you'll always come first with me, I promise you that.'

Eric talked his plans through with her then. They'd live with his mother to begin with. There was a bedroom that was never used next to his. He thought they could turn it into a little sitting room so that they could have privacy when they wanted it. The joy of this was that it could all happen quite soon.

'I don't want to wait.'

'Waiting is the last thing I want.' Greta's fingers squeezed his.

'It's more a question of giving our families time to get used to the idea. When we've known each other for six months, we'll tell them we're engaged. Then a few months later we'll get married. I mean, we're both old enough.' They'd both be twenty-four soon.

'If we waited I feel we'd just be wasting time, and what's the point if we've both made up our minds?'

Alice didn't stop going next door, though now she found it a bittersweet experience.

Eric seemed just as friendly as ever. If he realised how she felt, he gave no sign. She hoped, at first, that he'd change his mind about Greta. After all, Peter had a succession of girlfriends and was always changing his mind. Not that he ever took them home to meet Gran.

Auntie Nell didn't change. She encouraged Alice to have some sewing on the go all the time. She offered help and advice, and the use of all the patterns she used in the business. Alice was making all her own clothes now.

From time to time she found Greta there too. She found it hurtful to see her and Auntie Nell getting on so well together, but Greta's manner was always friendly towards her too. She dressed very smartly, and Alice told her so.

'It's working at Robb's. I can pick up on the latest fashions there.'

232

She explained how she and the other girls in the alteration room studied the expensive gowns that were on sale. Then they tried to make themselves dresses that looked similar.

'I make all my own clothes, and some for my sisters and mother too.'

The interest in sewing was something else Greta shared with Eric and Auntie Nell, but unlike Alice, Greta was an expert too.

Alice saw Greta there again after only six months, and she was wearing a ring on her engagement finger.

Greta smiled. 'A solitaire.'

She held her hand out so Alice could take a good look at the small but perfect diamond. It made Alice go cold with dread. Then came the mention of marriage. Only two months after she'd seen the engagement ring, they'd set the day.

'Right after Christmas,' Eric said with his usual grin. 'The day after Boxing Day. It's easier for everyone to get time off then.'

Greta said: 'Not a white wedding. It would be cold for white satin, and we don't want a lot of fuss. I'm going to make myself a smart two-piece. Something I can wear afterwards.

'Alma's asking to be bridesmaid, and Jane wants to be matron of honour. But one's enough for a quiet wedding.'

Greta's eyes smiled into hers. 'Would you like to be my bridesmaid, Alice?'

Alice felt her mouth go suddenly dry. 'Me?'

'Eric thought you might like to. He says you're like a little sister to him.'

'No.' Her voice was agonised. 'No, thanks all the same. It's lovely of you to ask, but no, I don't think I should.'

'He doesn't want you to feel left out.'

Left out? She felt abandoned, but the last thing she wanted was to be bridesmaid to his bride.

'I won't feel left out, Greta. You don't want to disappoint Alma.'

Alice couldn't get out of the house quick enough. She felt sick. Eric was hers. She knew him better than anyone else in the world, but she mustn't cry about losing him. She'd cried on his shoulder before and it hadn't made him love her. It had just made him sorry for her.

Chapter Twenty-One

July 1933

It was worrying Alice that the man who had frightened Dadda was accepted as a friend by Peter. Day after day he was coming into the bakery and being received with cups of tea and friendly banter.

Something about his manner was making her more nervous. She wondered if it was her imagination, or whether his light-blue eyes did turn to steel when he caught sight of her. She knew that at the back of her mind she blamed him for what had happened to her parents. She was afraid he'd prove as dangerous to Peter as he had to Dadda.

She hadn't wanted to talk about him to anybody, but bottling it up inside herself was making her more suspicious. She thought she ought to warn Peter, just in case Pat O'Neill tried to do him down.

Now she was working in the bakery Peter sent her home at one, in time to have dinner with Gran. By then, they'd finished baking and Harry had only to clean up. Peter didn't usually come home until after the shop closed. He said he had plenty to do checking his stores, ordering supplies and keeping his books up to date.

Today, when Alice woke from a nap on her bed, she decided to cycle back to the shop. She wanted to talk to him, and apart from the five-minute cycle ride at five in the morning, before she was properly awake, there seemed to be no other time she could catch him alone.

Peter had made what he called an office for himself from what had been a small storeroom in the passageway. The back wall was against the biggest oven, so it could be more than warm. He'd moved a desk in there, and an old bed chair. Now he owned a share of this business, he wanted to be on the premises should he be needed. Instead of finishing work early in the afternoon, he took an hour or so's nap here to make up for his early start.

When Alice returned, Flo told her Peter was asleep but that he'd asked her to wake him with a cup of tea at half past three, and she'd already put the kettle on. Alice made it and took two cups to his office.

She had to speak to him to wake him up; she watched him trying to force his eyes open. He yawned and asked:

'What are you doing back here? Is something wrong?'

'No.' She didn't know where to begin now.

'What then?' He pulled himself into a sitting position and reached for his tea.

'Do you like Pat O'Neill?'

'Yes, he's a good sort.'

'Uncle Frank used to bring him to our house. My mam and dadda were scared of him.'

She saw him stiffen. 'Were they?'

Peter listened, and watched Alice's earnest face. She was saying that seeing Pat O'Neill here had jogged her mind. She'd remembered that Frank used to bring him to their house and how once he'd terrified her when she'd got out of bed to see what they were doing.

She told him about the arguments between her parents and Frank, and how she'd listened, cowering under her blankets. She didn't know how old she was at the time, but it was long before she was nine. She thought it had been going on for years.

236

'I think that's why Dadda killed himself.'

'No, kid, surely not?' But Peter was afraid there might be something in what Alice was saying.

'Mam was more than scared. Dadda was a nervous wreck. Uncle Frank was pressing them to help him. I've always known; that isn't something I've just remembered. I blame him and Pat O'Neill for what happened. They caused all the trouble.'

'You've been worrying about it, have you? You should have told me before.'

'To start with I couldn't even think about Dadda. Couldn't talk about it. Too full up. It wouldn't have brought him back, would it?'

Peter shivered at the raw feeling in her voice. He didn't know how much credence he should give her story. Really it was nothing more than that Pat O'Neill had frightened her and she'd taken a dislike to him.

When Alice had gone, he lay back and thought about his brothers. They were fourteen years older than he was. In his earliest memories he'd seen them as adults. Almost as though he'd had four people taking care of him.

Dad had been easy-going, and he'd seen more of his brothers. Although they were twins, it was Frank who bossed him round. Frank had a stronger personality than his father, and a heavier hand when he'd delivered punishment. Frank had also bossed Len.

As to what Alice had said about Frank, it added up. As a child he'd been scared of Frank himself; it didn't surprise him that Len had been too. Frank was too forceful, too determined to have his own way. Peter had long suspected he wasn't entirely honest; for a family in their position, Frank and Cecily had too much money and were adding to it too quickly.

He wished he hadn't let Frank push him into having him and Pat as partners, but everything was going well. Pat was doing a grand job expanding their markets. Everything was fine. Peter was keeping the books himself and controlling the money. He was prepared to swear there was no monkey business going on. All the same . . . What Alice had told him added to his worries.

It was the end of term and the end of Alice's course. She looked round her classroom. The windows leaked when it rained, the school was in a dilapidated state and there was talk of closing it down, but she didn't want to leave. She'd been very happy here.

Neither did she want to lose touch with the boys and girls in her class. She'd spent three happy years with them, but now they were all on the point of starting work. Alice had certificates to prove she could type at sixty words a minute, and write Pitman's shorthand at a hundred and twenty words a minute. She'd also passed an examination in double-entry bookkeeping.

Local firms had vacancies for those leaving with the right qualifications. The school had been in touch with them and interviews were being arranged. Alice liked bookkeeping best and told her teacher she'd like to be an accounts clerk.

'Oh no, my dear! Your shorthand's better than average. It offers the better career. You'll lose your speed if you don't use it. Take my advice and get experience while you can. You won't regret it.'

Alice was told she'd be interviewed by the Globe Insurance Company, at their office in Hamilton Square. Maddy was allotted an interview with Lever Brothers in Port Sunlight.

'Lucky you.' Alice was a little disappointed. She'd have liked the chance to work at Lever's. Grandpa worked there and she thought it would be nice to have him on hand to show her the ropes. Also, she'd be able to travel backwards and forwards to work with him.

'They pay well too.' Madeleine grinned with satisfaction.

'Maddy might be coming to Lever's?' Grandpa almost choked when Alice told him at tea time.

'A very good firm,' Gran said, dishing up their Finnan haddock. 'Couldn't do better, could she, Monty?'

Grandpa looked a bit put out. 'Well – it's a long journey every day. There are other firms just as good. Cammell Laird's . . .'

It was clear to Alice that he didn't want Maddy to work in the same office. It surprised her.

'It's a good place to work, isn't it?' she asked. 'It must be, you've been there most of your life.'

'The pension . . . They pay good pensions.'

'And you wanted Dadda to work there.'

'Yes, well . . . When's Maddy coming? For her interview?'

'Tuesday, at four thirty.'

Monty hoped Maddy wouldn't be given a job, but he knew the company took on a lot of shorthand typists in July and August every year, when they were coming out of the schools and colleges.

If Maddy came to work here, he and Rita would have to be much more careful. He was afraid it wouldn't be long before she sized up the position. Maddy could be as quick as a load of monkeys. She had a loud voice and a forward manner too. He didn't want her shouting 'Grandpa' after him.

With a girlfriend of Rita's age, it made him sensitive about things like that, and the office juniors they were taking on these days were a cheeky lot. They'd all be calling him Grandpa behind his back before he knew it.

There was nothing he could do about it. Maddy would be selected or otherwise by the personnel department, and he couldn't influence their decision. She'd be bound to tell them her grandfather had worked for the company for thirty-two years. They liked their staff to stay, and that would encourage them to take her on. He tried not to think of the complications it would open up for him.

Rita just smiled when he told her.

'Even if she gets a job, it could be well away from us. There are lots of little offices round the factory.'

Monty was afraid Maddy would see him with Rita every dinner hour. Or worse, she'd come and join them at their table while they were eating. He wanted Rita to himself.

As Tuesday afternoon drew on, he found he couldn't concentrate on his work. Just knowing Maddy was here in the main office was enough to upset him, though the personnel department was in a different wing to where he worked and he wouldn't be likely to see her.

Ten minutes before the end of the working day, he watched Rita come out of her office and walk along the gallery above the hall where he sat. All the managers had their offices up there. She went to the ladies' cloakroom to comb her hair and powder her nose. Then she took her hat and coat back to the office with her.

Nobody dared leave their desk before the buzzer signalled it was time, but then there was a huge stampede for the buses. They all had to hurry if they didn't want to be left waiting at the bus stop.

He was relieved when the buzzer sounded. Seconds later, a hooter started up outside in the factory. All round him, books and papers were being tossed into drawers and keys turned in locks. Typewriters were being covered. Clerks left their desks to run along the corridors. Half the hall had emptied before the buzzer stopped.

Monty was carried along to the main entrance hall by the crowd. Rita always waited for him by the door. As he fought his way through to take her arm, he could see her smiling at him, looking as fresh at the end of the day as she did at the start. When they reached their bus stop, a long line had formed and was snaking back on itself.

'Just our luck,' she said.

A bus drew up at the head of the line and was filling up fast.

'We aren't going to get on this one.'

Rita nudged him in the ribs. 'Someone's trying to attract your attention. Over there.'

Monty froze. It was Maddy, waving excitedly. She was well ahead of them in the line. He let his hand fall from Rita's arm. His stomach turned over.

'Grandpa,' she shouted. 'I've got it. I've got the job.'

Rita tugged at his arm. 'Who's that?'

'I told you – it's Madeleine, my granddaughter. That's bad news.' He'd been hoping she wouldn't be offered a job here.

When Alice saw Maddy the next morning, she looked quite down in the mouth. She asked her how she'd got on in her interview.

'Great, I was offered a job there and then.'

'That's wonderful,' Alice said enviously. She'd been to the Globe Insurance and had two interviews: one in the personnel department and one from a Mr Hunt, the claims manager, who was seeking an assistant for his secretary. After both, she'd been told they'd write and let her know the result. She was still waiting.

'No it isn't,' Maddy said crossly. 'I was offered thirty-seven shillings and sixpence to start, with an increase after six months if I gave satisfaction.'

'That's good!'

'I know, but Dad won't let me take it.'

'Why not?'

'I told him I'd seen Grandpa with a lady friend.'

Alice giggled. She thought her cousin was joking. 'What d'you mean, lady friend?'

'You know, a mistress.'

'No!'

'My dad knew about her but he didn't know she worked at Lever's too.'

Alice couldn't see it. 'At his age? Don't be daft.'

'Honest.' Maddy was indignant. 'Dad doesn't want me to work there. Says it'll only embarrass Grandpa and make trouble with Gran. He made me write to say I didn't want the job.'

Alice found it hard to believe. 'What's she like, this lady friend?'

'She's very young – for him, I mean. Not much to look at: she's got a real snozzle.' It was Maddy's turn to giggle. 'But she was wearing a smashing suit. I'll get myself one like hers when I start earning.'

Alice was astounded. 'Who is she?'

'Dad doesn't know.'

'Grandpa's past all that! And what about Gran? I mean . . . ?'

'You mustn't tell her! Dad made me promise to keep my mouth shut. She doesn't know.'

'But for you – not to take a good job like that!'

'He said, "Better let sleeping dogs lie." Doesn't want Gran to be upset. Doesn't want her to know.'

Alice let out a long, shuddering breath. So that could be why Grandpa hadn't wanted Maddy to get a job there! All the same, she couldn't quite believe it. Maddy could be building it up to mean more than it did.

Alice received a letter from the Globe Insurance the following morning offering her the job. She was to start work next Monday and would receive thirty-five shillings a week.

'Not bad to begin with,' Gran said.

Alice felt apprehensive going down to Hamilton Square on her first morning. She hadn't taken to Mr Hunt when she'd gone in for her interview. He had a haughty manner and a grand office on the first floor. Miss Jones, his secretary, had the end of the corridor partitioned off to give her a little privacy. There was just room for two desks to be pushed together so that they faced each other.

242

Alice thought she might like Miss Jones. She came to the office in a black straw hat with silk flowers on the brim. Her dark dress formed tight creases round her stout figure.

'Worked here for six years, I have. Ever since Mr Hunt was promoted to claims manager.'

She was on the wrong side of fifty and had a flustered manner. Her dark hair showed a sprinkling of grey, and she wore it drawn back in a severe bun.

'Our office junior left without working out her notice,' Miss Jones told Alice disapprovingly. 'Said she had trouble at home and must leave to nurse her mother. She certainly inconvenienced us. There's more work than I can cope with alone, and Mr Hunt doesn't like his work being bandied about the general office. The last three weeks have been very hard for me.'

Having somebody with her again seemed to loosen her tongue. She never stopped talking. Alice had the story of her life as well as plenty of typing to do over the next three days.

'I'm a product of Rock Ferry Higher Grade School too,' Miss Jones smiled.

Alice was pleased to find they had something in common. She hoped Miss Jones would take to her. She'd been working for five days when Miss Jones mentioned that prior to coming to the Globe, she'd worked for ten years at Ledbetter's.

'Did you know a man called Pat O'Neill?' Alice asked before she could stop herself. She felt she'd worked herself up into a state about him by this time.

'Did I know him? I certainly did, only too well. He was supposed to be their best salesman. The trouble he caused!'

Alice had that sinking feeling in her stomach again. 'What d'you mean?'

It seemed Pat O'Neill had pinned a card on the firm's noticeboard asking for local lodgings because he was living at Crosby on the outskirts of Liverpool.

Miss Jones's mother, a widow at that time, had been

seeking a lodger to ease her finances. He'd lived in their spare room for three years, for which he'd been charged twenty-five shillings a week. For that he'd been provided with bed, breakfast and evening meal, with sandwiches to take out.

'I thought, knowing him through the firm, that he'd be all right. Some guarantee . . . He gave us references too, of course. Two women living alone, I mean, you can't be too careful, can you?'

'What happened?'

'Came to a sticky end, he did. Mam always said he seemed a bit of a rogue, but a likeable rogue, if you know what I mean.'

Alice swallowed. Everybody seemed to like Pat but her. 'What happened?'

'He got the sack. It was a nine-day wonder.'

'Why?'

'Between you and me, he was caught thieving,' Miss Jones whispered behind her hand. 'Selling off company products for his own benefit. It was thought he'd been taking stock for years.'

Alice's heart turned over.

'Nothing was ever proved against him, thank goodness. We wouldn't have liked to read our address in the paper if he'd been charged and taken to court. Such a disgrace to harbour a criminal.

'He got off scot free. Ledbetter's couldn't prove anything. His records were in order. They thought that when he collected stock from the factory, he took more than was on the order form.'

Alice was shaking. Of course! Why hadn't she thought of it before? Those crates that had been stored in their bedroom at home had been stolen goods. Pat O'Neill had been supplying Aunt Cecily for years. That could be one reason why she made such a profit from her business. No doubt if he stole goods from his employer, he could sell them on at a big discount.

* * *

244

Talking about Pat, finding out more about him, seemed to release more memories. They were going round in her head all afternoon and she couldn't keep her fingers on the right keys of her typewriter. She'd never made so many mistakes.

When she got home that evening, Peter was on his way out. He was going somewhere with Eric. Alice meant to stay awake to have a word with him when he came back. Grandpa went out too, as usual. She and Gran had cocoa at half past nine and went up to bed. She felt haunted by Pat O'Neill and though she kept the light on to make herself stay awake, she was in that halfway stage between sleep and wakefulness. She was remembering more. She'd heard her parents in the living room below her one night:

'It's stolen property, you fool,' her mother had shouted. 'Don't let that brother of yours talk you into having his spoils here. Why do you think Frank wants it to come? Yes, it's safer for him. If there's any trouble, we'll be the ones that get it, not him.'

And on another night:

'Your Frank's behind all this. He's forcing you to store stolen property until Pat can move it on. I wish you'd stay clear of him. He can talk you into anything. You live in each other's pockets.'

Dadda had moaned: 'He's my twin. How can I cut myself off from him?'

When she heard the front door scrape open and click shut, and then the stairs creak, Alice slid out of bed and opened her door.

Peter was creeping up in the dark. She dragged him into her bedroom where Gran wouldn't hear. He felt cold.

'You've got to watch Pat O'Neill,' she whispered urgently.

'I am, since our last talk. I go through his account book like a hawk.' Peter perched on the end of her bed.

'It's all right. He brings in the right money for what he's

245

selling. There's never any problem. He's paying whole-sale prices to the business but the three of us agreed them. They're fair. I always get Harry to help him load his van and then I check again what's being put on. I let him see me doing it. I tell him I don't want to send him out short of anything.

'I'll know if he tries anything on, really I will, Alice. He must have turned over a new leaf. Decided to go straight.'

'Perhaps.' She sighed. 'But all this talk about him . . . Miss Jones going on about him . . . it's making me remember things I shut out of my mind.'

Peter put a comforting hand on her arm. 'I'm sorry it's upsetting for you. If you could put it out of your mind when you were nine, couldn't you do it again now?'

'I don't want to. I'm older and I can face things. I want to get things straight in my mind. Why do you think Dadda killed himself? You were old enough to under-stand.'

'He was gassed in the war, Alice. It damaged his lungs, made him ill. That made him feel depressed.'

'That's what everyone says, but there were times when he played with me, when we were all happy.'

'That's how you felt, but did he?'

Alice shook her head. 'I don't know. I don't think my mam was happy. I remember her being terrified and shouting at Dadda: "Frank's pulling the strings and you're doing the dancing. Why don't you think about me and Alice? You know what Frank's like. He wants to be rich. He'll do anything for money."

'He brought Pat O'Neill round to our house and made them store his stolen property. They were putting pressure on my mam and dad.'

'I wish I'd thought about it more at the time,' Peter sighed. 'I don't know, Alice.'

'*I* know. That's how it was.'

*　　*　　*

Maddy found another job, as a typist with the Manchester and Liverpool District Bank.

'But I don't think I'm going to like it,' she complained to Alice when they next met. 'My boss is awfully strict.'

'So's mine.'

'I could see him eyeing me with a dreadful frown all morning, and then do you know what he said to me? "Your dress is a little flamboyant, Miss Luckett. Not quite what we expect of our employees at this bank. Could you wear something more businesslike in future?" I mean, what a nerve!

'I wouldn't mind but I'd have done better at Lever's, and they'd have paid me more. I wish I hadn't told Dad about seeing Grandpa with his lady friend.'

Book Three

Chapter Twenty-Two

December 1933 – February 1936

To Alice, things didn't seem to improve. She felt threatened by Pat O'Neill, and Eric's mind seemed wholly on Greta Judd. Everybody was talking about the wedding. Auntie Nell could think of nothing else. She was giving it more attention than Christmas this year.

'Greta's decided on a blue flannel two-piece. It's sensible to have something warm, and Eric is helping with the tailoring.'

The pattern was put into Alice's hands; she had to admire it.

'I thought tan and brown for me,' Auntie Nell said. 'I'll wear my fox fur too. What are you going to wear?'

'I haven't thought yet.' Alice didn't want to think about it. She didn't want to be there at all, but it seemed she'd have to be. Gran and Grandpa were invited, as well as Peter. There was no way she could get out of it.

Alice would have liked to wear blue, and it seemed fate that Greta had chosen her favourite shade of deep cobalt. She made herself a navy two-piece in rather a hurry. It had been cut on very grown-up lines, with a longer flowing skirt. When at last it was finished and she tried it on, the skirt didn't hang right.

'Don't worry,' Auntie Nell consoled her. 'If you unpick the waistband, I'll put that skirt right. It'll be just the thing to wear to your office afterwards.'

Christmas Day came and went, and then Boxing Day. The wedding was on her before Alice felt ready to face it. The day was dark and overcast, with an icy wind straight off the river.

Alice wore her navy suit, with her best cream blouse. She didn't have a coat other than her brown tweed to wear over it, and she felt that would prevent her looking fashionable. She felt numb with cold from the moment they set out to catch the bus into Birkenhead.

Eric had hired a car to drive his mother and Greta and some of her relatives down to the registry office in Hamilton Square. To Alice, it seemed to cut her off from the Ainslies.

Greta was a very elegant bride. Alice could hardly bear to look at her. Her cheeks were flushed with excitement and Eric was holding on to her arm. Every so often their eyes would meet and search each other's face.

Eric turned his attention from his bride just long enough to smile at Alice as they waited for the registrar to start the formalities. He looked very smart in the new three-piece suit he'd made himself. He'd bought the new white shirt from Robb's. He said the collar was so stiff it was cutting into his neck.

Seated between Gran and Grandpa, Alice kept her eyes tightly shut. She didn't want to see any more. It didn't stop her hearing Eric's responses, so clear and confident.

Greta's mother gave the wedding breakfast. Most of the guests were Judds. Peter had made the magnificent three-tier wedding cake, and provided many of the delicacies too.

Eric took Greta for a four-day honeymoon to Chester. It was cold, damp weather but that didn't seem to matter. They walked the brightly lit streets where the Christmas decorations already looked tired. He'd hired the car for the duration and used it to drive out into the surrounding countryside during the short, dark afternoons. They'd be back at their boarding house at dusk, in time for high tea. He took Greta to the theatre, and to the cinema on another night.

When they went home on New Year's Eve, he felt he'd had four days of luxury and pleasure. Greta said it had been wonderful.

It could be only four days, because she had to be back at work when the shop reopened on the second of January. The alteration room would be working at full stretch during their January sale.

Eric didn't want it to be longer. He and Mam had a lot of work on. Customers wanted party dresses at this time of the year and he'd never spent as much as a night away from her before. She'd prepared a special celebratory dinner for their return and seemed delighted to have them both with her.

'You should have given up your job,' she said to Greta. 'Then you could have stayed away longer. We can keep you busy here. We've plenty of work.'

Eric had already talked this through with Greta. He thought it would be easier if she kept her job on. Better for Mam if Greta wasn't always with them, at least to start with.

'I like working at Robb's,' she smiled. 'And I'm earning good money.'

She was on two pounds fourteen shillings a week. She had agreed that they'd save that. If things didn't go well, they might need it to set up home somewhere else. If they found they could all live together happily, he'd spend the money on a car. That was something they'd all enjoy.

Mam was looking at Greta. 'I'm not sure you should go on working now.'

Greta smiled. 'No reason for me to stop. I know lots of girls have to give up when they get married. Those in good jobs, like teachers and office workers and that sort, but Robb's don't insist on it. Not for alteration hands. One or two are already married.'

'Won't people say you're Eric's responsibility now? It

253

does make it look as though he can't afford to keep you, that our business isn't doing as well as we'd like. Some will say you're doing a man out of a job.'

Greta giggled. 'That sounds very middle class. All the alteration hands are girls. We have to put up men's trouser turn-ups too.'

She agreed with Eric. She wanted to take things a step at a time. She was happy to come and live with them, but to work with them too might be just too much straight off. Besides, she liked her job.

Eric thought of the years that followed as the best in his life. As the weeks went on, Greta seemed to fit in very well. When Mam caught bronchitis the following winter, he was particularly hard pressed trying to keep up with the orders they'd taken on. Greta and Alice helped him do her work. They sat sewing in the front room with him for two or three hours every evening. It meant Mam didn't feel pressurised to return to working a full day before she was well again.

Greta also turned her hand to the housework and did her share of the cooking. They were all invited to the Judd family home for tea from time to time, and Mam told Flo that Greta was a lovely girl, none better.

Eric was very pleased that everything was working out so well. The profits from the business continued to improve, and after two years he felt they could afford some form of transport. He wanted it mainly for leisure use, but it would enable them to slip down to Benson's much more quickly when they needed something.

For years, he and Peter had been talking about buying a car. Owning one had been their greatest ambition, but other things had had to come first.

Eric had toyed with the idea of buying a motorbike, but he'd have needed a sidecar if he wanted to take Mam out. He'd wanted to get married more, and it seemed sensible afterwards to save their money to buy a house.

Now, he didn't think there would be any hurry for that.

Greta had settled down in Mam's house. It was the best thing for them all. A motorbike no longer seemed practical.

Eric and Peter were having a glass of beer in the Halfway House one evening when Peter said: 'Our Frank's buying a new car. A Rover. Enough to make you turn green, isn't it?'

'What's he doing with his old one?'

'The Austin Seven? He wants to sell it. There's an advert going in the paper next week.'

Eric took a deep swallow of beer. He longed to own it. 'How much is he asking?'

'Fifty pounds.'

Fifty! Eric's fingers tightened round his glass. It would be possible! But . . . 'Is it worth it?'

'I think so. I'd love to have it, but I daren't think of it. Not yet. Got to be sensible and keep a bit of cash in hand. Anyway, I'd like to buy our Frank's share of the business, if he'll let me. Then, definitely, the first thing I'll go for is a car.'

'Tell me about this one Frank's selling.'

'It's a 1926 model, nine years old. He's owned it for six. It had only one other owner.'

'Why's he selling it? Has something gone wrong?'

Peter smiled. 'I don't think so. Bounces a bit, but they all do. You know our Frank, he's got big ideas. Wants something better. You serious about this?'

Eric took another swig of beer. 'Yes.' Never had he been more serious.

'D'you want to walk down and look at it now?'

Eric knew the car. He'd even ridden in it. Of course he ought to look it over for scratches, try it out. Perhaps talk to Greta first?

'Why not?' They drained their glasses and set off. It was dusk and not the best time to look a car over, but he had to see it. He'd ask if he could come back tomorrow in daylight to try it.

When he saw it he was bowled over. The maroon paintwork shone like new. There were no dents or scratches that he could see. The soft top of canvas looked very clean.

'Had to have a new hood last year,' Frank told him. 'It's all in good condition.'

It was small, tiny really, but there was a seat at the back. Room to take both Greta and Mam out.

'Cheap to run,' Frank urged. 'Road tax is only eight pounds a year. Cost you three times as much to tax the Model T.'

Eric was already persuaded. 'Here.' Frank put the keys in his hand. 'Try it, go on. I know you after all. It's as sweet as a bell.'

Eric climbed into the driver's seat. Impossible to wait until tomorrow. Frank swung the starting handle and showed him how to switch the lights on. He knew he'd buy it as he edged out on to the road.

Peter was right, it did bounce; it also swayed from side to side and wasn't as easy to handle as the Ford he'd hired. The brakes didn't seem all that good either.

'I've had them checked,' Frank assured him. 'They're all right. The mechanic said they're all like that on the baby Austins, but it's one of the first cars to have brakes on all four wheels.' He clinched the deal by reducing the price by a fiver.

Greta was thrilled with it, and Mam couldn't stop herself smiling. On Sundays after that, Eric took them both out for little outings. During that summer, he'd sometimes pack a picnic and pick Greta up from work. He'd take her out to Thurstaston and they'd climb the hill and eat their picnic taking in the view across the River Dee to Wales.

They'd been married for eighteen months when Greta became pregnant. If anything, Mam was even more thrilled than Eric was when it was confirmed. She bought flannelette to make nightgowns for the baby the very next time she went to Benson's.

'You'll have to give up your job now,' she said to Greta.

'Yes, in a month or two. When I feel it's getting a bit much.'

'You can come and sew with us. Do as much or as little as you like.'

They all knew now that there wouldn't be any problem.

'I'm so looking forward to this baby,' Mam said happily.

Greta worked until she was six months into her pregnancy, and kept well throughout. Once she'd given up going into Robb's every day, she wanted to spend her time in the front room, sewing with them. Nell and Eric refused to give her work, but found it impossible to keep her out.

Greta spent an hour or two each day working on the layette for her baby.

'I didn't realise a baby needed so much,' Eric laughed. Greta made gowns and bibs, hemmed cot sheets and napkins, while his mother made a fancy pram cover and quilted jacket. Meanwhile the Judd family knitted matinée jackets and bootees.

As her pregnancy progressed, Eric thought Greta looked more beautiful than ever, though she said she felt ungainly. She tired more easily now, and complained that she couldn't bend over.

'I'm tired of waiting,' she said. 'Fed up feeling like an elephant. I wish the time was up and the baby here.'

Christmas 1935 came round, and Greta saw to all the extra tasks it brought. She wrote Christmas cards, made and packed presents, and baked special cakes and puddings. They were all invited to the Judds' for dinner on Christmas Day, and Greta cooked a special meal for both families on Boxing Day.

For all of them, things felt a little flat once the festive season was over. Time seemed to crawl as January came and went. They were all counting the days of waiting that still stretched ahead. Greta was doing the household shopping now. Mam was always finding little errands for her to encourage her to get out in the fresh air.

But it was winter, and the weather was miserably damp and cold. Eric could understand why Greta preferred to huddle by the fire.

As the weekend came closer, the weather grew colder. On Sunday morning, it was icy, with hoar-frost on the windows. The scullery was icy too. Greta was wearing a cardigan over her pullover as she went out to wash the breakfast pots.

His mother went too, to get the Sunday dinner on. They always worked together, Greta usually preparing the vegetables while Mam made Yorkshire pudding and pastry for the apple pie.

As Eric sat at the living-room table, making up the accounts book, a shaft of wintry sun broke through the cloud and brightened everything up.

He went to the scullery door to say: 'We'll go for a run in the car this afternoon.'

'It's too cold for me,' Mam said. With the gas stove lit and the joint beginning to sizzle, Eric thought the scullery was beginning to feel much better.

'We're going round to my mum's for tea tonight,' Greta added.

Eric felt penned in. 'Do us good to get out this afternoon as well.'

Working at home was wonderfully convenient, but the downside was that he often felt caged indoors. He missed being able to get out and about and mingle with the crowds.

They were having a cup of tea after dinner when Peter came round.

'I borrowed Pat's van last night to come home and I can't start it,' he said. 'I think the radiator's frozen.'

Eric went out with him to have a look. 'Frozen solid,' he confirmed.

'I know I mustn't pour boiling water over it, I've heard that can crack the casing.'

'Should have given it an eiderdown last night.'

Peter smiled. 'That's no help now.'

'Hot-water bottles?'

'That'll take ages. I told Pat I'd go down and see him this afternoon to go through his order book with him. We never seem to find time in the week.'

'Well, I can run you there in my car. I was thinking of taking Greta out this afternoon.'

'Would you mind? But how d'you know you haven't got the same problem?'

Eric rented a garage on Storeton Road. They walked round to find out. The baby Austin started first time.

'Good little car this, it's never let me down.'

He drove it down into Woodchurch Lane and parked it outside his home.

'It's still below freezing.' Peter shivered. 'And with this wind . . . I'll get an old coat to cover it. Don't want any trouble now.'

'We'll be leaving in five minutes,' Eric laughed. 'Just as soon as we're all ready.'

'I'll not come,' his mother repeated. 'It's too cold for me.'

'You'll be fine tucked under the car rug,' Eric persuaded.

'I'm getting too old for it,' she smiled. 'I'd just as soon have an hour on the bed after dinner. Especially as we're going out for tea.'

'So would I,' Greta agreed. 'A rest on the bed sounds fine. You and Peter go. You can come back by five to take us down to Gorsefield Road.'

'No,' Eric protested. 'It's lovely out now. Sharp, yes, but the sun's out.'

It wasn't the golden sun of summer; everything was bathed in cold white light. The sky was of palest hazy blue, like ice itself.

'Come on,' he urged. 'After we've dropped Peter, we'll

take a run out to West Kirby and have a little walk along the prom.'

Reluctantly she said: 'I'll just wash my face and comb my hair then.'

He knew she was coming to please him rather than because she wanted to. He found their two car rugs. Out on the pavement of Woodchurch Lane, Greta shivered.

'I don't know about that walk along the prom. This wind cuts like a knife.'

The graceful Greta was awkward now. She eased herself into the front passenger seat and he tucked both rugs round her, encasing her arms underneath.

'You'll soon be warm.' The inside of the car felt icy and smelled of petrol.

Eric got in and started the engine. He remembered then about Peter's old coat and had to leap out to lift the bonnet and retrieve it. Peter slammed his front door behind him and came running over, his breath showing like steam in the frosty air.

Eric watched as he folded himself through the driver's door and on to the narrow back seat. Quite a feat for Peter, because he was so tall.

'I think this car's made for midgets,' Peter grinned, positioning his back into the corner behind Greta, and thus finding space for his long legs across the width of the car.

Eric put the engine in gear and they moved off. He loved driving. The car was his joy. He wouldn't hear a word against it, though today, he could understand Mam complaining it was draughty; the hood was flapping a little.

There was no traffic until he got down to Borough Road. There the car gathered a little speed. It didn't go fast, it was built for economy.

'Chugs along merrily, doesn't it?' Peter said. 'Our Frank said he needed something with a bit more go in it.'

Eric turned right and then left into Church Road. He

glanced at Greta and she smiled back. The pavements were almost deserted; the few people about were wrapped up in heavy coats and scarves. Pat had lodgings in a house at the bottom of Holt Hill.

Holt Hill was a high point. From the top Eric could see part of the town laid out below, bathed in the strange cold light. The steep hill stretched ahead. Automatically, he put his foot on the brake and was shocked to feel the car slide. Sudden fear shafted through him.

'Black ice.' Peter's voice came evenly from behind. 'Ice on the road.'

Eric gripped the wheel more tightly. What had he been thinking of? That there could be ice on the roads hadn't crossed his mind. He put his foot on the brake more gently, and at the same time applied the hand brake. It seemed to have no effect on their speed. The road fell away steeply in front of him.

'Take it easy.' Peter's voice was not so even now.

Panic gripped Eric. Everybody said the brakes on the Austin Seven were not very good and that it rolled badly when cornering. He no longer felt in control. The car was careering down the hill.

He put his foot down harder on the brake; the wheels screeched and the car skidded to the left. He had to ease off the brakes and fight with the steering wheel to keep it on course. They were nearing the bottom, where Holt Hill ran into Hinderton Road.

He wanted to turn left, but that was an acute turn because the road snaked to the right. He wouldn't be able to get round at this speed. He'd have to turn right. But that meant he'd have to avoid traffic going in both directions, and usually it was a busy road.

He was holding his breath. Beside him he saw Greta's hand come out to brace herself against the dashboard. He heard her deep intake of breath and knew she was as scared as he was.

He yanked on the hand brake, which controlled his front wheels. He had to slow them down.

The front wheels locked and the car went into a long skid. He heard Greta's scream of terror as they all saw the lorry at the bottom, travelling along Hinderton Road.

For a fraction of a second he thought he might just make it. He tried to go behind it and hoped to shoot through to the left-hand side of the road, but he was skidding out of control.

The left-hand side of his car hit the back wheel of the lorry. The recoil knocked the wind out of his body. He held on to the steering wheel, even though his arms felt as though they were coming out of their sockets and the noise of tearing metal was deafening. But worse by far were the screams of pain and terror that came from Greta.

He felt the car somersault and land back on its wheels the right way up. His head felt as though it had been jerked off his body. Everything was swimming round him and going black.

Chapter Twenty-Three

February 1936

Eric came round in the ambulance. He could see the attendant fixing an oxygen mask over somebody on the bunk opposite.

'Greta?' he croaked. His head throbbed.

'Hello. How are you?' The attendant adjusted the flow of oxygen. 'Not Greta. This chap was in the back of the car. What's his name?'

'Peter. Where's Greta?'

'In a different ambulance. Peter what?'

Eric told him. 'Is he badly hurt?'

'And your name?'

What had he done to Greta? 'Is the baby all right?'

'I'm afraid I don't know. Was she your wife? Somebody else is looking after her.'

Greta would be devastated if this made her lose the baby. What a fool he'd been to bring her out on such a day. What a thoughtless fool . . . Eric could feel himself drifting off in a sick stupor.

He kept coming round and worrying about Greta. He couldn't find out anything about her. It made him speculate, and his guesses horrified him. He knew he was in hospital now. He asked the nurse who was cleaning up the cuts and grazes on his face, but she didn't want to talk about Greta. She said she didn't know how she was but she'd find out for him. Then she gave him an injection that made him drift away again.

When the front door bell rang, Alice was setting out cups and saucers on the kitchen table for their tea, and Gran was cutting slices of the soda bread she'd made. Grandpa put down his newspaper and went to see who it was.

When Alice saw the policeman following him back up the hall, her heart missed a beat. He had his arm clasped round his helmet.

'Glory be!' Gran ejaculated. 'What's the matter?'

'Mrs Edith Luckett?'

'Yes.' Alice saw her moisten her lips.

'I'm afraid I've bad news for you. Please sit down.'

Gran collapsed on a chair. 'What is it?'

Alice was gripping the edge of the table in terror. At times like this, all her strength seemed to desert her. She felt as she had when she'd found her father dead. As though she was nine years old again.

'Peter Harold Luckett is your son?'

Alice closed her eyes as the police officer told them about the accident, about Peter's terrible injuries and Greta's death.

Greta's death! It conjured up images of tangled metal in her mind. An accident so bad she could hardly take it in.

'What about Eric Ainslie?' she whispered. She knew he'd been driving.

'Shocked, of course. Very shocked. He's hurt his neck, but compared with his passengers he seems to have escaped with relatively minor injuries.'

Grandpa's face drove home the horror of the accident. His eyes seemed glazed. Gran looked as though she'd had the stuffing knocked out of her.

'Have you told Mrs Ainslie?' Alice whispered.

'Yes.'

'I'll have to go to her . . .'

'Bring her in here,' Grandpa told her. 'She shouldn't be left on her own.'

Alice found Auntie Nell sitting quietly in her darkening living room. The fire had died down to a few red cinders. She was shaking and her hands felt like ice, but she was dry-eyed.

'I can't believe . . . It only seems a few minutes since they left.'

'They went straight after dinner.'

'I fell asleep on my bed. Greta dead! Poor Eric, he'll be devastated.'

'We're going to the hospital to see them.' Alice made up the fire. Auntie Nell would need warmth when she came back. 'You'll want to come too, won't you? We can all go together.'

It was only when she saw Nell sitting in the rocking chair in Gran's kitchen that Alice realised she'd never been in their house before. Gran poured the tea she'd made. Grandpa said there was a bus at six o'clock, they'd catch that.

'Eric's lucky to have got off so lightly,' Grandpa said.

'It'll destroy him,' Nell moaned. 'He won't be able to live with what he's done to Greta . . . And to Peter.'

Alice sat beside Auntie Nell on the bus going to the General Hospital. She could feel her shivering. Gran and Grandpa were sitting on the seat in front. Gran was sniffing into her handkerchief and mopping at her eyes. Alice was growing more apprehensive, dreading what they were going to find when they reached the ward.

She saw Eric as soon as they went in. She took Nell's arm and led her to his bedside, telling Grandpa she'd catch them up later. Eric's face was grey-white and without expression. He was staring into space and didn't see them come. Nell bent to kiss him.

Alice wanted to hug him but was afraid he might have wounds she couldn't see and she'd hurt him. His hands were clasped on the counterpane. She felt for one and squeezed that sympathetically. He hardly seemed to notice.

She felt sick. Greta's sudden and violent death had left her in an emotional turmoil. She'd felt torn and twisted like this when her father had died. When Greta had been alive she'd tried not to feel jealous and resentful. She'd wished something would happen to her, something to remove her from Eric's life. Most of all she'd wished he'd change his mind about her.

Now she was running with guilt that she had. She couldn't have wished this horrible violent death on Greta. She couldn't think of Greta's death. She mustn't let herself.

Eric was free again, but she couldn't feel glad. It was all so painful for him. She knew it would be years before he'd be able to think of anyone but Greta. Life wasn't as simple as she'd thought. This was making her grow up in a hurry.

'A terrible thing to happen,' she murmured. 'I'm so sorry.'

He was staring up at her with shocked glassy eyes. Alice didn't know what else to say. She was about to leave him to his mother when a nurse came.

'Could Sister have a word with you, Mrs Ainslie? Will you come with me to the office?'

Alice found the two small wards were run as one. Peter was in a side ward off a corridor that ran between the two. Both the office and the side ward had walls of glass. She saw Nell Ainslie being led into the sister's office, being offered a chair.

Gran and Grandpa were sitting one each side of Peter's bed, looking shocked to find him in such a state. Alice was appalled at his injuries. He was lying flat, without pillows, and had cuts and grazes on his face as well as an eye that promised to turn black.

Blood must have matted his hair; the nurses hadn't quite managed to wash it out. He had a saline drip running into one arm, which showed grazes and plasters. The other was covered with bandages and strapped to his side. There was a cradle over his legs to keep the weight of the blankets off them.

Alice stood gazing down at him, trying not to show the horror she felt. She'd always thought of Peter as having rock-like strength. She'd turned to him when in trouble, relied on him. Now he was reduced to a helpless wreck. They tried, one at a time, to talk to him. Alice watched him struggling to open his eyes, trying to focus. He managed a wavering smile.

Then the ward sister came in to speak to them. She told them Peter would be going down to theatre tonight for emergency surgery to reduce some of his fractures, and that he'd been sedated and was drifting in and out of consciousness.

A doctor joined them to say they would deal with his pelvis and femur tonight. He told them Peter's X-rays showed that his left arm had a particularly bad fracture. The bone had splintered into several pieces, some of which had pierced the skin. With deep wounds like these there was the added danger that they might become infected. To reset this was a specialist job and couldn't be done tonight. He'd have to go down to theatre again in a day or two.

Alice feared for Peter as she looked into the doctor's earnest face. He explained that Peter was very ill and would be in hospital for many weeks. With so many fractures it would take him a long time to get back on his feet.

She could see the colour draining from Gran's face. The next moment, Sister was pushing her head down between her legs. Even Grandpa looked ill. They were left alone with Peter then, but he seemed deeply asleep.

Eric could see that his mother was very distressed. She came very slowly down the ward from the office by herself, seeming not very steady on her feet. She slid on to the chair by his bed and took both his hands in hers.

'I'm sorry, love. So sorry.'

His heart wrenched with dread.

'They left it to me to tell you, but there's no easy way . . .'

He felt cold inside. 'Greta's . . . Greta's dead?'

He saw the tear roll down her cheek. Her voice was agonised. 'She was killed in the accident.'

He felt numb with shock, though he'd known it all along. The ward swam round him.

'I knew I'd killed her,' he whispered. 'And the baby?'

Mam was shaking her head. 'They said Greta died quickly of internal injuries. They took her to the maternity hospital in Grange Mount but they couldn't do anything about the baby. It was too late.'

The realisation that he'd killed her, that he could blame nobody but himself, was a weight on his chest that made it impossible to breathe. He didn't know how he was going to live without her. He certainly couldn't live with the guilt that he'd killed her. He'd been so thoughtless, careless and selfish.

'I knew she didn't want to come with me. I talked her into it. I killed her.'

'You mustn't say that.' His mother's face was gentle and loving.

'It's true.'

'It was an accident.'

'I was driving. She wanted to stay home with you. Why didn't I let her?'

Greta, who'd had such sparkle, who'd been so full of life, was no more.

'What about Flo Judd?'

'She knows. I'll go to see her on the way home. Aren't you going to ask about Peter?'

'The nurses told me.' The news wasn't good there either. 'He's here, in a side ward next to the office.'

'They say he's broken both legs and his pelvis.'

'And the rest,' Eric said hollowly. 'His collar bone, several ribs and his arm. I can't remember them all.'

'Have you seen him?'

'Yes, I walked down earlier. Mam, he didn't know me. He's in a bad way.' Eric swallowed hard. It didn't help that he'd escaped with nothing but a bruised knee and a whiplash injury to his neck.

His mother said softly: 'They tell me he'll mend, but it might take a long time.'

'What about his business?' It was a cry from Eric's heart. 'How's he going to run that over the next few weeks? Look what I've done to them. Greta and our baby, and Peter, the people nearest to me.'

'It was an accident,' Mam said firmly. 'An accident, you mustn't blame yourself.'

'But I do,' he moaned, turning his face into the pillow. 'I do.'

On the bus going home, Grandpa said: 'Couldn't have come at a worse time. Who's going to look after his business until he's on his feet again?'

Alice turned round in her seat to shake her head. Who indeed?

'Frank will have to do something,' Gran said. 'And that other partner of his.'

'Pat O'Neill?'

'Neither of them can do the baking,' Alice croaked.

The problem seemed enormous. She knew more about that part of the business than they did, because she'd worked there on all those Saturday mornings.

She could go in tomorrow at five o'clock and let Harry know what had happened. Help him for a few hours. Though they'd never be able to bake as much as he and Peter had managed together.

'It won't do to have the shop half-empty,' Grandpa warned.

'And the orders Pat has built up will have to be fulfilled. It'll harm the business if they aren't.' Alice shivered with dread. It would be a prodigious amount of work for one baker.

She had second thoughts. 'I know where Harry lives. I'll go round and tell him what's happened now. Warn him about tomorrow.'

She pulled up as another thought came.

'What about the Judds?'

'Nell said she'd go round to their house on the way home.'

'But will they feel like coming to work tomorrow? We can hardly expect it of Greta's mother. And even Alma? We'll need more help in the shop too. What are we going to do?'

'We'd best let Frank know,' Gran said. 'He doesn't go to work until tomorrow night. He can help.'

When Alice called at Harry's house, she found him and his wife listening to the wireless. They were shocked when she told them why she'd come. His wife insisted on making a cup of tea for them all.

'You mean Peter won't be able to work for weeks?' Harry asked.

'More like months.'

'We'll have to have another baker,' he said. 'I can't do Peter's work as well as my own.'

'Do you know anybody who'd come straight away?'

'Not off the top of my head.' He was frowning. 'I'll have a think.'

Alice said: 'I'll come in to help tomorrow morning. Could we start at four? With an hour's start, we might bake enough.'

She walked home with her head in a whirl. She needed to get to bed in readiness for her early start but she didn't know how she was going to cope. She was supposed to be at her desk at the Globe by nine.

Gran came home and said that Frank would ring Madeleine's boss and tell him she was ill. She would be at the shop by nine and serve there until the Judds felt able to return, and she might be able to get a friend to help her if needed.

Maddy had never settled in any job for long. She'd had seven different ones since leaving school. She was always chopping and changing, hoping to get a job that suited her better or paid more.

'All as dull as ditchwater,' she'd said to Alice. 'And I'm always unlucky with the boss. They've all been slave-drivers. I'd have been all right if Dad hadn't stopped me going to Lever's. They have all sorts of clubs for their workers there. They arrange tennis tournaments and dances and amateur dramatics and things like that. Are you happy at the Globe?'

Alice couldn't say she was. 'There's nothing like that there, nothing social, just work.'

'That might be all right for you.' Maddy had frowned. 'You aren't interested in boyfriends yet, haven't even had one. But I like to meet people and get about.'

Alice winced. Maddy was given to taunting her about her lack of boyfriends. She'd never wanted anybody but Eric. The trouble was, he'd been a non-starter.

Maddy had had a whole string of boyfriends; she was always talking about them. Alice had heard a good deal about Fred and Jeff and Don. Maddy had whispered that she was thinking of getting engaged to Don.

When Gran heard about it the following month, she'd exploded with disapproval.

'He's eighteen and still apprenticed. Nothing but a lad. He can't afford to keep a wife, not for years. Never be able to keep our Madeleine. Her mam's stuffed her head with big ideas. What's she thinking of?'

'She said she loves him.'

That made Gran snort with contempt. 'If Maddy put as much energy into her job as she did into finding boyfriends, she'd be able to settle and earn herself a decent wage. Plenty of time yet to think of getting engaged.'

Maddy was working in the council office at the moment, but wasn't enjoying it. She'd left some of her other jobs on the spur of the moment, so Alice wasn't concerned that she might leave this one.

'And Uncle Frank will help with the baking?' Alice wanted to know.

'No.'

'Then there mightn't be much to sell.'

'He said he knows nothing about baking and Pat will have to do more.'

That didn't ease Alice's worries at all. She was more than scared about what Pat would get up to. Especially now that Peter wasn't able to keep an eye on him.

It was too awful to think about. Greta was dead, Peter was in a terrible state and Eric was like a zombie. She felt sick as she realised what an impact this was going to have on her and the family.

For Alice, the next morning at the bakery seemed a chaotic scramble. Harry was past middle age and Peter had thought him a slow worker, but fortunately he'd been there long enough to know exactly what was needed, and he went about producing it methodically. Alice knew he was reliable and he'd do the best he could.

They started by making the bread dough, because that needed time to rise. Harry made their standard white dough for tins and cobs, while Alice made the wholemeal. When Harry mixed the lighter dough for the bloomer loaf, Alice made the Hovis brown. When they had enough bread dough, Alice started on fairy cakes, and put three batches in the oven. She made large sponges and chocolate sponges. She'd started to ice some of the fairy cakes before she had to rush off to her office job.

Alice hadn't watched the time carefully enough and was late getting to work. Mr Hunt was in a bad temper and told her off. She thought him equally as strict as the men Maddy worked for, but over the years she'd done her best to give satisfaction.

He dictated some letters, and for the first time she puzzled over the symbols she'd scrawled in her notebook and couldn't get the words back exactly as he'd said them. She did the best she could, rounding off the sentences to make sense. Her typing wasn't up to its usual standard either, and she had to redo some of the letters. Miss Jones didn't seem to notice; she prattled on about a film she'd seen over the weekend.

The problems Peter's business was facing were going round in Alice's head. She'd been working full pelt since four that morning and she knew she must do something about getting more help for Harry, otherwise she'd be doing it every morning.

At lunch time, she rushed round to an address Harry had given her, of a recently retired baker who was looking for part-time work. His wife told her he'd found a job, but that next door lived her fifteen-year-old grandson who was desperate for work of any sort.

Alice knocked there since it was handy, and liked the young lad. She offered him a temporary job because he'd be another pair of hands and was willing to start at five o'clock the next morning, but she explained that what she really needed was a trained baker.

She knew Uncle Frank would say she was getting too big for her boots; that it was not up to her to take on staff. But it seemed she could expect no help from him or Pat O'Neill with this. She wondered if she should advertise for a baker in the columns of the *Birkenhead News*.

When she got back to her office, she found she'd taken longer than the hour she was allowed for lunch, and the Cornish pasty she'd brought from the bakery was still uneaten in her bag. Miss Jones was cross with her, and Mr Hunt gave her a stern warning that she must never do it again.

The afternoon seemed long and wearisome, and when she got home that evening, she fell asleep at the table before she'd finished her tea.

Chapter Twenty-Four

The next morning, Alice found it a struggle to wake up, but she was at the bakery by five. Harry said they couldn't start every morning at four, it would kill them. He, for one, needed his rest.

Trevor, the young lad, turned up, and seemed eager to help where he could. Pat came in to collect his order before they had it ready. He felt their tea pot.

'No tea this morning?'

'We've had no time to make any,' Alice told him pointedly. 'Why don't you make a pot? We could all do with it.'

But he didn't. Instead, he pursed his lips and stood watching them scurry round.

'And don't go looking for new orders,' Alice said. 'We can't cope with any more work at the moment.'

'Do you know of an experienced baker looking for a job?' Harry asked.

'Peter's the only baker I know. How is he?'

Gran had phoned the hospital from the post office and had been told his operation had gone well.

Alice had four trays of cakes ready for Pat then, as well as the bread he'd asked for.

'Help me get these out to my van,' he ordered Trevor. 'I'll be back about midday for the rest. Can you manage that, Harry?'

Alice was on time getting to her office that morning and was able to keep her mind on the typing she was given. She didn't leave the office at lunch time, but even so, she felt Mr Hunt's manner was more distant than it had been.

On the way home, she called at Uncle Frank's house to let him know how difficult they were finding it to get more help in the bakery.

'I've just come from there,' he told her. 'Everything seems all right to me.'

'You've just been?'

'Yes, to cash up. Somebody has to empty the till at the end of the day.'

'Of course!'

Alice dropped her head in her hands. She'd forgotten what happened at the other end of the day. She couldn't leave her office until half past five. It was nearly six now.

She asked: 'How much did they take today?' and saw Frank's face change.

'What's it to you?'

That annoyed her. 'I just wondered whether the takings had gone down. Since Peter's accident.'

'I think they're about the same. I'm not sure.'

When Peter had first taken over the business he'd borrowed her school textbook on double-entry bookkeeping. He'd thought she knew more about that than he did and had discussed how best to set up his account books. They'd pored over Mr Best's books and tried to improve on his system. Peter had shown his accounts to her several times.

Alice said coldly: 'You could turn the page back to see what they took last week. Compare it with the same day.'

'We can only find his daily ledger.'

'That's the one you need.'

'But where are his other account books?'

Alice tried to think. Had they brought them back from the hospital with his clothes? 'Yes, he must have had them with him in the car at the time of the accident. I'll keep them up to date if you give me a note of how much . . .'

'I'll come over for the books some time. There's no need for you to interfere, Alice.'

Alice had never before lost her temper with Uncle Frank, but that made her see red.

'I interfere only in Peter's interests. I got up to work in the bakery at four on Monday and five this morning. It's desperate there without him. He ran that place, did most of the work. I'm shattered doing that as well as my own job.'

'All right.' Frank was holding up his hand. 'All right. I'm looking after the shop. Making sure they're managing there.'

Alice knew Alma Judd had returned to work. She took a deep breath and tried to calm herself. She was full of suspicions about Frank.

'I've taken on a boy to help temporarily, but we need somebody who knows the job. I came round tonight to see if you knew of anybody. It's either that, or advertise for someone in the newspaper.'

'What about a card in the shop window?'

'I put one there straight away, didn't you see it? It hasn't brought anybody in. We've got to get somebody, we can't let it drag on . . .'

'You should have let me know sooner. You could have come on Sunday with Mam and Dad.'

'I was arranging with Harry to start baking at four the next morning. I expected you to come to the shop. You're free most of the day and you own part of the business. I asked Alma this morning, she came in early, but she said she hadn't seen sight nor sound of you until closing time. You must have known what it would be like without Peter.'

'Pat said you were managing all right.'

'Pat! He doesn't understand. He came in and expected a cup of tea to be put in front of him. Didn't even notice we were all running round like March hares.'

'He's a good salesman.'

'Yes, well, we have to sort this out. Do you know a baker who wants a job for three or four months?'

'I might . . .'

Alice was having second thoughts. She was afraid Frank might put in another of his cronies. Peter wouldn't want that. Frank would take over if she wasn't careful; he was that sort. They had to get somebody Harry could work with. She wanted to keep the business running for Peter.

After her tea that night, she went round to see Auntie Nell to hear her news, and to pour out all the difficulties she was trying to sort out.

On Wednesday morning, Eric made himself walk down the ward to see Peter again.

This time Peter gave him a rueful grin. 'Hello, Eric.'

Peter's cheeks were grey. He had one leg in traction. Eric couldn't look at it.

'How are you feeling?'

'Not on top form. Nothing to eat or drink; I'm going down to theatre again this morning.'

'They told me.'

Peter indicated his left arm, which was heavily bandaged and splinted.

'Broken it to bits; the bone's coming through the skin. They're going to try and plate it.'

'I've made a terrible mess of you. Sorry, Peter.'

Peter was trying to smile, but it ended in a wince of pain.

It made Eric feel worse to see his friend suffering like that and to know he'd caused his terrible injuries. Especially when he himself had escaped so lightly. Too lightly. True, he had a whiplash injury to his neck and felt stiff and sore all over. He had plenty of bruises too, but what did that add up to by comparison?

Eric hadn't slept since the accident. His nights had been filled with terrible grief. He couldn't stop thinking of Greta. Her face was in front of him all the time. It made him feel sick to know he'd killed her, that he alone was responsible. Greta had only got into the car to please him.

Her funeral was due to take place on Friday, but if a thaw didn't come, it might have to be put off. The ground was frozen solid. The days and nights stretched ahead to Friday. He didn't know how he was going to get through them. He didn't know what he'd do if the funeral was postponed. Guilt was like a heavy weight on his chest; nothing would move it. He felt overwhelmed.

Sister had told him he'd probably be allowed home today. The specialist would see him on his morning round and decide. She'd arranged that his mother should telephone later on to find out. It seemed a mere formality. He was pronounced well enough to get on with his life. Mam hired a taxi to take him home.

Seated beside him, she said: 'You'll feel better once you're back with me.'

Eric didn't think he'd ever feel better. 'Mam, it's a miracle you weren't in the car too. I did my best to persuade you. Thank goodness you had the sense to stay home.'

'It wasn't sense,' Nell said. 'I didn't feel like going out that day.'

After such momentous changes in his life, it seemed strange to find nothing had altered at home. Here time had stood still; it was all so achingly familiar. Except that Greta was no longer here and the baby clothes that had spread from the front room to the living room had all disappeared.

'I put them away,' his mother said. 'I didn't want you to be reminded.'

But everything reminded him of Greta. The double bed in his room had been bought just before their wedding, and he still had to sleep in it. Greta's face cream was on her bedside table. The book she'd been reading was turned face down on the open page.

Her clothes would be in her wardrobe. He opened the door, waiting for a heart-rending tug. The hangers were empty; her clothes had gone.

'Mrs Judd's been, with Alma. They've taken some of her things.'

Eric sighed. 'How am I going to face Flo Judd after this?'

Mam was starting to cook dinner. She was busy, every movement she made was purposeful, while Eric could only hang around staring into space.

He felt he had to do something. Normally he'd have been sewing. He went to the front room and got out the grey worsted suit he'd started last Saturday. It was promised for a wedding in two weeks' time, so it had to be finished.

He lifted part of the jacket to his machine, but he had no energy and Greta's face was coming between him and the cloth. He was sitting over it, inert, when he heard light footsteps outside.

He knew it was Alice and was drawing back into himself. Nobody realised how hard it was to face people after what he'd done. How hard to look them in the eye, knowing he'd see blame there.

'Eric?'

She came behind him, put her arms round his shoulders and her cheek against his.

'You must be feeling terrible. I'm so sorry. I wish there was some way to help.'

'There isn't.' His tone was too brusque. He couldn't cope with sympathy. He'd had more than he could take from Mam, but when Alice straightened up, he felt he'd choked her off.

She crossed the room to her piano stool, took out some flowered material and started to sew.

'You helped me more than anybody when I went through my bad patch.' Her voice was soft, her eyes down over her sewing. 'You seemed to know what I needed then. I ought to know how to help you.'

'Nobody can help me. This is very different. My own fault. Nobody to blame but myself.'

His eyes were prickling; men weren't supposed to weep,

at least not in front of others. He'd wept in bed every night since. His tears were not far away now.

'Oh, Alice! If only I hadn't persuaded Greta to come with me. If only I'd thought about ice on the road. I could have gone round through town and avoided Holt Hill. If only I could put the clock back to Sunday dinner time.'

'We none of us can do that, but I wanted to when Dadda died. If only I'd gone home straight away. As soon as we realised he wasn't going to call for me on his way home from work. I could think of nothing else when we found him.' He could hear the agony in her voice. 'Neither could Gran and Peter.'

'Greta wanted to rest on the bed. If only I'd let her, she'd be here now.'

'With hindsight, we'd all do things differently.'

'I see her face in front of me all the time . . .'

'I saw Dadda's. I wouldn't let myself think of him. I knew, if I did, that I'd start crying again. I had to put him out of my mind.'

'You could do that?' He looked at Alice squarely for the first time. 'Put him out of your mind?'

'Not straight away.' Her voice was sad. 'It took time. Everybody thought Maddy would take my mind off my troubles, but to me she seemed like a bluebottle hovering round meat. I wanted her to go away and leave me in peace, but I couldn't get rid of her.'

'We all thought she helped.'

'In the end she did. She made me concentrate on my school lessons.' She smiled at him as she snipped the end of her thread.

'Do you know what helped me most?' Alice was rethreading her needle.

Eric tried to swallow the constriction in his throat. Nothing was going to help him.

'You did, you and your mother. I could feel the bond between you, the deep affection . . . Yet both of you had

281

time for me. You both showed me such kindness. I'll never forget that red velvet pinafore dress, or all those clothes you helped me make for Wobble.'

She was smiling at him. 'I loved coming here to your house. It seemed such a happy place. A refuge for me. I came whenever I felt low. You always cheered me.'

Eric was struck by Alice's confidence. Now she was strong, very different to the nine-year-old child he'd tried to comfort. Stronger than he was at this moment.

'Coming here took away the anger I felt, that it was my dadda who was gone. You gave me peace.'

He sat thinking of her words long after she'd gone, but they didn't banish Greta from his mind. He didn't want them to, not yet.

On Thursday morning, Alice almost went back to sleep after her alarm had gone off. She'd never felt more sleepy as she got out of bed. It was ten past five when she reached the bakery, but cycling in the cold, dark hours before dawn woke her thoroughly. Harry and Trevor had started work. She put on her apron and set to with them. It looked like being another very busy day for her.

Thursday afternoon between two and four was visiting time at the hospital. Alice wanted to talk to Peter about his business. She wanted his approval for what she'd done and his advice on how best to keep it running, but she knew Mr Hunt would not allow her time off on two consecutive afternoons.

Gran was planning to go in and see Peter. Grandpa had telephoned every day to find out how he was, and he was reported to be much better.

Although Alice spent much of her day answering the telephone in the office, she knew she'd be in trouble if she was caught using it for a personal call. On the way to work she stopped at a phone box. She rang the hospital to ask if she might visit Peter after work, explaining the reason. She was told this wasn't allowed now that Peter was off the acutely ill list, and if she wasn't free to visit on Thursday afternoons, then she must put it off until Sunday. She wished then she'd written a note to Peter and sent it with Gran.

Once at her desk, she worried about how she was going to ask Mr Hunt for time off on Friday. He seemed at his most forbidding this morning. Miss Jones was as chatty as usual, and told her about a forthcoming wedding in her family, a niece.

As the morning went on, lack of sleep began to catch up with Alice. She felt she could curl up on top of her desk and go to sleep. She pushed her shorthand notebook to one side and stood up. Walked to the window to wake herself up. She couldn't put off asking Mr Hunt any longer. Worrying about it was preventing her getting on with her work. Full of apprehension, she tapped on the door of his office.

'Come in,' he called. He always sounded fierce. His eyes raked her with displeasure. He didn't like being disturbed. 'Yes?'

'I was wondering if I might be allowed an hour or so off tomorrow afternoon.' She explained about Greta's funeral.

He was stern and unbending. 'Is she a relative? Normally we'd allow time off for the funeral of a close relative.'

'Not a very close relative,' Alice stammered. Her heart was hammering; she had to go. Eric needed her. 'I'll be happy to come back afterwards and work late to finish anything that's needed.'

'The office closes at half past five, Miss Luckett,' he said acidly.

She'd been toying with the idea of asking him for time off this afternoon as well. She lost her nerve. She'd have to put off seeing Peter until Sunday.

She was still waiting for his answer. 'I'm sorry, but I have to ask for this.'

He was drumming his fingers on his desk, undecided.

She felt desperate. 'I have to go.'

'Then I suppose you must. All right.' He let out a long,

exasperated sigh. 'I'm surprised you find time to work for us at all.'

She felt herself swaying on her feet. This week was packing an emotional punch that was knocking her sideways. She hadn't told him her working day was now starting at five in the morning, and that she was going very short of sleep.

Alice had never been to a funeral before and didn't know what to expect. When she went next door on Friday afternoon, Auntie Nell clung to her, terribly upset.

'Thank goodness you've come. I don't know how to comfort Eric. Greta seems everywhere in this house. I keep expecting to hear her laugh or come bouncing into the room. I can't believe she won't, that she's gone. It all happened so fast.'

Eric was a ghost of himself, grey-faced and over-smart in a dark suit and black tie. Flo and Alma Judd came, and they all watched from the front window for the hearse to draw up outside. When it came, Alice couldn't look at the pale coffin. There were so many flowers crowded round it.

Eric whispered: 'She's here. This is the end for Greta. The last time in this world anything will centre on her.'

'We'll all remember her,' Alice said gently as they walked out to the waiting cars.

'I'll never forget her. Greta trusted me and I killed her.'

'It was an accident,' Alice said fiercely. 'Greta will know that. Her trust wasn't misplaced.'

'Do you really think that?' He lifted his face to look at her for the first time.

'Of course.'

After a few moments he whispered:

'I won't see her ever again. That's hard to accept.'

The church was packed. Somebody whispered that it always was when somebody died young. Alice recognised a good many of her neighbours.

At the graveside, Alice clung to one of Eric's arms and Auntie Nell the other. He hardly seemed to know where he was or what he was doing. She'd never seen a man cry before.

After the funeral, they all went back to Nell's house. Edith had made sandwiches, and Alice had brought pies and cakes from the bakery and had helped Nell set them out on the living-room table.

Eric was withdrawn, Flo Judd looked downright ill, and everybody else was subdued. Alice couldn't eat anything; she felt shaken and upset. She handed round cups of tea, glad to have something to do, until Grandpa took her arm and asked if she wanted to go home. Gran whispered that it would be better to leave Nell and Eric on their own tonight. She was relieved to go.

To Alice, the funeral had brought throat-constricting emotion she couldn't handle. It had gone through her to see Eric weep. The world might consider his marriage over now he was a widower, but he didn't feel free. He didn't want to be free of Greta. For him, nobody else would do. Alice told herself she mustn't expect things to be otherwise.

Chapter Twenty-Five

February – March 1936

Alice went to bed early that night and wept into her pillow. She didn't know whether she wept for Greta or for Eric. She had to be up before five the next morning to go to the bakery.

Working there pulled her together. There was no time to think of anything else because they needed to bake more bread and cakes on Saturday than any other day. She reached her office in the nick of time, but sailed through the morning knowing she only had a half-day to work there.

She went home for the hot dinner she knew Gran would be cooking. Afterwards, she went to Peter's room and looked through the things they'd brought back from the hospital. The account books he'd been taking to Pat O'Neill's house on the day of the accident were amongst his clothes.

There was now a whole week of trading that needed to be entered. She did what she could, adding in the figures for what Pat had taken out. Then she cycled up to the bakery with them.

Alma Judd was taking another tray of freshly baked loaves into the shop. Alice thanked her for coming in. Harry had told her she'd turned up for work on Tuesday and been in every day since, except for Friday afternoon.

'I'd rather be at work,' Alma said. 'Gives me less time to think, and Mam was worried about both of us being off. She said it was letting Peter down when he couldn't do anything about it himself. It's bad enough that Maddy's had to give up her office job to come in.'

Maddy was behind the counter, serving a customer. The shop was busy this afternoon. Alice stood for a moment, watching her. Maddy had tucked her red hair under a white cap, but curling tendrils had escaped to frame her face. Her cheeks glowed, and she looked very pretty. She seemed to be enjoying herself, laughing with a customer. It made Alice wonder if office work suited her.

Alice heard the bakery door slam, and Pat O'Neill came up behind her.

'Got another order for Monday.' He pushed the paper into her hand and craned to look in the shop.

'Hasn't she blossomed? Ripe as a luscious peach, so she is.'

Alice didn't like that. She'd heard it said Pat had an eye for the girls, but she didn't think he should be ogling Maddy like this. She thought of him as Uncle Frank's contemporary, his friend. It hadn't occurred to her that he'd take this sort of interest in Maddy.

Pat seemed to be another Peter Pan. He never was going to grow up and act his age. He had a mop of brown curls, and over-innocent blue eyes. He'd never settled anywhere; never married nor made a real home for himself. She knew he moved from one lodging to another.

As the customer left the shop, Pat pushed past her.

'Hello, Maddy. It's on for tonight then? Where d'you want me to take you?'

Maddy turned to him with such a look of rapture on her face that Alice was left in no doubt about her feelings for Pat O'Neill. She was laughing out loud, more vivacious than ever.

Alice knew Peter had always checked his stores on Saturdays and ordered what he needed for the coming week. She had to take Harry to the storeroom with her to help make the list.

She knew who Peter's suppliers were; their bills were all neatly filed in his desk. There were standing orders with some. The only telephone was up in the Bests' flat and she knew Peter used that to phone through his orders.

The Bests were helpful, wanting to know how Peter was and how they were coping without him. Mr Best was much recovered. He'd spoken to both Frank and Harry and knew they were finding it difficult to get someone to take Peter's place.

'I'd love to come down and help,' he told Alice. 'I feel well enough now and it wouldn't be hard for me. I know the job like the back of my hand after all.'

'Absolutely not.' Mrs Best threw out her chest. 'I won't have it. I'm not letting you start that again. Getting up at five every morning. You'll kill yourself down there in that bakery.'

Alice said: 'Mr Best, you've been in the trade all your life. Do you know a good baker who'd come in and help Harry?'

'We were racking our brains last night, weren't we, Dora?'

'There must be dozens who've served their time under you,' his wife said.

'But are they free to come back now?' Alice asked.

'That's what I don't know. Look, I'll just write a note for you. Go and talk to this man; if he can't come, he might know somebody who can.'

Alice felt grateful. While she waited, Mrs Best chatted to her.

'You wouldn't believe the trouble I've had keeping him out of that bakery. As soon as he heard Peter was in hospital he wanted to go down and get his overalls on.

'He's better now, and before he takes another bad turn, I'm going to get him out of here. Right away, where he won't see what's going on. I think I've found a little house that would suit us. I'm taking him to see it tomorrow.'

With the note in her pocket, Alice ran back downstairs to

find the bakery had been cleared and scrubbed down. She took wages for Trevor and Harry from the shop till and put in a note of the amount she'd taken. She knew they'd want to be off home now.

Alma and Maddy would have to be paid, and she didn't know what she should do about Flo Judd. Uncle Frank came in then, so she asked him.

'She hasn't been to work at all this week.'

'But she's worked here for twenty-odd years.'

'Not for us, she hasn't.'

'I think Peter would want you to pay her. She manages the shop for him.'

'When she's here. I'll send half her wages home with Alma.'

Alice was writing the amounts down in the cash book.

'Here's a pound for you, Alice. You've been getting up early and all that. Only right you should be paid.'

'I was planning to take that up with Peter first,' she said. She thought Peter would want to be more generous.

The shelves in the shop were almost bare. A customer came in and bought the last two loaves. Alma collected the few cakes left on to one tray.

'We haven't had as much to sell today,' she said. 'Harry can't make as much on his own.'

'This baker you thought you could get . . .' Alice turned to Uncle Frank.

'No, no good. He's got another job.'

Alice told him about the note Mr Best had written for her. 'I'll go round and see him on my way home. If he comes recommended by Mr Best, he should be all right.'

'Don't forget to tell him it's only temporary.' Frank opened the cash register and started to cash up. 'It's nearly five, we might as well close. Maddy, divide the cakes that are left between us, we'll take them home.'

Alma was washing down the shelves. Frank was counting up the coins and packing them in the paper bags provided by the bank. Alice opened Peter's cash book and put it in front of the cash register.

'You might as well go,' Frank said to her. The tubes of coins were being packed into the leather pouch Peter used to transport the takings to the bank.

'You haven't entered the amount in the cash book,' she reminded him.

Frank raised his eyebrows, but he scribbled a figure on the page.

'Quite the efficient bookkeeper, aren't we?'

'You haven't entered any figures when you've cashed up all this week.' She ran her finger down the blank column. 'How will Peter know where he is if you don't do that?'

'I've got them somewhere.' Frank patted his pocket and took out a slip of paper. 'Well, I've got most of them.' He scribbled more figures in the cash book. 'I don't know what I did with Monday's . . .'

Alice said firmly: 'Until we know how much the shop's taken, we can't enter it in the ledgers. If we get behind with the accounting it makes it harder. Anyway, I want to take the accounts down to the hospital tomorrow. Peter will want to know how things have gone here.'

'Monday's figure was . . . Let me see . . .'

'I can get it from the bank,' she sighed. 'It'll be on the next statement.'

'The bank?'

Alice swallowed. 'You have paid it in?' She was afraid Frank wasn't paying the money into the bank as Peter did.

'It's all safe at home. You can't expect me to go running round to the bank every night. I've got to be down at the Carlton Hall before six.'

Alice watched him and Maddy climb into the very smart Rover he'd bought. She was afraid Peter could be heading for another disaster.

Alice was in bed by six o'clock that Saturday night and didn't

291

wake up until ten the next morning. She felt much better when she'd eaten breakfast, having had the sleep she needed.

She did her Sunday chores, making up her bed with one clean sheet and pillowcase. Gran didn't think it necessary to change both at once, it made too much washing. The clean sheet was the top sheet for one week and became the bottom for the next; it was quite good enough.

Then Alice gave her room a quick flick with a duster, brushed the lino and took her bedside rug down to the yard to shake. Gran expected that of her. She went next door as soon as she could. She wanted to see Eric. Auntie Nell was in the scullery, preparing dinner.

Eric was hunched over the living-room fire. Alice had never seen such a change in anybody. His hair needed washing and he hadn't even bothered to comb it. He looked totally downcast, staring into space, taking no interest in anything. She sat down on the other side of the hearth and talked, trying to cheer him up. He was apathetic.

She started to tell him about her difficulties at the bakery, mainly because they were uppermost in her mind, but it made Eric turn to her in greater misery.

'I've caused chaos in Peter's business, and that means everything to him; it's his way of getting a leg-up in life.'

Alice had to say: 'He won't see it that way, Eric. He won't blame you.'

'He can't blame anyone else.'

'He'll understand. He wanted you to go down Holt Hill. You were taking him where he wanted to go.'

Her heart went out to Eric; how could she not sympathise?

'Why don't you come with me to see him?'

'No, I couldn't. I've given you all this extra work and trouble too. A fine friend I've turned out to be.'

'I still see you as a very dear friend,' she choked. 'A friend who did all he could when I needed help.'

He let out a long and shaky sigh. 'Guilt is a terrible burden. I feel so low. Greta and all the other disasters are going round in my head the whole time. I feel as though I'm going mad. Do you think I am?'

'No. I'm sure I'd feel the same if I were in your place.'

Eric leapt up and poked the fire vigorously, though it didn't need it. She knew he was near tears again and struggling to control them.

She rushed on. 'But I'm not in your place, Eric. I can look at what happened as an outsider. I see it for what it was, an accident. An accident with terrible consequences, but an accident.'

He'd gained a moment's respite. He put the poker down and rested his hand on her wrist. 'Thanks,' he whispered.

'You've got to see it that way too. It could have happened to anybody.'

On the way out she stopped to have a word with Auntie Nell.

'Thank you for coming,' she said. 'You cheer him up.'

'I haven't this time. He's very low.'

Alice set out for the hospital as soon as she'd eaten her dinner. She wanted to get there early to talk to Peter. She was worried there were things she needed to straighten out. Gran and Grandpa were planning to come down to see him later.

When she arrived there were screens across the ward door and other visitors were waiting to go in. On the dot of two, the screens were pulled back and the doors opened.

She saw Peter through the glass, craning to catch sight of a familiar face amongst the visitors trooping past his side ward. He was propped up against a bank of pillows. The grazes on his face were healing and his drip had been taken down.

'Hello, kid,' he said as she went in. He seemed so much better she almost wept with relief. 'How are things? Mam said you were taking care of my business.'

She sat at his bedside and let the problems come pouring out.

'But I think I've solved one.'

She told him about the note Mr Best had given her to take to a baker he knew.

'His son's just out of his apprenticeship. He's agreed to come for a few months; his dad thinks it'll be good experience for him. I hope he'll be all right.'

'Cyril Wells, did you say? I know him! Worked with him when Mr Best was taken bad a year or two back. What's his son's name?'

'Hughie.'

'That's right, Hughie.'

'You know him too?'

'Only of him, but if he's anything like his father he'll be fine. Harry needs somebody young alongside him.'

'Thank goodness for that. It'll be easier next week.'

She told him how she'd gone in to help Harry every morning before going to the office.

'You can't work long hours like that.' Peter seemed overcome with all she'd done. 'It's killing. You've been wonderful to try.'

'I hope everything's going to be all right.' She told him about Frank and the suspicions she had.

Peter lay back for a few moments to think. 'He must know he can't take money belonging to the business. I'll have to have a word. Has Pat paid for what he's had?'

'I added up what he owes, but I didn't see him yesterday.'

'He always settles up on Saturday mornings,' Peter fumed. 'If we don't keep the accounts straight, we don't know where we are.'

'Perhaps he did, and put it in the till?'

'Nobody's put it in the cash book. It's impossible to run a business like this.' Peter frowned. 'Can't have everybody putting their oar in. There has to be one person in charge. Would you do it, Alice? Run it for me while I'm out of action?'

'Me? I can't control what Uncle Frank does. He's a law unto himself.'

'I'll tell him to keep away. Leave everything to you. He wouldn't come near if I was there. How d'you feel about giving up your job?'

Alice's heart turned over at the prospect. She'd told herself many times she must stay at the Globe Insurance. All the chopping and changing Maddy had done hadn't furthered her career, or even got her a job she liked better. But Mr Hunt was always carping at her. She wasn't all that happy there and she wanted to help Peter.

'It's a lot to ask of you. A lot to ask of anybody your age.'

'I'm seventeen.' Alice counted herself as grown up now.

'And it's just for a few months.' He looked worried.

'That doesn't bother me, but I don't know whether I could do it.'

'Of course you can! Frank won't keep the accounts straight. I'm afraid some of the cash might be going into his pocket. Pat ought to be able to, but . . . Did you order stores for next week?'

'Yes.'

'You've spent more time there than anyone else. You know how it runs. I can trust you. Say you will, there's nobody else.'

'Maddy's been serving in the shop. She's already given up her job.'

'She couldn't do it. You've done all the jobs there. You've more experience. More reliable too.'

'But Frank and Pat, they're your full partners. They just brush me aside.'

'I'll talk to them. They wanted to leave the running of it to me. It's too much like hard work for our Frank. I'll tell everybody you're acting for me. It'll get easier as you get used to it.'

'You're persuading me?'

'I'm not sure I should be asking you to give up your office job. You might not find it too easy to get another.'

'I'll risk that,' she smiled. 'Family has to stick together.'

'I'll pay you the wages you get now. No, five bob more, all right?'

'You bet.'

Alice looked up and saw Gran and Grandpa. 'More visitors for you. Oh! Here's Frank and Pat too. You will tell them?'

'I'll lay it on the line, don't worry. Thanks, kid, for all you've done. You're the tops.'

Sister was at the door within moments. 'Only two visitors at the bed at any one time. That's the rule.'

'I'll go.' Alice kissed him. 'I've had my innings. I'll come again.'

On Monday morning, Alice was at the bakery again at five. Hughie Wells turned up. He was young and energetic, just what Harry needed. She thought they'd make a good team. Of course Trevor turned up too, and she had to tell him he wouldn't be needed after today. She gave Harry the money to pay him off.

She left in good time to get to the Globe by nine. The first thing she did was write out her letter of resignation, giving the one week's notice that Mr Hunt had stipulated. That gave her some satisfaction. She took it into his office with the morning's post.

'Mr Hunt,' she began, 'I want . . .'

'Don't bother me now,' he snapped. 'Can't you see I'm busy?' She left her letter of resignation on his desk with the post.

Half an hour later, she heard his bellow of rage above the noise of her typewriter. He came to the door, waving her letter.

'I don't know what you young girls are coming to. None of you want to work. We put ourselves out to teach you the routine and this is the way you treat us. You're more trouble than you're worth.'

For the rest of the week, she thought he piled more work on to her than usual. He gave her copy-typing to do if there was nothing more urgent. Some of it didn't seem necessary. He was making sure she didn't have a minute to herself.

'You haven't got yourself a job with another insurance company?' he asked.

'No, a bakery. I'm going to work in the family business. I told you last week that my uncle was in hospital.'

Mr Hunt pursed his lips and looked as though he didn't believe her.

Alice felt more in control of the bakery now she'd talked to Peter and knew what he wanted. Now Harry had a trained assistant, she didn't get up at five, just popped in for half an hour before going to the office, to make sure they were all right.

She returned there straight from the office, by which time the shop had closed and everything was locked up for the night.

Maddy waited until she came. She counted out what was in the till and left it ready for Alice to take to the night safe. She said her dad had paid last week's takings into the bank and wouldn't be coming in to do anything in future.

Flo Judd didn't return to work. Alma said she was ill, that she couldn't get over Greta's sudden death and didn't have the energy to work. Since Maddy wanted to stay on, that wasn't a problem for Alice. Alma had been working there for years and was quite capable of running the shop.

On Saturday, Alice was paid off by the Globe. It gave her a sense of freedom to know she wouldn't have to go in again on Monday. Things would be easier now she could concentrate on the bakery.

She cycled up after she'd eaten her dinner, to pay the wages and check the stores. Later in the afternoon, when the bakery had been scrubbed out, she found Maddy there, giggling with Pat O'Neill. She felt another surge of dislike for him, but before she could ask, he paid her for the goods he'd collected to meet his orders over the last two weeks. She felt she could now bring the accounts up to date.

Alice felt so much better that she called in to see Eric. He was alone in the front room, sitting at his machine but not sewing. She told him what she was doing at the bakery.

'Peter's much better,' she said. 'Why don't you come to the hospital with me tomorrow to see him?'

'I don't know . . . Wouldn't he rather see his family?'

'Eric,' she smiled, 'you know he wants to see you. You two were always together.'

She heard Auntie Nell showing out a customer who'd come for a fitting. She followed her up the hall to the scullery, saying:

'Peter's still stuck in bed with his leg in traction, but to talk to, he seems almost his old self. It'll do Eric good to see how much better he is.'

'It'll do him good to get out.' Nell was filling the kettle to make tea. 'I can't persuade him to cross the doorstep.'

'Not since the accident?'

'Well – apart from the funeral. He doesn't want to meet people. If a customer comes here, he hides himself out of the way.

'You and me, we're the only ones he can cope with. He used to love getting out and about, but not anymore. Won't even go down to the shops, and he knows everybody here in Woodchurch Lane.'

'I'll come for him tomorrow.'

'What time?'

'Quarter past one, I won't let him say no.'

'I'm very grateful . . .'

Alice said: 'Why don't we all go to the pictures tonight? There's a good film on at the Carlton Hall. It would get him out and he won't have to talk to anyone.'

Auntie Nell was pleased, and Eric's gloom seemed to lift a little. Alice was looking forward to it. It seemed a long time since she'd had the energy to go to the pictures.

She watched Eric as he bought their tickets in the foyer.

Frank said: 'Hello, Eric, how are you? Our Peter seems

on the mend now, thank goodness. Living the life of Riley; waited on hand and foot in that hospital.'

Alice thought he'd said just the right thing to lift Eric further. Auntie Nell was beaming at them both; she thought so too.

Afterwards, they all said they'd enjoyed the film, but Alice knew her mind had wandered. She hadn't been to the Carlton Hall for ages and had rarely seen Frank at work. It was obvious to her now that his lifestyle didn't equate with his job.

Chapter Twenty-Six

March – April 1936

As the weeks went on, Alice thought she was managing the bakery reasonably well. Peter said he was delighted with everything she was doing. Pat was continuing to get more orders, and they were increasing both turnover and profit.

She went to see Peter on Thursday afternoons now, because that left more time on Sundays for those who had to be at work in the week. She took the cash book in with her and Peter checked the work she did in the ledgers.

'Frank hasn't been near,' she told him. 'He's left me to get on with things.'

'I told him he had to.' Peter grinned at her. 'And how about Pat? He's not giving you any trouble?'

'No . . . but I'm seeing more of him. He's always at the shop.'

'He has to come in, Alice. Every morning to collect his orders, and again in the afternoon if he has a new one.'

'More than that. He spends every lunch hour with us. He's always chatting up the girls in the shop.'

'Alma, you mean?'

'I kept asking myself what the attraction was. He keeps his distance from me, he knows I don't like him. It wasn't until Maddy started talking about him that I realised it was her he comes to see. She seems very fond of him.'

'She's too young!'

'She's seventeen, like me,' Alice told him. 'We're old enough to do adult work, but not old enough to have adult fun? Is that it?'

'I didn't mean that, kid. Pat's been around a long time. I'm not sure he's the type I'd choose for Maddy. He's over thirty.'

'Twenty-seven, she says.'

'What else does she say about him?'

'She thinks he's lovely. She doesn't like raw youths who still have to make their way in the world. He's taking her out in the evenings. Two or three times a week, and he's giving her a good time.'

'Does Frank know?'

'I don't know. Why shouldn't he? Pat's his friend, isn't he?'

'He may not approve of him taking Maddy out.' Peter pulled a face. 'I wish I could come home and get on with my life. It's like being in prison here.'

'How much longer?'

'Weeks, I'm afraid. Can't put much weight on my leg yet, but at least they're getting me out of bed. How are things out in the world?'

'Just the same. Eric's still very low; he says he'll never drive again.'

'Wait till I get out of here. I'll soon persuade him.'

About two months later, the Bests were ready to move out of the flat over the shop.

Alice was pleased for them and knew Peter would be too. He was making progress now and talking of being allowed home within the next couple of weeks. He could get round the ward on crutches and had been moved out of his side ward.

Peter planned to move into the flat over the shop, but Alice knew that even when he was discharged from hospital he wouldn't be well enough to live there by himself. The stairs were steep and narrow. Of course there were stairs at home, but they were easier. Even so, Gran was talking of having his bed in the front room for a week or two until he was stronger.

The day the Bests moved out was one of continual footsteps on the stairs and removal men shouting to each other as they took furniture and belongings down to the waiting van. When the doors banged shut for the last time and the van drew away, Alice went upstairs to look round.

Mrs Best had told her they were leaving the lino on the floor and the curtains at the windows in readiness for Peter.

'You don't want the place to look empty,' she'd said. 'Not when you've got all those stores down in the bakery.'

'That's not the real reason,' Mr Best had chuckled. 'She's set her mind on having everything new for the next house.'

Alice thought the flat would be ideal for Peter. It wouldn't need too much furniture, and it was in a good state of decoration. Mrs Best was house-proud. The kitchen was better than that at home, and there was a proper bathroom with hot water that came out of the taps. Gran would love that.

On Sunday, she went down to visit Peter and tell him that the flat was empty.

'Mam says I can take the furniture from my bedroom when I move in,' he told her. 'And she can fix me up with a few more things.'

'It'll be a little while yet,' Alice said.

'Not long. I think I'll be allowed home next week. I'd be able to use walking sticks if my left arm wasn't so weak. But I'll be walking without them soon. I'm working on it.'

On Monday morning, Alice was tidying the shelves in the storeroom before unpacking the new stores when she heard the door of the flat slam shut above her. She caught her breath and had fleeting visions of burglars. The strength was ebbing from her knees as she rushed to the bottom of the stairs. She recognised the tuneless whistle first, then Pat O'Neill came clattering down.

'What are you doing up there?' Her tone was sharp; she felt

indignant. Pat was everywhere in this business. She thought he had rather a sheepish look on his face.

'I've moved in,' he said.

'You can't do that.' Alice rounded on him. 'Peter intends to live here.'

'Frank said it would be all right.'

'Well, it isn't. Peter needs it. It'll be easier for him to run this business if he's on the spot.'

He said easily: 'Peter's out of action. Won't be able to live here yet awhile. Frank will fix it with him.'

Alice felt a rush of anger. 'Why didn't you say something? Peter doesn't know. You might have asked him first. You moved in here yesterday when you knew I wouldn't be about.'

'Sunday's the only day I don't have to work,' he said. 'The only day I have time to move. It'll be all right. We'll fix it with Peter, don't you worry.'

But Alice did worry. She was furious with Pat, and with Frank too. She felt Peter expected her to protect his interests, and she'd let this happen.

'Did you know Pat was moving in?' she demanded of Maddy the moment she came in.

'I helped him,' she said. 'Dad said it was all right for Pat to have it. Better if the flat wasn't left empty.'

Alice was displeased with Pat and Maddy. It didn't help that Pat stayed up in the flat instead of coming to deliver the orders they'd made up for him. Nor that trade in the shop was unusually slow, giving Maddy an excuse to go upstairs to him, leaving Alma to serve all comers.

At mid-morning, two hours late, Pat loaded his van and went to deliver his orders, while Maddy returned to the shop. Shortly after twelve he came back.

'I need to get myself straight upstairs,' he said to Alice as he passed her office. Maddy must have heard his voice, for the next moment she was following him upstairs.

'Aren't you needed in the shop?' Alice asked pointedly. There were several customers in at that moment.

'It'll be closing soon. Nearly lunch time.'

'I think you might wait until it does,' she said, but Maddy gave a little laugh and ran up.

Alice didn't know what she could do about it. She wouldn't be able to tell Peter until Thursday, and she knew if she did it would only make him feel more frustrated because he wouldn't be able to do anything about it either.

More customers were coming into the shop. More than Alma could cope with. Alice went to give her a hand. She found Alma was as cross with Maddy as she was.

'Always beetling off after Pat,' she complained. 'Never stops to think she might be needed here.'

When the shop closed at twelve thirty, Alice did what Peter always did: made a pot of tea and sat down with the rest of the staff round the big table in the bakehouse. He'd allowed the staff to eat whatever they chose from the newly baked stock.

Alice helped herself to a meat pie and a doughnut. When Maddy didn't appear, she felt frustration building up inside her. As soon as she'd finished eating, she wheeled her bike out of the yard and rode round to Frank's house. She meant to complain.

His Rover was parked outside his front door. Alice propped her bike against the front step and rang the bell. It surprised her when Cecily came to answer it.

'Oh! I thought Uncle Frank would be alone. I want a word.'

'Come in.' Cecily looked none too pleased to see her. 'I come home for lunch sometimes.'

Frank looked up from his meal. They were eating in the kitchen. 'She makes me fetch her.'

'From the Grange Road salon,' Cecily said, sitting down at the table again. 'I go to the Prenton one in the afternoons. With two to look after, it's the only way.

'Frank's teaching me to drive, so I won't have to bother him much longer.'

'Are you going to get a car of your own?' Alice marvelled at what Cecily was doing.

'Yes, I need to. Do you want a cup of tea?'

'No thanks, I've just had one.' They were both looking at her expectantly.

'It's about the flat,' Alice said, looking Frank in the eye. 'I don't think you should have told Pat he could move in. Peter won't like it.'

Frank chewed on his food for longer than seemed necessary.

'No point in leaving it empty for months. Pat's been put out of lodgings; he'll find somewhere else before Peter wants it.'

'He'd better start looking now then. Peter's keen to move in.'

Alice didn't like to think of Pat being there. 'It gives Pat the free run of the premises during the night hours.' She was afraid of what he might get up to.

'Pat owns one third of the business. It makes things more secure. I can't see the problem.'

'Peter won't like it. He's family, he's your brother. Surely you want to help him while he's ill?'

'Of course he does.' Cecily's voice was mocking. 'Frank feels strongly about family.'

Alice went on: 'You know how much this business means to him. He's worried stiff about what's happening to it. He's stuck in hospital and feels he can't do anything.'

'You forget, I own one third of it too,' Frank said sharply. 'I'll take good care of it.'

'But you aren't,' Alice blazed. 'What you're doing makes things more difficult for me.'

Frank laughed. 'I can't see . . .'

Alice felt her hackles rising. 'Maddy's supposed to serve in the shop, but she's spent most of the morning upstairs with Pat. And that's upsetting Alma.'

'Upstairs with him?' Cecily put her half-eaten sandwich down on her plate.

306

'In the flat. She's always with him. Surely you know? Pat's her new boyfriend.' They were both staring at her, astounded.

'Nonsense,' Frank said irritably. 'He's too old for her.'

Alice drew herself up; it wasn't nonsense. 'She said she was with him most of yesterday, helping him move in. You must know that?'

'She told us she was going to the pictures with you.'

Alice took a deep breath. She knew Maddy would be furious with her for opening her mouth. It was too late to stop now.

'Not me, I haven't been to the pictures for weeks. Pat's taking her out in the evenings. Maddy's always full of it. You must have heard.'

'No.' Cecily was glowering. She turned to Frank. 'Come on, I'm going back to work. You can go up and put a stop to it right away. I don't want our Maddy alone with him. You know what he's like.'

Frank felt his plans were spiralling hopelessly out of control. Cecily drove the short distance to Woodchurch Lane, but it didn't stop her letting fly.

'You men are all the same. Sex is the only thing you ever think about.'

'And money,' Frank added. 'Sex and money, you tell me that often enough.'

'It's the truth.'

He wished sex was more often on Cissie's mind. She was miserly in what she meted out to him, and he was failing to get it anywhere else. Not these days. Once or twice maybe, but not on a regular basis. Cissie was ruling the roost now because of that. She'd got the upper hand.

'I wouldn't trust your friend Pat within a mile of Maddy. You've got to stop it. He tried it on with me, years ago, the nerve! Thinks no woman can resist him. I sent him off with a flea in his ear. Well, I told you at the time.'

Frank sighed. 'Before we were married.'

'We were engaged! But there was Ena Worral last year, then Joan something, and Mary Thompson. He got her pregnant.'

'You don't have to tell me.'

'And he's never twenty-seven. That's what he's telling Maddy. Damn it, Frank, he's older than I am. He's nearer thirty-five and she's only seventeen. She'll be putty in his hands.'

'Perhaps Pat's serious about her . . .'

Cecily gave a hollow laugh. 'He's serious about all of them – for all of three months. Then he drops them like hot pokers because he's found another girl to be serious about. I know he's your friend, but he's a rogue. He'd make a rotten husband. We don't want Maddy mixed up with the likes of him.'

Frank felt even more strongly about it. 'Course we don't. We want her to have a good life, and she won't get it with him.' He wasn't sure how far he could trust Pat.

'We've got to take care of her. Maddy doesn't know what he's like.'

He knew Pat was a trickster and he didn't trust him; he wasn't sure he was getting his rightful share of some of the jobs they pulled. 'I'll tell Maddy to drop him.'

She sneered at him. 'You'll have to lay it on stronger than that.'

When Cissie got out at her salon, Frank drove straight on to the cake shop. Alice was surprising him. He'd thought of her as quiet and mouse-like, but she could come out as strong as Cissie when she was crossed. She was doing well with the business, bags of confidence in herself. Not a bit like Beryl.

The cake shop was just opening after lunch. When he parked outside he could see Maddy behind the counter with Alma. She was serving a customer, and with her bright hair tucked neatly under her cap, she looked every inch a model shop assistant.

There was plenty of bread on show, and the shelves were filled with delicious-looking cakes. As he went in, his head was filled with the mouth-watering scent of baking. Everything seemed to be running perfectly.

He nodded to the girls as he went through the shop and up to the flat to find Pat. As he climbed the stairs, he saw Alice had got back before him and was in the cubbyhole of an office.

'He's gone out,' she called after him. Frank hammered on the door, and when there was no answer, tried to get in. The door was locked. He went back to the office.

'Everything seems fine,' he told her. 'Maddy's serving in the shop and Pat's out working. Why make such a fuss?'

Alice sighed; he knew he hadn't soothed her.

'I've made out the list of stores we need for next week,' she said. Her finger tapped impatiently on the two-page list on the desk. 'But I've got to place the orders. Mrs Best always let me in the flat to use her phone. I shouted after Pat as he went out, but he didn't hear. Now the phone's behind a locked door. What am I supposed to do? Walk down to the post office?'

He drove her home to use his phone. Cecily had insisted on having one put in, so she could ring up and get him to fetch her. She treated him like her personal servant.

It took several phone calls, then he had to drive Alice back to the shop. Pat hadn't returned and Maddy was still serving. He decided to put off talking to her until he could do it at home. She'd fly at him if he told her to lay off Pat. He'd do it, but he wanted Cissie there to back him up.

It was partly Cissie's fault. She'd spoiled Maddy over the years by giving her everything she wanted; never saying no to anything. It was Cecily's way of getting Maddy to side with her, and against him. He felt pushed out of his own family.

He felt lost without Cissie's affection, only half the man he once was. He hated fighting with her, yet nothing he said would make her stop it. At one time everything she did showed her love for him; everything she said built him up. Now she was trying to make him look small, build herself up. He felt lost without her support and love.

But they were together on this. Neither of them wanted

Maddy mixed up with Pat O'Neill. They both knew him too well. He was far too randy for a young girl to handle.

That afternoon, Cissie rang up wanting to come home an hour earlier than usual. He told her how he'd found things at the shop, and she wasn't pleased that he hadn't yet warned Maddy off Pat.

'You've got to do it,' she insisted. 'We've got to stop it before there's any trouble.'

Cissie had left a casserole, with instructions to put the oven on at half past three. Now a lovely savoury smell was spreading from the kitchen. For a few moments, Frank stood at the door watching her chop cabbage, taking her irritation out on that. Then he went up to his bedroom to change into his uniform.

He stayed up there out of her way, contemplating his front garden from the window. It was one way to get the peace he needed.

Cissie had called up to say she was just about ready to put dinner on the table when he saw Maddy being dropped off at the gate from Pat's van. There was a spring in her step and a smile on her face as she came running up the drive.

'I don't want any dinner, Mam,' she called from the hall. 'I'm going out again.'

Cissie was out of the kitchen in a flash. 'No, you can't do that. Where are you going? You can't skip meals.'

'I'm not hungry.'

'If you're not hungry, it's because you've been stuffing yourself with cakes all day.'

Frank went slowly down. Maddy seemed to sparkle with youth and health. 'What's the rush?' he asked. 'Where are you going?'

'Just out with Alice. We thought we'd go down to the Savoy to see . . .'

Anger swept through him. 'Don't you mean with Pat O'Neill?' He watched her face fall. 'I've been talking to Alice today. I know you aren't going with her.'

'What's she been saying?'

'Enough.'

'The dirty sneak! She's been telling tales.'

'There's no point in telling lies about who you're going with.'

'Maddy, come and sit down. We want to talk to you.' Cissie's voice was heavy with assumed patience.

'I haven't time now. I want to get ready.' The sparkle had left Maddy, she looked alarmed.

Frank said: 'You aren't going out with Pat. Your mother and I think you should drop him.'

'Drop him? He's your friend! You must like him.' Her face was screwing with thought. 'Your partner too! You see a lot of him; why shouldn't I?'

Cecily had edged Maddy to the sofa in the sitting room.

'He's old enough to be your father, and he's always got some woman in tow. I don't want it to be you.' She went on to list Pat's previous girlfriends.

Frank went on to tell her Pat's faults. 'So now you understand what we're on about. You can phone him and tell him that what you were planning for tonight is off.'

'No! You can't stop me seeing him. You don't understand. He loves me, and I love him.'

Cecily groaned. 'We understand all right.'

'You can't just say "drop him".'

'We have,' Frank said. It was almost bravado that made him add: 'And that's that. You'll do as we say.'

He knew she'd flout his authority. Other men had daughters who obeyed their parents. Maddy wasn't the dutiful sort.

'You can't stop me seeing Pat.' Maddy's handsome eyes flashed defiance.

'I can stop you going out tonight,' Cecily told her.

Frank wished she'd been as strict over the last few years. It might have worked when Maddy was younger.

'But I'll see him again at the shop in the morning.'

'The shop! We're disappointed, Maddy, that you haven't

done better for yourself.' He knew Cissie was upset. She was ambitious for her daughter. 'A shop assistant! What sort of a job is that?'

Frank added: 'You were so clever at school, and with your training you could hold down a good job in an office.'

She turned on him with the fury of a tiger. 'And whose fault is it that I don't? Who stopped me taking the job I was offered at Lever's? I blame you, Dad. You and Grandpa.

'Last week, I saw a girl I knew at school. She's working there and loves it. They all do. She's been promoted to secretary, and earns three pounds twelve shillings now.'

Frank said stiffly: 'There are plenty of good office jobs about. You just won't settle down and do them.'

'Not good ones. You stopped me taking the best one I was offered. I'd have been happy there, I know. I'd have settled.'

Cissie was frowning. 'You aren't doing as well as Alice now. You're letting her get ahead.'

'Alice? I'm sick of hearing about her. What she can do and I can't.'

'You'd have been better in hairdressing, like your mother. Anyway, you won't be staying on at the cake shop. It was only meant to be temporary, until Flo comes back.'

Maddy bared her teeth. 'I like it. I'm happy there.'

'You're just an ordinary shop assistant.'

'It's a family business, isn't it? Why shouldn't I work there? You're always interfering, trying to stop me doing what I want. Telling me what I should do, and what I shouldn't. And you're wrong about me and Pat.

'There's no way you can stop us. We love each other. We want to get married soon. He's asked me.'

'What?' Cissie was aghast. 'Tell her, Frank, we won't give permission. Not to marry the likes of him.'

'You think you know everything,' Maddy sobbed at them. 'You're wrong about him. I love him.'

Chapter Twenty-Seven

April 1936

Frank hardly had time to eat his dinner after facing Maddy, but by then he had no appetite for it. What was the matter with his family? Everything he did was for them, and yet they were all at his throat. He didn't understand why Cissie and Maddy had turned against him.

All these rows were not good for him; they made him jumpy. He yearned for a calm and peaceful life. It was all getting too much for him.

He had to rush then to get to the Carlton Hall on time. That was bad for him too. There was no time for a Gold Flake in the cloakroom to settle his nerves. As he went upstairs to take off his hat and coat, he met Percy, the commissionaire, coming down to open the doors.

Shirley Temple smiled sweetly at him from huge photographs in the foyer. They were showing her in *The Littlest Rebel*. It wasn't her latest; they'd shown it before some time ago and it had done very well. It was the beginning of the week and unusual to get a full house, but there seemed to be a long line of customers, many with children, waiting to buy tickets.

He was short of money again; it seemed he was perennially short of it. It seemed to disappear faster than he was able to make it, and he was always desperate for more. Cecily was pressing him to get her a car of her own. He'd told her she could pay for it out of the profits of her shops; she could afford it. He knew she'd make him pay towards it. These days, she always did.

With that in mind, he had to sell as many of his own tickets as he could. Almost every time he was asked for balcony seats he unloaded his own. He didn't know how long it had been going on, but the line of people waiting to get in the cinema still stretched out to the street. It was only when he saw Hilary come flying down that he stopped to think what he was doing.

She knocked on the door to his ticket booth, which he had orders to keep locked for security reasons. She was thumping like a mad thing and calling his name. He had to count out change to the person he was serving before he could open the door. She was already at the ticket window.

'No more,' she hissed. 'Butterballs is on the balcony, he's watching me. No more.'

'What's he doing there?'

But she was gone in a flash of maroon serge, leaving him with a racing heart. Hilary had told him recently that the manager was spending more time walking round, watching them. As though he suspected they were fiddling. She was nervous about it. What had he been thinking of? He was usually so careful.

Percy was organising the queue into a more orderly formation.

'Could be heading for a full house,' he grunted to Frank as he marshalled the next customer at the ticket window.

Frank felt another tug on his nerves. 'Who'd have thought it, on a Monday?'

'Schools are closed. Half-term.'

That made him panic. He'd forgotten. He craned his neck but he couldn't see the end of the queue, and they were still asking for balcony seats.

The official ticket machine counted each ticket he sold. There were four hundred seats on the balcony, and he'd sold

314

two hundred and thirty official tickets. What he didn't know was how many he'd sold for his own account. He needed to stop and count up what he had left. It wouldn't do to sell more seats than were available. And if old Butterworth was watching, it was dangerous to sell more than could be safely lost amongst those holding genuine tickets.

At last the line of people had all gone in. Frank felt a nervous wreck. First house had started; he could hear the sound track. They were almost full. He'd heard Percy shout that there were only singles left in the cheap seats some time ago. More had bought seats in the back stalls after that.

According to the ticket machine, there should still be eighty-three vacant seats on the balcony. Keeping one eye on the ticket window, he furtively added up the cash he'd taken for himself. He reckoned he'd sold sixty-six. That was a near thing, and Hilary would have had trouble finding seats for couples to sit together. Surely Butterballs would see at a glance that there were not eighty-three empty seats?

Frank felt the sweat breaking out on his forehead as he filled in his book. Then he entered the number of tickets he'd sold into the three columns: front stalls, back stalls and balcony.

Now the big picture had started, there would be no more customers. They'd be waiting for the second house. Usually at this time he took the takings and the paperwork up to Mr Butterworth's office. Frank was worried that the manager might already have counted the few empty seats on the balcony and know there was a discrepancy.

He felt he'd been getting away with this for too long. It was a miracle old Butterworth hadn't rumbled it long ago. Frank thought he'd been looking at him oddly. Recently, he'd seemed to check his money and his figures more carefully.

It was time he left this job. He was fed up to the back teeth with it anyway. Even Hilary was getting him down, and she was jumpy too, saying the boss was always on the balcony, looking at the number of seats filled. Nothing had been said to any of the staff, but that didn't mean it wouldn't be tonight.

He wouldn't dare sell his own tickets for second house, not after this. He took them from the drawer and stuffed them in his pocket. He put his own money in the leather pouch he kept for the purpose, and put that in his pocket too. If Butterballs was suspicious when he saw the figures, he didn't want him to come straight down here and look for evidence of fraud. And if that happened, he didn't want it in his pockets either.

He slid out the drawer in which the official cash was kept. It was designed to come out in this fashion, and had a wire clip for bank notes and scooped hollows for coins. Then he went reluctantly upstairs towards the office.

The cloakroom for male staff was at the top of the stairs. He went in. It was a cold place, with a lot of white tiles and a sash window that had jammed three inches open. There was a row of pegs for outdoor clothes and pigeonholes for shoes, with a bench on top where they sat to smoke their fags. There was only one lavatory. He shut himself in.

Hilary had told him she wrapped the ticket stubs in toilet paper to flush them down the pan. He did that with his tickets and got rid of them all right. He was relieved to see them disappear. They were incriminating evidence. He brought them in with him every day, just enough. It was safer to keep his stock at home in case there was a spot search. He'd trained himself to be safety-conscious.

He also needed to hide the money he'd taken. It was mostly in small change and there was a lot of it. More than anyone would be likely to keep about his person in the normal way. He couldn't put it in his coat pocket either; that was another place that could be searched.

It came to him then that he could hide it in the water cistern above the lavatory, the ideal place, nobody would think of looking there. His leather pouch would be ruined by the water, but he could get a new one.

He stood on the seat and found he could just reach it. The walls and door of the stall were just high enough to provide for the modesty of the occupant, and from here he could see over

316

into the cloakroom. Not so good. Fiddling with the cistern, he'd be in full view of anyone there. Why hadn't he realised that? But he could think of nowhere else, and being in full view, wouldn't that make it safer? Besides, even if found, there was no proof it was his. It could be the property of any male member of staff.

This room was deserted for long periods; they were all pinned down by their jobs. He felt in his pocket for the pouch and was reaching up to lift the porcelain lid when the cloakroom door crashed back. The noise reverberated off the tiles, making him jump. He caught a glimpse of Bert Timmins, the projectionist, as he came rushing in, before he shrank down in a stoop. The tiles were cold against his back and his heart was pounding fit to burst. He was terrified he'd been seen.

'Hurry up,' Bert shouted. 'Is that you, Lucky?'

That made him freeze in greater panic. He *had* been seen! But he couldn't stay in a stoop over the lavatory like this; his legs felt stiff and weak. He lowered one to the floor and stood up, crushing the pouch back into his pocket. He must calm down and keep his wits about him. He took a deep breath, pulled the chain and picked up the official cash from the floor.

Bert said, as he drew back the bolt: 'Thank God! I can't wait. Have you got gut trouble too?'

'Yes,' Frank said as they changed places. He had to ask, 'How did you know it was me?'

'Saw the cash drawer on the floor.'

There was a foot gap at the bottom of the stall. He'd forgotten that they could always see when it was in use. Had Bert seen him step down from the seat? Frank felt a nervous wreck. The sweat was pouring off him.

Perhaps he'd been lucky that Bert had been looking down and not up. He wouldn't be able to hide the money in the cistern. He wouldn't be able to make himself stand on that seat again.

He had to go to the office. Already it was later than usual for him to take the money up. He wanted to get his breath back first, but he was afraid Bert might come rushing out again to get back to the projection room before the reel ran out. He gave the usual perfunctory knock on the office door and went in.

'Almost a full house this evening,' Mr Butterworth said with satisfaction.

That did nothing to reassure Frank. 'Almost, sir.'

Butterballs was studying the figures in his book. Always at work he wore a black bow tie on a white shirt, with a formal evening dinner suit. Being in the entertainment trade, he felt he needed to look dressed up for a good night out. He said it added tone to the Carlton Hall.

He drew in a long, thoughtful breath. 'I thought we'd done better than this.'

'Not bad, sir, for a Monday.'

The manager's finger stopped against the column for the balcony.

'I could hardly see an empty seat when the lights went down.'

What could he say to that? Frank's fingers closed over the money pouch in his pocket. It was heavy and dragging his trousers down on one side.

Butterballs pondered. 'Eighty empty . . . out of four hundred.'

'They throw their coats over the seat in front,' Frank hazarded, 'and they're milling about until the show starts. Can be misleading.'

Could it? How could he know? He must be more careful. He was never in the auditorium when it was filling up.

But the boss was starting to count the cash. Frank watched his hands spinning through the coins. He was expected to stay while the total was checked and found to agree with what he'd entered in the book. Did that mean the manager was accepting his figures? He'd certainly questioned them. He'd not done that before.

Frank swallowed. He wanted to give in his notice, get away from here before it was too late, but he'd like to go with more of the takings. He saw the coins spread out in piles across the desk. Old Butterballs was packing them in the coin bags provided by the bank. He'd been wondering how he could do it for years.

He'd been bringing the cash up to the office twice-nightly and watching the boss open the safe and put it inside. The safe had a combination lock and he'd watched very carefully. He knew the combination was changed weekly, but he hadn't understood how it worked until Pat showed him a cheap bicycle lock and spelled it out to him.

He'd gone to the office a few times to find the boss wasn't there, and had been able to have good look at the lock. To start with he'd had to work out where he must stand to see Butterballs' fingers as he opened the safe. If he stayed by the desk, all he saw was his back. Frank always hovered beside him now, holding out the cash in readiness.

It had been a challenge that had occupied him for ages, to work out the combination from the numbers Butterballs dialled as he twirled the knob back and forth. He always rushed back to his ticket booth to write down what he thought the numbers were. Then, when he went up again with the takings from the last house, he'd have those numbers in his mind and could check them.

The combination was changed every week and he had until Saturday to work it out. How much was in the safe depended on when the cash was paid into the bank. He'd had to work that out too. The safe was always empty on Monday night. Then again on Wednesday or Thursday. He'd decided long ago that Saturday would be the best night to go for it.

Frank considered he'd been capable of doing the job for years, but he had to look at it from every angle. To start with, he hadn't wanted to give up his ticket income. That had been steady over the years, but it couldn't go on much longer.

He was afraid that if he took the money from the safe,

suspicion would fall on him. After all, nobody knew better how much was there. He needed to make sure he had a watertight alibi.

He'd thought this through a hundred times and knew he wouldn't be able to do it without Pat's help.

Alice went to the hospital on the next visiting day. She needed to tell Peter that Pat had moved into his flat. When she went to sit at his bedside, he seemed more cheerful than he'd been for a long time.

'Sister says I'll probably be allowed home at the end of next week,' he grinned.

Alice was delighted at the prospect. She'd be able to talk to him every day, unload her worries.

'Thank goodness. You'll be more in touch with the business, know what's going on. Can you walk yet?' Alice had only seen him in bed during all the weeks he'd been in hospital.

He was quite excited. 'I can get about. I'm a whizz on crutches. I wanted to stay up to show you, but Sister makes us all get into bed to receive our visitors.'

'Will you want your bed downstairs?'

'No. Don't bother moving it. I'll start as I mean to go on.'

'It won't be a bother. Grandpa would help me. The stairs . . .'

'I'll get up them if I have to crawl on my hands and knees. I'm sick of being an invalid. I want to get back to normal. I want to get back to work.'

That reminded Alice of what she had to tell him. 'I'd love it if you could.' As she related how Pat had moved into his flat, she felt his cheerfulness fade.

'Already in? Without telling us? He's no business . . . I was so looking forward . . . That's why I have to cope with stairs.'

'I knew you'd be upset.'

He pushed his brown hair back from his face. 'It's not your fault, kid.'

'There's something else you don't know. Maddy thinks she's in love with Pat. She spends time up in the flat when she should be serving in the shop.'

Peter's lips straightened. 'That's making it harder for you?'

Alice nodded. 'A lot.'

Peter lay back against his pillows, looking defeated.

'I've put you in an impossible position, Alice. I knew it wouldn't be easy, having Pat and Frank as partners. It was the last thing I wanted.'

Alice sighed. 'Running the business would be easier if it weren't for them. They take no notice of me – do exactly what they like.

'Frank took the takings from the till that first night and he's never paid them into the bank. I nagged at him, so he gave me a figure to put in the books, but it's the money I want to see. Nobody can run a business this way. It would be different if you were there.'

Peter was shaking his head sadly. 'Not necessarily. I have to fight like a tiger to get my own way about anything. Frank treats me like a child. I can't cope with them either, that's the truth. I wish I had the money to buy them out.'

He stared silently at the blank wall in front of him for a long time. 'What am I going to do, Alice?'

Alice had been lost in thought too. His words stayed in her mind. If he had money, it might be possible to buy them out.

She'd worked in the claims department of the Globe Insurance for two years. She'd typed enough letters to be familiar with compensation claims. Possibly he could get money that way.

'Peter, it might be possible for you to claim against Eric. His car insurance policy probably covers it.'

Peter's blue eyes fixed themselves on her face. 'I can't claim against Eric. He's my friend.'

'His insurance company would pay.'

'Eric's upset enough now. Won't it make him feel worse? How's he getting on?'

Alice shook her head; she'd thought of that angle too.

'But you do have a claim against him. You've been in hospital for ten weeks up to now. You've suffered pain and serious injuries, and it'll be a while yet before you're properly on your feet. Your business is suffering. You're having to pay me and Hughie to do your job.'

'Yes, but Eric blames himself for doing this to me. He's not on an even keel because he blames himself for what happened to Greta too. If I claim on his insurance, it looks as though I'm heaping more blame on his head.'

Alice didn't answer.

Peter went on: 'I know Eric. He's agonising about it. I don't think I can add to his burden, make things seem worse. Not to Eric.'

When Alice next looked up, Gran and Flo Judd were coming up the ward. Flo looked much better. As soon as the greetings were over, Peter told her so.

'When do you want to come back to work? Are you feeling up to it yet?'

'I'd be glad to get back,' she said. 'I'm still under the doctor, but I think I'll be signed off soon.'

'The sooner the better for us,' Peter told her. 'We need you there.'

Alice stood up. She knew only two people were allowed to visit at one time, and she'd had her turn.

'I'd welcome you back,' she told Flo. 'As soon as you feel well enough.' Even though she was sure Maddy would make a fuss when she told her she was no longer needed. No other job would suit Maddy now. She'd want to stay close to Pat O'Neill.

Chapter Twenty-Eight

Alice went straight to the Ainslies' house. The placards were outside, inviting everybody to come in. She found Eric alone in the front room, sewing buttons on a green coat. His cuts and grazes had long since healed. He still complained of aches and pains, particularly in his neck. Physically he was in good shape compared to Peter, but he wasn't over the mental trauma. He looked dejected.

'Hello, Alice. Mam's doing a fitting.'

She could hear Nell's voice in the middle room. 'It's you I want to talk to.' She was glad he was alone. 'I've just been to see Peter.'

'How is he?'

'Getting better. Hoping to come home next week.'

She told him they'd talked about the possibility of Peter claiming compensation for the accident and his need for money to buy out Pat and Frank. Eric said nothing, but continued to look downcast and to sew intermittently.

'He still sees you as a friend, Eric. He's afraid it'll upset you more if he makes this claim. I've told him he should do it. It's the only way he's going to get Frank off his back. But he doesn't want to, he's afraid it will upset you. You know what Peter's like.'

'A good sort,' Eric choked.

Alice pushed him gently in the ribs. 'More than that.'

His smile was lopsided. 'The tops.'

'But he really needs this compensation. If you want the best for him . . .'

'You know I do.' Eric's dark eyes burned with sincerity.

'Will you see him, bring the subject up? Because he won't. Tell him you're happy to have him do it? It's asking a lot of you. I know you feel burdened down with guilt. It's like asking you to take the blame . . .'

'I am to blame, Alice.' He was blinking hard. 'That's what makes it difficult, I am to blame.'

Alice put her hand on his arm. It was wringing her out to see Eric like this. She wanted to put her arms round him, protect him from all the bad things in the world. He needed time and he needed peace, and here she was pushing him, but she had to for Peter's sake. He had needs too.

'You don't mind if he . . . ?'

She could see Eric was trying to think it through. 'If he puts a claim in, is he likely to get anything? Mam made me fill in a claim for the car, it's a write-off. I think they're going to pay what it's worth.'

'I'm pretty sure he will. At the Globe, all the letters I typed were about claims. About every sort of claim. I saw all the correspondence about how they were settled. Yes, I'm sure.'

Eric sighed. He sounded as though he had all the worries of the world on his shoulders.

'Here I am all woebegone about my own problems, not giving a thought to poor Peter's.'

'That's understandable.'

Eric was still grieving for Greta, but she didn't want to say that to him.

'It's inexcusable. I ought to be doing all I can to help him.' Eric drew himself up; he seemed less lethargic than he'd been over these last weeks.

'I'll get another claim form and take it to him. Tell him I want him to go ahead. I don't want him to suffer any more than he has. I wouldn't want him to forgo compensation just to spare my feelings. That would make me feel worse.

'Thanks for pointing it out. What would I do without you, Alice?'

She smiled. 'I'm good at interfering, aren't I? Always busying myself with other people's affairs.'

'I need somebody like you to peg me in the land of the living,' he sighed.

Maddy had been told to start work at quarter to nine, but she was getting to the shop earlier. The cakes were always ready on their trays, waiting to be set out in the shop. She went about the job briskly, filling the window, doing more than her share of the work before Alma arrived.

The bakery staff would be sitting round the table finishing their breakfast at that hour, and a new pot of tea would be brewed for the shop staff coming in.

Maddy got into the habit of running up to the flat and giving the door three sharp raps to let Pat know it was time he was out of bed. When she returned a few minutes later with a tray set with two cups of tea and freshly baked rolls and butter, Pat would be yawning at his front door, his mop of curls still dishevelled by sleep.

'Good morning, my love.' He always covered up with a smart dressing gown. 'Breakfast! You are good to me.'

He'd kiss her, and she'd have a blissful fifteen minutes. First she'd watch him eat, then she'd follow him to the bathroom door to watch him shave.

'Got to rush,' he told her every morning. 'I'm supposed to be out delivering orders by now.' He'd go to his bedroom to throw on his clothes, then give her another kiss and a quick hug and go clattering down the stairs.

First thing in the morning, the shop was never very busy. It took another hour for most shoppers to get out and about. Maddy was sure Alma could manage perfectly well by herself.

She liked to stay in the flat to make Pat's bed and tidy round. She liked to think she was getting a taste of what married life would be like. Of course, when they were married they'd have a much nicer home than this. Pat had come from furnished rooms in Beckwith Street, and the place looked bare.

Maddy had really enjoyed helping him buy the basic necessities he needed. He'd taken her to the furniture department at Robb's and let her choose his bed and the two easy chairs to put one each side of the fire here in his living room.

'You're like a little girl playing house,' he'd laughed, and encouraged her to go on choosing pots and pans for his kitchen. The flat needed more furniture, and he talked of taking her on another shopping expedition to get a table and a bookcase.

She went to see if his bedroom needed tidying too. He had loads of clothes strewn around; he needed a wardrobe for them. She picked them up and hung them on hangers from the picture rail.

His bed looked as though he'd tossed and turned all night. She set about making it. She'd chosen these linen sheets and Whitney blankets for him, and Pat hadn't even glanced at the price tags. The only thing he'd quibbled about was the eiderdown. She'd wanted him to have one of rose-pink satin, but instead he'd picked out this plainer and cheaper green one. She shook it out.

A red-backed exercise book fell to the floor. She picked it up, curious as to what it was. Half the pages had been filled up with his handwriting, and many had diagrams too. She sank down on his bed to study it.

On the first page was what seemed to be the plan of a grocer's shop. It showed the position of the till, the shelves where cigarettes were displayed, and the internal and external doors. The name of the proprietor and the address were given. This one was in Kendal Street. He'd noted down the opening hours and the make of the till.

Mystified, she turned the page. There was another plan, this time of a tea shop near the old workhouse on Derby Road. Again the position of the till was shown, the opening hours and the position of the doors. She flicked through the other pages, which showed much the same details.

She heard Pat coming back. He pulled up short when he saw what she was doing.

'Give me that,' he said, and his voice had lost the playful tone he usually used with her.

'What is it?'

'Never you mind.'

'Are those the shops you deliver cakes to?'

Speculative blue eyes fastened on hers.

'Yes, it's what I came back for. I've got the van loaded. I'm ready to start.' He pushed the book into his pocket and kissed her again. 'You're doing a good job here. The place looks great.'

When he'd gone, she stood at the window, thinking hard, looking down at the busy street. A few moments later she saw the top of his van pass beneath her.

She knew he spent all day visiting grocer's shops, trying to wholesale cakes and bread to them. He must be calling on tea shops too.

She didn't think the details of the shops in his book were the ones he delivered orders to. There was a list pinned to the wall in the bakery from which the orders were made up, and she didn't recognise the names in the book.

She'd read in the local newspaper of a series of thefts from small grocery shops. Generally, the thief struck in the late afternoon when the till contained the day's takings. Sometimes he helped himself to some of the stock too.

Maddy went back to the shop, thinking hard. There was only one reason to make a diagram showing the position of the till and note its make. She knew Pat was no better than he should be. She'd heard her mother say as much, knew he used to supply her hairdressing needs at half the usual price.

There was a recklessness about him, an air of daring. He was loads of fun and seemed to have a limitless supply of money. She thought she knew where it came from now.

She'd known he wasn't truly honest, not like Grandpa and Peter. Mam and Dad had been going on about what he did, making out he was a criminal, but he wasn't really bad. All right, he bent the rules a bit. Sometimes took what didn't belong to him.

Pat was more of a rogue than she'd realised. A lovable rogue who took everything in life at a tremendous pace. It would be the pace he wanted, the thrill of doing what was forbidden. It wouldn't be just the money. To think of what he was doing excited her, gave an added dimension to life.

Frank was in the pay box at the Carlton Hall. The first house was not yet over, but he'd delivered the takings to Butterballs. Now he had the best part of an hour before he'd have to start selling tickets for the second house.

He'd bought an *Evening Echo* on the way to work because he'd definitely made up his mind to look for another job. As he turned to the situations-vacant page, his eye caught a heading: THIEVES STRIKE AGAIN. He smiled to himself and read on:

Local Grocer Robbed: Small shops all over the district are on red alert. Two men, both wearing flat caps and mackintoshes, walked into a grocer's shop on Derby Road on Tuesday afternoon, while the proprietor, Mr Albert Jones, was alone in the shop. One lured him outside saying boys playing in the street had damaged his property, while the other took the day's takings from the till. Both got away before Mr Jones discovered the loss and raised the alarm.

Similar thefts have occurred in twenty-one other shops all over Liverpool and the Wirral. Police are asking all shops in the district to be on their guard.

Frank smirked. Actually, they'd done twenty-five shops; it pleased him that they'd got that wrong. But Albert Jones's till had had only seven pounds in it, less than they'd expected. For three pounds ten each, it wasn't worth the risk, and to keep doing similar jobs in the same area must be asking for trouble. This was another sort of job they'd been doing for far too long. Shopkeepers were being warned; they couldn't keep getting away with it.

Pat thought his good planning guaranteed they would. He was able to assess the risk when he called on them to offer bread and cakes from the bakery at wholesale prices. He couldn't steal from those who put in orders. He had to go back every day to make deliveries. From those who declined, he picked out those he thought were the safe targets, and he always allowed several weeks to pass before they did the job.

Pat preferred shops that were run by one person, but most had family accommodation above, and that could prove a problem.

Sometimes Pat deflected the owner's attention while Frank, posing as a customer, lifted goods. He only ever took tobacco and alcohol. Nothing else was worth enough to justify the risk. Pat always marked on his layout plans where they'd be displayed.

Frank sighed. He needed to do fewer but bigger jobs. He'd already mentioned to Pat that he'd like to have a go at the safe here at the Carlton Hall.

'During a performance? With all the staff around?'

'Yes.'

'But the public aren't allowed near the office.'

'There's a door cutting that passage off. It's marked "Private. Staff Only." It's not locked.'

'But I couldn't be seen anywhere near.'

'There's nobody much to see you during a performance.'

'The manager's there.'

'Yes, but I'll lure him down to the pay box.'

'What else is on that passage?'

'Storerooms, staff cloakrooms, but the staff won't be about.

329

The projection room's up another flight, but Bert can't go far if a film's showing.'

'Wouldn't it be safer to do it when the place is closed? The money's left in the safe overnight, isn't it?'

Frank frowned. 'Yes, but I can't get in once the cinema empties for the night. The place is locked up like a fortress. The commissionaire even does a round of the wash rooms to make sure nobody's left inside before he locks them. He finds the odd down-and-out hiding sometimes. They see it as a warm place for a night's kip. Plenty of sweets and chocolate to eat too.'

'When does the money go to the bank? Couldn't we follow your boss, or whoever takes it? Snatch it then?'

'He takes Percy with him for protection, and he's a big chap. You'd be seen; there's always people about in the street. I couldn't have anything to do with it, they'd both recognise me. Much easier to do it before second house finishes.'

Pat pulled a face. 'Better if you do it then.'

'I'll give you the combination to the safe and Hilary will act as look-out. You'll be fine.'

'I don't know . . . You know your way around the place, and it wouldn't matter if you were seen near the manager's office.'

Frank thought it would. He wanted an alibi for this, particularly if he was going to leave immediately afterwards.

He said: 'Come in and see the layout. When everybody settles down for the big film, you can pretend you're heading for the gents'. I'll draw you a map so you can find your way round. You could try and take a peep at the office.'

'I don't like the idea of being inside a big building. Of not being sure which way I should run if things go wrong.'

'Downstairs and through the foyer. The way you go in.'

'There's no other way out?'

'Not during a performance. Percy opens the fire exits at the end of the show. There's two, so the audience in the stalls can get straight out into the street. Relieves the congestion through the foyer. But the doors are kept locked most of the time. We have to be careful nobody gets in that way.'

'That's what I mean. I don't want to be trapped inside. I'd rather do another shop. Look, there's this one in Greasby, it's a lock-up. It'll be easy.'

Pat brought out his red book, and opened it to show Frank his notes and diagram.

'No other shop nearby. Let's drive out and I'll show you the place. You could go in and buy something, take a good look. Once you've seen it, you'll agree. We could do it next week. Say Friday afternoon.'

Frank felt a rush of irritation. 'It won't be worth it, Pat. Not enough in the till. Better if we did the Carlton Hall. We'd get a lot there, enough to set us up for a while.'

Chapter Twenty-Nine

Frank couldn't get over his irritation with Pat. He'd fallen in with Pat's ideas time and time again; it was only reasonable to expect Pat to fall in with his. Especially one that would bring such a good return as the Carlton Hall safe.

He pondered and pondered, but he couldn't see any way of doing the job without Pat's help. Hilary might be able to open it and get the money out, but she couldn't walk out through the foyer with it, not if old Butterballs was there with him.

A member of the audience occasionally went out early if he didn't like the film, but even so, it was unusual and would attract the eye. Pat would need to lie low until the coast was clear.

Staff were not allowed to go out during the performance, so it would immediately put suspicion on Hilary if she was seen doing that. He'd thought of all the places they might hide the money inside until later, but none seemed safe.

All the toilet cisterns were in full view of the cloakrooms, even those in the ladies'. Anyway, Hilary was quite small and could barely reach it even if she stood on the seat. Throwing the money out of the window was the only possibility, but then there was no guarantee it would still be there when they went to pick it up. For Pat to do it with him was much the best thing.

They needed each other for the jobs they did; they were mutually dependent. It wasn't easy to find another partner. Why couldn't Pat see this?

He decided that when he finished work tonight, he'd call

round to see him again. If he could persuade Pat to come in and see the Carlton Hall, he'd be sold on the idea. A shame not to take that money when he'd spent so much time figuring how to open the safe. He'd like to do it before he left. Silly not to. Much better than doing the small grocery shops.

He opened his newspaper and ran his finger down the situations-vacant column. There was a vacancy for a cashier at the Regal in Wallasey, but Wallasey was further to go. Perhaps he should try something different?

The first house came to an end and he had to open his ticket window again before he'd seen anything he wanted to apply for. This job had become a drag; he'd had enough of it to last him a lifetime. He really wanted to open the safe and hand in his notice.

Although he had no more to do once he'd passed the takings over to Butterballs and had his figures checked, he wasn't supposed to leave until the performance was over and they were locking up for the night. He'd been told off for slipping away early more than once. He hung around while time dragged. What was the point of it?

At last he was free to go. Having a car made it easier to get about, especially late at night. The streets were almost devoid of traffic at this hour. He was up in Prenton very quickly. As he drew up outside the bakery, he could see the lights were on in the flat above.

There was a door bell to the flat on the top of the shop door frame. He pressed it but could hear nothing; he didn't know whether it had rung or not. Nobody seemed to be coming down. He was afraid it wasn't working. He hammered with his fist against the door, but that didn't bring anybody either. He looked round for a small stone to throw up at the glass, but in the dim light from the streetlamp, he could see nothing suitable on the pavement.

Frank decided to go round the back to the bakery. He thought there was another bell there. It meant a short walk round the block, and once away from the streetlights it was so black he couldn't see anything. He was stumbling along, wishing he hadn't bothered. He was tired now, and sorry he hadn't gone straight home to bed.

He'd reached the bakery door and was feeling round for the bell. He couldn't remember where it was, and in the dark he couldn't find it. But he could hear footsteps inside, running to the door, though no light was put on. Suddenly the door was pulled open. Somebody came rushing out straight into his arms.

She knocked the wind out of his body, making him gasp with shock. He knew it was Maddy.

'Dad!'

His arms tightened round her. 'What are you doing here at this time of night?' He was angry. 'I told you to stay away from Pat, didn't I? It's half past eleven!'

Pat was coming back from the shop door, brown curls all awry, looking sheepish.

'Hello, Frank.'

Frank moved inside and kicked the door shut behind him. He felt for the light switch.

'What have you two been up to? No, don't tell me, it's obvious!'

'Hold on a minute, Frank . . .'

Maddy said: 'We've done nothing wrong.'

'You hold on. Maddy, I told you, and your mother told you, you were not to hang around Pat's lodgings.'

She was staring back at him defiantly.

'I've lost my job here. Flo Judd wanted to come back and Alice said I had to go.'

'What's wrong with that? You knew it would happen.'

'The only time I can see Pat now is in the evenings. You don't understand, Dad.'

'It's you who don't understand, you silly fool. Go and sit in my car. It's parked round the front. Oh yes, you saw it from the window, that's why you tried to leave in a hurry. Silly

335

bitch, you've got to learn to do as you're told. It's for your own good!'

'I . . . Pat and I, we're in love. Tell him, Pat.'

Frank felt like wringing her neck.

'Go and sit in my car.' He gave her a little push. 'You're coming home with me.' He turned to face Pat.

'No need to go over the top, Frank.'

'You and I are supposed to be partners,' he ground out. 'What are you doing to me? You knew I didn't want Maddy coming here. She's just a kid. I don't want you playing round with her. You're always talking about the women you have. I don't want Maddy to be one of them.'

'I'm sorry.' Pat looked contrite.

'She'll be lucky if she isn't already pregnant.'

'No.' Pat tried to laugh. 'Nothing like that.'

'I'll kill you if she is.'

'She isn't, Frank. I've taken good care of that.'

Frank surveyed him, bristling with rage. Then he punched his fist hard into Pat's face and watched him stagger back against the wall.

'Stay away from my daughter. I won't have you playing about with her. Do you hear? I'll not have her hanging about your flat at midnight. Don't ever let her in again.

'In fact, you'd better find somewhere else to live. Peter's coming home. He'll be wanting to move in here.'

Pat eased himself upright and mopped at his face with a handkerchief.

'All right, I said I was sorry, didn't I? No need to go off the deep end. I tell you, no harm's done, so I do.'

Frank stared at him, not convinced.

'I'll make sure she doesn't come near me again. I swear to you I will. We're partners, aren't we?'

'We were.'

'Don't let this come between us, Frank.' Pat was pleading. 'We're friends too, so we are.'

'I'm not so sure about that,' he said, thinking about what

had brought him here. He had no appetite to go into that now.

'We need each other, don't we? We neither of us would be any good on our own.'

Frank drove home with Maddy slumped on the seat beside him, fulminating all the way.

'Wait till your mother hears of this. I suppose you told her some fib about where you were going? You give Pat a wide berth in future.'

'Dad, he's lovely.'

'He isn't honest. What sort of a life would you have with him? If I catch you with him again I'll belt the living daylights out of you.'

Maddy thought she'd had a bad time from her father in the car, but when they got home her mother was furious.

'I've been worried stiff,' she raved at her. 'Wondering where you'd got to. Do you know what the time is?'

Maddy had told her she was going to the pictures with a girl she used to work with, and the time had gone so fast while she was with Pat.

'Telling lies about where you're going and who you're going with. I'm not standing for it, Maddy. It's wild behaviour and you're only seventeen. Far too young to be going to Pat O'Neill's rooms. You'll end up in terrible trouble if you don't watch out.

'From now on, you're staying with me. There'll be no going out at night.'

'Mam! You can't keep me in all the time.'

'Well – let's say you can go out if your friends come here to collect you. I want to see who you're going with, and they'd better be respectable. And since you don't have a job, you can come to work with me and make yourself useful about the salon.'

'No! I'll get myself a proper job. I don't want . . .'

'Until you do, you come and work a full day with me. I'm

not having this nonsense, Maddy. Goodness knows what you'll get up to if I don't keep an eye on you.'

Maddy stamped up to her room in a rage. She felt hard done by. Pat was a lovely person; he wouldn't let her parents interfere like this. He was a grown man, not some half-baked youth. He could afford to get married, he had plenty of money; more than Dad, she was sure. He had more sense too, he wasn't always working like a slave. Mam never stopped. He was much more fun.

Maddy got into bed and wondered what Pat would do now. He wouldn't stand for never seeing her again, she was sure about that. He loved her. He'd want to marry her even though Mam said she wouldn't give permission. They could elope, go to Gretna Green. Anywhere with Pat would be wonderful. She started thinking about her clothes, deciding what she'd pack for the trip.

What she needed to do was to see Pat, straighten all this out. What really mattered was where she stood with him, not what her parents wanted. They didn't understand. She'd have to give Mam the slip.

It was four days before she managed to get away. It was like wearing a ball and chain. Maddy had never had such a bad four days. Mam had been on at her the whole time; it had been do this and do that. Mam thought she was bestowing a privilege by letting her wash clients' hair, but she still had to make the tea and sweep up the cuttings from the floor.

She was needed full time in the Prenton salon because one of the girls was off sick and they were short-handed. Her chance came when Mam had to go down to the Grange Road salon. At lunch time, Daisy wanted her to stay in the shop with her, but she told her she was going out to buy a pork pie and a sausage roll. Where better to go than up to the bakery?

She went in through the bakery door at the back, and was delighted to see Pat's van parked there. Luck was on her side for once; he was at home. The staff were already round the table, eating.

'Is that you, Maddy?' Alice got up with a cream bun in her hand and followed her to the bottom of the stairs.

'You can see it is,' she said, and raced up. She was smiling in anticipation when he opened the door.

'Hello, Pat.'

It was a shock to see the way his face fell, but she stepped inside and reached up to kiss him.

He put his hands up to fend her off. 'You can't come here!'

She shivered. That felt as though he'd thrown a jug of cold water over her. 'But I have.'

He was frowning. 'You've got to stay away from me. You heard what your dad said.'

Maddy felt rebuffed. 'You're not going to take any notice of him?'

'I am. We're partners, I don't want to fall out with him.'

She tossed her red hair off her face in a rush of anger. 'For God's sake! What about falling out with me? You can't just drop me.'

'I can, Maddy.' He took her by the arm and turned her back to the door.

'Come on, I don't want you up here with me. Alice and Alma and that lot have seen you come up. Now let them see you leave.'

'But we've got to talk. I want to know where we stand.'

'You're just a kid. You knew it was nothing serious.'

That was like being stabbed. 'You said you loved me.'

He laughed. 'We were just playing.'

He was turning the knife in the wound. She couldn't believe this. 'You said we'd be married.'

'Just part of the game, love. Big girls know that.'

It felt like the end of the world; she'd had such high hopes, felt so sure of him. They were out on the landing and he was leading her downstairs. Every face turned from the table in the bakery as they passed the door.

He was throwing her out and they were all watching.

She wanted to die with shame; this was far worse than the other night.

'Your dad's right, Maddy.' He lowered his voice so nobody else would hear. 'You're a pretty wee colleen, so you are, but you need to grow up.'

'You bastard,' she hissed. 'You bastard.'

'Grow up. Come on, there's no harm done. You were wild for it too.'

Maddy let out a squeal of rage. 'You're an old man, a dirty old man, a pervert. I should have known better.'

It reduced what she'd felt for him. He'd been using her. She was running with embarrassment and rage. They were out in the yard. He went to his van, opened the passenger door to take his order book from where he kept it tucked between the two seats. Maddy saw his red exercise book, which had been hidden behind it.

He opened the rear door of his van then and took out a stack of empty cake trays, lifting them up on his shoulder. 'Go on, and don't come back, ever.'

That seemed the last straw, to be shooed away like an annoying puppy. She started to back away as he turned and took the trays into the bakery.

Through the passenger window of his van, she could see his red exercise book. Her first thought was to deprive him of something he found useful, to make things difficult for him. She was overwhelmed by the rush of loathing. On the spur of the moment she opened the door, reached across and took it, pushing it down into the pocket of her coat.

She understood at last what her mam and dad had been on about. They'd been right; she should have listened to them. Pat was horrible, but she'd get even with him. So help her, she'd make him sorry. He wasn't going to treat her like this and get away with it.

She was upset all the same. She couldn't stop the tears running down her cheeks. To be dropped like that! To be told he was just playing with her!

She'd thought he loved her. He'd said so a dozen times, and kissed her and fondled her and done what was totally forbidden. In the last few minutes, all the love she'd felt turned to hate.

Mam had called him a petty criminal, and he was. She had proof, didn't she? He'd used her for his own ends, but she'd get her own back. She'd take his little red book to the police. She'd fix Mr Pat O'Neill. He'd be sorry he'd treated her like this.

Monty was in dreadful trouble. He didn't know which way to turn. He'd thought Rita was acting strangely. She'd always been relaxed in public, and loving when they were alone.

At lunch time today, she'd been restless and edgy in the cafeteria. Now tonight, at home, she couldn't sit still, and she moved her face away when he tried to kiss her. It was out of character.

'What's the matter?' he asked.

Rita's voice was panic-stricken. 'I think I'm having a baby.'

Monty's heart jerked. This had always been his worst nightmare. Of course he'd been very careful, getting his supply of French letters from his barber every time he went. Careful about using them too.

'What are we going to do? I'm scared.'

'I've been so careful. Are you sure?'

'Of course I'm sure!'

'You said you thought . . .'

'I'm sure. I wouldn't have said anything if I wasn't sure. I've suspected for some time. Oh, I know you're careful, Monty, but it can still happen. They aren't a hundred per cent. They don't come with any guarantee.'

'No.' His heart was still thudding.

'What are we going to do?' Rita wailed. 'I won't be able to work . . .'

'How far on?'

341

'Two months.'

Monty swallowed hard. Rita wasn't thrifty. She earned a good salary and believed in getting all the enjoyment she could from it. Her house was filled with glossy magazines and fresh flowers. She spent a lot on clothes and the new cosmetics.

'Say we'll be married, Monty,' she implored. 'Please.'

Her hazel eyes were wide with agony; he could see the green flecks in them. His heart was pumping away and he could feel the blood throbbing in his head. He'd have to tell Edith. Have to marry Rita. That was his duty, Edith would see that now.

'I'm so sorry. . . Yes, we'll have to be married now.' There was no other way round this. He said more cheerfully: 'Of course we'll be married, love.'

Even as he said the words, Monty worried about how he was going to make it come to pass. He'd been trying to tell Edith about Rita for the past eight years.

He'd imagined dozens of scenarios, each worse than the last, each bringing cold, gripping fear to his gut. He'd tried and failed to do it for so long that he knew in his heart he couldn't. The task was beyond him.

Edith looked up to him. He was the head of the family, and the family was everything. If he left Edith, she wouldn't just lose her husband; it would shatter her faith in the family.

Yet if he didn't find the courage, and courage was what he needed, then what would happen to Rita? He'd started a second family, and he felt stretched like a piece of elastic between the two. And yes, stretched until he was on the point of breaking.

His nights were agonised and wakeful. Edith was asleep within five minutes of getting into bed, but if he wasn't careful, his tossing would wake her again, and that brought more unwelcome questions. He told her he had indigestion, that was something she understood. He'd even got up and pretended to follow her advice to take bicarb of soda.

342

He'd longed to move in with Rita and enjoy a more glamorous and comfortable life with her. Now he didn't know what he wanted. He'd worried about it too long, mulled over what he should or shouldn't do. He'd scared himself rotten. He couldn't make up his mind to do anything.

On top of that, there was more trouble. He couldn't stop thinking about that dreadful accident. He was sick with sympathy for Eric, who'd killed his own wife. Such a young and pretty girl, and not long since she'd been a bride.

Monty felt very bothered about Peter. They couldn't be sure yet he'd make a complete recovery. His business was in jeopardy because he couldn't run it. Frank ought to be doing more to help him. What could a child like Alice do? It was ridiculous to leave it to her. She kept asking him for advice, and he couldn't begin to think about baking, not when he had Rita's predicament on his mind. Monty hated the indecision and lack of direction. He liked having things cut and dried, and yet he couldn't bring himself to make any move.

Rita had told him she'd always been attracted by mature men. Her husband had been seventeen years older than her, but age had not prevented him being killed in the last months of the Great War. She'd been married for only three years at the time.

Her father had died when she was four. Monty thought she saw him as a father figure. Her mother had married again quite quickly; her stepfather was three years younger than her mother. Rita had never really got on with him.

He'd tried to speak to Rita about the coming baby. To get rid of it would be the easiest thing all round, then nothing need change. They could go on just as they were.

'I don't want to get rid of it.' She'd been upset. 'I want things to change. I'm getting older, Monty. I want a husband and child. I'm thirty-nine, I might never get another chance. When are you going to tell Edith? I wish you would.'

He'd tried to explain how he saw the problem of Edith.

'I'm the one with the real problem, Monty,' she'd said, in a tone that was rather cold for Rita.

He kept eyeing her figure. Rita was thin. Stringy thin really, and though she said she was putting on weight, Monty couldn't see it.

'Should you be drinking now?' he asked when she wanted a third glass of sherry.

Although Rita said she wanted change in her life, as far as he could see she was carrying on exactly the same as usual. The weeks were passing, and still Monty felt torn. One moment he felt he should pluck up courage to do it, and then not.

Rita kept saying: 'When we're married we'll take a long holiday. France, I'd love to go to France.' Monty had never been out of England, and didn't want to.

'We could just go away together now,' she suggested. 'Stay away, have a lovely lazy time.'

That sort of talk terrified Monty. He only had four months to go to retirement. He didn't want to retire, but he wasn't about to disappear now, when his pension was almost due. He couldn't afford to turn his back on that. He'd been paying into it for years.

'Where's the money to come from?' he demanded. Rita was irritable and less inclined to let him make love to her these days.

Chapter Thirty

April 1936

Tuesday was the day Edith did her ironing. As soon as the breakfast dishes had been cleared away and washed up, she got out the old ironing blanket and spread it on the kitchen table.

Peter had given her one of the new-fangled electric irons. Instead of having to heat her flat irons in the fire, all she had to do was to take out the light bulb over the table and plug it in. She enjoyed ironing these days.

She made separate piles of newly ironed clothes for each of the family. Peter's was all pyjamas these days; she packed them in a carrier bag to take to the hospital. She took two other piles upstairs. The one belonging to Alice she put on her bed. Usually Alice did her own ironing, but she was doing so much for Peter at the moment, this was the only way Edith felt she could help.

She looked round with approval. Alice always made her bed before she went to work, even when she was getting up early and going out before breakfast. She kept her own room spick and span.

Not like Monty. He expected her to run round after him. She put his pile of ironing on his tallboy. He'd worn his blue pullover last night and let it slide to the floor. She folded it neatly and put it in his drawer. Then she made the bed they shared, tucking in the blankets carefully on

Monty's side, fluffing up the crimson taffeta eiderdown to make it look nice.

Monty had been reading last night's *Echo* in bed. She picked it up from the floor and opened it at the property pages. They were building everywhere these days.

Edith sighed at an artist's impression of a new building site in Bebington. Perkins Brothers were advertising what they called Perkins' Little Palaces for sale. Mostly they were semi-detached houses, but there were some lovely bungalows too. One of those would be absolutely perfect.

She decided she'd go into town now she'd tidied up, and pay what she'd saved into their account at the Liverpool Savings Bank. She started to get ready, sitting on her side of the bed so she could see herself in the glass on her dressing table. She didn't have time to do her hair properly first thing in the morning when she had to get Monty off to work. Her hair pins had worked loose and let wisps escape. She pulled the pins out and her hair rolled down over her shoulders. She looked at it with dissatisfaction. There was less of it than there used to be, and it was getting greyer.

She combed it carefully and then remade the stiff little roll that sat on the collar of her blouse. After years of pondering about it, she'd asked Cecily to give her a Eugene perm, but Cecily had been very off-hand with her and put her off. Without actually saying so, Edith was given to understand that the offer had been withdrawn.

She frowned at her reflection and wondered what had upset Cecily. She was a changed woman; there were times when she was quite nasty. She was never pleased to see any of them these days. Edith didn't know what had come over her.

Perhaps it was just as well she hadn't had a perm. Edith had heard that Mrs Gorton down the road had gone to the best hairdresser in Liverpool and now had two bald patches on her head because they'd let the perming machine burn her.

Before going downstairs, she took a last look round to make

346

sure everything was tidy, and realised she hadn't put Monty's ironing away.

She opened the drawer where he kept his underwear. It was full of garments he no longer wanted to wear, though they were far too good to throw away. There was barely room to put in what she'd just washed.

Once he'd worn whatever she bought for him. He'd always worn long-john combinations of pure wool in winter. What could be more sensible? But over the last years he'd complained, said they were itchy and far too hot now the office was centrally heated. Now Monty had very extravagant ideas about his underwear.

She'd got him some interlock cotton combinations such as he'd always worn in the summer, but he'd made her take them back to the stall in the market. He said they were old-fashioned and cheap and she was trying to be too thrifty. He'd torn a piece from his newspaper showing the very latest Aertex briefs and singlets, advertised as up-to-the-minute wear for sportsmen. He'd told her to buy those for him, and very expensive they'd been.

They kept their shape a bit better than the interlock, but they were never worth what she'd had to pay. She didn't know what had come over him.

She pulled out his handkerchief drawer and wondered why he had to use two or three a week when he didn't have a cold. It never occurred to him that he was making unnecessary work for her.

She sorted his handkerchiefs to one side of the drawer and his socks to the other, and was about to put the clean ones in when she saw the corner of an envelope sticking out from under the left-over wallpaper she'd used to line it. She pulled it out, a brown business-size envelope without a stamp. It was marked 'Personal' and formally addressed to Monty. It was creased and grubby, as though he'd been carrying it round in his pocket for weeks. She sat down on the bed again to read what was inside.

It was an official letter from the personnel department at Lever Brothers. Edith felt a surge of interest as she groped for her glasses. It was about Monty's retirement!

She sat staring at the letter, alternating between delight and disbelief. His pension would be three pounds ten shillings a week! That was better than she'd supposed, and she'd heard talk of the state pension going up too.

Monty had said nothing about it to her. How silly he was, not wanting to retire when they were going to pay him to do nothing. The date was here too, 30 May, his sixty-fifth birthday. All this was going to happen in the next few weeks!

She lay back against her pillow, feeling as though the breath had been knocked out of her body. There were figures showing how his pension was worked out. It gave in black and white the amount of salary he was earning. Five pounds fifteen shillings a week!

She certainly didn't see her fair share of that. Not many men told their wives exactly what they earned, but Monty had gone out of his way to say he was earning less. He'd said four pounds five. She felt cheated; she'd always played fair by him.

She'd been living with careful thrift all these years, making his money go as far as she could. She'd been saving for his retirement and though he'd said he'd get a pension he'd never even hazarded a guess as to how much it might be. He'd certainly known exactly for the last two months, because there was a date on the letter. Edith gave a grunt of displeasure. He should never have kept her in ignorance like this.

Then it came to her. With this sort of pension to live on, they could easily afford to move to a nice bungalow. There was no reason not to. When Peter was better, he'd want to move into the rooms over the bakery. He said it would be easier to manage if he lived on the spot. Easier to rest, as well as keep an eye on the business.

Two bedrooms would be exactly right for them. Alice

would be with them for another few years. She was actually quite a help now she'd grown up. Edith had never had a daughter; having Alice might be a comfort to her in her old age.

She decided against going to the bank. She'd go instead to see Perkins' Little Palaces on yet another new estate being built in Bebington. When she found it, she realised it was further from any shops, but the bungalows backed on to open fields. It would be like living in the country.

They were not very different to the ones she'd seen before. Perhaps they were a little bigger: the living room was better proportioned, and they had good-sized gardens back and front, with wooden fences round.

She went inside one and liked it better than any others she'd seen. She sniffed at the smell of new paint and plaster and imagined her own furniture here. Her dining table up that end of the room and her three-piece suite here. They had far too much furniture for this house. She'd only have room for the best of her things. She could make it look beautiful.

She talked to the man in the site office, who showed her the plan. They were going to build two more at the end of the row and they hadn't yet been reserved.

She'd talk to Monty tonight. If they put down their deposit now, they'd be able to move in as soon as he retired.

Edith felt full of resentment as she prepared Finnan haddock for tea. She set the table for three, but she hoped Alice wouldn't be home in time to hear what she was going to say to Monty.

She read the letter again. A pension of three pounds ten; all that and he was keeping quiet about it. She couldn't get over the fact that he was earning five pounds fifteen shillings. What had he spent all that on? He'd wasted it: frittered it away on beer and newspapers.

She set the letter beside his plate. She was going to confront him with what he'd been keeping from her. He was going to get a piece of her mind.

She heard his key in the lock. Good, he was here before Alice. Monty's step was slow. He looked cast down as he came into the kitchen.

'What's for tea?' He always said that as though he was starving.

'You're cheating on me,' she told him straight out. 'A pension of three pounds ten a week, as well as the state pension. What are you keeping the good news to yourself for?'

He sat down at the table. Pulled the letter towards him, then folded it roughly and pushed it back in the envelope.

'Don't nag me about looking at bungalows,' he said. 'I've got too much on my mind, what with our Peter . . .'

'You've got to think of retirement some time. I'd have thought you'd be glad not to go to work and still have all that money coming in.'

'Perhaps I will,' he sighed.

'You didn't tell me you were getting five pounds fifteen a week either. I haven't had a rise in my housekeeping for years.'

'I didn't tell you because I knew you'd nag like this if I did,' he said with a show of spirit.

'There's no reason why I can't have a bungalow, not when . . .'

'Not now, Edith. I can't think about that just now. Perhaps later. I've too many other things bothering me.'

'What? What have you got to worry about?'

'Well, our Peter . . .'

'It's not you that worries about Peter.'

'There's a lot on my mind.'

Monty didn't know which way to turn. He found no peace with Edith, but none with Rita either. Nothing seemed to be going right for him.

He went to Rita's house on Saturday afternoon, though for

350

once he wasn't looking forward to it. Once their afternoons together had seemed magical; now Rita never stopped trying to persuade him to leave Edith. It was tearing him to pieces. Today she was irritable too.

It hadn't been one of their better afternoons. Monty felt it was turning into a nightmare when he saw her step-father's bull-nosed Morris pull in to the pavement in front of her house.

'Rita!' He was panic-stricken. 'Look who's coming.'

He felt her nudge against him as she came to look out of the window. 'Not again!'

Rita had been doing her best to discourage her parents from visiting when she wasn't expecting them. Since the last time this had happened, she said she'd devoted two nights each week to them.

This time they were dressed: they'd each had a bath. Separately, though once they'd have got in the large white bath on Queen Anne legs together.

'I'll get rid of them as soon as I can.' She fastened the belt of a new summer dress printed with scarlet poppies.

'You stay here. I wish this didn't have to be a hole-and-corner affair. Stay out of sight and don't make any noise.' She was glowering as she turned to go downstairs. 'I'll probably have to make them a cup of tea. An hour at the most.'

Monty lay down on her bed again. It hadn't been made and it was the only comfortable place to pass an hour. He looked round for something to read. He didn't feel so anxious. It wasn't an entirely new experience.

He could see a book pushed out of sight under her bedside cabinet. He hooked his fingers round and pulled it out. He was surprised to find it was a textbook on midwifery.

Well, not really surprised, because Rita was having a baby. He found a large sheet of notepaper had been slipped inside the pages. It was covered with Rita's neat script.

The words 'morning sickness' were heavily underlined.

She complained about that a lot. All the other familiar symptoms of pregnancy were listed. She'd spoken of having all of them.

Suspicion flared in Monty's mind. Somehow she didn't seem pregnant. She never mentioned any plans for the baby. She wasn't knitting bonnets and bootees.

Why copy the signs and symptoms from a textbook? She'd mentioned all the ones listed here, but was that just to convince him? Was she trying to make him believe she was with child?

A faint gust of laughter eddied up from below. Monty asked himself if Rita was making a fool of him. He had that awful sinking feeling she was. He counted up the time since she'd first told him. He couldn't believe he'd been worrying about this for over two months, and at the time she'd said she was already two months gone.

It had dominated his life in that time; he'd thought of nothing else but how to manage this crisis, how to tell Edith. He'd been torn in two.

It meant Rita must be four months gone now. She wouldn't bath with him like she used to, but he saw enough of her body in bed to know it was still reed-slender. Surely, by this time, her breasts should no longer be the tight virginal buds they were?

It was a very long time since Edith had been pregnant, but he was certain that by this stage, her body had looked in full bloom. The visible signs had been unmistakable.

A door opened downstairs and there was another gust of laughter. Monty felt his anger building, and yet he wanted to cry too. He was sure Rita was taking him for a ride.

The visitors were leaving. Rita was out on the front step. He stood well back from the window so as not to be seen, watching her parents get into their car. With much waving they drew away from the kerb. He heard the front door slam shut and Rita's footsteps coming up.

Her cheeks were slightly flushed; she was smiling. Her

ill-matched features for once seemed a more cohesive whole. She had never looked more attractive.

'They've gone. Come on down and have a drink.'

He threw the textbook on her bed. 'You aren't pregnant at all, are you?' He was surprised at the sound of his own voice. It sounded agonised, bereft of hope.

Her head went back with shock. Her flush deepened.

'It's a lie, isn't it? I know it is.'

'What if it is?' Her hazel eyes challenged his.

'Rita!'

She turned on him then. 'You were sitting on the fence doing nothing. You wouldn't make up your mind. I wanted to give you a little push. I wanted us to be married. You wanted that too.'

Monty held up his hand. 'Don't . . .'

'You can't deny that!' She was getting angry now. 'You wanted it but you wouldn't do anything about it.'

'It's not as easy for me. I've been married for nearly forty years.'

'Lucky old you. I've nobody but you. I got tired of sharing you. Tired of being kept out of half your life. I want to go out and about, have a good time with you. You want to hide me away as though you're ashamed of me.'

'You're trying to cheat me, rush me into doing something without . . .'

'Rush you? Don't make me laugh!'

'It's not fair, telling me lies like that.'

'I had to do something to urge you on. I wanted you to make up your mind, I wanted you to tell Edith and come and live openly with me.'

'Thank goodness I didn't!'

He saw her stiffen. 'I should have known nothing would make you move. You're an old stick-in-the-mud, Monty. Deep in your rut, and you won't get out for anything. You want both of us, me and Edith, that's your trouble.'

Monty knew there was truth in that, truth in all she said. 'But to lie like that! It's underhand.'

'What about your lies? Don't tell me you never tell them. Or are yours always white?'

'I don't tell lies. I don't scheme like you.'

'You lied to me about your age.' Her hazel eyes were accusing. 'I know you're due to retire next month, but you never mention it. You pretend you're much younger than you are. And you told me you earn more than you do; that's another lie.'

Monty was taken aback. 'How did you find out?'

'I was sent to personnel, to check on somebody else. While I was there I had a look at your file. Just curiosity.'

He felt cold inside. Angry that he'd been caught out. 'I wanted to appear more attractive to you,' he choked. 'I loved you and I wanted you to love me. That's quite different . . .'

Rita's eyes flashed green fire. Her face was working with rage. 'Should I just have spelled it out? Throw over your marriage or get out of my life? It was always going to be one or the other. I was much too patient with you, always trying to jolly you along.'

'You didn't jolly me, you nagged.' Monty couldn't stop himself, although he felt the bottom was falling out of his world. He'd never crossed words with Rita before.

'Nagged?' The colour had left her cheeks. Her eyes burned with vengeance. 'That's it. I've had enough. After all these years, I never thought it would end like this.'

'It doesn't have to end,' Monty protested. It was the last thing he wanted.

'It does! You're not getting away with calling me a liar. Everything's changed anyway. I've been out once or twice with Edward Blackwood; it's not just lunch in the staff dining room now.'

Monty didn't believe that. 'When have you had time to go out with anyone else?'

'When I told you I was seeing my parents on Wednesdays and Fridays.'

He knew that must be the truth. 'That's why they came round to see you! Another lie you've told!' Anger and frustration were building up inside him.

'You wanted all my time. Edward's a manager, he's got a car and he's a lot more fun than you. You can get out of my life. I've had enough. You're too old for me. Too staid. You take everything and give nothing in return.'

To Monty, it felt like a kick in the stomach. He felt cut down in size.

'Go on, get out. You're just an old grandpa. You were never going to be any good to me. I was a fool to think you would, but I had nobody else then.

'Edward Blackwood's my generation, just three years older. My class too. You're nothing but a tuppenny-halfpenny clerk. I must have been desperate to want you.'

Monty wanted to scream with fury but was afraid she'd poke fun at him if he did. He took a deep breath, fought to stay calm.

'All right, I'll go. I know when I'm not wanted. I hope your new boyfriend can dig your garden for you and cut your grass. I hope he's willing to mend your lawnmower and fix your new-fangled electric gadgets when they go wrong.'

'Of course he is. He knows all about electricity.'

'I'll take my things with me. Then I'll not have to bother you again.'

Monty started to collect the things that belonged to him. His gardening manual was on her bookshelf, and the pair of fancy slippers he'd brought here were by the bed. He leapt to the bedroom door and unhooked the velvet smoking jacket that hung there, and then remembered Rita had given it to him and flung it on the bed.

'You can keep your presents. You can wrap them up again for your new boyfriend.' He could be nasty too.

'Don't be silly.' Her tone was disdainful.

He raced to the bathroom for the new razor he'd bought because she complained his chin was scratchy when he kissed her. Grabbed that together with his brush and comb. He'd been too fastidious. Worked too hard to make himself acceptable to her.

He went down to the hall. She threw after him a sleeveless Fair Isle pullover Edith had bought him several Christmases ago.

'Don't forget this. Nobody under retirement age would want to wear such a thing.'

That made him see red. He liked it, he felt smart in it.

'Cecily admired that. She said it was distinctive.' Rita knew Cecily; she'd been doing her hair for years.

'It's hideous,' she said. 'Cecily's just being polite, as I've been.'

Monty was boiling with hurt. 'You're not being polite now.'

'Don't forget your umbrella. It's been here for the last three weeks. Now, what other rubbish did you bring?'

He caught at her dress and swung her round. 'There's no need to be so . . . so hurtful.'

'There is. I want to make sure you don't come back.' Her hazel eyes taunted him. 'I'm just sorry I have to see you at work. But it won't be all that long before you retire, thank goodness. I won't feel happy until you're out of that office. Let me alone.'

She shook him off. His fingers slid off the smooth material of her dress. He grabbed to get a firmer hold, but she jerked back out of his reach.

She was goading him too far. She tried to dodge under his arm and escape. He grabbed at her again; she needn't think she could get away easily.

'So I'm too old, am I? I'm still a lot stronger than you.' He caught her round the waist, backed her up against the wall.

'You can't frighten me.' Her face twisted with scorn. Fury welled up in his throat and exploded within him. He wanted to get his own back for this and hardly knew what he was doing.

'Don't bet on that.' He ground the words out. His hands were round her throat. The long, slender throat he'd thought so beautiful. 'That frightens you, doesn't it? Doesn't it?'

She was tearing at his hands, trying to pull his fingers away. He tightened his grip, wanting to hurt her as she'd hurt him. She was fighting hard, making terrible guttural noises that only made him strengthen his grasp.

The next thing he knew, she'd gone all limp and was collapsing at his feet.

'Rita?' He bent over her. Her face was deathly white. There were red marks each side of her neck where his fingers had bitten into her flesh.

Terror rolled through him like a wave, leaving him weak. 'Wake up. It's no good pretending.'

But he knew she wasn't pretending. He tried to stand her on her feet but she was unconscious. The blood was pounding in his head, and he could hardly breathe. He knew he'd strangled her. She was dead! He'd killed her!

He was in a blind panic then. He'd killed her! What was he going to do? He couldn't even look towards the heap of flowered material lying at the bottom of the stairs. Methodically, he collected his belongings up. He mustn't leave anything to give the police a clue as to his identity. He must stay calm.

Calm was the last thing he was; he was shaking all over. He could think of nothing but that he'd killed Rita. He was running with sweat. He was terrified. He'd murdered her!

Chapter Thirty-One

Monty felt like a soul tormented. He thought he'd been worried about whether to ask Edith for a divorce or not. That was nothing to the torture he was going through now.

He'd been petrified ever since he'd banged Rita's front door behind him and left her body in a crumpled heap at the bottom of the stairs. Every minute at home, he'd been expecting a policeman to knock at the door. By breakfast time the next morning, he couldn't believe one hadn't come.

He told himself he hadn't been thinking clearly. She mightn't be found for some days. Her parents had been with her half an hour or so before; they wouldn't be likely to make contact again for some time.

For once he didn't want to go to work, but he made himself stick to his routine. He set out to catch the bus. As it drew up at his bus stop, he looked inside as he always did. Usually Rita got on a couple of stops earlier and kept a seat for him. Today there was no sign of her.

The worst thing about it was that he missed her terribly. He really had loved her, and somehow it had all gone wrong. She'd turned on him and he'd done the unforgivable. He hadn't meant to kill her. Not Rita! He really didn't know how it had come about.

When he reached his desk, a young clerk he'd taken a dislike to because he was always wisecracking looked at him kindly.

'Are you all right, Mr Luckett?'

'Yes, I'm fine,' he said brusquely, but he wasn't. He felt

terrible. He must look terrible too. To liven himself up, he got to his feet and walked down to the gents'. Swilled his face with cold water and used the comb he kept in his jacket pocket to smooth out his thick pelt of white hair.

His face was paste-white. He looked ready to go to the scaffold. He made himself smile; that was better. He'd forget his problems, concentrate on his work when he got back to his desk, that was the best thing. But of course, he couldn't do it.

He was so used to watching for Rita that he couldn't help lifting his eyes to the gallery every time somebody walked along it. Rita would have been missed by now. He saw Mr Blackwood arrive with his briefcase and wondered if he was disappointed not to be lunching with her today.

It occurred to Monty then that the police could just as easily come into the office to find him. After a murder, they'd be bound to make enquiries in her place of work; about who her friends and associates were. They'd be bound to search out the men in her life. Everybody was used to seeing them eat their lunch together, they'd been doing it for years. Sooner or later, the police would question him. It was inevitable.

His affair with Rita had been hidden from his family, but he'd spoken to the man next door in Carlaw Road several times when he'd been out digging her garden. Earlier this year, Monty had given him some lettuce plants and received sprout plants in return. That man would recognise him, point him out as the fellow who visited Rita so often. Then there was Frank. He knew he had another life, another woman.

At lunch time in the cafeteria, while he was trying to eat his usual sausage roll, somebody asked him where Rita was.

'I believe she's off sick,' he said, as noncommittally as he could.

He was on tenterhooks waiting for something to happen, but nothing did. When the buzzer signalled the end of the working day, he went home on the usual bus, fighting at the bus stop in the crowd all eager to push on. Usually he put his arm under Rita's to help her. A woman he didn't know asked: 'Where's Mrs Hooper today?'

'I believe she's off sick,' he said yet again.

Edith had made faggots and peas for tea. Alice was all excited. He felt exhausted by the emotional pressures.

'Aren't you going down to your allotment?' Edith asked as he settled on the rocking chair with his newspaper.

'Not tonight.'

'Aren't you well or something?'

'I'm all right.' He heard the edge of irritation in his voice. He felt as though the net was closing in on him. Surely they wouldn't be much longer now?

Tuesday came, and the waiting seemed worse. Monty's head throbbed. Everybody kept asking the same question. 'Where's Mrs Hooper today?'

At lunch time in the cafeteria, a young girl said she'd heard Rita was off with a sore throat and wanted to know if she was better. Monty wondered what she'd say if he told her he'd left her dead at the bottom of her stairs on Sunday night.

He bought the local newspaper, half expecting to find a picture of Rita beneath a headline. Yet reason told him that the police would surely question him first.

Monty felt at the end of his tether. He couldn't get on with anything. After all, what was the point? He'd be down at the police station soon. Then on remand in prison until his case came up. It didn't look good for him, a man of almost sixty-five having a woman of thirty-nine as his long-term lover.

He wondered if they'd hang him, or whether her taunts could be considered mitigating circumstances. Either way, it would be dreadful. Life imprisonment could be worse.

Wednesday came, and still Monty had heard nothing. He felt ill; he couldn't eat his breakfast of porridge and boiled egg. He left five minutes early to buy a newspaper. He was all of a shake when he opened it, quite certain by now that he'd find her death plastered over the pages. There was nothing about it anywhere. He felt stiff with tension and his head throbbed.

The working day stretched ahead; each hour seemed as long as three. He kept watch on the gallery to see if any strangers visited her boss. That would surely be police routine when they found her body? So far as Monty could see, no detectives came to the office.

But it couldn't last. This awful waiting couldn't drag on much longer. On Wednesday evenings, Rita had told him, she went to her parents' house for her tea. Surely when she didn't turn up they'd call round at Carlaw Road to find out why. But no, that *had* been a lie, she'd admitted she'd gone out with Mr Blackwood. In that case, surely he'd go round to her house?

Monty reasoned that the police would come for him at home on Wednesday night. At the latest, it would be Thursday morning in the office. He rather hoped the latter, so he'd be spared seeing Edith's face when they took him away. She'd be mortified.

He felt a nervous wreck. He hadn't slept properly for three nights, hadn't eaten properly either. The police would certainly come and question him. All this waiting was making it ten times worse. Apprehension was like a pall; he knew he was terrified of what was creeping nearer and nearer.

'What is the matter with you, Monty?' Edith asked when he'd failed to eat his tea again. 'Are you sickening for something?'

'No,' he said. Not being able to talk about what had happened was making it worse. It was all bottled up inside him and going round in his head.

'You're mooning around here like a lost soul. Why don't you go up to the Halfway House for a drink? I'm not used to having you under my feet like this.'

'I don't feel like it.'

'Go down to your allotment then. The fresh air will do you good.'

Monty felt at his wits' end.

'I could do with some more of those carrots and parsnips. You could bring a cabbage too, if there's one ready.'

'No.' He could stand no more.

'Surely there's one with a bit of heart?'

He took a deep breath. 'I haven't got an allotment, Edith. I haven't had one for the last eight or nine years.'

'Course you have.' She was looking at him as though he'd gone out of his mind. 'You grow good cabbages. Those carrots last week were top-notch.'

'I gave it up ages ago. It was just an excuse to go out all the time.'

She snorted with derision. 'When have you needed an excuse to go out?'

'I had to give some reason. You don't understand. I've had another woman for the last ten years. A young woman I worked with. Thirty-nine she was.'

He saw her smile in disbelief. 'Oh come on, Monty.'

He had to convince her. Better that she knew it all now. Better to prepare her for when the police came. Anyway, he had to tell somebody, to stop it all going round in his head.

'I murdered her on Sunday,' he said. 'Strangled her because she tried to pretend I'd got her pregnant.'

He couldn't believe his eyes and ears: Edith was choking back a laugh. 'At your age,' she chuckled.

'I'm telling you the truth. Listen to me, woman!'

He gripped her wrists. Pinned her down to tell her all about the book he'd found and the row he'd had with Rita Hooper who lived in Carlaw Road.

'One of those posh new houses?' He saw incredulity on her face. 'She's got one of those? A young lass like that, why would she want to trouble herself with an old man like you?'

'I'm telling you, she loved me and I loved her. It's the truth.'

Edith had a very funny look on her face.

'You ask our Frank if you don't believe me. He knows

about her. I had a mistress and I've killed her. I'm in trouble. Big trouble.'

Edith was backing away from him.

'Always knew it was your side of the family. Our Len, he inherited his trouble from you.'

'Don't be daft,' he burst out.

'I think you'd better have an early night. You haven't been sleeping well at all. Twisting and turning all night, you've been.'

Edith thought he looked half-asleep already. 'Have a little read by the fire and then I'll make you a cup of cocoa. You'd better have a couple of aspirins too. See if that'll help.'

Monty had gone to bed, dragging himself upstairs like one half-dead. Edith sat on alone by the fire, feeling full of resentment.

Alice had come home for her tea, and as soon as she'd eaten and helped to wash up, she'd gone next door to see Nell and Eric. With Monty sitting by the fire within earshot, Edith hadn't been able to say anything to Alice.

Monty was in a terrible state, out of his mind. She didn't know what to make of his story. Having a mistress of thirty-nine! It sounded more like wishful thinking than fact to her.

It was that terrible accident that had upset him. He'd not seemed normal since then. It had been too much for him.

But he'd said he'd killed his mistress! Edith pulled herself up straight in the chair as she remembered that. If only Peter were here. She needed to talk this over with someone.

She heard Alice coming back. She said: 'Grandpa's gone to bed. I don't know what's come over him.'

'I thought he looked off colour, but he said he was all right.'

'Well, he isn't.' Edith let what Monty had told her come pouring out. 'What d'you make of it?'

364

'Killed her? You've got it wrong, Gran. Grandpa wouldn't hurt a fly.'

'But a long-standing mistress? Living in one of those fine houses in Carlaw Road.'

Alice's face gave her away. She was pulling a chair up close, feeling for Edith's hand.

Edith tensed. 'You knew about her?'

'I did hear something about a mistress.'

'Who from?'

'Madeleine. Uncle Frank stopped her taking a job at Lever's – you remember. Because his mistress worked there.'

'No! So everybody knew but me?'

'Shall I make you a cup of tea, Gran?'

It all fitted in now Edith thought about it. All that fancy underwear he wanted. What a fool she'd been. The last to know, and it had been going on for nine years.

All the lies he'd told, and she'd believed him. Even giving up the allotment and bringing her cabbages from his mistress's garden. Edith was furious, with herself and with Monty.

A cup of tea was being pressed into her hands. 'Drink it, Gran, and go to bed. Things will look different in the morning.'

'You go up, Alice. Good night.'

Edith listened to her footsteps on the stairs. She'd never have believed it of Monty if Alice hadn't said . . . She'd almost decided he was no longer sane. All that talk of killing . . .

If that was true, then he'd hang for it. She sat shivering over the low fire until it went out.

Edith switched on the bedside light before leaning over to switch off the alarm clock.

'Come on, time to get up. It's quarter past seven.' She said exactly the same thing every morning, making her voice as raucous as she could.

Monty's eyelids seemed stuck down; he was struggling to open them. More gently, she added: 'How d'you feel this morning?'

'Terrible.' He looked as though he wouldn't be able to stand upright.

'You slept well enough last night. No talking in your sleep or anything.'

'Have I been talking in my sleep?' His face was creased with anxiety.

'You did the night before, and the night before that.'

He choked out: 'What did I say?'

'It didn't make sense. Come on, it's time to get up.'

The mattress creaked as she heaved her weight off it.

'I don't think I'll go to work today. What's the point if the police are going to . . .'

'Oh, come on now.' Edith had no more patience with his stories. 'You're not ill, are you? Just troubled in your mind. Has something gone wrong in the office?'

'No, I told you what happened.'

She looked up from fastening her corsets. 'You're well enough to sit at a desk. No point in losing a day's pay if you don't have to.'

Edith had made up her mind. She'd been a fool to wait this long, expecting Monty to agree about the bungalow. He'd never been able to make up his mind about anything.

She didn't know whether he was out of his mind, or whether he had killed this woman. Either way, she'd have to look after herself. She'd go out this morning and put this house on the market. Then she'd draw out twenty-five pounds from her bank and reserve one of Perkins' Little Palaces in Bebington.

She had the cash. It was hers, she'd saved it. She'd put the bungalow in her own name, not jointly with Monty.

She was kinder than usual to him. 'Shall I do you a bit of bacon for breakfast?'

'No thanks.'

'Try a little porridge then. That'll slide down.' At the table she pushed a plate with only half as much as usual in front of him.

It was no good relying on Monty anymore. If he objected to the bungalow, she'd tell him to go to his fancy woman. If he was to be believed, he'd been cheating on her for years. But . . . impossible to believe he'd murder anyone.

True, he could blow up like a volcano without much provocation. But if he'd killed her last Sunday as he'd said, the police would have been here by now asking questions.

Temper or not, she didn't think Monty was the sort to kill. Wasn't the sort to have a fancy woman either. No, the whole thing was a figment of his imagination. His mind had turned. That was much more likely.

Chapter Thirty-Two

It was another wet morning. Monty didn't know why he was going out in it to catch the bus. The police would come to his house if he wasn't at work. There was the usual line of people waiting for it. Some worked in the same office. He said good morning, just as though it was an ordinary morning.

The bus slowed as it came to a halt at the head of the waiting line. Monty usually took an interest in the buses he travelled on. This was one of the 'warriors' the Corporation had acquired in 1930. Already there were plenty of passengers on it. It stopped, and looking down from the window right in front of him was Rita's affronted gaze.

Monty let out a moan of agony. Everything was swimming round him in a sea of black spots. The line of people ahead of him had boarded the bus.

'You all right, sir?' A young man was taking his arm, leading him forward. The conductor helped him aboard. Urged forward by the passengers behind, he went down the bus.

It really seemed to be Rita. She was wearing her green mackintosh; he knew it well. He'd thought he was having hallucinations. It was second nature to sit next to her. She'd always kept him that seat. Now she was staring out of the window, pretending she hadn't seen him.

Monty's mouth was dry. Rita seemed solid enough. Water dripped off her mac on to his sock. He asked: 'What are you doing here?'

'What d'you think I'm doing here? I'm going to work.' Her

tone was cold. 'You've got a nerve, coming to sit next to me after what you did.'

'What did I do?'

She turned on him then and hissed angrily, 'You know very well what you did.' The bus's engine accelerated noisily. 'You tried to strangle me.'

Monty covered his face with his hands. He'd thought he was going mad. It had happened then, in the way he thought.

'Look what you've done to my neck.' She pulled back the georgette scarf she wore under the collar of her blouse. Her long neck was discoloured with bruises that ranged from navy blue to yellow.

'I haven't been able to come to work with these great weals on my neck.'

He hadn't killed her then! Miraculously he hadn't killed her! It seemed she'd just lost consciousness. It felt like a ton weight lifting from his shoulders.

'I couldn't come to work. The red and the bruising went right up to my chin and I hurt myself when I fell. I'm bruised right up my leg as well.'

'Did you fall?'

'You know I did,' she hissed again. 'I blacked out. You wanted me to choke, didn't you? You were strangling me. Here's the imprint of your fingers on my neck. Then you went off, leaving me on the floor. You knew there was nobody to help me. I think that was callous. You very near finished me off, then you walked out.'

Monty could hardly speak. He managed: 'I'm sorry.'

'Sorry! I'm thinking of going to the police. Making an official complaint about you, while I've still got these weals on my neck to prove it. You assaulted me.'

'I'm sorry,' Monty said again. Assault didn't sound too serious. Not when he'd been thinking it was murder. 'You're all right?'

'No thanks to you. I'll trouble you never to sit next to me again on this bus, or come anywhere near me. I think you tried to kill me, but you got scared and couldn't do it.'

Monty moistened his lips. 'No, I was just angry, I didn't mean to . . .' He couldn't tell her that he thought he'd left her dead.

Her eyes flashed with contempt. 'I'd be frightened of any other man who tried to kill me, but not of you.

'You never manage to do anything properly, do you, Monty? You're ineffective, that's what you are. Feeble and weak.'

Monty sat at his desk for an hour with an open card index in front of him. He stared at it but saw nothing but Rita's angry face in front of him.

He couldn't wait to get out of this place. When he retired he'd never have to see Rita Hooper again. Sweat was streaming from him at every pore. Relief, too, that he hadn't killed her. He hadn't killed anybody.

He didn't think she'd go to the police and complain he'd assaulted her. She'd have to explain the circumstances, and that would ruin her reputation. She wouldn't want the new boyfriend to know she'd had a lover for years. Much better for her to keep quiet about him. His life was still his own and would go on as it always had.

But would it? He sat back in his chair in horror as he remembered how he'd confessed everything to Edith last night. He should have kept silent. Why, oh why, had he opened his mouth? He'd even told her to talk to Frank if she wanted confirmation of his story.

What a fool he'd been to do that. He couldn't believe he'd been so silly. He needed Edith; hadn't they been married for over forty years? He couldn't manage without her.

When he went home that evening, he told her so.

'It was all a mistake. I didn't kill her.'

'Course you didn't. How daft can you get?'

The table was set for three as usual. He took heart. He'd

been afraid she'd throw him out, but perhaps nothing would change here after all.

He said: 'I'm not going to work tomorrow. They know I'm not feeling well.'

Alice was worried about Grandpa. He hadn't missed a day's work in years, but now he said he was too ill to go. He stayed in bed for most of the day, and when he did get up, he spent the time sitting by the fire, staring into it. She brought him newspapers, which he'd always read, but now he hardly opened them. He was eating very little.

'Shouldn't we take him to the doctor?' she asked Gran.

Edith was acting strangely too. She was almost ignoring Grandpa. It was left to Alice to take drinks and meals up to his bedroom on a tray.

There was a new determination about Gran. She'd put the house up for sale and was cleaning and polishing with tremendous energy. The house had always been clean; now it sparkled. She'd already had two couples round to see it.

'The doctor?' Gran stared at Alice in surprise. 'Do you think he's ill?'

'Yes. He's not himself.'

'I can see he's not himself.' She drew herself up to her full height. 'That's not the same as being ill.' Alice knew she was upset because she'd found out he'd had a mistress.

'Go on then, ask the doctor to call. Monty's been on his panel for years and never troubled him. We won't have to pay.'

Alice was at the bakery when the doctor called. When she returned, Gran had given Monty some lunch and seemed more sympathetic.

'What does the doctor say?' Alice asked.

'Reckons he's had a nervous breakdown.'

'Really? A nervous breakdown?'

'Doctor's given him a note to stay off work and says he

needs rest.' Gran gave a grunt of disbelief. 'Would you believe he needs rest? It's not as though he ever did much.'

'Poor Gramps . . .'

'Poor me too,' Gran said sharply. 'I'm the one that'll have to wait on him hand and foot and do everything for him. All the same, the doctor's taken a weight off my mind. Now I know it is a nervous breakdown he's had.'

Alice watched her tight little smile come and go. 'Should have known, shouldn't I? Our Len must have inherited it from one side or the other.'

Frank was in bed. Nowadays he enjoyed a peaceful hour or so when the front door slammed behind Cissie. He felt he was entitled to it because he worked late at night.

She'd learned to drive and even managed to pass the new test that had come in. Now she'd gone off to work in his car and taken Maddy with her.

Cissie was being a pain in the neck. She wanted a car of her own. He'd had to agree to help her pay for it in order to get his marital rights. She was making plenty of money now from her two salons, but she was careful not to let much of it come his way. He thought that mean, considering he'd helped to set her up. She was earning it all legally too.

When he heard the door bell ring, Frank slid out of bed to look through the window. He was none too pleased to see Pat O'Neill's van in the drive. He wasn't feeling friendly towards Pat.

As he pushed his arms into his dressing gown, he reflected that if he had any sense, he'd give Pat a wide berth. The time had come to give up working with him, as well as give up his job. He ought to make a fresh start. Do something quite different. Pat was becoming difficult.

He opened the front door. 'You're round bright and early.'

Pat had been in the habit of coming a couple of times each

week, but not so early as this. Frank hadn't seen him since the fracas about Maddy.

'I wanted to say I was sorry.'

'Oh!' Frank thought Pat looked anxious and on edge. He'd never apologised for anything before.

'Come in.' He led the way to the kitchen to put the kettle on for tea.

'I won't let Maddy near me again.' Pat was defensive.

'You're damn right you won't.'

'She came again, Frank. She came round to my flat the other day.'

'What?'

'I sent her off with a flea in her ear. She won't be back. Had to make myself unpleasant.' Pat was running his hand through his brown curls, looking contrite.

'I'm glad you did.'

'And I've found some rooms to rent in Gladstone Street, but it'll be another month before the present tenant moves out. Is that all right? I'll definitely be going, it's all fixed.'

Frank looked up from the bread he was cutting to make toast. Pat couldn't keep still; he was pacing up and down the kitchen.

'Well, I don't suppose our Peter will need it for a month.'

'I don't want to fall out with you, Frank. We've been mates for a long time now. Good friends. We can trust each other, can't we?'

Frank was somewhat mollified. 'Partners. Do you want some toast?'

'Yes please.' Pat pulled out a chair and sat down at the table. 'It's not that easy to get another mate you can trust. We both know that.'

'Yes. I suppose you're wanting to do another job?'

'I need rent money to put down. About that shop in Greasby . . .'

'I wish you'd think seriously about the safe at the Carlton Hall instead. Forget the shop in Greasby.'

'I think I'll have to. I've lost my form book.'

'Not that red one with all the details in?' Frank was aghast. 'The Greasby shop was in it?'

'Yes, the layout and the usual stuff.'

'It couldn't have been taken? The book?'

'No, no, I thought it was in my van, but I've turned that inside out. I must have put it somewhere . . . I'm usually very careful . . .'

'You need to be. It could get you into trouble.'

'Frank! I haven't written my name and address in it. There's nothing to tie it to me.'

'But you've written the addresses of all those shops we did. Plans and diagrams, everything. They'd be recognisable.'

'With lots of others.'

'I wouldn't do the Greasby shop until you find your book,' Frank warned. 'I wouldn't do any shop you've included in that book.'

'It must be in the flat somewhere,' Pat worried. 'Though I've looked and looked.'

'Look some more.'

'Yes, better if we give the shops a rest and do your safe instead.'

'Much the best idea.' Frank buttered his toast. 'Anyway, there wasn't enough in the till at that last shop. It wasn't worth the trouble. The safe now, that'll be different.'

'I'll come to the Carlton Hall for a look round tonight. First or second house, which would be best?'

'Second.' Frank got up to find a pencil and paper. 'I'll sketch the layout for you. Wait till the big picture's well under way, and then pretend you're looking for the gents' and have a good nose round. See what you think.'

When Pat had gone, Frank poured himself another cup of tea. He was pleased; he really wanted to get into that safe before he left. He'd watched Mr Butterworth like a hawk. He was going to the bank on Monday and Thursday mornings. That meant that by Saturday night there would be the takings from eight performances in the safe.

Frank had seen a job in the paper he thought he'd like. A toll collector for cars going through the Mersey Tunnel. He'd written after it and had high hopes; after all, he had exactly the right experience.

Pat came that night, as arranged. As he bought his ticket for the second house, Frank winked at him, but they acted as though they were strangers because Percy, the commissionaire, happened to be close.

Since the beginning of the week, Frank had been watching closely as the boss opened the safe. He saw him do it twice-nightly; three times a day if there was a matinée. On Monday he concentrated on getting the first four numbers of the combination. As soon as he was back in the ticket office, he wrote down what he thought he'd seen.

When he saw it done again during the second performance, he checked that he'd got them right. Then he went on to the final four numbers.

On Thursday he had a stroke of luck. When he took up the takings from the matinée, he found the office empty. Immediately the blood started pumping in his head. This was a chance he hadn't expected. If he just dared . . .

With his heart in his mouth, he checked there was nobody in the corridor and then almost closed the door. He crept over to the safe and with shaking fingers fed in the numbers he'd worked out as being the combination for the week.

It clicked open effortlessly. Frank tingled with triumph. He could now guarantee he was giving Pat the right combination. He glanced inside. There was no money at all, just the rolls of tickets that were used in his machine. It was what he'd expected. By Saturday night, when Pat opened it, it would be different. He could add up exactly how much would be inside. Everything he took between now and then.

He pushed the door until it clicked shut. Then he polished up the handle and the lock with his handkerchief. He wanted to laugh out loud. He wasn't called Lucky for nothing. That was a good omen if ever there was one.

He left the matinée takings on the desk and went to stand in the doorway, looking up and down the passage. It remained deserted for another five minutes. He tingled with excitement as he waited.

He heard Butterballs coming up the stairs. When he was close, Frank stood back from the door to let him go inside and said: 'I've brought the takings up, Mr Butterworth.'

Chapter Thirty-Three

May 1936

Alice had been delighted when at last Peter came home, but it had shocked her to find how much help he needed. Her heart had gone out to see him struggling up the stairs.

'Just need a bit of practice,' he'd puffed when he'd seen her watching him. 'I'll do it.'

He'd practised doggedly, going up and down more times than he needed. 'I'll get the hang of it soon.' As the days passed she was relieved to see him getting stronger.

Eric often came round to see him. Though Peter needed help to start with, he soon managed to get next door. Everything began to seem more hopeful.

Now that Peter was at home, Alice felt he took all the responsibility for the shop off her shoulders. She was able to tell him every evening all that had happened during the day. He took over the bookkeeping, adding in the figures she brought home.

Things were easier in the bakery too. Flo and Alma Judd were running the shop and there were no problems there. Pat said he'd found himself somewhere else to live, and eventually Alice was able to report that he'd moved into rooms in Gladstone Street and that the flat over the shop was ready for Peter as soon as he felt able to move in.

Gran was delighted to hear from her estate agent that a young couple had made an offer for her house. She wrote back by return, accepting it. She was on top of the world about the bungalow she was buying, and couldn't stop talking about it. It was in the process of being built and she was down there every week to see how much progress was being made. She took Grandpa with her, and one day Alice went too.

'It'll be ideal,' she told her, looking round the living room. 'You'll not have to black-lead this grate every week.'

'Are you coming to live here too?' Gran asked. 'You could. For a while. Until . . .'

'I don't know . . .' Alice shook her head. Gran didn't sound as though she wanted her. It seemed suddenly that everyone was making plans to move house that didn't include her.

She decided she'd ask Peter if she could go with him, but at the tea table that evening, Gran raised the problem again.

'Alice, how can I decide what furniture to take till I know whether you're coming or not?'

Peter turned to her straight away and said: 'Come to the flat with me, Alice. I'd be eternally grateful if you would. I'll need help, won't I?'

She was relieved. 'I'll keep house for you, cook your meals. You won't want meat pies for every meal.'

Gran looked pleased. 'Much the best thing for everyone,' she said with obvious satisfaction. 'You go and help our Peter. He'll need you.'

'We rub along very well, don't we?' Peter asked Alice. 'You've been wonderful to me since the accident. I couldn't have coped without you. I'd like to have you there, not just for what you do but for company and all that.'

'Course,' Gran said. 'He won't want to pay you to work in that bakery once he can manage it himself.'

Alice didn't need to be told that, she'd already started to look for an office job.

'It'll seem dull, I expect, after running your show,' she said to Peter. 'But I'm doing less for you. There's no sense in paying me wages if you can do it yourself.'

Peter and Alice were sitting in the front room for once. Gran had complained there were too many people under her feet in the kitchen.

'Put a match to the fire in the parlour,' she told Alice. It had been laid in the grate straight after Christmas. 'We might as well burn it before we leave.'

The room was warm and the fusty, unused smell had gone when Eric came round to say that his insurance company had sent him a cheque for his car.

'Buy another,' Peter advised. 'Are you going to?'

'No.' Eric wouldn't look at him. 'I don't think I want to drive again.'

'Course you do,' Peter told him. 'You used to love it.'

'That was before the accident.'

'You'll do it again.' Peter sounded confident. 'I wish you would. Our Frank ran me up to the bakery once, but he was hanging around with his hands in his pockets, looking impatient. He hated waiting around to run me back, but he knew he had to, because I couldn't get back on my own.'

'Pat collected you in his van once,' Alice said.

Peter sighed. 'Things were a bit strained between us, him being in my flat and all that. Anyway, I don't like asking him for favours.'

Eric had a wry smile on his face. 'You're prepared to let me drive you again?'

'Why not?'

'Aren't you scared?'

'No,' Peter said stoutly. 'There's no ice about now. You'll be perfectly all right.'

'Well I'm scared. I'd have to screw myself up to drive.'

'The first time perhaps, but you'd soon get over that.'

'Do you think so?'

'It's a well-known fact. Shall I ask our Frank if you can have a go in his? Just to get your hand in again.'

'No! I've never driven a Rover. What if I pranged it? It's an expensive car. No.'

Alice knew Peter was keeping on at him.

'What sort of a car do you fancy? I wish I could afford one.'

He asked her to buy a car magazine from the newsagent, and to call in at the showrooms down town and bring back what brochures she could find. Every time he saw Eric he talked about cars.

He got Auntie Nell on his side; even she thought Eric should get another.

'I miss it,' she told him. 'It was very useful to collect the trimmings and things we needed from town, and it saved us time.'

Eventually Eric agreed to do it and settled on a Morris Eight tourer. Alice was glad to see him taking Peter out in it. He brought him to the shop regularly now, and collected him later. He ran his mother into town too.

One Sunday, Alice saw him washing it outside his house and asked him: 'When am I going to get a ride in your new car?' He looked up, frowning.

'You don't have to screw yourself up to take me, do you?'

She saw him swallow. 'Nothing personal, Alice. It's all in my mind. I couldn't bring myself to ask you, persuade you . . . just in case . . . The first move had to come from you.'

Her heart turned over in sympathy. 'It has, now.'

'You're not worried – about getting into a car with me? Driving you, I mean?'

'Peter's come back safe and sound. And your mam.'

'Right then, give me five minutes to put away my wash leathers. Let's go straight away before I lose my nerve.'

It was a sunny day, and Eric folded the hood down. He drove her to New Brighton and all along the prom. He went on to Hoylake and West Kirby, where he parked so they could have a walk and a cup of tea in a small café. Alice enjoyed it very much.

Eric had colour in his cheeks again when they got back. He seemed more himself from that day, and began to put on the weight he'd lost.

Grandpa improved slowly, though he seemed to have little interest in anything. All his bounce had gone. Gran prepared his meals as she always had. She even took him out for little walks.

He went back to work eventually, but by then it was only a week before he retired. He was presented with a gold watch.

'Not as good as the one you bought yourself,' Gran snorted when she saw it.

But Grandpa wore it all the time and said he preferred it. He also said he was glad he didn't have to go to work anymore.

'He'll pick up when the new bungalow's ready and you can move in,' Alice said.

The bungalow was nearly ready; Edith was preparing to move. The walls were going to be distempered. Mr Perkins, of Perkins' Little Palaces, didn't advise wallpaper for at least six months. She'd chosen the colours she wanted, and Nell Ainslie was making new curtains for the living room.

She'd measured up the rooms and decided which of their carpets were worth taking, and she'd gone round her house thinking about what she wanted to do with her furniture.

'You can have the kitchen table and chairs,' she told Peter. 'And the rocking chair. We won't have room for them. There's that sideboard up in the spare bedroom that belonged to our Len, and a lot more of his stuff up in the attic. You'd better decide what pieces you want to take.'

He laughed. 'How do I get up there, Mam?'

'Well, it'll have to be cleared out now the house is sold. Your dad won't feel like it. You know, he doesn't feel like doing anything.'

'I'll go up and take a look,' Alice offered.

'You?' Peter smiled. 'You won't have the strength to lift the stuff down.'

'I can see what's there. See what you can use.'

'It'll all have to come down,' Edith said.

'I'll get Eric to come round. Give you a hand.'

Eric came with a big torch the following evening and carried up the ladder from the yard. Alice found another torch and changed into a pair of old slacks. She knew it would be dusty up there. Peter braced himself against the stair rail and held the ladder steady, while Eric went up and pushed back the trap door. He pulled himself up and disappeared from view. Alice followed him up the ladder.

'There's a set of dining chairs,' Eric called down. 'Four of them. Not bad, they'd polish up.'

'I can use those.'

Alice could see them in the light of Eric's torch. 'A good chest of drawers . . .'

Her heart seemed to stop and then beat twice as fast. These things were ghosts from her past, though everything seemed smaller and shabbier than she remembered. This was furniture that had come from her old home.

'I feel so damned helpless.' Below, on the landing, Peter exploded with impatience.

'Dad?' he called over the banisters. 'Dad, would you mind coming up for a minute? Eric, you can hand the light stuff down to him. We can make a start.'

Gran was following Monty up to the landing. Alice heard her say:

'You'll have to stack it in the spare bedroom out of sight.' Her voice was severe. 'I don't want a mess anywhere.'

Alice climbed up into the loft. She'd seen something else that struck an even deeper chord. While Eric started lowering the chairs down, she shone her torch on a tin trunk. She remembered that very well. She scrambled over to it, running her hands over the cold surface. It was gritty with dust.

'Mind you don't put your foot through the ceiling, Alice,' Gran warned.

Once this trunk had belonged to her mother; the thought brought a lump to her throat. She'd demanded to have it in her bedroom all those years ago. Cried and howled for it, but Gran had said no, it would only upset her. Gran had had it put up here in the loft, where she couldn't get at it, and here it had stayed.

'This belonged to my mother,' she said to Eric. He turned and shone his torch on it, while she tried to lift the lid.

'Is it locked?'

'I don't know. Perhaps it's just stuck.'

'Let's take it down.'

There was a handle on each end. She helped lift it over to the trap door and Eric slid it down the ladder. Grandpa took the weight as it came down.

It was years since Alice had thought of this trunk, but now she could feel a ball of excitement in her stomach. Eric helped her carry it to her bedroom.

'It doesn't seem to be locked.' He pulled at the lid. 'The hinges are rusty . . .' He forced it, it creaked loudly and he was able to lift the lid back. Alice shivered. It was painted blue inside, just as she remembered.

'It'll be a load of rubbish,' Gran said.

By now they were all crowding round to see what was inside. Alice stared at the collection of oddments on top and picked out a framed photograph of her mother. It brought a mist of tears to her eyes. Underneath, neatly folded, was a dark-green dress. Had she seen her mother wear that? She recognised her father's battered alarm clock, a fur tippet, a black silk shawl and an imitation-leather writing case, shabby and well-used. All gave off a strong smell of moth-balls.

'Eh, I remember that.' Edith reached across for the writing case. 'We gave it to Beryl one Christmas. It had nice writing paper and envelopes inside. She was always writing to her mother in London.'

She opened it, and a sealed envelope slid to the floor. Alice picked it up. It was addressed to Mrs Edith Luckett.

Edith took the envelope between limp fingers and sank down

385

on Alice's bed. Her legs suddenly felt as though they were buckling under her weight.

'It's our Len's writing.' She was sure of that.

'Oh my goodness!' Alice's voice was awed. 'I remember tossing that case inside the trunk on that terrible morning after Dadda died. When we were emptying our house.'

Edith opened the envelope carefully and drew out the letter.

'Dear Mam,' it started. The writing seemed to shimmer before her eyes. It was a moment before she could go on.

I've got to put the record straight before I go, but this is family business and needs to be kept from prying eyes.

Me and Beryl are getting all the blame and that's not right. I know Frank is your favourite and you don't want to think ill of him, but he's caused terrible trouble for us.

You think you're doing me a favour by looking after Alice. She's a sweet little thing really and deserves better than she's had from any of us. You tell me often that I should be grateful for what you do for her, and I've been on the point of telling you many times.

The favour you do is for Frank, not me. He's her father. He doesn't want it known and will probably deny it because it wouldn't do for Cecily to know. He got her and Beryl into trouble at the same time and this was his idea of sorting things out. I wish he'd done it without involving me. He made me accept responsibilities that should have been his.

The baby Beryl's expecting now is his too. He wouldn't leave her alone and I can't go on and get myself saddled with another.

Make Frank look after her and Alice. Be kind to them. Don't let him turn his back on them. It's what he always wants to do.

Frank thinks twins should be very close. Almost one

person. He wants to live his own life but he wants mine too. He thinks he has a right to call on my help for the most dreadful things. He wants to be too close. He hounds both me and Beryl, we can't get away from him.

Forgive me Mam for what I do. I can't go on like this.

Edith couldn't get her breath. She felt as though she was suffocating. It was like a voice from the dead.

'What is it?' Alice and Peter asked together. It was Peter who took the letter from her fingers to read.

'My God! Alice . . .'

'No,' Gran croaked. 'Don't let her see.'

'Why not?' Alice was craning forward.

'She has a right to know,' Peter said quietly looking at Alice with troubled eyes.

'She's grown up now, you can't forbid it nor fob her off with fairy stories. Read it, Alice.' He put the letter in her hand. 'I think you should know.'

'I can't stand this.' Edith headed downstairs. 'I need a cup of tea. I'm going to put the kettle on.'

But she flung herself on the rocking chair in front of the kitchen range, tossed her apron over her face and wept.

Poor, poor Len. All those years ago he'd tried to tell her why he wanted to do away with himself. If only she'd known. If only she'd read his letter at the time of his death, she'd have seen things differently. It hurt that it was her own fault she hadn't.

That dreadful Sunday when Frank had brought the trunk, she could think only of putting it where she wouldn't have to see it. She'd been blaming Beryl for his death and wanted no reminders of her. She hadn't allowed Alice to have any reminders either. Perhaps she'd been wrong about that.

Edith's family had always been important to her; she'd wanted them to be happy and stable, loving and law-abiding.

She'd wanted to be the perfect mother, and a perfect mother didn't bring up children to do the things Frank had done.

There was a lump in her throat Edith couldn't swallow. Poor Len, why hadn't she realised what was going on? Frank wasn't the saviour of the family as she'd thought. He'd caused so much misery. She'd turned to him for help and thought him generous when he gave a few shillings. Poor Alice too; she should have been more gentle with her.

It had been a mistake to call her twin sons after her dead brothers. In her worst moments, she could fancy they were the same persons returned.

Her brother Frank had been domineering and bombastic. He'd died a hero's death in South Africa, but her brother Len was shot for cowardice. She'd never admitted that to anyone, not even Monty. It was a terrible shaming secret she'd always kept to herself. The two Lens, such a tragic pair. And the two Franks? She didn't know how she was going to face her son after this. He'd done a terrible thing.

As she read the letter, Alice felt her whole world had shattered.

Eric asked: 'What is it, Alice?' She gave him the letter to read.

'Uncle Frank is my father! I can't believe it. Not Frank!'

She sank down on her bed. Peter sat one side of her and Eric the other; they each put an arm round her.

'He's always talking of how important the family is, yet he tipped all responsibility for me on to Dadda – I mean Len.'

'He helped Mam with your keep,' Peter said. 'And shelled out for presents for you.'

'There's more to being a father than that,' Alice wept. 'I could feel something different in the way he looked at me. Almost as though he owned me. It was always there between us like a fence.

'He loved Maddy much more. I could see he loved her. I

was always in awe, a bit scared of him. I've been closer to you, Peter.'

He gave her a comforting hug. 'I like to think I'm the same generation, only ten years older, and you and I have always lived here in the same house.'

Eric gave her his handkerchief. 'I've never known any father,' he said. 'And here you are with two.'

That brought a half-smile to her lips. 'It's a shock all the same. Uncle Frank! I shall let him know his secret is out.'

'I bet he thought he was safe after all this time,' Peter said. 'How lucky he was that Len's letter to Mam wasn't found.'

'I think I was lucky too,' Alice said. 'It would have been harder to take then.'

'You wouldn't have been told,' Peter said. 'Your gran would have seen to that.'

Straight after breakfast the next morning, Alice went round to Frank's house on her bike. She was burning with indignation. She knew she'd got him out of bed; he was wearing his fancy dressing gown when he opened the front door.

'I hope you haven't come to make trouble again,' he said. She knew he wasn't pleased to see her; he turned away, shuffling in his slippers to the kitchen to fill the kettle for his morning tea.

Alice followed him and said coldly, 'The trouble is never of my making.'

'What is it then? Something's wrong at the bakery?'

He looked at her squarely for the first time. Alice met the gaze of his bossy blue eyes and felt full of revulsion. She flung the letter across the kitchen table to him.

'Read this.'

'What is it?'

'A letter from Dadda explaining a few things to Gran.' She watched the colour ebb from his face.

'It's been lying in my mother's tin trunk. The one Gran didn't think I should have. We've only just found it.'

Frank had always had the upper hand, not only with her but with the rest of her family. Now she could see a slight tremor in his fingers as they groped for the letter. As he read it, she could see him folding up, his power gone. He stared down at the letter for a long time.

At last he said quietly, 'Now you know, you'd better call me Dad.' He looked shamefaced.

Alice felt something explode within her. 'I'll never call you that. You keep saying you pride yourself on being a family man, but it's all talk, isn't it? You battened on Len and Gran, made them take on your responsibilities. Some father you've been.'

'I'm sorry . . .'

'Sorry! You watched me grow up thinking both my parents were dead. Even after Len died you couldn't bring yourself to tell me the truth. You let your mother bring me up. I needed you then.

'And now you say I'd better call you Dad! Never in a thousand years. I'll always think of Len as my father. I blame you for his death, and so do the rest of the family. You drove him to it. You won't be able to talk your way round this.'

The kettle boiled behind him, sending clouds of steam up into the room. 'Get out,' he growled. 'If you can't take it like an adult, I don't want you near me.'

Alice leaned across the table and scooped up the letter.

'I won't be bothering you again. I leave it to you to tell Maddy we're half-sisters, not cousins. I do hope the news doesn't upset Aunt Cecily.'

'She knows. She's accepted it.' He was blustering.

'Well, I can't.'

Alice was more upset than she wanted him to know. It had come completely out of the blue. She turned on her heel and rushed out of the house, slamming the front door behind her. She ran down the path with her bike and out on to the pavement, not looking where she was going. She almost cannoned into Eric, who was waiting at the gate for her.

'Hey,' he said. 'Are you trying to run me down?'

'Didn't expect . . .' She blew her nose. 'Didn't expect to see you here. Oh, Eric!'

He took her bike and wheeled it towards his car.

'I was worried about you. Your gran said you'd come to see Frank. You're all right?'

She nodded and swallowed hard, watching him lift her bike on the back bumper and strap it to the spare wheel. Then he opened the passenger door for her.

'It's all history, isn't it? Silly to be upset.'

He got into the driver's seat. 'I don't want you to be.'

'I'm not,' she denied.

He put an arm round her shoulders and pulled her closer. 'I think you are a little.'

Alice sighed. 'Who wouldn't be? Who'd want Frank for a father? I'll always think of Len . . .'

'He gave you love?'

She nodded. 'And tried to care for me – in his way.'

'Forget Frank. We care for you, Alice, we always have. Peter and Mam, and especially me.'

Alice felt warmed by his concern. She'd always wanted Eric to care about her. She felt very close to him, pleased that he'd come to meet her. He was looking at her intently, his face only inches from her own. He came closer and kissed her.

'Alice, we are good for each other. I feel we're drawing closer.'

Her heart turned over. She'd never given up hoping that one day she'd hear him say something like this.

'Might we be happy together? I know I'm not the romantic type, but we could comfort each other.'

His dark eyes were tender. Alice knew she could be very happy with him. She wanted it so very much.

'What are you saying? Are you asking . . . ?'

He smiled, his face hopeful, expectant.

'I suppose I'm asking if you'll take me on permanently; take pity on a broken reed like me. If you'll marry me.'

Alice drew back with a jerk. Disappointment flooded through her. She didn't want a husband who thought of himself as a broken reed. He wasn't in love with her. He wasn't over Greta yet.

'I'd expect more than comfort from a husband.' She wiped her eyes.

He drew back, hurt.

'Yes, selfish of me. I was thinking of myself. And it's not the moment, is it? You're all upset about . . . finding out about Frank. I'm sorry.'

'No need to be sorry.' Alice roused herself. 'You were romantic once. You swept Greta off her feet.'

'Yes, well – a long time ago. All that's gone now.'

'I want you to learn to live again.'

'It's not easy. You've no one else? A boyfriend?'

'No, only you, Eric. But this isn't the right moment for you either. You aren't over Greta yet. We both have to come to terms with what fate has doled out to us.'

'But we have an understanding?'

She nodded, unable to say any more. She wanted him to say he loved her, to be wholehearted about it. She wanted to feel he loved her as much as she did him.

Chapter Thirty-Four

Frank hadn't moved; he was supporting himself against the kitchen sink. He felt gutted. Alice knew, the whole family knew. It was the last thing he'd expected to happen. He'd thought all that was behind him years ago. Finished and over.

Once Cissie knew, nothing had been the same; he'd lost her love and her support. He was afraid the same would happen with the family and they'd treat him differently now. He crawled with consternation. They'd shame him, make him grovel.

He'd seen the look of disdain on Alice's face. She was blaming him and it wasn't his fault. He'd tried hard to bring her up, hadn't he? He would have done if Cissie hadn't dug her heels in.

He heard the post come through the front door and plop on to the mat. He moved automatically to see what had come.

There was a letter asking him to attend an interview for the tunnel job. At any other time it would have pleased him. This morning he was too upset to think of anything but Alice's boiling indignation when she'd said: 'I blame you for his death . . . You drove him to it.' His mother would feel exactly the same; she'd never forgive him for that.

He was still sweating. This couldn't have come on a worse day. He particularly wanted to have a quiet mind and all his wits about him, and here he was in a blue funk. Today was the day Pat was going to open the Carlton Hall safe.

He was expecting Pat to come round later that morning to

finalise their plans. All his instincts were to put it off, but he knew he had the right combination for the safe. Next week he might not be able to check it out first. The chances were he wouldn't. He heard Pat's van draw into his drive.

Frank tried to pull himself together as he took Pat into the dining room and put the gas fire on. They always sat facing each other across the table. It made it seem like an ordinary business meeting.

He'd carefully written out the code for the safe on a small piece of card. 'Handy for you,' he said, sliding it across the table. 'It'll fit in your top pocket.'

Pat seemed confident and fully in control of himself. 'I'll memorise it.'

'Keep that with you, then I know you'll get in. The safe's easy to open, I've tried it.'

'What did you take?'

'Nothing! How could I when we were planning this? Anyway, there was no money in it then.'

Pat said: 'I got as far as the office the other night. I saw the safe.'

'Good, you won't have to waste time looking for it then. You'll need strong bags to carry the cash.'

'I've bought two Rexine shopping bags; they'll fold up in my coat pockets.'

'Go for the bank notes first. I changed as much as I could to notes, to make it easier. Don't miss them. They're clipped together in two bundles, on the left of the top shelf. The coins are all sorted and packed in paper tubes, the sort you get from the bank. You can see which are half-crowns and which are pennies at a glance. It's printed on them. Pick up the silver first.'

Pat grinned. 'I'll make sure I take the right tubes.'

'Where are you going to park your van?'

'Not too far away. All those coins are going to be heavy. I won't be able to move fast.'

'You don't want to be seen getting into the van.'

Peter had wanted Pat to get a sign-writer to put the bakery name on his van, but very wisely he'd resisted that. It was a small black Ford. There were lots of them about. It didn't stand out in any way.

'Douglas Street is the safest place. I leave my car there. Double back behind the Carlton Hall; there's a narrow passage running back to Henry Street. Go to the end and cross Market Street, and you'll see another back entry into Douglas Street.' Frank was making a sketch for him.

'I'll check that out this morning.'

'You'd better, you'll not find it easy in the dark. No streetlights down the back entries, but you're less likely to be seen.'

'Right.'

'Buy a balcony ticket for the second house and watch the film until quarter to ten,' Frank ordered. 'That should give me time to get the takings for the last house into the safe.

'At quarter to ten exactly make contact with Hilary. She'll be watching out for you and will act as look-out. If the boss comes back while you're in his office, she'll head him off. She's going to cause a flood in the ladies' powder room. The one used by the audience on the balcony. She'll take him to see the damage. That should give you time to get away before the alarm's raised.'

'Right,' Pat said. 'And you'll come round to my flat on Sunday morning to count up what we get?'

'I'll know exactly how much we'll get,' Frank told him. 'There's a hundred and twenty there now, and three more performances to go.

'I might come round on Saturday night when we close, but that could be very late. The place will be running with police once the safe's found empty. We'll all be kept hanging about being questioned. Sure to be.'

'Be careful what you say.'

'I'll say I saw nothing out of the ordinary. Don't forget to leave the safe door swinging open when you've taken the money,' Frank told him. 'That's important.'

His alibi depended on the theft being discovered immediately. All he had to do was to stay with old Butterballs from the moment the money was locked in the safe until it was found to be gone.

When Pat had gone, Frank sat over the gas fire, watching the hands of the clock crawl round. He couldn't get what Alice had said out of his mind. He'd always blamed himself for Len's death; how could he do otherwise? For Beryl's death too. He dreaded seeing Mam, and half-expected her to come round to give him a piece of her mind.

Cissie brought Maddy back when her salon closed for lunch. Neither seemed in a good mood and they didn't want to speak to him, but a meal was put on the table for him as usual. He was expected to eat with them.

Frank had to force himself. His stomach felt full of wind and he had a dreadful foreboding that his luck had run out at last. He tried to tell himself he was being silly. Alice had given him the jitters, that was all it was.

He went to work, sat in his airless box and prepared to sell tickets for the children's matinée. All the staff hated the Saturday matinée: screaming kids who wouldn't do as they were told, all pushing to get in.

He told himself twenty times that it was Pat who was going to open the safe, not him. He'd already done his share by setting it up. All he had to do now was to act normally, and after the second-house takings were in the safe, stick close to old Butterballs.

Hilary looked flushed. He knew she was keyed up, but she'd be all right. He could depend on her.

Time seemed to stand still that afternoon. The matinée seemed endless, so did first house. He felt sick with apprehension when he saw the queue for second house growing outside.

He hardly recognised Pat when he came to the ticket window. He wore a workman's flat cap on his head, covering his curls. A pair of glasses and a big loose mackintosh completed his outfit. Frank gave him a tight little grin, and told himself Pat would be all right too.

They were showing Clark Gable in *Call of the Wild* and were heading for a full house. He hadn't sold his own tickets for some time, so from that point of view it didn't matter. All the more cash would find its way into the safe.

Frank watched the clock. Timing was important now. He totalled up the takings and made up his book. His last job was to feed the nut from a small screw into the ticket machine. He'd already tested it to make sure it would go through the slot the tickets came up. He heard it drop inside. That surely would cause a problem.

He was ten minutes early. He sat on his stool and waited. It was the longest ten minutes he'd ever lived through. The sound track sounded distorted. There were loud bursts of music. He wondered how Pat was feeling. Impossible for him to feel more on edge than he was himself.

At twenty-seven minutes to ten precisely, he went up to the office. Mr Butterworth was at his desk. So far so good. If he'd not been there, Pat would have had to wait in the wings.

'Almost a full house tonight, sir.'

He crashed the money down on the desk and pushed his book forward for inspection. Old Butterballs studied it for what seemed an age.

'I'm having a bit of trouble with the ticket machine,' Frank said smoothly. 'It's stuck once or twice tonight. I was afraid it was going to give up the ghost before the second house was in. Making a fearful noise too. Will you come down and look at it, sir? Perhaps we should get somebody out to fix it on Monday morning?'

Butterballs was counting the coins. Stacking them up in piles along the edge of his desk. Frank wished he'd hurry up. He couldn't stop his gaze going anxiously to the clock every few seconds. Two more minutes and Pat would be on his way.

'There's a new machine ordered,' Butterworth said at last. 'A much-improved model. It's a till as well. Should make this job easier.'

All Frank registered was that he hadn't said he'd come down to the foyer to see the old one. He didn't care what machine was brought in now; he'd be leaving soon.

'More accurate too.'

Frank could feel himself shaking. He didn't like the way the manager looked up at him when he said that. 'It won't be here by Monday though?' He had to ask.

'No, about three weeks.'

Butterballs still didn't say he was coming with him. Slowly he began putting the coins in the paper tubes he got from the bank, and piling them back in the cash drawer.

Frank watched him initial his book to confirm all was correct. Then he went to open the safe. Frank carried over the drawer of money so he could stack it inside. The safe was full, and the coin bags had to be pushed in hard.

Butterballs turned round. 'So what exactly is the matter with your machine? I suppose I'd better take a look.'

Frank felt relief flooding through him. He'd done it. The office would be empty when Pat came up. Another glance at the clock told him he was spot on time. Everything was going like clockwork. As he skipped downstairs, he could hear ponderous footsteps following him.

'This machine's given a lot of trouble.' Butterballs was breathing heavily as he bent over it.

Frank wasn't surprised; he'd regularly abused it. He'd been in the habit of half-depressing the button when he sold his own tickets from the drawer. The half-hearted whirring sound was nothing like its usual rolling roar, but it gave the customer the impression he was using the machine when he wasn't.

It was time to demonstrate the problem to Butterballs. He

398

pressed for a one-and-threepence ticket; it came up, but with a terrible grating sound. The nut was doing a wonderful job inside. Even if the manager found it, he'd think it was part of the mechanism.

'Get Percy,' he ordered. 'Tell him to bring his tools. We'll take a look inside.'

Frank shot upstairs. His head was thumping, but he knew everything was going well. The top corridor was empty, the office door shut. Pat was probably in there this minute, but it was each to his own job now. He daren't absent himself for long. Percy was in the cloakroom, having a quiet fag, as he'd expected. He gave him the message and went straight back to Butterballs.

'I don't know what you do with this machine,' the manager grumbled at him.

'Something's the matter with it, sir.'

Percy was coming down, Frank could hear the chink of his tool bag. There was hardly room for three in the tiny space. He kept well back out of the way of Percy's elbows, watching the stairs. Pat would be coming down with the money any minute now. The foyer was empty. He couldn't believe Butterballs wouldn't notice him if he crossed to the door. It was closed now, and it creaked when it was swung open.

They had the top off the machine and were shining a torch in at the works. There was a gasp of triumph from Butterballs.

'Here's the trouble.' He put the nut up on the counter.

'Where's that come from?' Frank asked. 'The whole thing's falling apart.'

The torch shone inside for a long time. They were pressing for the tickets to come up and watching the mechanism. It sounded normal again.

Then Frank saw Pat on the stairs, looking down into the foyer. He felt the hairs sticking up on the back of his neck.

For God's sake! Pat couldn't stay there, looking as guilty as hell. They had only to glance up!

He signalled to him to move and saw him slip through

the door into the back stalls. It was one of the options they'd discussed. It would be dark in there and everybody's attention would be on the screen. Nobody would notice his heavy shopping bags weighing him down.

'Everything seems all right.' Mr Butterworth sounded doubtful. He was pressing for tickets to come up at all prices.

'Doesn't sound too healthy, but as long as it's working . . . It only needs to last another three weeks.'

They had to wind the tickets back on their rolls then, but at last Percy was screwing down the brass plate on top.

Frank could feel himself breaking out in a sweat again. He was holding his breath. The boss was backing out, about to head back to his office, a pleased smirk on his face that he'd managed to improve matters. On cue, Hilary appeared and led him off to see the flood she'd made in the ladies' powder room.

Percy was throwing his tools back in the bag. Silently Frank implored him to get out of the way. The commissionaire took his time, but at last he headed for the stairs. Frank locked up the ticket office, taking his time. The coast was clear. Silently he implored Pat to come now. Exactly on cue, Pat was quietly crossing the foyer, weighed down with his bags. The heavy glass doors creaked, Pat slid out into the night and was gone like a shadow.

Frank realised he'd been holding his breath. Now he let it out slowly and straightened up. His heart was thumping nineteen to the dozen, but they'd got away with the money. There was almost three hundred there if Pat had taken it all. A nice little nest egg.

He mopped his forehead dry, then wiped the palms of his hands on his handkerchief. He had to calm down. He'd go up to the cloakroom and have a Gold Flake with Percy. The commissionaire would be changing out of his uniform, ready to go home, not knowing that another job awaited him in the ladies' loo. Frank still needed an alibi and had to stay close to other people. In the next few minutes, Butterworth would return to his office and notice the door of his safe was wide open.

He started for the stairs. Behind him he heard a scuffle at the door and two policemen came in. He could see more police outside. Suddenly the sweat was pouring off him again. Had the alarm been raised already? Old Butterballs must have phoned for the police.

He was afraid Pat hadn't had enough time to get away. It was only moments . . . Then through the glass doors he saw Pat being held between two more police officers. He craned his neck. Yes, it was Pat. His legs felt weak, his head swam with shock.

He was turning to get away. Up to the cloakroom, anywhere to get away from the police. One of the officers was in front of him. The place was suddenly swarming with them.

'Do you know where Mr Butterworth is?' the policeman demanded.

'Probably in his office,' Frank mumbled. He was in a lather, aware now that everything had gone desperately wrong.

'Take me to him,' ordered the policeman, but there was another officer behind him.

'Are you Frank Luckett?'

What could he say but 'Yes.'

'We'd like you to come down to the station with us. We think you can help us with our enquiries.'

His whole world collapsed at that moment. Nothing this bad had ever happened to him before. He'd gambled on doing the big one and lost. So had Pat. He was escorted through the foyer, past Hilary, her eyes wide in panic. He wanted to tell her he'd keep his mouth shut about the help she'd given him. If he could.

What he didn't understand was what they had done wrong that had caused this.

Chapter Thirty-Five

1936–1938

On Sunday morning, Edith was salting the piece of pork she was going to roast for dinner.

The removal van was ordered for a week on Tuesday, and she was getting excited about moving. She felt they'd all turned the corner, that everything was picking up after the setbacks they'd had.

When the front door bell rang, she called: 'See who that is, Monty.'

Alice was with her in the scullery, peeling potatoes for her, and her hands were wet.

'It's Cecily,' he said, leading her back to the kitchen. Maddy followed them, her face tear-stained and solemn. Edith's heart missed a beat. She knew immediately that something was terribly wrong.

'Isn't Frank with you?' Cecily never came to her house without Frank.

'Oh, Mother . . .' Cecily was upset too. She always used to call them Mother and Papa. She always used to be sweet and friendly and couldn't do enough for them. She'd changed completely when Len died. Edith thought she knew why now. Cecily had found out then that Frank was Alice's father, and that had turned her against all the Lucketts.

'He's been arrested,' Maddy said, bursting into tears. 'Pat too, and it's all my fault.'

'Come here,' Peter said from his seat at the table, and he gave her a hug. 'What's all this about?'

Alice came from the scullery, drying her hands.

'Get the kettle on again,' Edith told her. 'We'll have more tea.'

Monty ushered Cecily into his rocking chair. She looked white and strained; for once she'd paid little attention to her appearance.

'Frank's been asking for it long enough. Sailing close to the wind. Maddy's in a state of hysterics; she thinks it's her fault, which is silly. She wasn't to know that her dad was hand in glove with Pat O'Neill.'

'I told the police about Pat,' Maddy whispered, clearly horrified at what she'd done. 'They were watching him for days. Saw him come round to our house and found out Dad was his accomplice. They caught Pat red-handed as he left the Carlton Hall. He had the money on him. They'd have got away with hundreds of pounds if I hadn't . . .'

'Maddy, nobody's blaming you.'

'Dad will.'

'They'd have been caught sooner or later. I keep telling you that. They've been at it for years.'

'Where are they now?' Peter asked, aghast.

'Down at the police station, still being questioned. Hilary's at our house. She's in a terrible state, expecting them to come for her every minute. I blame Frank for involving her. She's just a kid out for a lark. She didn't know what she was doing.'

Edith swallowed hard and sank down on a chair. She'd thought her troubles were over. Now this! She shivered. All the neighbours would know. She'd be glad to get away from here, go where the Lucketts weren't known.

'Fancy our Frank,' Monty said. 'Hundreds of pounds?'

Edith looked at him, afraid for him. She didn't want Monty to go downhill again. Just when he was on the mend and getting over his nervous breakdown.

'Serve them both right,' Alice said as she brought in

the tea pot. 'Look what Uncle Frank did to Dadda and my mam.'

'And to you.'

'What about Hilary? He didn't have to involve my sister.' Cecily's eyes were wide with horror. 'I'll never forgive him for that.'

'What's she been doing?' Peter asked.

'Helping him for years. I thought they'd both given up selling their own tickets. Not that Frank's ever given her much. I pray they both keep their mouths shut about her now.'

'He's had a very good run,' Monty said slowly.

'They called him Lucky at work,' Cecily said. 'He's had the luck of the devil up till now.'

The move to the bungalow went without a hitch. Edith was determined not to let Frank's problems spoil things for her, not now she'd finally got what she'd wanted. She wouldn't let Monty mention it.

Of course, she didn't like to think of Frank being sent to prison for two years. His friend Pat had been given the same sentence. He was a bad lot; she was sure he'd led their Frank into it. They'd confessed to stealing from shops over the previous eight years, and that had been taken into account. Even the judge said they'd had a tremendous run of luck, but that it was over now.

Edith looked round her pretty little house and marvelled that Monty was so much better. She'd talked to him about buying a car, and he was quite keen. He hadn't quite made up his mind what sort they'd get, but he was going round garages looking at them. They'd need a car here; it was a long walk back from the shops when she had a lot to carry. Monty would be able to drive them out into the country for day trips. They were both looking forward to that.

It would give them a bit of status with their new neighbours too. Not many of them had cars, nor had they paid extra for a garage at the back.

Edith was delighted to hear that Peter was much better now. He and Alice had moved to the flat over the shop.

'He's getting up and downstairs all right, and he's started putting in a few hours in the bakery. He feels he's in charge again, and that's as good as a tonic to him.'

Alice had been round to see them yesterday, and had brought some of Peter's cakes for them.

'It's great living with Peter, playing at being a house-wife. I love doing the cooking and deciding what we're going to eat.

'Eric comes round almost every evening. He and his mother are coming for dinner on Sunday. Oh, and I've found myself a job as a shorthand-typist with the Liverpool Savings Bank. You used to take me there when I was small, to pay money into your account.'

Edith smiled. She'd been in and out of there so many times she felt she knew the place. 'You'll be happy there, I know.'

Eric smoothed out the huge yardage of pinstripe suiting on the cutting-out table. A very stout gentleman had ordered a formal three-piece lounge suit.

Last night, he and Mam had been invited up to the bakery again for supper. Alice had given them steak and kidney pie and both she and Peter had been in great form.

'It's taken several medical examinations and more than a year,' Peter had grinned at him, 'for your insurance company to pay up on my claim.'

'Thank goodness they have,' Eric said. 'I'm relieved.'

'The cheque came last Wednesday,' Alice told him. 'As soon as he got the money, he went to visit Frank and Pat in Walton Jail.'

'I'd arranged that weeks ago,' Peter said. 'I was just lucky with the timing. Guess what? They've both agreed to let me buy them out. This bakery will soon be all mine. I can't wait.'

Eric knew Peter had been doing more and more of the work

406

in the bakery himself, and that he felt well. He was expanding the business fast, and now employed a driver to drive a new red van with the bakery name emblazoned on both sides.

Flo and Alma Judd were all right too. Last year some time Peter had said:

'I'm back on my feet, I can walk; now I'd like to see if I can dance again. There's a do on at the rugby club next Saturday. How about taking up our Saturday-night dancing again?'

Eric had been delighted that Peter wanted to do more. They'd been going to the pub for an occasional drink for some time.

'An excellent idea, but I want Alice to come too. She'll wheel you round gently to start with.'

'I don't need wheeling round gently.'

'All right, there's another reason. Alice wouldn't want me to take up with anyone else.'

'Eric, it's not Alice you're thinking of – it's yourself. You don't have to pretend to me.'

'Yes – well.' That had made him think. He'd begun to see things more clearly after that.

'Of course we'll take Alice.'

Several days later, it was Alice who suggested to Peter: 'Why don't you ask Alma Judd if she wants to make up a foursome?'

The four of them got on very well. They often went out together after that. Peter said he'd also been taking Alma out by herself, to the music hall and the pictures. Flo encouraged them. They were all getting on well in the shop.

'Listen, Eric,' Peter had said to him. 'We're all back on our feet and going strong. You can give your conscience a rest. You don't have to worry about us any more. We're all over that awful accident, back to normal.'

He'd sighed: 'But I wonder if you are.'

Eric had laid out his pattern now. He took up the scissors and made his first cut into the pinstripe suiting.

These days he could think of Greta without going into paroxysms of grief and rage at losing her. Life was very different now. Peter was living it to the full again, and so must he.

He put down his scissors and went to look for his mother. She was preparing something for supper.

'I'm going to meet Alice from work,' he said. 'It's a nasty wet evening.'

Alice felt she'd settled into her job. At first she was glad it gave her less responsibility than running the bakery. Now she was beginning to think she'd find dressmaking more interesting. She worked with two other lady typists, both nearing middle age. All the bank clerks were men.

All afternoon it had been blustery and rain had been hurtling at the windows. She'd been glad to be in a warm office. Now, in the depths of winter, she was at work before it was properly daylight, and it was dark again before she went home.

At half past five, she covered her typewriter, put on her mackintosh and went to the door. The clerks were already streaming out.

She didn't see Eric waiting near the step until he called her name.

'Hello.' She laughed out loud with pleasure that he'd come to meet her.

He took her arm. 'The car's just down here.'

'Lovely, a ride home.' The wind buffeted her. 'It's terrible weather.'

'Alice, I'm a fool,' he said. 'What am I thinking of? Letting you work in that place amongst all those handsome bank clerks?'

She laughed again. 'I'm well chaperoned. Not allowed near them, nor they near me. I work with two lady typists who see to that.'

'I'm dragging my feet. I've spent far too long struggling

with my own problems. I've made heavy weather of them, haven't I?'

They reached his car. It was hard to open the doors against the wind. He switched on the headlights, and they glistened on the wet road.

Alice said softly: 'It takes time to get over an accident like that. It wrecked the life you had.' She knew it had locked him in grief, brought him self-blame and guilt.

'You've been wonderfully understanding, Alice. Given me time.'

His attention was on the road ahead. The windscreen wipers swished rhythmically. In the semi-darkness, she watched him push his dark wavy hair back from his forehead in a gesture she knew so well. She'd loved him since she was nine years old.

'I've needed an awful lot of time – to see you were offering me another chance of happiness.'

'I'd wait for ever for you.'

'That's a lovely thing to say. I've always felt very close to you. Even when I was married to Greta, you were very special to me.'

'I didn't want to be your little sister,' she told him. 'I always wanted more than that.'

Eric drove straight into the bakery yard and took her in his arms. 'I love you, Alice. You've given me the strength to put all that behind me. I want to look to the future. I want us to be married.'

Alice knew there had always been a bond between them, ever since he'd taken her hand in his the day they'd found Len. She remembered his tenderness and his kindness, and the love she'd always had for him.

'It's what I've always wanted. To be your wife.'

'Soon,' he said. 'Let's do it soon. I've wasted too much time already.'

'As soon as possible.' She kissed him. 'Come on, let's go in and tell Peter.'

When he heard the news, his smile stretched from ear to ear. 'About time.' He gave Eric a playful punch in the abdomen. 'Alma was getting impatient. Me too, I suppose.'

'Why?'

'You're very sweet, Alice, but naturally Alma and I want to start married life on our own. I couldn't turn you out, not when I'd pleaded with you to come and look after me. Only last year too.'

'Peter!' Alice hugged him. 'Have you got that far already? I'm so happy, for both of us. Where's Alma?'

'Gone home. It's the end of the working day.'

'I can't wait to see her, to tell her . . .'

'Let's go and tell Mam,' Eric said, putting a hand on her shoulder. 'She'll want to know too.'

Nell was sewing in the front room when they got there. She leapt to her feet, throughly excited, to kiss Alice.

'It's what I've been hoping for, for a long time! You know how I feel about you, Alice. You belong here. I've always thought you and Eric would suit each other perfectly.'

'So have I,' Alice said, smiling up at him.